YOU LIED FIRST

ANNABEL KANTARIA

ONE PLACE. MANY STORIES

HQ
An imprint of HarperCollins*Publishers* Ltd
1 London Bridge Street
London SE1 9GF

www.harpercollins.co.uk

HarperCollins*Publishers*
Macken House, 39/40 Mayor Street Upper
Dublin 1, D01 C9W8, Ireland
This edition 2025

1
First published in Great Britain by HQ,
an imprint of HarperCollins*Publishers* Ltd 2025

A catalogue record for this book is available from the British Library.

ISBN: 9780008238766

Set in Sabon LT Pro by HarperCollins*Publishers* India

Printed and bound in the UK using 100% Renewable Electricity at CPI Group (UK) Ltd

For more information visit: www.harpercollins.co.uk/green

Praise for Annabel Kantaria

'A nail-biting read that absolutely gripped me. A real page-turner!'
***Sunday Times* bestselling author Susan Lewis**

'Haunting, dark and wonderfully atmospheric, *The House of Whispers* will quickly have you under its spell.'
***Sunday Times* bestselling author B A Paris**

'Beautifully written, *The House of Whispers* is a dark and inventive tale. Utterly compelling.' ***Sunday Times* bestselling author Lesley Kara**

'So, so good! A brilliant tale of artistic temperament and toxic friendship but so much more than that too. Just fabulous.'
***Sunday Times* bestselling author Catherine Cooper**

'Unsettling and creepy, *The House of Whispers* is a gothic yet very modern tale of a descent into madness. But whose decline are we witnessing? Anna Kent kept me guessing at every turn, right up until the last shocking page' **Alice Clark-Platts**

'Dark, creepy and atmospheric. I loved it, especially all the details of the art – I could really see each painting as it came alive. I'm sure this book will be haunting me for days to come – in a good way!'
Melanie Golding

'An atmospheric and unsettling psychological thriller that had me second guessing myself.' **Nell Pattison**

'I found myself totally immersed in this unsettling, tense and thought-provoking novel that explores the deep resonances of buried guilt. With excellent characterisation, pitch-perfect prose and heart-wrenching detail, this is a fresh new psychological thriller that – like Grace – completely got its hooks into me!'
Philippa East

'Filled with intrigue, suspense and a sense of foreboding, this expertly written domestic thriller will keep you enthralled from its opening page to its shockingly good last. Chilling and atmospheric, with some dark moments – it really does pack a punch.'
Sam Carrington

'A chilling and original take on toxic friendship, with a proper gasp-inducing ending' **Roz Watkins**

Annabel Kantaria is a British journalist who now lives in Dubai with her husband and children. She has edited and contributed to women's magazines and publications throughout the Middle East and returns regularly to the UK.

Also by Annabel Kantaria

Coming Home
The Disappearance
The One that Got Away
I Know You

Published under Anna Kent

The House of Whispers

For you

Breaking News:
Hope for family of Brit missing in Oman

Activity was today detected on the mobile phone belonging to a British national missing in Oman, bringing fresh hope.
Royal Oman Police have not released any further information at this point.

1
SARA

The holiday to Oman is not my idea. Call me unadventurous, but no part of the Middle East has ever been on my holiday bucket list. New York, Rome, Barcelona, Sydney, or even a week on the Costa del Sol, absolutely, but now I'm in a taxi speeding along a highway through Muscat city centre behind the Forrests' hired Land Cruiser – which is being piloted by Margot since Guy apparently drank a skinful of champagne on the flight – and Liv and I are sitting in exhausted silence. She fiddles with her phone while I stare out of the window at palm trees and the exotic architecture of the city, taking in the Arabic road signs, the surprising amount of greenery, and the unfamiliar stretch of minarets towards a deep blue sky. It's not how I imagined Oman would look, even though I pored over internet guides until my head spun, terrified that one of us would unwittingly break the law.

'Just remember you can't hug or kiss Flynn in public,' I remind my daughter, even though I've already spelled it out to her multiple times. 'It's not like back home.'

'Yeah.' She doesn't look up.

'Please remember that when we're out in public.'

'Mum!'

'Liv! It's important. I don't want either of us to end up in jail, okay? And you can't take pictures of any locals without asking permission.' I'm treated to teenage side-eye for that.

My biggest worry, though, is about the cost of the holiday. Guy and Margot are not known for their thrifty tastes.

'By the way, I thought that if the Forrests want to eat out every night, maybe we could do our own thing sometimes,' I suggest. 'With Flynn, of course,' I add quickly, but I realise as I say it that inviting myself to be a gooseberry between her and her boyfriend won't be any more welcome to her than the thought of she and I staying in while Flynn goes out with his parents.

Liv turns to look at me and lowers her sunglasses with a small sigh. 'Let's see.'

'Okay,' I say mildly, but I really hope we manage to carve out some time just for us. She's the one who pushed for me to join the holiday and the point in me being here is for us to spend some time together – all going well, she'll be off to university in less than a year – and we have so much lost ground to catch up on.

Liv turns away and I remind myself to look on the bright side. I'm here with Liv. We're going to have a great holiday. Together. Experiencing new things. Getting to know her boyfriend's family. And, with the sun now high in a cloudless sky, the weather bodes well, too. I picture myself tanning by a swimming pool and feel the beginnings of pleasant anticipation.

The taxi exits the highway and the streets become more residential, fringed with villas. We turn into ever-narrower residential streets until the Forrests' car slows to a crawl before pulling left into a carport. Behind it, our taxi comes to a halt outside a white wall over which glorious bougainvillea tumbles. Guy appears on the pavement, nodding and indicating with two thumbs up that this is the right place. His trousers and linen shirt are creased from the journey but the sunshine suits him, as do his Aviator sunglasses – he looks alive in a way I'd not noticed in our few interactions back home.

'Livvie? I think we're here,' I say.

'Finally.' She shoves her phone into the Longchamp bag Michael bought her just for this trip and yawns. 'That took forever.'

'Maybe we should have gone to Munich, after all!' I laugh to show I'm joking but Liv rolls her eyes. Once she'd been offered the chance to join Flynn in Oman, my planned trip for the two of us to the Christmas markets hadn't stood a chance.

'How much?' I ask the driver. There's a meter, but I want to check.

He turns and holds up eight fingers but, as I poke around in my wallet trying to understand the unfamiliar notes, my car door opens and Guy hands the driver a note. Liv and I climb out of the cab, blinking in the harsh light as Guy opens the boot and hauls out our bags. Liv grabs hers and goes straight to Flynn. My eyes sting with lack of sleep. I'm more than ready to fling off my travel clothes and stretch out on a proper bed.

'Here,' I say, offering Guy the ten-riyal note I finally located, but he waves it away.

'It's nothing. Right. Let's go.'

I smile at Margot. 'I'm impressed you found this place! Those last streets were like a maze.'

'Google Maps is a wonderful thing,' she says and turns to follow Guy through the gate towards the front door. Wearing a casual two-piece set with trainers and a baseball cap, she looks as immaculate here as she had when we'd met yesterday at Birmingham Airport.

'We used to live here,' Flynn says. 'Same compound.'

'Ah.' I pick up my bag and follow, closing the gate behind me. Guy finds the key box and retrieves the front door key.

'Welcome, welcome!' he says as he swings open the huge double doors to the villa. He throws out his arm expansively as if welcoming us to his own home, which I suppose in a way, he is. The air in the hallway is warm and stagnant, and the smell is musty, undisturbed; the scent of an unlived-in residence in a hot country. I let my bag drop and take in the sprawling entrance hall and the balustraded staircase as Liv and Flynn rush through to the open-plan living area, their footsteps echoing on the marble tiles. Through the sliding glass doors that Flynn's scrabbling to unlock, I can make out a pretty garden with an outdoor dining table and, beyond that, a flash of glittering blue: the promised and much yearned-for swimming pool.

The living area is bright and airy. I follow Margot through it from the sofas to the dining area to a white-panelled kitchen with jazzy blue tiles. Margot's head cranes forward as it swivels left and right, taking in her new quarters.

'It's lovely!' I say.

'Mmm.' She nods, her lips a tight line and throws a small smile my way.

Too tired to decipher her mood, I turn back to the hall and ask Guy, 'So ... what do we all want to do now? Unpack? Sleep? Eat something?' but, as the words come out, I kick myself. Am I going to dance around the Forrests the whole week just because they invited me to join their holiday? Because they paid for the villa? Now that we're all here, how is this actually going to work? Margot, always cool, always aloof, is a mystery to me. I barely know these people.

'Let's get the bags upstairs so we can freshen up,' Guy says.

He picks up two of the Forrests' gleaming hard-shell suitcases, one in each hand, so I grab my own bag and follow him and Margot up to a landing so big it has its own sofa and television. The first bedroom we enter is enormous, with a bed that looks eight feet wide, an en suite bathroom, and sliding doors to a balcony that overlooks the pool. A cream leather sofa, two armchairs, an oriental rug and a low table create a gorgeous sitting area at the far end of the room.

'Wow,' I say, thinking that a whole family could live in this room. 'It's stunning.'

'Isn't it just.' Guy throws his bag onto the bed. Margot's already opening the built-in, mirror-fronted wardrobes, assessing where to put her things.

'You can pick your room,' Guy says. 'There are three more. Come, let me show you.'

I follow him to another pool-facing room which, although smaller, is still larger than my living room at home, and is decorated in tonal shades of blue.

'This is probably the next best,' Guy says. 'It has a good

balcony with a pool view and the main bathroom is literally outside your door.'

'It's lovely,' I say. 'Perfect. Thank you.'

'Great,' he says, rubbing his hands together. 'And I thought the kids could have the front principal. It's got an en suite but it faces the street. I doubt it will bother them if there's a bit of noise outside. They'll probably be making half of it!'

'Oh! Er ...' I'd naively assumed that Liv and I would be sharing, or we'd be in single rooms. Liv had said nothing to the contrary.

Guy peers at me.

'Oh. Oh, my bad,' he says, placing his hand on his heart. 'I'm sorry if I assumed ... It's just that, well, I think that horse has long bolted.' He pulls a cringing expression. 'I mean, we always let them stay together when she sleeps at ours ...' He pauses, and takes a step towards me, his voice now sounding more serious, more responsible. 'I'm sorry. I shouldn't have assumed.'

I turn away, pretending to look at the view. Although I probably should have guessed, I didn't know Liv was sleeping with Flynn. She hasn't lived with me full time since she was fourteen, yet the realisation that if she'd confided in anyone about the status of her first serious relationship, it will have been in Michael and/or his new wife, Nancy, knocks the breath out of me. I assumed Michael would tell me if he had that conversation with Liv but clearly he hasn't. I hate the way father and daughter still lock me out; still punish me via a thousand paper cuts. But I try to look on the bright side. I'm here. She wanted me to come on this holiday. She wants to build bridges with me. I breathe in deeply and try to smile as I turn back to Guy, even though I can feel tears welling.

'Of course,' I say. 'Ignore me. I'm just tired.'

Guy slides his arm around my shoulders and gives me a reassuring squeeze, as if he understands the subtext.

'We all are,' he says. 'Let's get unpacked and then let's get this holiday started.'

2
MARGOT

Margot slides the French door back and steps out onto the balcony, breathing in the heady botanical scent of the garden, which mixes with the familiar scent of chlorinated water warmed by the sun. She runs a finger along the balcony guard rail and absently notes the pale coating of dust – not her problem this time. Below her, the light dances on the surface of the pool and she watches as Flynn and Liv flick off their shoes and dip their toes in the water, exclaiming with pleasure when they discover the water's heated. Seeing her son down there takes her back to the times she used to spend on the balcony of the adjacent house, as she watched Guy in the pool with a much younger Flynn.

Her 'boys' had been so close when Flynn was growing up. Margot, as a stay-at-home mum who spent every waking hour – and often the sleeping ones, too – with Flynn attached to her, had been very conscious of making space for father and son to spend time alone together for the scant few hours a week that Guy was home from work. But that hadn't meant she hadn't kept a watchful eye. While they roughhoused in the pool, she'd bring a book and a glass of iced mint-lemonade up to the balcony and pretend to read while discretely making sure

Guy didn't throw their son too far, too hard, too deep. Flynn's screams of joy would bounce off the walls of the surrounding villas, causing her to worry that the noise was a nuisance to their childless neighbours. In those days, Flynn couldn't get enough of his father's attention. She wonders when they lost that closeness. Had the shift been so insidious that she hadn't noticed it happening?

Now, her eyes move to the villa directly opposite. All the doors and windows are closed. It's impossible to tell if it's occupied, let alone by whom. Sweat beads on her hairline and she wipes it away with the back of her hand. It's the warmest part of the day and the balcony's in the full glare of the white-hot sun. She turns back to the bedroom and dials the air conditioning as low as it'll go. It's nice to be in Oman. But here? She's disappointed.

Yes, it's a lovely villa; yes, they used to live here; and yes, until the end, they were largely happy here but, when Guy had told her he was going to surprise her with the accommodation, she'd pictured a five-star beach hotel with a spa, not self-catering in the compound where they used to live. Guy's reasons for wanting to come back might be oblique, but right now the bigger question she faces is whether any of their old neighbours are still here. Margot very deliberately lost touch with them and is in absolutely no hurry to reacquaint herself. Back in the room, she tries to stifle her huffs as she unpacks her things.

'Oops,' Guy says, appearing suddenly behind Margot. 'Think I just put my foot in it.'

'How?' Margot shakes out her clothes as she hangs them, hoping that any creases will vanish, and she won't have to resort to using her travel steamer. Under her baseball cap, her hair feels rank. The clothes she'd put on at home the previous day are too warm, and she's hanging for a shower.

'I think Sara thought Liv would be in a separate room to Flynn.'

Margot winces. 'Ouch.'

'Well, if she didn't know before, she does now,' Guy says. He unlocks his case and starts making piles of clothes on the bed. He's a fastidious packer and an even more fastidious unpacker, a quirk that contradicts his usual *laissez-faire* attitude to life.

'I'd love to know why Olivia doesn't live with her mum,' Margot says. 'I know they say it's because the dad's house is bigger and he works from home so he's around more, but it's odd, isn't it? That she doesn't live with her mum? Especially a girl at that age. I'm sure there's more to it. Something must have happened.'

Guy waves his hand dismissively. 'I'm sure it's all very civilised or Liv wouldn't have wanted her mum to join us.' He opens his side of the wardrobes, wipes the surface with a tissue, then lines up his T-shirts in a stack on the shelf with the precision of a civil engineer. 'It's none of our business, really.'

'Well, I hope they keep it civil while they're here,' Margot says. 'I don't have the headspace for drama. It's our holiday, too. Did you bring a proper shirt in case we go somewhere smart?'

'Mar, please stop worrying. Everything will be fine. You saw how excited Flynn was when Liv agreed to come. And, yes, I did bring a shirt. Two, actually. And shoes.'

Margot turns away. She's used to being the only woman in her son's life – the sun around which his love orbits – and adjusting to Liv's encroachment is not easy.

'Let's try to remember it's supposed to be a family holiday,' she says. 'Happy families – okay?' She gives Guy a bright smile then turns away but his fingers land on her sinewy shoulders, massaging them from behind. She stills under his touch.

'I'm actually looking forward to getting to know the mother of our son's girlfriend,' Guy says. 'Liv is lovely so I'm sure Sara will be as well. Also, as I said when we discussed this *ad infinitum*, I thought it would be nice for you to have the extra female company – to not be outnumbered by men as usual. It's going to be fine. No – it's going to be better than that – it's going to be *fantastic*!'

They both turn as Flynn thuds into the room, shadowed by Liv. 'Mum! I saw it! Our old villa. It looks just the same!'

'Glad to hear it hasn't been sucked into a third dimension,' Guy says. 'Especially given we're right next door.'

'Where are we sleeping? My old room?' Flynn nods his head towards the room Sara's in. He hooks his fingers over the door frame, showing off the full extent of his six-foot height as he stretches his shoulders revealing a couple of inches of taut, muscled abs. When the Forrests had left five years ago, he'd not been able to reach the frame at all.

'Liv's mum's in there, so either of the front bedrooms,' Margot says.

Liv is standing shyly behind Flynn. 'Thank you,' she says. 'And thank you for inviting us. It's very kind of you, Mr and Mrs Forrest.'

Margot smiles benignly. 'You're welcome, Olivia. It's a pleasure to have you here.' She searches to find it in herself to ask the girl to call her by her first name, but she can't, not yet.

'So what's the plan?' Flynn asks. 'Swimming? Food? Both?'

'Do you ever stop eating?' Margot says. 'We ate practically the entire way over here.'

'I don't know about you, but I could do with a nap,' Guy says.

'How were the beds on the plane?' Liv asks, her eyes alight.

There'd been much excitement about the Forrests being in business class on the Birmingham to Dubai leg of the trip; a lot of oohing and aahing over the lie-flat beds, the privacy and the comfort of the A380 aircraft. Guy had asked Margot if they should upgrade Liv and Sara to join them, but Margot had sunk that idea as quickly as it had surfaced – and she hadn't felt guilty even when she'd seen how tired and crumpled Sara had looked in Dubai airport this morning.

'Flynn's father was far too busy propping up the bar to sleep,' Margot says.

'Free-flowing champagne!' Guy smiles with a wink that makes Liv giggle. 'I mean, what kind of human being would waste their time sleeping?'

One who wasn't busy flirting with the cabin crew, that's who, Margot thinks.

3

SARA

The sun is setting and I'm adding the finishing touches to the dining table in the garden when Guy appears at the sliding door looking rested. He's changed into a polo shirt, linen shorts and leather flip-flops, and his hair's damp from the shower. He rubs his hands together, every inch the successful businessman enjoying the holiday he's earned.

'Hey, hey! This looks incredible!' he says, surveying the fruits of my labour.

I've used the villa's crockery, cutlery and glassware but added candles and cheerful paper napkins, along with a couple of strings of fairy lights, which I've tangled around a centrepiece of bougainvillea and threaded among the glasses. The garden already has a great set of string lights that fans out like splayed fingers from the house to the fence at the rear of the garden. Underwater LEDs light up the pool, making it look even more inviting in the evening than it did during the day. The effect, even though the sun is yet to set fully, is enchanting.

'It's nothing,' I lie.

If Guy knew the amount of thought and planning I've put into this he wouldn't believe it. I'd even brought the paper napkins from home. He and Margot appear to be the type of people for whom things just fall into place. But when the idea for us to join the Forrests on this holiday had first been born, Guy had absolutely refused to let me pay for our stay in the villa. It would cost them the same whether or not Liv and I came, he said, so I'd decided the least I could do, to make a contribution, was to make myself a useful house guest. The table setting is the first of my surprises. The second is dinner.

'Did you manage to sleep?' I ask.

'Like the dead.'

'And Margot?'

'She'll be down in a minute. How about you? Did you get some sleep?'

I nod, although I hadn't slept a wink. I was both too tired and too wired. My head had started pounding, the blood whooshing at my temples, so I'd got up and gone for a short walk around the area to get my bearings. Although I'd spotted various hypermarkets on our way through Muscat, it seems we're in a residential area that has no shops within easy walking distance. Guy's said several times that I'm insured to drive the Land Cruiser but I've never driven a left-hand drive on the 'wrong' side of the road. The last thing I want is to get into an incident in a country where I don't understand the language.

'Do you think people are hungry?' I ask. 'Dinner's ready to go – it'll take about ten minutes.'

'Dinner? What do you mean?' He peers at me. 'You've cooked?'

I feel myself blush. 'Just something simple. I didn't know what would be available on our first night, so I brought some bits with me. Everyone likes pasta, right?'

'You are an absolute angel,' says Guy. 'In that case, I should see about opening a bottle of wine to match this feast.'

Like moths to a flame, the others find their way to the garden in time for sundowner drinks, so I boil up the pasta and heat the jar of Tesco Finest sauce I brought in my luggage. I even remembered to bring Parmesan cheese because Liv won't eat pasta without it.

'I thought we'd all be too tired to go out, so ta-da! Dinner is served!' I announce. I carry the platter of simple pasta as if it were a banquet, and Guy, Flynn and – to my absolutely joy – Liv clap.

'Is it aubergine and ricotta?' she asks, peering at the sauce, and I nod as my face splits with a smile.

'Of course. And there's Parmesan, too,' I say. 'Liv's favourite,' I add for the others.

'Well, thank you,' Margot says. 'Although you do know you don't have to do this every day, don't you?'

I smile at her, happy at first, but then unsure of what she means. Is she telling me that she'd rather do the cooking herself and that I've stepped on her toes as the hostess? Or does she intend to eat out every night? Have I done something wrong by cooking at home? I'm lost.

'Dig in,' I say, offering the bowl.

'Leave some for everyone else,' Margot warns Flynn.

'What?' he says. 'I'm hungry.'

'Just to let you know, the only thing I have for dessert is Wispas!' I smile at Liv. It's homage to the 'picky teas' I used to prepare on Sunday evenings when she was a kid, back before everything happened. The Wispas were her favourite part.

'This is delicious,' Guy says, nodding, after he tastes his first forkful. 'And so thoughtful. Thank you, Sara.' The smile he gives me is warm. He's way easier to read than his wife. 'So, what shall we do this week? I'd love to get in a round at the golf club …'

I notice Margot look down at her plate as if she expected nothing less. A golf widow maybe? Interesting.

'… and maybe catch up with Tom and Di. I think they're still here. Maybe Tom will bash a ball with me.'

'Well, I'd like to go to The Chedi for a spa and beach day,' Margot says. 'I'd also like to take a look around the Opera House – I used to love going there. And I always love having a look around the fish market.'

'Liv wants to go shopping,' Flynn says.

'I've seen some amazing malls on TikTok!'

'I wouldn't mind looking around a souk,' I say. 'Maybe it's something we could do together, Liv? What's good to buy in Oman?'

'Silver,' Margot says. 'Gold. Jewellery. Arabian perfumes. Carpets, if you need any. Frankincense. Omani daggers, but I don't advise trying to get those home in your luggage.'

'Makes a change from Marks and Sparks!' I say, and only Guy laughs.

'It's best in the evening,' Margot says. 'But you need to know what you want and then you need to haggle. They'll see you coming a mile off.'

'Do you want to do any sightseeing?' Guy asks. 'I mean, we've done most of it, but there might be things you'd like to see.'

'I don't want to get in your way if there are people you guys need to see. I'm happy to take Liv off for a bit here and there. I've done some research and there's a hop-on, hop-off bus we could take. See a bit of the city? Flynn, you'd be welcome to come with us, of course. And I'm sure Liv'll want to top up her tan, so we can hang out by the pool, too.

'Nonsense!' Guy says. 'We're happy to show you around, aren't we, Mar? We could start with a bit of sightseeing around town tomorrow. Why don't we all go out together and then you can take it from there?'

'That sounds terrific. Thank you,' I say, smiling at Guy.

Margot's chair scrapes on the tiles as she stands to gather the empty dishes and I sit back, finally beginning to relax: this holiday might actually be wonderful.

4
MARGOT

Sara didn't use the extractor fan when she boiled the pasta, so it's stuffy in the kitchen and sweat pools in Margot's lower back as she rinses the plates before loading them into the dishwasher. She thinks about the dinner Sara 'cooked'. How difficult is it to chuck some pasta and a jar of sauce in a pan? The cleaning-up is far more work. As she stacks plates, Margot is surprised, then affronted that Sara doesn't come to help.

When Margot returns to the garden, she sees that the teens have wandered back down to the pool and are sitting with their feet dangling in the water. Sara and Guy are still in their seats, and Sara is laughing at something Guy's said.

'Mar, be a love and bring another bottle,' Guy calls, so Margot goes back in and pulls out the third bottle of the four they picked up at duty-free. She plonks the wine next to Guy, then starts to fan herself with her napkin.

'There's only one bottle left. When we run out, you'll have to ask Tom for more because we don't have a licence,' she says, aware that she sounds snippy.

'I know, I know. I'll sort it.'

'I bought two as well,' Sara says.

Margot's seen Sara's choices; the words battery and acid

come to mind. At the very least, they lack taste – a bit like the string lights from the pound shop that Sara's littered all over the table.

'That should see us through tonight then!' Guy laughs as he tops up the glasses.

Margot sits back and lets the sounds and smells of Muscat wash over her. She's missed the place dreadfully since they left and now, as the velvety night air strokes her skin like a needy lover, she has a satisfying sense of coming home. She breathes in deeply the scent of jasmine and frangipani that wafts in the evening air. She even loves the distant hum of traffic, which blends with the comforting sound of crickets and the occasional splosh as the kids mess around by the pool. To her, these are the sounds of home; of where she should be. Maybe Guy was right after all about staying in the villa rather than the frigid environs of a hotel. They had been so happy here.

She and Guy had met as expats in Oman, and it had always been their plan to stay long term. They were saving to buy their 'forever for now' house on the coast, but life, of course, has a way of disrupting the best-laid plans. Guy had been sacked, which led to the family losing their residence visas. The increasing frailty of Margot's elderly father was the smokescreen they used to brush Guy's misdemeanour under the carpet. But the suddenness with which they'd had to rip up their lives still bites.

'So, I hear you have a YouTube channel,' Guy says to Sara. 'How did that come about?'

Sara breathes in deeply through her nose and lets the air out slowly. Margot waits. She knows the answer because she's done her research, but she wants to see how Sara frames it.

'Well, I run a little agony aunt website where people can get advice for free – it's kind of my way of giving back, if you know what I mean. Anyway, then I thought that if I gave my answers in video form, I might reach a younger audience,' Sara says. 'Because, you know, teens like Liv and Flynn, they don't really read websites, do they? It's all videos these days, but they might not know where to turn when they need serious advice. So, I started a YouTube channel to see what happened. People email me with their problems and I make little videos giving advice. I get more traction there than I do on the site these days. The Gen Zs have apparently got a bit of a thing going on with my tagline: *What would Sara say?*'

Guy leans forwards, steepling his hands like a student interested in a lecture. 'That's amazing. Well done, you! So, is that the age group you aim at?'

'I don't really aim for any age group but that's the way it's grown organically. And now …? Well, it seems to be working,' Sara shrugs, a smug little smile tugging at her lips.

'Don't you need qualifications to do that?' Margot asks. 'I mean, can anyone just tell people what to do?'

'I'm a trained counsellor,' Sara says. 'That's actually my day job. And I only reply to questions where I feel I can add something. If it's out of my reach – which some problems to do with gender identity can be – I refer on to other, more suitable, sources of advice. Specialists and so on.'

'It all sounds very noble.' Margot leans back in her chair.

'Anyway, I'm super impressed with your website,' Guy says. 'I'm going to use that phrase: *What would Sara say?* It has a ring to it. Shall we open another bottle of wine? *What would Sara say?*' he laughs and pats her hand. 'Love it!'

And then, as if the evening hasn't been testing enough, Margot hears a sound she assumed she'd never hear again in her life; a sound that is surely set to ruin the delicate balance of this holiday.

'Yoo-hoo!' calls a voice from the pool area. 'Guy Forrest! Don't tell me it's you hiding in this villa! I just saw Flynn by the pool! What the hell are you guys doing here?'

Oh, Jesus, Margot thinks as her stomach plummets: now I see exactly why he booked this villa.

5
SARA

The woman yoo-hooing at the edge of the garden is wearing a knee-length swing dress and espadrille wedges that show off her long and lean legs. Her brown hair is tied back in a shiny ponytail that swishes left and right as she walks towards them. Guy's eyes flick to Margot's for a fraction of a second then he shoves his chair back and meets the woman with his arms wide open.

'Celine Cremorne! Good God! Look what the cat dragged in,' he says, looking her up and down as if she's an apparition. He gives her a big hug and a showy kiss on each cheek as he holds her shoulders. 'Who on earth would have thought you of all creatures would still be here?'

He leads her back to the table. 'Celine, this is our friend Sara – the mother of Flynn's girlfriend. Sara, our old friend Celine. And, of course, you remember Margot.'

'Flynn has a girlfriend? Get out of here! He's old enough for that?' Celine says, laughing.

'Celine!' Margot smiles limply. 'What a surprise!'

Celine grasps Margot's hand in both of hers. 'How lovely to see you! My God, it's been ages.'

She then comes around to me and reaches for my hand, which

forces me to half stand, banging my thighs on the table and sloshing the wine in all the glasses. Celine's wrist is stacked with gold bracelets that glimmer in the fairy lights and her nails are perfect ovals of orange-red polish. I get a waft of floral perfume.

'Lovely to meet you,' I say. She's pretty, mid- to late twenties, with dark eyes, dimples when she smiles, and very white, very even teeth.

'I just got in and I saw someone by the pool,' Celine says. 'I think to myself, "That looks like little Flynn all grown-up!" But then I'm like, "No, that gorgeous apparition surely can't be!" So I come over, and there he is. I couldn't believe it! I haven't even been in the front door yet.'

'Will you join us for a drink?' Guy asks. 'I want to hear what you've been up to.'

Celine pulls out a chair for herself. 'Ha ha. You know how it is. Same old, same old. But yeah, sure! Why not? Chardonnay, if there's one going.'

Guy disappears into the villa to get her a glass and there's a moment of awkward silence before Celine says, 'So … here on holiday?'

'Yep,' Margot replies. 'Just a week. Back home for New Year.'

'Cool. So, how's your dad?' She beams at Margot in a way that looks overly innocent.

'Stable, thanks,' Margot says, maintaining eye contact with Celine.

I wait for her to elaborate but she doesn't and I wonder what the hell is going on.

'How do you know each other?' I ask because the conversation about Margot's dad hasn't led anywhere.

'We were neighbours when these guys lived here,' Celine says. 'They were in that villa.' She twists around and points. 'Diagonally across from me.'

'Oh,' I say. 'That's nice.'

'It was!' Guy says as he returns to the table. 'We had a good time, didn't we?'

'My lips are sealed,' Celine says.

Margot coughs. 'Went down the wrong way,' she says putting her hand to her chest.

Guy pours wine for Celine and tops up his own glass after waving the bottle questioningly at Margot and me. 'So, tell us. How *are* you? What's been going on since we left?'

Celine laughs. 'You know me. Trying to stay out of trouble!'

'Still teaching?'

'Yeah, same school. I'm head of year now. Year four.'

'Congrats. That's brilliant.'

'Thanks. And what about you guys? How's it going in Blighty? Are you still making those toy houses, Margot?'

I cringe. Margot makes replicas of people's homes as doll's houses – small maybe, but they're not 'toys'. In fact, they take months to make, cost so much that people joke about mortgaging them, and even become family heirlooms. I've read about her company, Margot's Mansions, in the paper.

Margot smiles peacefully, not rising to the bait. 'Indeed I am.'

'And she has a new boss now,' Guy says, his eyes twinkling. 'I'm the CEO, in charge of the company's direction and disciplining my sole worker!'

Margot's smile widens. It's clearly fake, and when Guy tries to pat her hand, she pulls it away.

'Don't worry,' Guy chuckles, 'we all know who the real boss is.'

I smile uneasily.

'That's great!' Celine says. 'I remember when you were first starting out and it was just a hobby.' She clucks her tongue and shakes her head in admiration. 'I'm glad it's working out. I bet it's difficult to get away when you're self-employed. So what have you got planned this week? You *have* to have breakfast at Nana's. It's my new favourite place.'

'We're going to drive around a bit tomorrow, see old haunts, see what's new, show Sara the lay of the land,' Guy says.

Celine turns to me. 'Nice. And what about you? Is it your first time here? Is there anything in particular you want to see?'

'I'm just happy to be here,' I say. 'I'll do whatever you all advise. You're the experts. It'll be nice to look around tomorrow. Get my bearings.'

'Well, I mean, if you need a tour guide, I'm free tomorrow. Why don't I come along?'

'Really?' I ask. I'd love her to join us – she seems fun.

'Yes, why don't you?' Guy says. 'The more the merrier. The car seats seven, so … *yalla! Let's go!*'

'*Yalla*,' echoes Margot, but I notice that big smile is gone.

6
MARGOT

Margot thinks it's bad enough trying to get Flynn up for school back home, but the combination of the four-hour time difference and sleepy teenage brains means the adults – all dressed, ready and waiting in the hallway – have shouted up the stairs multiple times before Liv and Flynn finally make their way down. Margot's itching to get going, mainly to avoid Celine, but also because she wants to make it to the fish market before it closes around lunchtime. Immediately, she sees a problem. Liv is wearing tiny denim shorts that are wholly inappropriate for the souk.

'Is that what you're wearing, Livvie?' Sara asks gently.

Liv shrugs. 'Yeah.'

For a moment Margot thinks Sara might say something, but then she turns towards the door. 'Right – shall we?'

'Umm.' Margot takes a breath. She doesn't want to make a scene, but she can't let the girl go to the souk dressed like that. 'Liv, you look lovely, don't get me wrong,' she says, 'but that outfit isn't really appropriate for today. I think you ought to pop on something longer. Below the knee at least.' She smiles to soften her words. 'It's not you. It's just how it is. We're going to some traditional areas. You won't be told off, but you might get some strange looks and stares, and that can feel uncomfortable.' She shrugs. 'It's your choice, of course, but I wouldn't like it.'

'Margot knows what she's talking about,' Sara says.

Liv looks from Margot to Flynn, to her mum and back.

'Yeah, maybe she's right,' Flynn says. 'Sorry, babe.'

'Okay, Mrs Forrest. I'll change.' Liv turns back up the stairs.

'Just throw on a pair of trousers, not a whole new outfit!' Margot calls after her.

The doorbell rings and her hopes are dashed when Guy opens the door to find Celine on the steps.

'Morning!' Celine says with a huge smile. 'Are we all ready?'

'Morning! We're almost ready,' Sara says. 'Liv's just putting on something longer.'

Celine's in wide-leg linen trousers, a T-shirt that's somehow modest while also showing off her figure, and strappy flat sandals that reveal elegant, tanned and polished toes. She laughs.

'Middle East 101. So, have you guys eaten? I was thinking we could begin at Nana's. It's not far and it's such a nice spot to have breakfast. Fuel us up for the day.'

'Why don't we just get going?' Margot says. 'We've lots to see.' She rattles the car keys in her hand.

'I'm hungry,' Flynn says, and Margot stifles a sigh. She knew he'd be hungry. He's always ravenous when he gets up. That's why she's been calling him for breakfast for the past hour.

'I could do with another coffee, to be honest.' Sara hides a yawn behind her hand. 'It's five-thirty in the morning for us right now.'

'Perfect!' says Celine. 'Don't worry. They're quite fast there.'

And so, when Liv reappears in more suitable clothing, they climb into the four-wheel drive. Margot takes the wheel and after a few minutes, with Celine navigating, they reach a pretty café with a flower-bedecked patio facing a strip of park and a vast expanse of bright blue sea. Margot can't deny that it's beautiful but she doesn't want to chew the cud here; she wants to get on with the day: a quick walk around the grounds of the Opera House taking in the play of shadows on arches before the sun gets too high in the sky; a drive to Muttrah to walk along the corniche; an early lunch, and then a chance to buy her fish before the market closes, and home to relax mid-afternoon. Muscat's not huge; if they don't hang around, they should have time to fit in everything but, at Nana's, croissants are ordered along with iced lattes and hot Americanos, and Margot has to stop herself from fidgeting while everyone laughs and chats. She can just picture them arriving at the fish market after it's closed.

'What a great start to the day,' Guy says leaning back in his seat. 'This is what a holiday's all about. Just taking your time and going with the flow, eh, Mar? It's so good to be back.'

'I swear this view lowers my blood pressure,' says Celine.

Margot can feel her own blood pressure inching up by the minute. She catches the waiter's eye and signals for the bill.

But Sara gets up and says, 'Back in a sec.' She walks over the grass towards the beach, and when she comes back her face is glowing as the wind coming off the sea whips her hair.

'It's gorgeous!' she says. 'The tide's out and the path goes for miles. The beach is so wide! I had no idea the sand would be so dark!'

'Maybe we should walk off the croissants if we're going to be driving around all day,' Celine says, and Margot could quite literally throttle her.

'Good idea,' Guy replies. He pays the bill and then takes Margot's arm. 'Remember how we used to walk here when you were pregnant?' Margot does, but now's not the time.

They set off, and while everyone exclaims about the view, she mutters to herself, 'God's sake. It'll still be here tonight.'

7
SARA

'Sorry about the shorts,' I say to Liv as we make our way back towards the car. She's now wearing a maxi skirt that swishes around her ankles. 'I thought they looked great, but you know ...'

'It's okay,' she says. 'No biggie,' but I'm still feeling inadequate for not being the one who sent her back to get changed. I should have handled it better. I had one job, as they say.

'By the way, I couldn't get my seat belt to work on the way here,' Liv says.

'What?' I ask. Maybe this is my chance to show some good parenting. 'Why didn't you say something?'

She shrugs.

'It wasn't far,' Celine says and I feel a flash of irritation. Liv is my child, not Celine's, and what she's just said goes against everything I've ever taught Liv about getting into cars. I'm very aware that now she's seventeen her friends are starting to learn to drive, and I'm haunted by images of cars packed with teens not wearing seat belts and distracted by mobile phones. It's a critical time for me to push home all the safety messages I can. I also want to teach her that it's okay to stand up to pressure from others in this type of situation.

'Livvie, it's important. You must always wear a seat belt! No exceptions.'

'Let me take a look,' Guy says. He stretches into the last row of seats and pulls and pushes and pants before backing out, shaking his head. 'I can't get it out. It's jammed.'

'Okay, well, we have seven seats so I'll just squish in the middle with Flynn and Liv then everyone has a seat belt,' I say. 'Better safe than sorry.'

'"Sara says" don't get in a car without seat belts, eh?' Guy says, laughing. 'You're on holiday now! You can take a break from doing the right thing.' He puts his arm around me and gives me a little squeeze aiming to take the sting out of his words, but I'm appalled that he'd be such a bad role model to Flynn and potentially Liv, too.

'Laugh if you want but I'd rather be laughed at than dead,' I say.

'Right, if everyone has a seat belt now, can we please get going?' Margot says, and so we all pile in. 'As we'll be going past the Royal Opera House anyway, I think we should make a quick stop there. It's a beautiful building. We can walk around a bit and take in the architecture. Just a few minutes, please. You can get some photos. It's really something.'

'Sounds great!' I say because no one else seems enthusiastic.

When we get there, I see that Margot is right: the structure and its grounds are stunning. We walk around, taking pictures of the walkways and arches then head back to the car.

'I'll drive you through Muscat so you can see different

districts, then over to Muttrah,' says Margot. 'It's not terribly far, but we'll go through the mountains.'

'Muttrah is where the souk is,' Celine tells me. 'It's better to go in the evening, though. A different vibe. There are all these little alleyways. It's so atmospheric. You'll feel like you're in a movie. I absolutely love it. If you want to come back another time, I'll happily come with you.'

I throw her a smile. 'Thanks! I might take you up on that.'

We drive past an amusement park.

'Is that Marah Land?' Flynn asks. 'We used to go there, didn't we? I have a memory of this ride ... God, I thought it was a dream but it was here, wasn't it?'

'Yes, we took you once,' Margot says. 'You loved it.'

'Can we go?' Flynn asks. 'I'd love to see it again.'

'Not now,' Margot says.

Guy turns to face us and winks. 'Can't you see someone's got a bee in her bonnet? Muttrah's been there hundreds of years but she's worried it won't wait another hour.'

He laughs at Margot and it makes me feel awkward. I don't want to laugh along with him, as she does seem stressed. I'm aware that she's doing this tour for me and Liv, and I don't want to be the cause of any unpleasantness between her and Guy.

'This is a beautiful road,' I say. I'm surprised how green everything is – the rows of roadside flowers and trees – how clean it all is, and how exotic the architecture looks. 'I love all these decorated domes. They're so beautiful.'

I can't stop looking at the mountains – the way they've been cut to allow the road to pass through, and the channels engraved into them presumably to let water run down when it rains. Then we're through and I see a clutch of white buildings and the sparkling blue of the sea beyond.

'That's it: Muttrah,' says Margot. 'I'm going to park at one end of the corniche so we can walk along. It's so interesting.'

'Why don't we drive along the corniche first?' Guy says.

'It's easier to park, then walk,' replies Margot getting into the left lane.

'Turn right, turn right!' says Guy, flinging his arm out, and Margot suddenly swerves the car right so we're driving along with the sea on our left. The corniche curves around, fringed with shops, apartment blocks, restaurants and small hotels.

'Is that a cruise ship?' I ask, indicating the largest of two huge boats in the marina.

'That's the Sultan's *second* ship,' Guy says. 'Imagine. The other one you can see used to be his as well. Though I think he put it up for sale a couple of years ago, so I don't know if he still owns it.'

'Wow,' I say.

'And on the right you'll see the entrance to the Muttrah Souk …' says Guy.

My head flicks this way and that as I strain to see all the sights. The area near the souk is full of people – locals in their round caps, women in Indian and Pakistani dress, tourists. They throng across the road and stream around the vehicles, which move slowly forwards in the traffic. Then Margot slams the brakes and we're all thrown forwards.

'Shit!' she says.

'Did you hit her?' Guy asks.

'I don't know. She fell over. She's on the ground.'

They stare at each other, almost as if they're having a silent conversation.

'I'll check if she's okay,' Margot says eventually. 'Stay here.'

She opens the car door. I go to open mine, but Celine puts her hand on my shoulder.

'Stay here, too. I know exactly what's going on. I'll sort it.'

8
MARGOT

Margot is so pissed off with Guy for making her drive along the corniche that she can barely breathe. But she knows why Guy is nervous: he's keen not to draw police attention to himself after his brush with the law when they lived here. She grits her teeth and tries to establish how bad this is. There's a woman in a bright *shalwar kameez* sitting on the side of the road, a bottle of water in her hand and a circle of people gathering around her. Margot can't actually see anything wrong with her, and there's no sense of urgency or any serious concern on the faces of those helping her. It really was nothing more than a soft bump. They weren't going at any speed and they definitely didn't run over her. At worst, Margot feels the woman got nudged by the car. Still, Margot's legs are shaking.

'I'm sorry,' she says, squatting down to the woman's level. '*Ana asef.*' She doesn't even know if Arabic is the woman's language. 'Are you okay?'

The woman looks blankly at Margot. She's not clutching any part of her body. She doesn't look like she's in any pain. But a man who's with her turns on Margot, shouting angrily. She can't understand his words, but she gets the sentiment.

'Police!' He barks and gets out his phone, but Margot puts her hand over it.

'No,' she says. 'Please. She's okay. Look. She's fine.' She smiles encouragingly at the woman.

Celine appears around the car. She's holding out a fifty riyal note. The man reaches for it but she snatches it away.

'She's okay?' Celine nods to the woman. 'Are you okay?'

The man shrugs. 'She's okay.'

'No police,' she says, miming her words at the same time. 'Okay?' The man grunts, and Celine hands him the money. 'Deal? All good?' The man nods. Celine turns to Margot. 'Right, come on. Let's go.'

Margot is blindsided by how quickly Celine solved the issue. It's obvious that money would sort it, but in the heat of the moment it hadn't crossed her mind. And Guy wasn't much use, hiding in the car.

'Thank you,' Margot mutters faintly.

'No worries,' Celine says with a little smirk.

Back in the car, Margot starts the engine, but she's still trembling.

'All okay?' Guy asks.

'Yep.'

Margot pulls away forgetting to check her mirror. Behind them, there's the blast of a car horn, and she slams on the brakes as a car speeds by, too close for comfort. She desperately needs a coffee.

She pulls away again and says, 'Can you direct me on how I turn around and get to the car park behind the fish market?'

'Do you want me to drive?' Guy asks, but Margot shakes her head. 'I'm fine. Just tell me where I can turn around.'

'You know the road! Surely you remember?'

'Just tell me!' Margot snaps.

'I've got it on Maps. Keep going straight for now,' calls Sara from the back. 'Then take the next U-turn. It doesn't look far.'

Margot hears Celine telling the kids what happened on the corniche.

'I gave him fifty riyals not to call the police,' she's saying. 'About a hundred quid. There's not much money can't buy in life.'

'But what if he still does call the police?' Flynn asks.

'He won't.'

'So it's like a scam?' Liv says. 'Like those moped riders back home? I've seen them on TikTok. They fake an accident so you give them money.'

'Dunno,' Celine says. 'I don't think it's like that here. They probably didn't plan it but just seized the opportunity to make a little cash. I always tell the new teachers when they arrive, "you're not playing in your own backyard now". Things are different here. Things that are okay at home can get you into so much trouble here.'

'It's like I was telling you,' Sara says to Liv. 'And like with your shorts this morning. You just need to be aware of where you are and be a bit respectful of the local culture. I don't want you going to jail for holding hands.'

'That's a bit dramatic,' Margot says. 'You're not going to go to jail for holding hands. Though I wouldn't advise you to do it in a traditional place like a souk out of respect, that's all. But you'll be absolutely fine doing it in a hotel or around the pool at home.'

'Always err on the side of caution. Just to be safe,' Guy says, swivelling his head before turning back to Margot. 'Here's the U-turn, Mar. Then go back along the corniche and the car park is on the right after the roundabout.'

'But that bloke just now – could he have taken our number plate,' Flynn says. 'What if there really is something wrong with that woman? Will the police come after us?'

'What's done is done,' says Celine. 'Let's not think the worst. Okay?'

Behind the fish market Margot pulls into a parking space and closes her eyes for a moment as she inhales with relief. She's not enjoying the driving today – it feels different to when they lived here. Then she used to zip around town confidently, from school run to supermarket, play date to tennis lesson. But the first day driving in the city was never going to be easy. She could let Guy take over, but that would be worse. He's an aggressive driver and lane weaving doesn't make for a relaxing passenger experience.

'If anyone's hungry we could have some food here,' Celine says, already walking off past the fish market towards the corniche. 'Have you ever tried Omani food?'

'No, but I bet it's lovely,' Sara says.

They walk straight past the coffee shop that Margot thought they'd nip into and head along the corniche towards one of the local restaurants, the type where the menu is a book with plastic pages that Margot wants to cleanse with antiseptic wipes. She growls inwardly. Celine stops outside one that has a patio. She reads the menu enthusiastically and starts pointing things out to Sara, and Margot sees once more that she was absolutely right when she thought that their holiday would be different because Sara and Liv were joining them. Had it just been the three of them, they'd grab a coffee here then eat at one of their old haunts. She has a list of places she's missed since they moved back and she wants to visit them all. She nudges Guy and they hang back from the others.

'What?' he asks.

She nods her head towards Sara and Celine. 'You want to have lunch there?'

'I thought you wanted to stop?'

'I just wanted a moment after what happened. I'm shaken. I *hit* someone.'

'I get that. You can have a moment at the restaurant.' He points towards it. 'It'll be cool and quiet.'

Margot sighs. 'I only meant a coffee. If we have a huge lunch no one will want to go out for dinner and I'd really hoped we could go to ...'

Guy stops abruptly, wrenching her arm back painfully, which forces her to stop, too.

'If you don't want to be here, say it, and we'll go home. All right?' He glowers at her. 'The point is this is what our guests want to do and that's why I'm going along with it. I'm being a polite *host*.'

They stare at each other, then Margot starts walking towards the restaurant.

'Okay,' Guy says after a beat. 'Good.'

9

SARA

'I've no idea what to order,' I say once we're all seated. 'There's so much. I like hummus. But is hummus and bread enough, or should I get something else as well? Does anyone want to share a salad?'

'Tell you what, why don't I order for everyone?' Celine says, looking around the table. 'We can do sharing plates.'

'Tell you what. Why don't you do just that?' Margot puts her menu down. 'But count me out.'

'Are you sure?' Celine asks. 'The food here is insane. You'll be missing out!'

Margot smiles. 'I'm good, thanks. I'll just have a coffee.'

When the food that Celine's ordered starts to come, it doesn't stop. Dish after dish appears from the kitchen: hummus and tabbouleh, plates of fresh Arabic bread, Fattoush, za'atar flatbreads and kibbeh, followed by platters of kebabs and diced fried potatoes laced with garlic and chilli. Somehow the waiters squeeze them all onto the table.

'Did you order the entire menu?' Guy asks, smirking as yet another dish arrives.

'Whoops,' Celine says, not looking contrite at all as the plates are passed around. 'I want Sara to try everything and we have two teenagers here! Flynn's a growing lad, aren't you? You must be eating for England to get those muscles! We can pack it to go if there's too much. It'll always get eaten. It's even better the next day.'

'It's delicious. A feast! But I feel bad that you're not eating,' I say to Margot. 'Can I tempt you with a bit of hummus?' I hold it out for her but she shakes her head.

'No, thanks. There could be pine nuts in it.'

'Oh!' says Celine. 'I forgot about your allergy.'

'No worries.' Margot takes a sip of her coffee.

'Is it a serious allergy?' I ask. 'I mean, all allergies are serious, but do you carry an EpiPen?'

'Of course,' Margot says. 'I haven't needed it for years but I always have it with me. Flynn, can you please put your phone down now the food's here?'

'Sorry,' he says. 'We were just checking Liv's mum's website.'

'"Your gut knows right from wrong",' Liv says. 'Very deep, Mother.'

I remember that one. The message had been from a young girl who'd stolen a lip gloss from a small corner shop because her friends had dared her to. She'd been wracked with guilt and messaged to ask if she should take it back and own up, or just put it back. In the heat of the moment, with her friends all stuffing things in their jackets while another diverted the owner, one cheap lip gloss hadn't seemed like a big deal, so she'd wanted to know why she felt so bad she couldn't sleep – and what to do next time she found herself in the same situation.

'Well, listening to your gut is always good advice,' I say. 'You would do well to remember it.'

'We'd all have far fewer problems if we bore that in mind. Wouldn't we?' Margot says to Guy.

'Indeed,' Guy says smoothly as he passes her a plate. 'Do you want to try the flatbread? I'm pretty sure it's nut-free.'

'Pretty sure?' Margot asks with one eyebrow raised. 'Do you want me dead?'

'Course not, Mar.' Guy chuckles and shakes his head as he moves the plate away from her.

'How do you know what to tell them, Mum?' Liv asks.

'Sara is a counsellor and agony aunt to Gen Zs,' Guy says to Celine.

'Well, some things are just common sense,' I say. 'If you listen to your gut, it really will guide you. But many people have got out of the habit of listening to it. They get egged on by others or are motivated by stronger feelings like greed or envy – or fear or anxiety – or they just react in the heat of the moment. They don't tune in to their inner self, which would normally give them the right answer.'

'Go Mum!' Liv says, and I can see from the way she's smiling that she's proud to be the one whose mum's a counsellor. Proud to be the one whose mum listens to her gut feelings and makes the right decisions – for once – and that makes me very happy. For the first time today I feel like I'm as good a mum as Margot. I look down at my food and I can't stop a smile from creeping over my face. This is exactly why I agreed to this holiday. I may have preferred it to be just the two of us elsewhere, but if this precious time with my daughter helps me to earn back her trust, it'll be worth it.

We eat enthusiastically, Liv and I exclaiming over the tastes and textures of the unfamiliar food and, as I finish the last bits on my plate, I lean back in my chair and groan, absolutely sated. I don't even want to think about fitting into my swimwear.

'I can't eat another thing. But that was absolutely delicious. Great choices, Celine. Thank you. I feel well and truly initiated.'

Celine gives me a sunny smile. 'You're so welcome. I'm glad you enjoyed it. I knew we'd eat it all.'

'Did you have any of the lamb?' Guy asks and I shake my head. 'No, I missed that one.'

'Oh, you must try it. It melts in your mouth. I've never had lamb like it.' He puts his fingertips to his lips and explodes them in a chef's kiss.

'I'm good, thanks,' I say. 'I don't think I'll eat again for another year.'

'Come on! Try it!' Guy spears a piece from his own plate and holds out the fork to me.

'No. Really, I can't,' I say, but Guy leans over, presenting the fork to me the right way around so I have no choice but to open my mouth. As I do so, out of the corner of my eye I see Margot turn away, and it leaves me feeling dirty, as if I've just made a huge faux pas.

10
MARGOT

'Right, straight home for a siesta?' Guy says, rubbing his hands together as they leave the restaurant, but Margot's not ready to go back to the villa.

'The fish market – remember?' she says. 'I'd like to pick up some fish. Maybe for dinner.'

'I can't even think about food,' Sara says.

'Well, at some point tonight I expect people will start to be hungry and I imagine no one will want to go out for a nice dinner now,' Margot says without managing to hide the edge of disappointment in her voice. 'So …'

She starts walking towards the building that houses the indoor fish, fruit and vegetable market. She honestly doesn't care if the others come inside with her or not; she needs a bit of time to herself after the circus that was lunch – *Oh, you must try it. I've never had lamb like it.* This is one of the things she's looked forward to doing in Oman. She used to come here once a week to buy fish; she knew some of the sellers by name and they'd send her pictures of the morning's catch if they got anything special. To this day, she salivates when she thinks about the fish; literally from sea to plate in hours. If everyone else is too full to eat tonight, she'll slap it in a pan and enjoy it on her own.

Margot glances back towards the door – no one is following her into the market. She can see them standing around outside in the sunshine. Celine is vaping and they're all laughing at something Guy's said. As usual. If only they knew what he was really like. But, after all these years, Margot is used to the huge disparity between the face Guy presents to the world and the face he shows to her. Jekyll and Hyde.

Inside, the familiar briny smell of fish envelops her and she's hit by the blissfully cool air. Margot takes her time browsing the vast steel sinks, taking in the huge variety of seafood on offer. She can identify Japanese threadfin bream with its pinky colour, mackerel, sardines, squid, kingfish and the local brown-spotted hammour, but some she has to ask about. In the end, she decides to plan as if the others will want to eat, and chooses a crowd-pleaser for dinner – sheri. Guy will no doubt insist on throwing it on the barbecue, and she'll serve it with a salad. Tesco pasta sauce be damned.

She's getting the fish wrapped and bagged when Sara comes up to her.

'It's amazing in here,' Sara says. 'So many fish.'

Margot gives her a tight smile. 'Well, it *is* a fish market.' She could say that the best time to be there is early morning when the fishermen unload their catches; that what she sees here is a fraction of what would have been on offer earlier in the day – but Margot is a woman of few words.

'Do you know what they all are?' Sara asks and Margot shakes her head.

'Not all. But enough.'

'What did you buy?' Sara asks.

'Sheri,' says Margot, not expecting Sara to have heard of it.

'Ah. Okay. So, umm, the kids are itching to get back. They're talking about going to the beach. It's a beautiful afternoon.'

Margot knows she can be stubborn at times, and this is one of those moments.

'Well, I just need to pick up some fruit and veg,' she says. Sara and Margot both look towards a different section of the market. Pyramids and piles of vibrant produce stretch as far as they can see.

'Okay,' says Sara, looking doubtful. 'Do you need a hand?'

'No, thanks. I'm good.'

'If you're sure. Well, I'll see you back outside.'

Browsing the fruit and veg is like therapy for Margot. She wanders through the main aisle of the market, feeling the satisfying weight of a melon and assessing the firmness of a banana. Next she potters over to the chilled section and picks out a variety of salad leaves, a couple of bunches of fresh spinach, Omani mushrooms, big juicy tomatoes and a box of dates, and she starts to get a grip on her feelings. It's not the others' fault she feels this way, she tells herself. And she can see that Sara is trying – she's really trying to connect with her.

But Margot's problem is that, over the course of her marriage, she's become a loner. Before Guy, she used to be gregarious, daring, adventurous and always into something or other – but her world has shrunk and sharing her emotions and making friendships no longer come easily to her. In her more reflective moments, she understands that her problems likely stem from the fact she plays her cards too close to her chest and people simply don't know what she's thinking or feeling, and then she's left feeling lonely because she has no friends. And, God knows, she could do with a friend right now.

Margot sighs. Everything always leads back to bloody Guy. Margot had never planned to marry, never dreamed about the dress or the bridesmaids or Prince Charming, but then Guy Forrest had happened. Like a cyclone making landfall, he'd torn into her life, blasting her off her feet, and now here she is all these years later, suddenly wondering: how did I get here? What happened to *me*? Where did I go? And whispering to herself: *how can I get out*?

She shakes her head as she realises her thoughts are rambling. The others will be feeling the heat outside by now. She'll try to make an effort with Sara. The last thing she needs is her becoming best friends with Celine bloody Cremorne, and it looks like it's going that way already. She gathers her bags and heads back to the door. Time to go home.

11
SARA

'Shall we head down to the pool?' I ask Liv when we get back, but she shakes her head.

'Me and Flynn are going to the beach. He reckons we might be able to hire a jet ski or a kayak or something.'

'Something more exciting than hanging out with your old mum,' I say, trying to hide my disappointment with a laugh, but I'm unnerved to feel the sudden burn of tears.

'Aww, Mum,' Liv says, pulling me into a hug. 'Don't be like that. I'm so glad you're here. Are you enjoying it so far?'

I hold her longer than she probably wants.

'Of course I am!' I say when she pulls away. 'It's so nice to be with you. That food today was amazing, wasn't it? And Celine seems fun.'

'Yeah, why don't you hang out with her this afternoon?'

'Maybe I will. Anyway, have fun at the beach. Check the water for riptides. You got that video I sent you on Instagram, didn't you? You know what to look for?'

'Mm-hmm,' she says in a way that implies she didn't even open it. 'Right, see ya.'

I flop onto my bed for a moment before heading out to the pool. The food's made me drowsy and I could do with some alone time to process everything that happened this morning, not least the mini accident we had down by the souk. I shudder as I imagine what I'd have done if that had happened to me out driving on my own. It makes me double down on my decision not to get behind the wheel of a car over here. Follow your gut and all that.

As my muscles relax, my mind starts to drift. The Forrests really are a strange pair. On the surface they look so together, so glossy, but the moment you look closer, you can see tension roiling between them. I feel there might be more to Margot than the demure side she shows. And if there's one thing I know about relationships, when one person is always backing down it'll all blow up at some point. Hopefully not while we're here.

'Right, come on, Sara,' I say as I haul myself back up. I can lie on a bed anywhere but it's not every day I get to lie in the sunshine by a sparkling turquoise pool. I put on the bikini that I bought specially for the trip but, as I stand in front of the mirror and think about Guy and Margot seeing me in all my flabby forty-eight-year-old glory, I see that I'd been way too optimistic in the Marks & Spencer changing rooms.

I turn this way and that, sucking in my belly and pulling at the flab at the top of my thighs, but the fact is I've put on half a stone since I last wore a bikini – and it's too late to do anything about it now. I know I shouldn't compare myself to Margot, or the spritely child that is Celine for that matter but, in reality, if Margot lies next to me by the pool and I'm in this bikini, I'll shrivel up with mortification. Margot's about five foot ten to my five foot five, plus she's lean. In that liminal space when I'd first met Guy but was yet to meet Margot, I'd stalked her social media and my heart had sunk at the sight of her lanky frame at various upmarket social occasions looking angular in maxi dresses or cigarette trousers, accessorised with hats and spiky heels. Hers is a body borne partly through good genes, but I suspect also through ironclad discipline. Mine, not so much. The lunch we've just had being a prime example. I can't believe she didn't eat a thing. Maybe she controls her own world so meticulously as a way of pushing back against Guy. The way he'd mentioned being responsible for the 'disciplining' of his employee had felt weird, like it was more than a joke. It's an odd partnership, that's for sure.

I pull off the bikini and put on my tummy control swimsuit, tie a wrap around my lower half and go down to the pool. Margot and Guy are nowhere to be seen so I stretch out on a lounger and close my eyes. It's December. The weather back home is vile but I'm lying in the sun by a pool, my daughter is on holiday with me and, for now, in this moment, life is good.

I don't know how much later it is when I come to and hear the sound of Celine's voice.

'Hello-o!' she calls. 'You look relaxed! Fancy some company?' Without waiting for me to respond, she plonks herself on the lounger next to mine. 'My villa's so empty.'

'Well, I'm here!' I say, genuinely happy to see her. Celine complements our group in a way that works for me. When she's around, I'm no longer the odd number, the mother of the bride, the gooseberry to the two couples. Celine is someone for me to talk to. And she's so easy to be with. 'Thanks for the tour this morning,' I say. 'Your commentary was great.'

'You're welcome,' she says. 'I love showing people around.

'And I'm so impressed with how you handled the accident.'

She shrugs. 'You learn these things when you live here.'

'Do you think you'll ever move back?'

'You can never say never, can you? But I don't want to,' she says, stretching out her tanned limbs on her lounger. 'I live for the sunshine. The salary's tax-free, and I earn more here than I would back home.'

'When you put it like that ...' I say, laughing. 'And you can afford to live somewhere really lovely like this.'

'Oh, I share with three other teachers. But I'd rather do that and have all this than be in a studio or one-bed on my own.'

'Fair enough,' I say, trying not to compare the grounds to my own muddy patch of grass back home. 'I'd love to wake up to sunshine every day.'

'I know, right? I find people are just more cheerful here and I'm sure it's because of the sun.' She pauses. 'So how do you know the Forrests?'

'Just through Liv.'

Celine swats a fly off her arm. 'Is that all? I got the feeling it was more than that. With Guy anyway.'

I give a little shrug. 'No. I barely know him.'

'You sure?' Celine says. 'Because Margot's got her eye on you.'

'Got her eye on me? In what way?'

'You haven't noticed the way Guy looks at you? His whole face lights up.'

I scoff. 'Stop it! That's not true.'

Celine pulls a face at me. 'Isn't it? "Come on, Sara! Try the lamb!"' She mimes Guy holding out his fork earlier. 'Well, in my opinion, you're on Margot's radar.'

'Oh. That's not good.' I shift awkwardly on the lounger.

'They've been so kind inviting me here. I'd hate for her to feel uncomfortable. About nothing!'

'Oh, trust me, Margot Forrest is always uncomfortable about something. That woman is never happy.'

'Really? She's so successful and she has a lovely family. Though I do feel like I barely know her …' I hope Celine will take the bait and tell me more.

She snorts a laugh. 'It's not you, it's her – trust me. I don't think anyone knows her properly, not even Guy. It's just how she is. So buttoned up.'

'How long have you known them?'

'Since I moved into this compound, so I knew them for about two years before they left, which was just before Covid.'

'Do you know why they left? They seem to miss it so much. Margot especially.'

I don't want to gossip but it's tempting to pick the brains of someone who knows the Forrests better than I do.

'The official answer is it was because of Margot's dad,' Celine says. 'He's getting on and was no longer able to live independently. He was going to move in with them. That's what they told everyone anyway.'

'Fair enough.'

'But when they got back, they put him in a block of really fancy assisted living apartments, which – because I googled – I know is only available to rent and costs an absolute fortune. It even has a swimming pool. Anyway, as far as I know, Guy's paying for it out of an inheritance he received when his parents passed away.'

'Ah. That's nice of him.' But even as I say it, I'm wondering if it's as generous as it sounds. Guy spending his inheritance on her dad's home would definitely skew the balance of power in their relationship, if it wasn't already skewed to begin with. I like Guy, but it doesn't take a lot for me to imagine him holding that over her if he wanted to.

'Isn't it just? Well, that's the party line on why they left,' Celine says with a naughty smile. 'But, if you think about it, her dad is in a lovely place, so that really isn't a reason to leave here, is it? It's not like he moved in with them.' She pauses and licks her lips. 'So that brings me on to the unofficial reason.'

'And?'

Celine examines her nails. 'Let's just say Guy did something. Got in some trouble here, lost his job and had his visa cancelled, so they had no choice.'

'Oh ... do you know what it was?'

Celine pulls an imaginary zip across her mouth. 'I could tell you, but I'd have to kill you.' She laughs. 'No, look. It was an internal matter at his work. Harassment of a junior employee is what I heard. Female, of course.' She rolls her eyes. 'The police got involved but Guy was never charged with anything. It was probably just wishful thinking on her part!'

I laugh uneasily. For it to be bad enough to have the police called ...

'Anyway, keep it zipped because it's not something that they let be widely known.'

I immediately want to know how she knows. I don't see Margot telling her, so it must be hearsay – unless Guy told her himself.

'No, of course,' I say. 'I understand. But I wonder why her dad couldn't just live with them? In Cheltenham, I mean. I've seen their house. It's huge.'

'Guy can't stand the dad. He'd rather fritter away his inheritance so he's the only alpha male in the house. Other peoples' lives, eh?' Celine laughs.

'But things are okay between Guy and Margot, aren't they?'

'You saw them today at lunchtime. I mean, what do you think?' Celine shakes her head and smiles. 'Refusing to eat was typical Margot. And Guy, well, is Guy, as you've probably noticed ...'

She doesn't get to say anymore because Liv and Flynn appear around the pool. Flynn takes a running dive straight into the deep end and Liv holds her nose and leaps in after him before Sara's able to warn her that the pool's only five feet deep.

12

MARGOT

When Flynn and Liv come in, Margot's cooking. She's decided to make a creamy potato dauphinois laced with garlicky sautéed mushrooms to go with her fish and salad. The oven has heated up the kitchen to what feels like fifty degrees despite the extractor running so fast it sounds like it's going to take off. Under her hair, Margot's scalp feels wet with sweat and she keeps blotting her forehead with kitchen roll. If the others hadn't had that stupid lunch, they'd probably be getting ready for drinks and dinner somewhere nice right now. Maybe that Indian they used to go to. It was always nice there.

Flynn and Liv have beach towels knotted around their hips and wet hair.

'How was the beach?' Margot asks. 'Try not to drip on the floor, please.'

'Sea's quite cold but the pool's lovely,' Flynn says. 'What's for dinner? I'm actually starving.'

'Flynn Forrest, I swear you never stop eating. I've got fish. Olivia, are you hungry, too? Do you need dinner?'

'Yes, please, Mrs Forrest. I didn't eat much at lunch, to be honest. Fish sounds lovely. Do you need any help?'

Margot smiles. 'No. Thank you. I'll just throw a few extra veggies into the salad and Flynn's dad can barbecue the fish, so no problem. Thanks for offering.'

'Cool,' Flynn says. 'Babe, you go on up, I'll be up in a minute.'

Margot's mum-radar springs to life. Her son has been glued at the hip to Liv on this holiday. She's always had a very close relationship with him, but she can feel her influence starting to swing to Liv, and it gives her an unnerving feeling of being untethered. No longer needed. She turns to face him with a soft smile.

'You all right, darling?'

Flynn's face creases in the way it used to when he was upset as a child. 'Yeah. But. Well ... it's Celine,' he says. 'I mean, is she going to hang around with us all the time?'

Margot tries not to show her own opinion. 'Does it bother you if she does?'

'I just ... she's ... uh, I don't know. I just don't think it's right. It's our holiday, yeah?'

'It certainly is.'

'So ... why is she always here?'

Margot blows air out of her mouth in lieu of the words she can't say. *Because your dad wants her to be.*

'She lives here, and she's excited to see us,' Margot says mildly. 'All her friends are away. She's probably having quite a lonely time.'

'But still.' Flynn's tone is petulant and Margot wonders what Celine has said or done to get under his skin like this. Nothing surprises her when it comes to their ex-neighbour.

'Come here.' Margot pulls Flynn into a hug, breathing in

the swimming-pool smell of his skin. It takes her back to the days when he was small enough for her to squat down and envelop his whole body in a warm, dry towel after he'd been in the pool.

'I want you to have a good holiday, too,' Flynn says when she lets him go. 'That's all.'

He catches her eye, and she freezes, then quickly turns her back and checks the oven while she gathers herself.

'Okay,' she says. 'Well, look, I certainly won't be inviting her to join us for anything, but I can't speak for your father.'

'Exactly,' Flynn huffs.

Margot pretends not to hear.

'Right,' Flynn says after a beat, 'I'm gonna have my shower.'

'Nice chatting!' Margot calls to his back.

Moments later, Sara appears in the kitchen. She's freshly dressed in a linen shorts-and-shirt two-piece that Margot recalls seeing in the sale in a shop in the Regent Arcade.

It hasn't escaped Margot's notice that Sara spent time with Celine this afternoon and she really doesn't like that. Celine knows things that Margot would rather weren't discussed. She tried to catch what was being said from the balcony, but only got snatches of sentences thrown on the wind. Though she's sure she heard her name and Guy's name. What was Celine telling Sara? Margot doesn't like the idea of them talking about her. Doesn't like the idea of them being friends. Paradoxically, she doesn't like being excluded, yet she knows she can hardly expect to be included in their blossoming alliance, given how standoffish she's being.

'Mmm, something smells yummy,' Sara says. 'I can't believe I'm hungry again. Is there enough fish for one more?'

'Of course,' Margot says, forcing a smile.

'Oh, great! Because if there isn't, I can fix myself a sandwich or something.'

'No, it's fine. The kids are hungry, too, and it's best if the fish is cooked today anyway.'

'What can I do?' Sara asks.

Margot slides over a bunch of celery. 'Can you dice that and mix it though the salad?' Celine has not been invited over tonight, but Margot is sure as the sky is blue that her nemesis will turn up. Celine loathes celery and Margot just can't help herself: small victories.

When Guy comes down and sees that Margot's cooking for everyone, he insists – as she knew he would – on barbecuing the fish. It's not to do with kindness; it's about being the centre of attention; it's about the showmanship of producing the meal for everyone, despite the fact that it was Margot who chose the food, bought it and worked away in the sweatshop of the kitchen.

Margot gives Guy a chance to get the barbecue lit, then loads up a tray with crockery, cutlery and glasses and steps through the patio doors into the balmy evening, pausing to inhale the scent of jasmine and frangipani that have cooked all day in the gentle warmth of the winter sun. Flynn and Liv, showered and dressed, are now sitting on the edge of the pool, their feet once again dangling in the water, ripples spreading across the surface.

Flynn turns on hearing her footsteps. 'Hey. When's dinner?'

'Fish ETA five minutes,' Guy calls from the barbecue.

'Sara's just setting the table if either of you want to help,'

Margot says. To their credit, both the kids haul themselves up and come to the table, painting wet footprints across the tiles as they set the places and light the candles.

'Lay a place for Celine!' Guy calls, and Margot screams silently. Her husband is like the bloody Pied Piper, she thinks – his group of fans and hangers-on grows by the day.

'Sure!' Sara says. 'I was chatting to her by the pool this afternoon. She's so nice! She was telling me all about her life here. It sounds amazing.'

'I bet it does,' Margot says. 'What else did she say?'

'Oh, nothing much. Just girl chat, you know how it is.'

Margot wishes she did. She glances at Celine's villa. Like the others around the pool, it's cast in darkness and that gives her some cause for hope: maybe Celine's gone out. She goes back into the kitchen and brings out the salad. Liv and Flynn take their seats at the table while Sara lingers, looking to see if anything else needs doing, and making sure she doesn't sit before Margot does. Margot understands why she's doing that, but it still irritates her. She could do without the pressure of being the hostess.

'Thanks, Sara. I think that's everything.' Margot sinks into a chair. She wishes she could bottle the heady evening scent of the plants and take it back to Cheltenham with her. She misses this place so much her chest actually aches, and the familiar resentment about having to leave rolls over her again. She reaches for the wine Guy got this afternoon via Tom and pours herself a generous glass.

'Right! Grub's up!' Guy calls as he slides the grilled sheri onto a serving plate and brings it over. He looks around.

'What, no Celine?' He sounds disappointed, as if it won't

be a decent evening without her. As if the people already there are worthless.

'Her lights are off,' Margot says placidly, 'so maybe not.'

She exchanges a quick glance with Flynn and they smile.

'Let's dig in,' Guy says, and then Margot hears it:

'Yoo-hoo, guys! Got space for a little one?'

13

SARA

'Come on over! The more the merrier!' Guy shouts. 'We set a place for you!

'Yay!' Over the other side of the pool, Celine does a little cheer with her fists in the air and wiggles her hips. She's wearing a flowing white maxi dress with gold jewellery at her throat, wrists and ears, and high-heeled mules that clack on the tiles as she skirts around the pool. Her lip gloss matches those red-orange nails and her dark hair is loose, but held back from her face with a casual clasp so it catches the breeze as she walks. The overall effect is one hundred per cent Greek goddess. I feel utterly inadequate in my crumpled shorts and shirt set. It had looked so nice on the mannequin in the shop, but I hadn't really thought ahead to how it would look once I'd sat in it for a bit. In the heat. I hope there's no sweat marks when I stand up.

'Hey, hey, hey!' Celine sings as she gets closer. She kisses her fingers and waves them around the table in a greeting. Her hair actually bounces like it's in a shampoo ad.

'What a treat,' she says to Margot. 'You were on the nose about being hungry later. This looks absolutely delicious.'

'You look very smart. Don't let us hold you back if you had plans,' Margot says.

'Oh, no. Not at all. Absolutely everyone and his dog went away for Christmas. I've been Billy No-Mates for the last week. I've practically forgotten how to speak.'

'I love your dress,' I say, although I do wonder why she's all dressed up if she has no plans. Had Guy invited her on the sly?

'Thanks! Outnet sale,' Celine says. 'Absolute bargain. You look lovely, too. I adore linen.'

Guy offers her the platter of fish and we all start passing food around.

'So what did you two get up to this afternoon?' she asks Guy. 'Anything you can talk about in front of the kids?' She winks at Flynn, who looks at his plate.

'I slept off lunch in time for dinner,' Guy says with a chuckle, 'and Margot, I think – what did you do, Mar?'

She waves her hand at the table, presenting the food as her reply.

'Well, it all looks lovely,' Celine says. 'Sara and I hung out by the pool. I tried to persuade her to move here. So, did it work? Have you been googling one-way flights and residence visas?' she asks me.

'Ha ha!' I laugh. 'I wouldn't need much persuading!'

'What about me?' Liv says, and I open my mouth then close it again. Is she worried I might move abroad? I smile and reach over to squeeze her hand.

'I'm not going anywhere, don't you worry.'

'Good!' Liv says, and it lights me up like a Christmas tree.

'How about you guys?' I say to the Forrests without thinking. 'Would you ever come back here to live? Maybe after Flynn's A-levels?'

Flynn glances at Margot and they both look away. I can't believe I put my foot in it just like that.

'We're settled in Cheltenham now,' Guy says smoothly. 'For Margot's dad. And it would be too difficult to run the business from here. Margot does a lot of home visits.'

Margot's staring at the salad, her face inscrutable.

'Of course,' I say, wishing the ground would swallow me up.

'Well, if you won't come back, maybe I can tempt Flynn back once he's finished school,' Celine says with a grin. There's a beat of silence before she says, 'So, what are you all up to tomorrow?'

'I've got a round of golf booked at the Club,' Guy says. 'And I think Mar's got her own plans.'

'I'm having a pool and spa day at The Chedi,' she says.

I looked up The Chedi the first time she mentioned it – it's a five-star hotel that looks absolutely divine. I thought about joining Margot but she hasn't said anything to lead me to believe that she wants me there – besides, it's pretty pricey.

'Maybe we could do something,' I say to Liv. 'Explore a bit?'

But Liv and Flynn exchange a look. 'Flynn and me are going to some of his favourite places from when he was growing up,' she says.

'Oh! Maybe I could come with you? Would that be fun? I'd love to see.'

Liv gives her head a tiny but definite shake as she mouths, 'No!'

'It's only Marah Land,' says Flynn with his hand over his mouth because he's chewing. 'It's not very exciting.'

'And then we're going to the mall,' Liv says.

'Oh, lovely – have lunch there. Put it on the credit card,' Margot says to Flynn, and irritation flares inside me. Can't Margot see that I want to spend time with my daughter? Isn't it obvious that's why I'm here?

'So what will you do, Sara?' Guy asks. 'Do you play golf? Want to join me?'

I shake my head. Again, I'm the odd one out. 'Don't worry about me. I'll lie by the pool, or maybe go down to the beach. I'll be grand.'

'So what else do you have planned while you're here?' Celine asks. 'You go back early next week, don't you?'

'Yes. We want to get over the jet lag before the kids go back to school. They've got their mocks,' Margot says.

'I'm sure you're hard enough to cope with a bit of jet lag,' Celine says, raising her eyebrows at Flynn. 'You should stay longer. Let the others go back, and stick around till after New Year. I'll look after you.' She chuckles. 'Remember the fun we had when I used to babysit? This could be the grown-up version!'

'We need to revise,' Liv says glancing at Flynn. 'Exams start the first week back.'

'What's the desert like?' I ask, trying to deflect the conversation from whatever was making Flynn blush. 'Is it worth a trip? Is it far?'

'It's magnificent,' Guy says. 'Actually, you're right. You can't come to Oman and not see the desert. It's magical. You should see it at least once in your life. Watching the sun sink into the dunes is one of the seven wonders of the world. At least it should be.'

'How would I even do that?' I ask. 'Can I just ask a taxi to take me there? Is there somewhere I should head to, or a scenic route I should follow? I don't really want to drive myself.'

'*Yalla*, James! Take me to the desert!' Guy says in a posh British accent. He's poking fun at me, and it makes me feel silly. But how am I supposed to know?

'No, seriously,' he continues. 'It's about a hundred and fifty miles. But we could head out that way. We might get to see some camels, and it'll be nice for Liv to see some desert, too.' He scratches his chin thoughtfully. 'But you want to be out there for sunset, really. Nothing beats that silence when you're in the middle of nowhere and the sun's just gone over the horizon.'

'It makes you realise how small and insignificant your problems are in the general scheme of things,' Margot says.

'I find the desert experience is vastly improved if there's a glass of champagne on hand,' Celine says. 'Or, even better, a couple of magnums!'

I laugh with her. 'I like your style!'

'Sara and Liv could go on a desert safari,' Margot says. She turns to Sara. 'I think they go to Wahiba Sands, which is stunning. It's a full day. They take you out in a four-wheel drive, throw you about a bit over the dunes, show you a traditional Bedouin house and give you a chance to swim in a wadi. But it's a long way in a day,' she muses. 'You could go overnight, then you'd have a traditional Arabic dinner and there's usually some belly-dancing and some camels to ride – stuff like that – and you'd stay in one of those "luxury" tents. It'll give you a real taste of the desert and you'd see the sunset. I think you'd love it.'

Guy sighs and clucks his tongue. 'Too touristy. But I tell you what.' His foot starts to jiggle and his eyes narrow thoughtfully. 'We could do it ourselves. We could rent another four-wheel drive and camp in the desert.' He turns to Margot, eyes shining. 'You can get to some decent bits of desert within a couple of hours from here ... we could borrow gear from Tom and Di. I'm sure they'd lend us their camping stuff. I mean – why not?' He's nodding slowly as he runs through the logistics in his head. 'If we put our minds to it, we could make it happen. What d'you reckon? Do you fancy a night under canvas?'

I look at Margot. 'It sounds fun. What do you think?'

Margot opens her mouth then closes it again. Then she sighs and starts clearing the plates.

14
MARGOT

Margot gets up early the next day, packs her day bag quietly, makes a quick coffee and creeps out of the house before anyone else wakes up. She knows there are women who like to go to the spa with girlfriends and catch up in the sauna and the jacuzzi or sip ginger tea while wrapped in white robes, and she realises this might have been a good chance to bond a little with Sara, but she's been looking forward to this alone time for so long she can't sacrifice it. How on earth would she manage to talk to Sara all day?

She closes the front door quietly and takes the Land Cruiser – it's a given that Guy will drink at the golf club and therefore won't drive. She cranks up the music and opens the windows and, less than half an hour later, she's passing through the hotel's elegant white gateway. Already the tension and stress sitting in her neck from the tonne of responsibilities she always seems to shoulder are starting to dissipate as she anticipates stretching out in blissful solitude on a lounger next to one of the three beautiful pools. The childfree one that faces the sea, she thinks.

As the hotel's ever courteous staff welcome Margot and usher her through the lobby, her insides are twisted once more by the pang of regret that Guy didn't book them into a hotel. Yes, they have the garden at the villa, but what they don't have is all this luxury and service – the things that make *her* life easier for the week. *And* they wouldn't have bumped into bloody Celine. It needn't even be somewhere as fancy as The Chedi. Muscat has plenty of gorgeous beachfront hotels. It would have meant that she, too, could have a proper holiday rather than simply hosting guests in a different location, which is what self-catering in an Airbnb feels like to Margot.

'Enjoy,' the pool butler says, after unfurling a thick towel onto the lounger he's arranged for her, partly in the sun, partly in the shade, just as she requested. Margot slips out of her kaftan and lets her body sink onto the lounger. This is what a holiday should be like, she thinks. This is what she craves. It hasn't slipped her notice how she's most content when Guy isn't around. Everyone else finds him charming but his bonhomie – the exact thing that attracted her to him in the first place – has begun to grate on her. Perhaps it's because she can see through it. Perhaps it's because he turns it on for everyone, like a lamp. He's not discriminating and, as someone who is very discriminating, Margot finds his chumminess phoney.

She lets her head fall back on the lounger, fixing her hair off her face with her sunglasses, and, as the sun warms her eyelids, she lets her mind wander properly for the first time since they arrived. When Guy had first brought up the idea of coming back to Oman she'd had mixed feelings. Of course she wanted to come, her love for Oman is enmeshed in her soul and she was keen to soak up that Gulf winter sun. But equally she didn't want to be reminded of the way in which they'd had to pack up their lives, of the indignity of quitting the country where they had, very publicly, said they wanted to stay for the long term, by pretending it was their choice to leave to take care of her dad. Humiliated beyond endurance, she'd turned her back on friends, who'd been almost as close as family, as she and Guy had wound up their expat lives. Always presenting a united front: the Forrests' family motto, voiced most loudly by Guy, was 'one for all and all for one'.

Once Guy had the idea that they should come to Oman over the Christmas school holidays, he'd ridden roughshod over her objections until, in the end, Margot had allowed herself to look forward to the holiday.

What she wasn't expecting was to go back to the precise scene of their old lives – not just that, but to find Celine still there. Margot is not naive enough to imagine that was a surprise for Guy. So, is this his cack-handed way of trying to tell her that nothing happened between them – back when she chose to look the other way in order to keep the family together? That the red lingerie she found trapped down the side of the spare-room bed was not Celine's? That the figure she'd seen Celine kissing in her shadowy bedroom window was not Guy? Because the alternative – that he was and still is carrying on with Celine – is too monstrous to consider. Besides, she's seen the way he's now looking at Sara of all people. The images of Guy passing her his fork, of admiring her work and complimenting her student-standard cooking slide into Margot's memory like unwanted DMs. Sighing she resolves not to let these thoughts ruin her perfect day.

When the sun's temperature on her skin starts to border on uncomfortable, she places her wide-brimmed hat on her head, slips into the pool and, with languid breaststrokes, swims over to the infinity edge. There, facing the sea, she leans on her elbows, stares out at the endless horizon and lets her mind drift.

She's pleased with how well Margot's Mansions is doing although, if she's honest, she could do without the huge pressure she's now under to produce models to deadlines. When Flynn was tiny, she'd started making the doll's houses as a creative outlet that she could fit around childcare. She liked doing things with her hands and was captivated by making things in miniature. She made one for a friend and that led to another until it started to give her not just a small income but a legitimate reason to spend time apart from Guy in the evenings. Perhaps that's why she put in so much time, she thinks ruefully, and became so good at it.

But Guy couldn't let her have it. He couldn't bear that she had something without him. When he was sacked, he took over her hobby and now she's stuck at home with him 24/7. She can't even go to the bathroom without him knowing. It's suffocating, and her hobby is no longer her respite. She can feel the pressure building, and she has no idea how it'll end.

15
SARA

With the pool and villa to myself for most of the day, I'm a pig in clover. For a few hours, I don't need to be the perfect houseguest; I don't need to worry about stepping on toes, offending egos, making faux pas and worrying about what Margot thinks of me. I find a local English-language radio station and boogie around the kitchen as I make breakfast, pretending to myself that the villa with the glittering pool is mine – that the life here in the gorgeous sunshine is all mine, mine, mine. And maybe it could be! I've always hated the dank greyness of the British winter, the short days, and the endless rain that leaves everything wet for weeks at a time. Maybe I *could* make this work. I do some visualising, trying to send a message out to the universe that I'd be open to life in Oman. Maybe Liv would come with me once she finishes school. They must have universities here. I smile to myself as I think about Michael taking that and shoving it in his six-holidays-a-year pipe.

I see that Margot's bought some flour and we have milk, sugar and eggs, so I whisk up some batter and make a stack of pancakes which are just about ready as Liv and Flynn come down. I haven't been this domesticated in years, and the pancake recipe is a bit hit-and-miss but who's watching?

'Ta-da! Breakfast's ready – if you fancy some,' I say, and the look on Liv's face is one I know I'll cherish. Selfishly, I hope news of the wonderful pancakes I made for the teens filters back to Margot.

'Oh, wow, thanks,' Liv says. 'Flynn loves pancakes!'

'Great! What do you have on them?' I ask. 'We don't have syrup but there's Greek yoghurt, bananas and blueberries. Oh, and dates?'

'Amazing,' Flynn says. 'A bit of everything, maybe?' As they both sit down and start helping themselves – and I whip out all the fruit and start slicing bananas and pass over the Greek yoghurt – I experience for the first time in forever what a joy it is to feed people who want to eat. I can be a good mum. I know I can. I just need to be given the chance. Maybe it's true what they say: the way to someone's heart is through their stomach. Well, with Liv, maybe it's through her boyfriend's stomach, but at least I've had another chance to impress her.

When their taxi comes, I wish the kids a fun time at Marah Land and start clearing up the kitchen. I'm tempted to leave it till later since I know Margot will be out all day, but the thought of the look she'd give me if she came back to a messy kitchen is enough to motivate me. Before long, I'm stretched out on my towel on a lounger by the pool, thinking how wonderful it would be to have this as an everyday thing. Imagine getting up in the morning and being able to have a swim before breakfast! Imagine the weekends lying by the pool!

I lose myself in my book, make a sandwich for lunch, and continue my day by the pool. Who needs the expense of The Chedi when you have this in your backyard? People who have money never seem to ask themselves if there's a perfectly good, free option for what they want to do. What will Margot be doing over there? Exactly what I'm doing here, but for loads of money.

That thought gets me wondering what she thought when I didn't offer to go with her. Did she think I was being a cheapskate? Or that I was giving her space? I've moved from being slightly scared of her to feeling like I might want, maybe, to be friends with her. If things continue with Flynn and Liv, Margot and I will be seeing a lot of each other in the coming years. But Celine's words about me being on Margot's radar have rattled me – now I feel I need to prove to Margot that there's absolutely nothing between Guy and me. Speaking of which, perhaps I should have just gone with her to The Chedi, after all? Was she waiting for me to offer? Or being polite and not inviting me in case I couldn't afford it? For a counsellor, I sometimes surprise myself with how socially inept I can be.

'Yoo-hoo! Sara!'

In one movement, I scramble to sit up, get my sunglasses over my eyes and arrange my legs in the most flattering pose I can think of, like I'm modelling for a magazine cover. As I do so, I notice that the sun is significantly lower in the sky. I must have fallen asleep. My skin feels hot. I bet I'm red as a beetroot.

'Celine! Hi! Oh, and hello, Guy!'

They both stand over me, blocking out the sun.

'Had a good day?' I ask. 'How was golf?'

They look at each other.

'Great,' says Guy. 'Celine was at a loose end, so I persuaded her to join me.'

'Oh, nice,' I say. 'I didn't know you played.'

She laughs. 'I hacked my way around to keep him company. He hates playing alone. Anyway, "Celine says" we've earned a glass of wine, so how about you fetch us all one, G?'

'Amen to that,' he says. 'I'm on it.' As he disappears off into the villa, Celine sits on the lounger next to me. She stretches her fingers out and looks at her nails.

'By the way, look, it's nothing suspicious or anything, but maybe best not to mention to Margot that I was with Guy today.'

I take a moment before I reply because the funny thing is, I hadn't been suspicious. Yes, a part of me wondered how they ended up playing together, though it really is none of my business. But now it sounds entirely like she's covering something up. My mind rewinds at high speed through the times I've seen them together: is there something going on between these two? Has there ever been?

'Of course,' I say. 'But – should I be suspicious?'

Celine closes her eyes and puffs out a little air. It seems as if she's not going to say anything else, so I wait. I know that silence is often rewarded with further elaboration, and I am not wrong.

'Who, in such a long marriage, is actually happy?' she says eventually. 'Show me that person, and I'll show you a liar.' She laughs and looks towards the villa.

Ouch, I think. Messy.

16
MARGOT

As the sun starts to sink towards the horizon, turning the sky a soft apricot, Margot picks up the pool bar menu and thinks about a crisp glass of Chablis and a little dish of olives. She would give anything to have a drink here, in solitude, before she goes back to face her husband, her teenager and her houseguests. She knows she'd be fine to drive after one glass, but there's absolutely no way she'll risk breaking the law. Anyway, Guy said he'd be back by four latest and they spoke about going to the souk at six, so she puts the menu down and reluctantly begins to gather her things. Her day in blissful solitude is over.

The sky turns pink then slides into purples and mauves as Margot drives back to the villa, her foot easing up on the gas the closer she gets. But she can't delay the inevitable and, before she knows it, she's opening the front door. She hears at once the laughter coming from the garden, and sees the shapes of several people out there. In the kitchen there's already an empty wine bottle on the counter and anger flashes through her: either they've forgotten that they were going to the souk or Guy has assumed, as always, that Margot will refrain from a sundowner so that he can have six, and that she will be the designated driver.

For a few moments, she watches them all through the window: Guy, Celine and Sara. They look perfect together, complete somehow, as they talk and tease and throw their heads back with laughter while sipping their drinks. She sees how Celine watches Guy, her fingers fluttering on and off his arm as he speaks; how Sara belly-laughs when Celine tells a story; and how her husband's face lights up when Sara speaks. Where does Margot fit into this picture? There is no space for her.

She takes a deep breath and steps outside.

'Margot! How was it?' Sara calls, the first to notice her. 'Did you have a lovely day?'

Margot smiles. 'I did, thank you. How about you?'

Sara babbles on about having a brilliant time doing nothing and feeling so ridiculously lazy and how it's all just been absolute heaven. While Margot waits for her to finish, she notices that Celine has sunburned cheeks that match those of her husband.

'What did you do, Celine?' she asks lightly, and every cell in her body is receptive to the frozen microsecond that occurs before Celine replies.

'I lay in the sun here, too. Can't you tell,' she says, waving her hand at her face. 'Fell asleep and got a bit too much.'

She notices Sara's eyes flick to Guy and then away as Celine speaks, and that tells Margot all she needs to know. Celine was out with Guy, whatever they were doing – golf or something else.

'Where are the kids?' she asks.

'Upstairs having showers,' Sara says. 'They haven't been back long.'

'So, what about the souk at six?' Margot says briskly, looking at her watch. 'It's getting late …'

Guy slaps both hands on his thighs. 'Oh, shit! Completely forgot about that!' He looks at his wine glass and pulls a face. 'Whoops!'

'Liv wanted to go, didn't she?' Margot asks Sara.

'Yes,' Sara says. 'I'd love to go, too. But we can take a taxi. Please, Margot, have a glass with us.'

'No, don't even think it,' Guy says. 'Margot will drive.' And Margot knows that this is her moment; he won't argue with her in front of the others. She's been dreading the souk trip. She hates walking down the narrow lanes looking at the same touristy stuff in all the shops: the 'OMAN' tote bags, the silver trinket boxes, the pashminas, the silver coins, the kaftans, the Omani hats and the evil-eye necklaces. She hates the men who try to pull you into their shops to look at knock-off handbags. She can't stand the push and rub of the evening crowd and she's dreading the innocent amazement of Sara and Liv; the slow progress they will make as they stop and look at every item in every shop. Neither of Margot's available choices may be rosy, but she knows which is the lesser of the two evils.

'Actually, why don't you get a taxi,' she says, omitting the question mark. 'There's only four of you, so you'll fit in one.'

'I've been meaning to go there, too,' Celine says. 'I need to get some gifts for when I go home. My mum needs a new pashmina, and she loves those glass evil-eyes. But I can go another day …'

Guy, predictably, won't hear of that, and a plan is made for them to go together in two taxis. No one tries to persuade Margot to come.

‘Oh, and by the way,’ Guy says when everything is agreed. ‘I forgot to say: we’re all good for camping. I sorted everything.’

‘Yay! Road trip!’ Celine and Sara cheer and clink their glasses, and Margot turns away. Course you did, she thinks. Course you bloody did.

17
SARA

The cabs drop us on the corniche outside a shop selling Omani silver. I see necklaces, bangles, coffee pots and daggers glinting in the bright lights of the window and wonder if the souk takes Apple Pay. I don't have a lot of Omani riyals on me. I didn't even think that I might need cash. Around us, the shops offer up carpets, silks, textiles, handicrafts, gifts and 'treasures'. Liv's already peering at the handicrafts shop while Celine is pointing out something to Flynn. I notice some of the men around giving Liv more than an appreciative glance and I'm glad she's not in one of her tiny skirts.

Guy slings an arm around my shoulders.

'Right, my lady,' he says. 'Are you ready for an adventure?'

'The main entrance is over there.' Celine nods towards a spot down the street.

Guy cocks his head at her. 'We're not tourists, Leen. This isn't our first rodeo! Let's live a bit!'

He ushers us up a narrow alleyway between two shops and it's like entering another world: crooked alleyways that divide off each other, the backs of buildings, vibrating air conditioning units, secret courtyards, overhanging rooftops, wiry cats beneath our feet, the occasional stench of rubbish, tiny stairways, and shopfronts piled with Indian and Arabic clothing, sandals and fabrics. Even though it's striking, I'm a little disappointed – it's not really the shopping that I expected. But then we pass through that area and the shops morph into jewellery stores with heavy gold pieces glimmering behind glass windows. Alongside sets and trays of bangles and necklaces, I see a piece that would cover your entire chest in shimmering gold.

'Keep walking!' Guy says, throwing a glance over his shoulder. 'The moment you stop, you'll be sucked in, and before you know it, you'll be re-mortgaging your house. This shit's all real.'

He takes a turn and leads us down another narrow alley past shops selling stacks of the hats the Omani men wear. Laughing, Celine grabs one and jumps up to shove it on Guy's head. The shop assistant immediately appears, offering prices and deals for multiple purchase, but Guy hands it back, apologising, and we continue into an area that eventually opens out into more of what I imagined the souk would be like. The pathways are wider and there are multiple shops selling the sort of things that look like they'll be more in my budget. My eye catches a clutch of tinkling silver wind chimes shaped like camels, but there's everything you could imagine in every shop: brass, silver, pashminas, clothes, bags, home ornaments, Aladdin's lamps, carvings, walking sticks, plates, coffee pots – even a suit of armour – plus the cloying smell of *oud* and incense. It's a sensory overload. I wouldn't know where to begin.

Guy stops to the side of a central area, off which five or more alleyways run. All around us are shops and swarms of people.

'Right, this is the main part,' he says. 'Are you looking for anything in particular?'

'Oh, just browsing, I think,' I say. 'This is just …'

'Too much?' Guy asks.

'Exactly.' We exchange a smile.

'I want a tote and I'd love to look at beaded necklaces,' Liv says, pointing to a shop where clusters of necklaces in every colour, length and size hang from the ceiling. She seems oblivious to the looks she's getting from men all around.

'I want to look at the fake trainers,' Flynn says. Celine is lifting up pashminas outside the shop next door.

'*La, la, la*, best price. Last price. Not tourist price! I live here,' I hear her telling the shop assistant.

'Well, this looks like a good place,' Guy says, so we enter the shop and disperse as we look around. The shop is crowded, the ceiling is low with things hanging from it and there's just too much for me to focus on any one thing. I wander around aimlessly, picking up old coins and silver trinket boxes, feeling the beading of necklaces and peering at framed scorpions and hairy spiders as big as my hand as I dodge other customers reaching for treasures hanging above my head.

'Boo!' Guy says, appearing next to me. He stands close, and I can feel the heat of him. 'What have you found?'

'Nothing really. But I wouldn't mind looking at some wind chimes I saw on the way here.'

'Come on then,' he says, so I ask Celine if she'll stay with Liv and Flynn, and Guy and I wander over to a shop with wind chimes hanging outside. I start examining them, trying to picture them in my house, and trying out the tones of all the chimes and, when I finally feel I've selected the right one, I look around for Guy but he's not there.

'You like?' an assistant asks me. 'This one?' He picks it

from the display and holds it lovingly, as if I've selected the golden ticket. 'Beautiful!' He jangles it and cocks his ear. 'You want? Where you from? America? Only one hundred riyal for you! Special price!' He laughs, revealing gleaming teeth.

I smile nervously and look again for Guy but I can't see him. As far as I can work out, with my panicky mental maths, the man's just asked for about two hundred pounds. Did I make a mistake? Is this one of those shops where everything is solid gold?

'Okay, I do you deal, only fifty for you!' The man laughs again, his eyes sparkling.

'It's nice, but I don't know,' I say. Margot had said we'd have to haggle, but I can't do it. Even if I offer half of what he's asking, it's too much. 'It's fine, I'll leave it.' I turn to walk away, disappointment slugging in my chest.

'Okay, lady! I make joke. Ten riyals!'

I pause. That's about twenty quid, give or take. I'm about to say yes but I picture myself regaling the story to Margot later and turn back to him. 'Eight?'

The man clutches his chest like I've murdered his child, then says, 'Okay. For you, just this one time, special price.' He's wrapping it for me before I've managed to ask about Apple Pay, but he brings over a card machine and it works. I swing the bag as I make my way back to where I can finally see Guy standing in the central area.

'Sorry,' he says. 'I had to take a call. Got them?'

'Yeah. All good. I haggled!'

'Good girl!' Guy says admiringly, and I bask for a moment, feeling like I levelled up in my Middle Eastern competency. I'm getting the hang of this place.

'Where are the others?' I ask.

'They'll be around,' Guy says. We linger around a perfume shop, sniffing the paper strips the shop assistant keeps wafting under our noses.

'Do you think Margot minded not coming with us?' I ask.

He gives a little shrug. 'She could have come if she wanted.'

'Mmm,' I say. As Celine said earlier: other peoples' marriages.

'But how about you? Are you enjoying seeing Oman?'

'Oh! Yes! Absolutely! It's not like I imagined at all. It's so … exotic, and colourful, and surprising. I can't believe how green it is, and how neat and orderly – not here in the souk, obviously!' I babble. 'Thank you for inviting me.'

'You're welcome, Sara. I'm glad you're here. And I know Margot is, too.'

'Thanks.'

And then, in among the crowds I spot Flynn's head.

'Oh, look, there's Flynn – and Celine!' But, even as I say it, I can see that something's wrong. There's a sheen of sweat on Flynn's forehead and Celine's hurrying to keep up with him. He strides through the shoppers, dodging this way and that to get to us. He looks flustered as he swivels his head around.

'Is Liv with you?' he asks as soon as he reaches us. 'I can't find her anywhere.'

18
SARA

'She was with you!' I say, without bothering to temper the accusation that seeps into my voice.

'I know,' Flynn says, 'but then we lost her. I thought she'd have come back here.' He spins to face Celine and snaps quite savagely, 'I told you we should have waited for her!'

Celine holds up her hands. 'I'm sorry. I thought she was right behind us. Have you messaged her?'

'She doesn't have data. I told you that!'

'Let's just wait here,' Guy says calmly. 'I'm sure she'll find her way back.'

But I'm not so sure. The place is a maze and, if I know Liv, she would have been focusing on everything but the route along which she walked.

'Where were you when you last saw her?' I ask. 'Did she say what she was looking for?'

'She was after a tote bag – something cute, not the naff ones,' Flynn says.

'Where are the tote-bag shops?' I ask, hoping that, as with the fabrics and the jewellery, they're all in one area, but Guy shakes his head.

'Everywhere. Most shops have them. But look, don't worry.

The souk isn't huge. If she has any sense of direction, she'll make her way back towards the road where we came in …'

'She has no sense of direction!' I snap. 'She could end up coming out the wrong side completely! And then what?'

Tears bloom in my eyes and I turn away, embarrassed. I'm picturing what Michael's going to say. His anger when he hears that I lost Liv in a Middle Eastern souk. His 'I told you so. *This* is why she lives with me'. How could I blow it like this? How do other parents keep an eye on their children at all times?

I'm hot, sweating, and my heart's racing. The souk takes on a different feel: gone is the benign fun of a tourist trip. I spin around, scouring the crowds for Liv's face, her hair, her walk. I know my daughter's seventeen but she's still my baby, and memories of the Madeleine McCann story flash through my mind. A lapse of parental attention. A snatched child. The people-trafficking signs stuck on the loo doors at the airport in Birmingham. Liv's blonde hair and grey eyes. Rape. Sex rings. All these men milling about, watching us with hooded eyes, but doing what? Those narrow alleyways, the tiny staircases leading up – to where?

Guy's hands land on my shoulders and he turns me towards him, giving me the tiniest of shakes as he does so.

'Do you want to look for her? Would you rather be looking?'

I nod, silently grateful.

'Okay, Celine: you stay here with Flynn,' he says. 'We'll work our way around the main touristy area and then head down towards the road in case she does make it there. Stay in touch with your phone, okay? Right, come on, Sara. We'll find her and we'll be laughing about this before you know it.'

He steers me down one of the pathways of the souk and

we peer into each shop we pass, him looking left and me to the right. After we reach the end and emerge onto the street without finding her, I stop. The beauty of the nighttime port and corniche is completely lost on me.

'This is useless! How are we going to find her? There are so many people! It's a rabbit warren, Guy! Why didn't Celine stay with her? She had one job!'

'Hey, hey, hey. Come here.' Guy pulls me to him in a hug. My ear presses against his chest and I can hear the solid thump of his heart, a contrast to the racing staccato of my own. It's calming, but he's hot and I'm even hotter. I pull away.

'I need to find her!'

I plunge back into the souk, taking a different alley this time, and I try to find my way to the wider pathways, the more touristy ones with the more commercial shops that I know would appeal to Liv – and then, suddenly, there she is, standing outside a shop, looking left and right, her eyes panicky and the sheen of tears shining on her cheeks: my baby. The girl for whom I would do absolutely anything.

19

MARGOT

When the others have left, Margot pours herself a large glass of wine and sits out in the garden, propping her legs up on another chair. She breathes in deeply and exhales slowly, absorbing the fragrance of the evening plants and the caress of the warm air on her skin. How long has she got, she wonders, until the rabble returns?

And then she feels bad because she's including her son in that description, but the group is more than the sum of its parts. Despite the attention Guy's giving to Sara, she thinks Sara's harmless enough. She has quite a soft spot for Olivia, she adores Flynn, obviously, and Guy is Guy. It's just lying, cheating, fake Celine who makes her teeth grate. But when they're all together they become something worse; something she wants to avoid. Much as she loves being here, a part of Margot is actually looking forward to the day they get on the plane and she no longer has to be bound with this particular group.

How bittersweet that is: she's finally returned to the country that stole her heart – and here she is looking forward to going back home. Maybe there's a way she can come back to Oman by herself, she thinks. Maybe she can try to get clients here and fly out on work trips. Or maybe she'll actually leave Guy. A little snort escapes through her nose as she thinks that. Guy's made sure there's no way she can do that, not unless she's got an alternative plan for her dad.

But it's more than that. Margot's always been determined to find a way through any difficulties she's had in her marriage – which, to be honest, have been quite a few. But she can't deny that something is shifting inside her. Maybe it's the famous menopausal drop in oestrogen, the 'caring', domestic hormone. But she has a feeling that wasn't there before – a slowly surfacing knowledge of who she is and what she wants – and she's realising she wants far more than to spend the rest of her life pussyfooting around Guy Forrest. She's had enough of him taking charge; of him telling her what they'll be doing; of him making – and ballsing up – all the decisions that they should be taking as a couple. She wants to rise up and be seen for herself. But how?

Yet, for now, she pulls open the fridge and wonders what she can throw together for dinner. Another night self-catering when they should be eating out. With a weary sigh, she pulls out a big pack of chicken breasts and locates some vegetables that would roast well. She chucks them all in the oven for a tray bake, and she's had another glass of wine and only just finished roasting the chicken in the hot, stuffy kitchen when she hears car doors slamming outside and her heart sinks at the knowledge that her peace is about to be shattered.

'How was it?' she asks as Guy crashes through the front door with all his noisy energy.

'Oh my God!' Flynn says. 'Liv got lost!'

'It's okay,' Liv says. 'It wasn't for long.'

But Margot can see from her puffy eyes that she's been

crying and she understands that this was a big thing. She looks at Sara, who widens her eyes at her, and half-rolls them as if there's more to the story.

'The main thing is, we found you,' Sara says to Liv. 'Oh my God, when I saw you there outside that shop, I could have died of relief.'

'I think we all need a drink,' Celine says.

'Too right.' Guy grabs a bottle from the fridge and they both head out to the garden. Flynn goes to the bathroom, leaving Margot, Sara and Liv alone.

'So what happened?' Margot asks.

Sara and Liv look at each other.

'Celine dragged Flynn off,' Liv says.

Margot can see by the way she says it that this is not the first time that Celine has irked Liv.

'I'm sure she didn't mean to,' Sara says placatingly.

Margot rolls her lips to stop herself from speaking. In her opinion, Sara might be better off sticking up for her daughter instead of standing up for her friend of half a second.

'You should have seen her!' Liv says. 'It's like she *wanted* to lose me.'

Margot raises an eyebrow. 'Right.'

'Guy came with me to get my wind chimes.' Sara holds up and waggles a plastic bag. 'I asked Celine to stay with Flynn and Liv, but …' she shrugs. 'Anyway, Livvie. It's all over now and you're safe and nothing happened.'

'It's a very safe country,' Margot says. 'You'll have been fine in that respect, Olivia, but I know it must have been scary. It can be quite intimidating on your own in the middle of the souk, especially if you don't know where you are.'

'What's actually scary is the way Celine looks at Flynn,' Liv says. 'Have you noticed that as well? It's like she's always flirting with him, or glancing at him.'

'You can say that again,' Flynn says, re-entering the kitchen.

Sara frowns. 'Maybe she's just trying to be nice.'

Liv scowls and Margot realises it's upsetting her more than she's letting on.

'Do you want me to say anything to her?' she says to Flynn. 'Because I can.'

But Flynn shakes his head. 'It's fine.'

'Well, if you're sure. Anyway, dinner's ready, so would you just help me bring out some bits for the table and then we can eat?'

'Oh …' says Flynn. 'We ate in Muttrah. In one of those cafés on the corniche, you know?'

Liv sees the look on Margot's face and puts her hand over her mouth. 'Sorry, Mrs Forrest. We didn't think.'

20
SARA

I don't know how Guy arranges it, but by mid-afternoon the following day, our group is in possession of three tents, bedding, enough food and drink to feed a starving army, a camping stove, cooking equipment, head torches, two Land Cruisers, a quad bike on a trailer, two turtle doves and a partridge in a pear tree. I bite my lip as I look at the assembled gear. It's only for one night.

'I'll pull the trailer,' Margot says. She's been quiet all morning, but I put it down to the fact that she's been getting together all the kitchen supplies we need. I tried to help her but, with no idea what we'll need, I'm only as good as the orders I'm given, and I get the impression that Margot prefers to do it alone.

Flynn leads Liv to Margot's car, so I get into the other one with Celine and Guy and, before you can say *yalla*, we're bowling through Muscat towards a road that slices through different mountains than the ones we drove through the other day. The mood in the car is upbeat and carefree with Celine's phone playlist connected to the audio, Guy beat-boxing like a YouTube rapper and all of us singing along, and it makes me realise how much I've been tiptoeing around Margot.

'It's not the most picturesque drive,' Guy says, 'but it shouldn't take more than two hours, especially if Margot keeps up.'

'It might not be chocolate-box pretty,' I say, looking at the scraggy mountains, 'but it's very striking. And so alien to me. I don't drive through mountains very often.'

'I don't suppose you do,' Guy says. I don't think he means to put me down, but I feel gauche because I remember Liv telling me that the Forrests drive down to the Alps each year to ski.

As we leave the town behind us, the traffic quietens. Guy settles back in his seat, leaving only one hand loosely on the wheel, which makes me feel a little uneasy at 120 kph, but I tell myself that he knows what he's doing. Ahead of us, the six-lane road snakes through grey mountains. We pass a quarry and an oasis of palm trees. We speed past the odd truck and several low-slung sedans with number plates written in Arabic, and then, when I see a sign to a prison, Guy exits that road and joins a different one.

Céline turns the music down. 'So, I know you two met through your kids, but did you ever come across each other before that? At the school gate or events or anything?'

I smile to myself. The closest I'd got to the Forrest family before the teens had fallen in love was reading the article about Margot's Mansions in *The Cheltenham Post*. Even now, on the very rare occasions I drop Liv off at school, I might see Flynn climbing out of a navy Range Rover and catch a glimpse of Margot's cap of ice-blonde hair through the window, but that's about it.

'No,' I say.

'I'd seen Sara around,' Guy says, 'but our paths hadn't properly crossed, had they?'

'Nope. Not really.' I suspect Guy's lying, but I appreciate the kindness. 'I'm not there much, to be honest.'

'Don't you all go for coffees or something after drop-off? Or tennis mornings?' Celine asks. 'The mums at my school are always yacking in the coffee shop.'

'It's not like that at secondary school,' I say. 'Most of the kids get there independently.'

'Of course, and am I right in thinking that Liv doesn't live with you? So you wouldn't be doing drop-off anyway.'

'Mmm-hmm,' I say.

'So tell me about that!' she says. 'I'm fascinated. Why him and not you? If you don't mind me asking.'

'Oh, it's nothing, really,' I say. 'We got divorced and, well, his house is bigger than mine and I was busy studying for my counselling qualifications and out at work, while he works from home, so we just thought it made sense, really. He's around more than I would be. I see Liv on the weekends.'

'Really? It's just because his house is bigger?' Celine asks, shaking her head. 'Don't you miss her? Wouldn't you want her with you as much of the time as possible?'

'Celine,' Guy says in a warning tone.

She throws her hands up and gives me a grin. 'Sorry. I just find it interesting. Not having kids myself, it's hard to imagine.'

'Well, anyway. Just think,' Guy says, 'if Liv and Flynn hadn't locked eyes across a crowded chemistry lab or something, we wouldn't be here now. So I'm grateful to the little shit for that.'

We all laugh.

'And how's Margot's dad?' Celine says. 'She wasn't very

forthcoming when I asked her. I hope he's all right?' She's got her feet up on the dashboard, a portrait of relaxed.

Guy pretends to scream. 'He's Margot's dad, that's how he is. Living in the fanciest old people's home you've ever seen, with an indoor swimming pool and a gym, and refusing to consider moving anywhere else, even though he knows how much it's costing me.'

'Ouch,' Celine says. 'Couldn't he live with you?' She turns back and gives me a wink. I lean forward a little so I don't miss what Guy says.

'Nope. No way. And, furthermore, Margot thinks that if we try to move him anywhere else, he'll take himself off to Dignitas.'

'And you wouldn't let him?' Celine says cheekily. 'I mean ...' She shrugs one shoulder and bites her lip.

Guy laughs. 'Much as I might be on board with that plan, you can imagine that Margot isn't. So, yes, the upshot is we continue ploughing recklessly through money that should have been my retirement fund. And that, Celine, is the answer to the question of how Margot's dad is: ridiculously healthy and bloody annoying.'

The topic moves on, so I tune out and let my mind drift on to what the next twenty-four hours will bring. I'm really looking forward to seeing the desert, but I wish we hadn't brought the quad bike. A fifteen-year-old girl who lived just outside Cheltenham broke her neck a couple of years ago, being driven by a boy who rolled it over accidentally. It had been all over the news and it really struck a chord with me, like sometimes these things do. That poor, innocent girl. If anything ever happened to Liv I don't know how I'd carry on.

I turn to look out of the back window and see Margot doing her best to keep pace with Guy, whose speedometer is tinging its disapproval at the fact he's over the limit. Liv's in the front seat next to her, and the two of them look totally badass in the big four-wheel drive, their sunglasses glinting in the sunlight. I smile to myself, hoping she's put yesterday's souk trip far behind her, and then there's an almighty bang. Celine screams and I gasp as the car rocks and veers hard across the road towards the central reservation. I don't even have time to brace myself.

21
MARGOT

Margot sees the explosion of Guy's tyre at the exact same moment as the Land Cruiser swerves across the highway. There's no time to think, although she sees everything in her mind's eye: the car hitting the central reservation barrier and launching through the air; a truck coming the other way; a crumpled, steaming wreck; bodies ejected through smashed windows and scattered on the dusty tarmac. A thought flashes, *Imagine! – Guy gone just like that!*

But none of that happens. Within moments, Guy has the car back under control and is guiding it towards the hard shoulder as he slows down. Luckily the traffic on this road is sparse. Margot steps on the brakes and follows her husband until both cars come to a halt. She presses her hand to her chest and takes a moment to get her breath back. She's as rattled by the feeling of relief from thinking Guy might die just as much as she is by the shock of the puncture.

Guy's already outside examining the damage. Behind him, Celine and Sara are clasped together in a hug.

'Oh my God! I thought that was it!' Celine says as they pull apart. 'I literally thought we were going to die. All I could see was the barrier coming towards us.'

'I'm still shaking!' Sara says, holding out her hands to demonstrate. 'I had no idea what'd happened. But Guy, you were amazing. I mean, you saved our lives!'

Guy shrugs off the praise, as Margot knows he will. 'Instinct.' He straightens up. 'Well, this tyre is well and truly fucked. Let's hope we have a real spare and not one of those toy wheels because that won't get us far in the sand.'

Celine's on her hands and knees peering under the car. 'It's here. It looks okay. Do you know how to get it out?'

Guy says he doesn't know off-hand, but there's nothing you can't find on YouTube. He locates the Toyota tool kit and orders Flynn to get a how-to video up on his phone. Margot joins Liv, Sara and Celine, who are sitting on rocks at the edge of the hard shoulder, buffeted by the force of the occasional car that speeds past.

'Do you think they'll be able to change it?' Sara says.

Margot shrugs a shoulder. 'I imagine so.'

Guy's yet to meet a physical challenge he hasn't risen to, but a good half an hour later, he's drenched in sweat and snapping orders at a snarling Flynn. Even after the spare's been extracted; the car jacked up; the tyre replaced; and the jack released, the news is not good. The car is leaning down on one side, like a wounded animal. The spare, it turns out, has barely any air in it.

Guy aims a vicious kick at the tyre. 'Fucking pile of shit!' he yells. 'Good for nothing fucking hire company!'

Margot sees Liv exchange a nervous glance with Sara. She edges closer to her mum, who puts her arm around her and presses a kiss to her hair. But Celine steps forward and touches Guy's arm, as if to calm him down.

'Can we limp it to the nearest petrol station, do you think?' she asks.

'We passed the last one a long way back,' Flynn says. 'I checked on Maps. There's no more between here and where we're going.'

Guy tears his hands through his hair. 'I swear. They're supposed to check the spare. Fucking bunch of cowboys. Excuse my French.'

He paces three steps up and down the dusty tarmac, while the rest of them stand staring at the car, as if their collective willpower could re-inflate the tyre.

'There's no pump in the boot?' Celine asks. 'I always keep one in my car. Just in case. And a tow rope.'

'You think I didn't look?' Guy snaps.

'Are there any rescue people we could call?' Sara asks. 'Like the AA? Is there a number on the rental papers?'

'We're in the middle of nowhere!' Guy scoffs. Then, seeing Sara's face fall, he softens his tone. 'I'm sorry. It's just: how long is that going to take?' He looks at the sky. 'It's not getting any earlier and we still have a good forty minutes to go on this road. Plus off-roading and setting up camp, which I certainly don't want to do in the dark.' He looks around. 'Any other bright ideas?'

Margot shrugs. Guy wipes sweat off his brow.

'Well,' he says. 'If the closest petrol station is behind us, to be honest, maybe our only choice is to turn back.'

'You mean just go home?' Margot asks.

She's surprised how the idea disappoints her. Despite the undisputed hassle of erecting the camp and disassembling it again in the morning, she realises she's actually been looking forward to spending the evening in the peace of the desert under a canopy of stars. And she spent so long this morning prepping the food.

'That's exactly what I mean,' Guy says. 'What does "Sara Say"?' He grins at Sara now, and she laughs, clearly relieved to have Guy back on familiar territory.

'It sounds like the sensible option, to be honest,' she says. 'From where I stand, it doesn't look like we have any other choice.'

Margot waits for Guy to ask her opinion, but he doesn't. She addresses the teens. 'You two all right with that? If we turn back?'

'You mean, that's it?' Flynn asks. 'No camping?'

'Well, yes,' Margot says. 'Not unless you do it in the garden.'

'Aww,' Liv says, pulling a downturned face. 'I was really looking forward to it.'

'I know,' Margot says, surprising herself by reaching out to touch Olivia's hand.

'Look,' Guy says, 'by the time we've driven, slowly, back to the petrol station and inflated the tyre – assuming it's not got a hole in it – it's going to be very late by the time we actually get to the desert. It's going to be pitch black. We can't pick a spot in the dark. We need to see where we are to put up the tents.'

'Could we try again tomorrow?' Flynn asks. 'I really want to drive the quad bike!'

'Maybe,' Margot says, and she starts to think through the logistics and timings but then she hears a car slowing and they all turn to watch a Land Cruiser with Arabic plates pull to a stop behind them. Out gets an older man wearing the traditional Omani *dishdasha* with a *masar* turban tied around his head, followed by three younger men, similarly dressed, who Margot imagines could be his sons.

''*Allo ... mushkila?*' the older man says, pointing at the deflated car as the others gather around it, examining the tyre. The man's beard is flecked with grey and his face weathered. Margot remembers the word *mushkila* from what little Arabic she'd learned at her ladies' morning lessons – 'problem'.

'Yes, *mushkila*,' Guy says nodding vigorously. He points at each wheel in turn: one on the ground with a massive hole in it and the other flat as the proverbial and gives an exaggerated shrug. 'Do you have a pump?' He mimes hand-pumping and points to the air nozzle, but the man shakes his head. He fires some Arabic at the young men, who scurry back to their own car.

'What's happening?' Sara asks, as if Margot is the font of all knowledge.

'I think,' Celine says, her eyes on what the men are doing, 'they've thought of a way to help us.'

22
SARA

Celine is not wrong. In under half an hour, the man and his sons have fitted their own spare wheel onto our car and taken our flat spare wheel as their own replacement: a straight swap. There follows a lot of hand-shaking and back-patting. Guy tries to give the man some cash and, failing that, take his phone number, but he shakes his head. The Omanis pile back into their car and drive off, leaving us looking incredulously at each other.

'Did he seriously just give us his own wheel?' Liv asks.

'Arabian hospitality at its best. Lucky for us,' Guy says. 'Right, come on, let's get going.'

The mood in our car, as we get back on the road, is reflective as we process all that's just happened – both the tyre blow-out and the help. I'm still reeling. I believe in signs and a part of me feels like the double knock-back of the puncture and the flat spare was the universe telling us to turn back. I feel like we've gone against what's meant to be by carrying on. I can't shake off a feeling of impending doom.

'I suppose it works for him,' Guy says. 'Our spare looked unused, so I guess he didn't lose out. I wanted to pay him, or swap it back, but he wouldn't hear of it. You saw how he was.'

'I can't imagine that happening back home,' I say.

'You can always call a breakdown service back home, to be fair,' Celine says. 'And well driven, G, by the way. I think we both owe you a thank-you.' She gives Guy's leg a pat. He reaches down and holds her hand for a moment, and I'm almost a hundred per cent sure, watching that, something's happened between them.

'Any time,' Guy says. 'Right, I reckon we'll be there in about forty minutes and, if everyone pulls their weight, we should have camp set up just in time for some very welcome sundowners.'

'Amen to that!' Celine says with a huge sigh. 'I'm looking forward to this so much.'

'Do you know the site? Have you camped there before?' I ask.

Celine smiles gently as she peers back at me. 'Oh, Sara, you're so sweet.'

'What?'

'Umm,' Guy says. 'You know there is no "site" as such, don't you? It's just desert. We're going to drive off-road until we find a nice bit – maybe with a big dune or two for some bashing with the quad bike – and then we'll stop and pitch our tents. Just like that.' He pauses. 'You're not expecting showers or anything, are you? There aren't even toilets. We're going off-grid for twenty-four hours.'

'The full Bear Grylls!' Celine says.

'You'll be picking sand out of your scalp for the next month and I'm not kidding,' Guy says. 'But it'll be fun.'

'I'm not planning on rolling down the dunes,' I say drily.

'It just gets everywhere. You can't help it,' Guy says. He

chuckles. 'Camping here is quite the experience. You'll never forget it. That much I promise.'

'Can't wait.' I lean back on the leather seat and look out of the window.

The road snakes ahead of us, a line of tarmac as far as the eye can see. We see the odd settlement of white houses clustered around a mosque, but there's not much besides sand and an expanse of clear sky so big it almost gives me vertigo. After another fifteen minutes, Guy slows the car a little and then turns off onto a smaller road, then again onto a sand track.

'Now for the fun bit,' he says as we rattle along the track far faster than I think is appropriate for a rental car, especially one that's just had a flat and now has no spare. 'You might want to hang on tight. Things are about to get very bumpy.'

23
MARGOT

Once Guy's selected the perfect camping spot, nestled among a few softly undulating dunes near a clutch of trees, he indicates to Margot where she should park. As long as she does what he tells her, Margot and Guy are a good team when it comes to setting up camp – the things that need to be done coming back to them almost like muscle memory, but it's hot work despite the breeze. The sun may be on its way down, but heat still radiates off the top layer of the sand and fat flies buzz around, attracted by the sweat that runs down the side of Margot's face as she scrambles around. She's panting by the time she's rammed the last tent peg deep into slippery, soft sand. The large tent looks solid: it has two self-contained, zipped rooms and a shaded veranda that Guy is calling 'the terrace'.

Arranged around it are the two one-man, pop-up tents and, in the middle of the campsite, Celine and Sara have set up the table facing the spot where they predict the sun will sink below the dunes, arranged six chairs around it, and dragged over the large cool box that contains much of the alcohol.

'Good job, team,' Guy says as they survey their handiwork.

'This is incredible. It looks so cosy,' Celine says, looking enviously inside the big tent.

Guy points to the two small tents. 'You and Sara are in the "desert suites". No en suite though. Bathroom's that way.' He points to the trees. 'But please dig a hole. Don't just leave it lying there. Okay?'

Flynn and Liv aren't really listening. They're circling the quad bike, their eyes lit with excitement. Flynn climbs up onto the trailer, leans in, put his hands on the handlebars and gives the brakes an experimental squeeze.

'Wanna have a go?' he asks Liv.

'Hell, yeah!' Liv says.

Margot sees Sara sidle over to her daughter and hears her ask quietly, 'Are you sure? You don't have to.'

Liv swats Sara away. 'Can you please not be so overprotective?' she says in that way teenagers have. 'I'm nearly eighteen. And yes, before you ask, Dad would let me.'

Margot watches as Sara takes a deep, slow breath.

Sara turns to Flynn. 'Well, maybe wait till your dad's reminded you how to use it. We don't want any accidents.'

'We're in the middle of nowhere,' Flynn says. 'Like, what's gonna happen?'

'I don't know. Roll-overs?' Sara says. 'Anyway, being in the middle of nowhere isn't actually the best thing if something *does* happen.'

Sara's anxiety surprises Margot. Apart from the thing about the seat belts on the first day, she's come across as quite easygoing so far.

'Don't worry,' Margot says. 'Flynn's been driving these since he was yay high.' She waves her hand towards her knees though obviously that's an exaggeration. In fact, she thinks he's only done it once, and that was on a trip supervised by professionals. But Flynn's not an idiot and he's got good spatial skills.

'I wouldn't ever forgive myself if anything happened,' Sara says. 'But, more importantly, neither would my ex.'

'I get that,' Margot says. 'But we have to let them live a bit. Right? This is my Danish roots speaking.'

Guy's voice booms across the campsite. 'Who wants a drink? I'm parched!'

He strides towards the cool box, flurries of sand thrown up with each huge stride, and Margot has to admit, he does look magnificent. He's in his element: the endless sweep of sand, the battle to survive in an inhospitable landscape, Guy Forrest imposing his will on nature. With a stab of bitterness, Margot hopes that he misses all this as much as she misses their life in Muscat.

'G&Ts?' he calls. 'Wine? Kids, you want a beer or a Coke?'

'Should we wait till after everyone's driven that thing?' Sara says, nodding towards the quad bike. 'Just in case? I'm sorry, I can't help it. It's my job to be sensible.'

Guy laughs and pats her arm. 'There's no police in the desert. It'll be fine.'

'That's not the point,' Sara turns away.

Celine rummages in her bag and stands up brandishing a huge bottle of champagne like a trophy. 'I brought this as my contribution. Shall we open it?'

'A magnum? You absolute treasure,' Guy says. 'Why not?'

And so the bottle's opened, sending a spurt into the air that lands with a hard splat on the sand. Celine splashes champagne into everyone's glasses, but Margot puts her hand over hers.

‘Not for me. Thanks.’ She adores champagne and would have loved a glass if anyone else had brought it, but ‘absolute treasure’? She picks up the Thermos of double, maybe triple, gin and tonics she mixed at home and wonders if she can just stick a straw in it.

‘Suit yourself,’ Celine says. ‘Bottoms up!’

The others chink glasses and Liv and Flynn raise bottles of beer.

‘Cheers to a fantastic holiday,’ Guy says.

‘Cheers!’ everyone echoes.

24
SARA

Having drunk his first glass of champagne in pretty much one gulp, Guy climbs up onto the trailer and releases the quad bike.

'Well, we haven't dragged this thing here to look pretty so we may as well have a go. Who's first?' He sits astride the machine and pretends to rev it. 'Maybe I should take her for a spin to check everything's okay.'

'Dad!' Flynn snaps.

Liv's jiggling her leg in a way that shows me that she's also desperate to get on. My heart twists. You want to give your kids everything; you want to do anything you can to make them happy, but you also want to do all you can to protect them; to keep them safe. It's in a mother's DNA.

'Okay, go on then,' Guy says.

Half a second later Flynn's seated on it, revving it up and then zooming across the sand like he's trying to break the land speed record. Just before the bigger dunes start to swell, he spins the bike around in a full circle, spraying a doughnut of sand in the air then he heads back, not breaking his speed until he's practically on top of us.

‘Whoah!’ Guy holds up his hands as sand showers us. ‘Mate! Who invited Lewis Hamilton?’

‘Come on!’ Flynn calls to Liv.

With a sheepish look at me, she climbs aboard, winds her arms around Flynn’s waist and they roar off, Liv’s hair flying out behind her like a pennant. It’s only then that I think: we don’t have helmets. I watch – my eyes glued to them as they head straight for the dunes. Flynn starts racing up and down them, the bike tipping this way and that as he crests them over and over. Liv’s screams echo across the sand.

‘So how did Liv get the head injury?’ I imagine Michael asking me. ‘She was wearing a helmet, wasn’t she? When you let her loose on a quad bike driven by a teenager who’d been drinking?’

‘Top up?’ Celine asks, plopping herself down next to me and offering the enormous champagne bottle.

‘I shouldn’t,’ I say. ‘One of us should probably remain sober. Just in case.’

‘Aww, babe. They’ll be fine. And we’ve got this massive great bottle to get through. My parents bought it for me, and I’ve been saving it for a special occasion. Come on …’ She pours more into my glass anyway. ‘Isn’t this just incredible?’

‘It is. I’m really glad we came.’ I touch her arm. ‘I know I sometimes worry too much. But Livvie, she’s … she’s delicate. I’ve been protecting her so long, I’ve forgotten how not to.’

‘Delicate? Really?’ Celine frowns. ‘In what way?’

I sigh. I don’t usually talk to people about Liv’s issues. But I feel like I can talk to Celine. She works with kids – maybe she’ll have come across similar cases.

‘She had a lot of anxiety when she was younger,’ I say. ‘I’ve no idea why. It came from nowhere. Crippling anxiety. She was on medication for a while. Not anymore, though. Flynn has been amazing for her. I could literally kiss the ground he walks on. I don't know how he does it, but he knows how to handle her. She's been so much better since they've been together.'

Celine nods. 'I'd never have guessed.'

'It's been a work in progress. But, oh my God, the things I did to protect her over the years. To smooth her way in life.' I laugh. 'Quite ridiculous when I look back, but they seemed big things at the time.'

'Like what?'

I take a sip of the cold champagne and feel the burn as it slides down my oesophagus. Should I really share this with Celine? I've never told anyone about all the ways in which I've smoothed Liv's path through life. Until it all went wrong, of course, and I lost her to Michael.

'One example,' I say. 'So, when she was in year four, there was this kid who she really, really didn't like. Rory, his name was. I'll never forget. I don't know why she didn't like him, but every morning Liv would invent tummy aches, headaches, anything to try and get out of school. It was awful. I used to really dread school mornings.'

'So, what did you do?'

'I did what any decent mother would do: I had the other kid moved out of the class.'

Celine chuckles. 'Oh yeah. You wouldn't be the first.'

'Okay. But … I might not have been entirely truthful when I spoke to the teacher. I might have exaggerated things a bit.' I pause. 'Implied the other kid was bullying her. And blamed the teacher for not noticing.'

'Ouch,' Celine says, and the champagne must have started to go to my head because, instead of reading the room, I carry on.

'When she was younger, I used to do her homework for her myself. If it was difficult, like an essay or a project, I'd pay a tutor to do it for her. We'd pre-prepare exam questions and, if the questions had ever been leaked – which they sometimes were – we bought them online. What else? There was the time I might have shagged an admissions teacher in order to get her into the senior school we wanted when we were too far down the waiting list. You get the idea.'

I stop talking as I realise that Celine is looking sideways at me, and not in a nice way.

'Whoah,' she says. 'You're a dark horse for a counsellor, Sara. Er, any other confessions you want to get off your chest while we're here?'

My stomach drops. Does she know what happened? The time I 'accidentally' pushed the teacher who always picked on Liv down the stairs, causing her to break her wrist? The real reason why Liv left home? I open my mouth, unsure what to say, but Celine laughs and clinks her glass against mine.

'Just kidding!' she says. 'Cheers to the tiger mum who'd do *anything* for her cub. Fight for who you love, eh? I'll drink to that.'

'To the tiger mum! And to fighting for who you love,' I say, taking a gulp of champagne.

'What are you two ladies nattering about?' Guy comes up behind us. 'Girl stuff, or can anyone join in?' He drops into the chair next to Celine, and Margot flops down next to me.

'Ssh, Sara, no more gossiping about Guy,' Celine says. 'It'll only go to his head,' and I almost faint with gratitude to her for covering up what we really were talking about. But I suddenly feel uneasy, like I revealed too much.

'So, what are you doing for New Year?' Guy asks Celine. 'Let us live vicariously through you. We'll be back in cold old Blighty.'

'Not much on New Year's Eve as my friends are still away, and I'm not big into New Year's Eve anyway. Everything's so overpriced. But I've booked into a beach club for New Year's Day. I'm going to spend it stretched out on a sunlounger, drinking champagne and working on my tan.'

'I can't tell you how jealous I am,' I say.

'I used to love New Year's Eve here,' Guy says. 'Remember that pot-luck party we had around the pool?'

'That was so much fun!' Celine says. 'We haven't done anything like that since you guys left. It's not the same. The new people aren't as friendly.'

Next to me, Margot gives a little snort, which I take to mean that she either knows or suspects about Guy and Celine, but the others don't hear. We continue chatting, our tongues loosening as we drain the magnum, while birds reel overhead and screech their evening song. Guy spots a desert fox and starts telling us about the wildlife we might get to see – sand fish and owls and little things that scrabble around in the dark, and I try to focus on the raw beauty of this incredible landscape – not on the teens, who've now been on the quad bike for what seems like an eternity.

25

MARGOT

'Right,' Guy says, stretching his arms back behind his head. 'I suppose I'd better go and hunt down some food.'

'Yes, off you go, you hunter-gatherer,' Celine says. She rolls her eyes at Sara. 'He loves it, really.'

'I'll help,' Sara says. 'Margot, you prepared so much this morning. You relax.'

Guy and Sara go off to unpack the food that Margot had got ready this morning: the marinaded kebabs; the par-boiled potatoes neatly wrapped in foil; and the peppers and juicy big Portobello mushrooms ready to roast. Margot, left alone with Celine, scrabbles for something harmless to say but the problem is, all the things she really wants to say – about husband-stealing and dishonesty – won't make good conversation. In the end, Celine's the first to speak.

'So, what's it like being back? Are you having a good time?' she asks after a few moments have passed.

'It's good to be back in Oman,' Margot says.

'Nice. And I'm glad we've made it out to the desert. That's something you can't do in England, isn't it?'

'Horses for courses,' Margot says. 'There are other things that are good about the UK.'

'I know! But nothing like this.'

Margot thinks about saying something about camping in the UK. It's not something she's experienced, and neither is she keen to thanks to the British weather, but she imagines the joys might be similar. Celine is quite tipsy now and Margot feels an edge to her, like the air around her is bristling, so she decides not to say anything.

'No,' she agrees.

Celine glances over her shoulder before she speaks. 'So, what do you make of Sara?' she asks quietly. 'I gather you didn't really know each other before this trip.'

Margot takes a moment to think before replying. It's a good introduction to find out if Celine knows anything more about why Liv doesn't live with Sara, but that would mean lowering her defences against Celine, which is not something she's prepared to do. Margot doesn't trust her for a minute. She doesn't trust the way Celine is chumming up to Sara, which she knows is probably only to irk Margot. But, on the other hand, Margot has noticed how Celine watches Guy when he smiles at Sara, and she finds Celine's jealousy quite amusing. She chooses her words deliberately.

'I think she's lovely,' she says sweetly. 'It's quite incredible how well she's slotted in with Guy and me on this trip. I'm so glad we invited her.'

'Hmm.' Celine's big toe circles in the sand, flexing her calf muscle. 'There's more to her than meets the eye, I can tell you that.'

'Surely not,' Margot says, turning away to hide her smile.

'I can't believe some of the underhand things she's done in the past.'

Margot gives a little laugh. She's dying to hear them, but she won't beg Celine for information.

'Usually to do with Liv. Buying leaked exam papers, having kids moved out of the class if Liv doesn't like them, sleeping with admissions tutors … I could go on.' Margot raises an eyebrow but says nothing. 'Do you know why her daughter doesn't live with her?' Celine asks.

Ooh, Margot thinks. Here we go. But she feigns disinterest as she says, 'The dad's house is bigger, I think that's what Flynn said.'

Celine laughs. 'You believe that, do you? Oh, Margot. She was convicted of assault. Actual bodily harm.' Margot's breath catches. 'Went to court and everything, but she'll never tell you even if you ask her. Believe me, I tried.'

'It must have been provoked. She's so easy-going.'

'If you don't believe me, look it up. You can find it if you look hard enough.'

'Not sure I want to,' Margot says. 'The main thing is she's mended bridges with her daughter and turned things around. Now she's a counsellor herself. So, good for her.'

'Hmm,' Celine says.

'You have to go through a lot of training, as well as work on yourself, when you get a counselling qualification, I think.'

'As I said: hmm. I'm not sure it's possible to train out your natural instincts like that.'

'Well … what would I know?' Margot says. 'I just make toy houses.'

Celine raises her glass. 'Touché.'

And then, maybe because she's having the longest conversation she's ever had with Celine, or simply because the gin has fully kicked in, she decides to jump right in with a question of her own.

'So, do you have a boyfriend, or partner, or whatever you call it these days?' she asks.

'Nah,' Celine says with a sigh. 'I'm happy just doing my own thing.'

'But, you know, don't you want to settle down at some point? Have kids?'

'Don't need to be married to have kids these days,' Celine says.

In the darkness, Margot's left eyebrow lifts. 'Not in Oman,' she says. 'I'm pretty sure that's illegal.'

'So, I'd leave?' Celine says.

'Or just get married, I suppose,' Margot says. 'If you love your life here as much as you say you do.'

But Celine shakes her head. 'Nah. Marriage isn't for me. Why would I buy the restaurant when I can get all the food for free? From every restaurant, if you see what I mean.' She chuckles. 'I'm a free spirit in case you haven't noticed.'

Margot, mid sip of her drink, tries not to choke.

'To be honest, though,' Celine says, 'I'm not prepared to make the sacrifices I see married women make.'

Over the side of the deck chair, Margot's fingertips are trailing in the cooling sand. She grasps a handful, squeezes it hard and lets it trickle back out. 'Oh?' she says as mildly as she can. 'Like what?'

'Margot,' Celine says. 'You know what I'm talking about. There's no shame in it. Horses for courses, as you say. It's just not what I want for me.'

Margot's blood is suddenly racing in her temples. She holds

herself very still, not trusting herself to speak. It's one thing for her to criticise her own marriage, but it's absolutely not all right for Celine to do so. Celine of all people. How dare she? But Celine carries on.

'Forgive me – maybe it's the alcohol. But I'm talking about you moving country because *he* fucked up. I know that's not what you tell people, that's not the party line. But, come on, I know about the harassment case. Just as I know your dad's perfectly fine in that assisted living place. You didn't need to go back for him. You had a good life here, and you were forced to leave because of your husband's mistake. Well, I'd hate ever to be in that position. I just wouldn't let it happen to me, to be honest.'

Squeezing that cold sand in her hand again, Margot forces her words to come out calmly.

'It's not always that black and white.'

Celine snorts. 'Well, I wouldn't have done it. That's all I'm saying. If it were me, I'd have divorced him and stayed here.'

'Hey, hey,' Sara says, suddenly behind them. 'Everything all right?' She looks from Margot to Celine and back.

'Everything's super,' Margot says. 'Celine's just telling me what it's like to be married.'

Sara looks baffled for a moment, then says, 'Well, I came to say that everything's on the barbecue – great prep, Margot! I was just wondering if you think the kids are ever coming back or if they've disappeared off to Timbuktu on that thing.'

'They'll be back when they're hungry,' Margot says as she stands. 'If you'll excuse me, I'll go and check my husband's not "fucking up" the food.'

26

SARA

'What was that about?' I ask Celine after Margot stalks off. 'She seems upset?'

Celine shakes her head. 'She's supersensitive sometimes. Doesn't want to hear the truth. It's nothing.'

I don't want to pry so I just say, 'Are you two good? Or do you need me to mediate?'

Celine laughs. 'Don't waste your energy. She'll get over it.'

We sit with our drinks as the light starts to turn from orange to a hazy apricot. The sun grows larger and redder as it slips slowly downwards and then, eventually, the kids reappear on the quad bike, looking windswept and sandy. They get off and Guy climbs on.

'Shotgun! Or whatever you call it!' Celine shouts and jumps on behind him, throwing her arms around Guy's waist. I steal a look at Margot but her back is turned as she's fixing something on the table.

'Do you want a go, Margot?' I call over to her.

'Later!'

'Oh my God, Mum, that was so much fun!' Liv says. Her face is radiant with excitement. 'Can we go quad-biking back home?'

'What, to Tesco?' I say.

Liv tuts. 'I'm sure they have places in the country where you can ride on tracks. I bet there's one near us.'

'I'll look into it,' I say. And I will, because Liv's happiness is my priority. Every weekend she spends with me, we try to do something special. Quality over quantity, that's what I tell myself. It's the only way I've been able to get through her living with Michael and Nancy.

I step closer and drop my voice so Margot won't hear.

'So, err ... how am I doing? With the Forrests, I mean. I'm not embarrassing you or anything?'

'No! You're doing really well.'

'Really?'

'I mean – yeah! And Guy's so impressed with *Sara Says*.'

'That was cool, wasn't it?'

'Cold. Oh, and I meant to say, I had a message from Sophie.'

'Sophie, as in ...?'

'Yeah, Sophie from school. Look.'

Liv opens her phone and navigates to a message, which she shoves in front of my face. I squint and push the phone away, the black letters a blur at such close range. Sophie is a friend of Liv's, who came to me as a client for some help dealing with her parents' acrimonious divorce.

'What did she say?'

'Oh my God, she thinks you're amazing. You've really helped her. She was saying that the techniques you taught her have been so useful.'

'That's so good to hear. Thank you.' I beam at her.

'It makes me feel really proud. Everyone's jealous that I have such a cool mum.' She winds her arm around my waist and rests her head against mine. My arms snake around her, too. 'I'm sorry,' she says.

'For what?'

'For being so awful when all "that" happened. For moving out.'

There's a lump in my throat. These are words I've waited to hear for so long. I thought I never would.

'It's okay,' I lie. 'All that matters is that we're in a good place now. And that we're here together, having fun. Okay? It's all water under the bridge. Gone.'

'Aww,' Liv says. 'I'm so glad you came. It's the best holiday ever, isn't it?'

I bask in the glow of Liv's pleasure, hoping that Margot glances over and sees us standing there with our arms around each other. I've been feeling a little jealous of her closeness with Flynn and I want her to see that I have it with Liv, too.

Liv drops her arm and nods towards the dunes where we can just about make out the quad bike zipping around. It looks like Guy and Celine are doing doughnuts. 'You seem to be getting on really well with *her*.'

'She's nice,' I say.

'You sure about that?'

'Yeah? I mean, she's been really lovely to me.'

'Flynn says she's a fake friend. He says you should be careful. She's a snake.'

'No! She ...'

'I'm just telling you what he said, that's all. He really doesn't like her.'

'I thought they got on really well?'

We have no chance to continue the conversation because

Celine and Guy are suddenly back, flushed and full of laughter. Celine dismounts, and Guy turns his attention to me.

'Hop on!'

'Oh, no,' I say. 'Not me. I'm cooking.' I'm nowhere near the barbecue.

'I'm sure Margot can spare you,' Guys says, hiding a smile. 'Just there and back. No tricks, I promise I'll go slow. Best way to face your fears is to ... face them.'

'You may as well, while you're here,' Margot says.

'Go on, Mum!' Liv says, 'You'll love it.' I can see how badly she wants me to join in with everyone else and not be the boring mum, so, reluctantly, I straddle the quad bike behind Guy.

'Hold on tight,' he says, so I slide my arms loosely around his waist.

'Tighter,' he says. 'I'm not being funny. I can't have you falling off the back.'

I tighten my arms and peer over his shoulder as he moves the quad bike away from the camp.

'You okay?' he asks.

'So far, so good.'

'Shall I floor it?'

'Nothing crazy, okay? We have children!'

Guy laughs and opens the throttle gently, easing us away from the camp.

'You okay to go a bit faster?' he asks.

He sends the bike leaping forward, which forces me to cling on to him even tighter. I shriek, and the rest of the ride's a blur of sand as we crest dunes and plunge down them again. Sand in my hair? It's everywhere; I can even feel the crunch of it in my mouth. Back at the camp, I dismount with shaking legs and grab my drink, glad it's over.

'Margot?' Guy asks, revving the bike suggestively. 'Your turn?'

'No, thanks,' she says, so Guy gets off and Flynn climbs back on.

'Livvie?' he asks.

She stops gulping water to shake her head. 'I'm good.'

Flynn's about to drive off when Celine yells, 'I'll come!' and climbs on behind him, slinking her arms around his waist. I see Flynn roll his eyes at Liv. They roar off and then, with the ever-changing colours in the darkening sky and the birds wheeling, silhouetted, across my view of the sinking sun, the accident I've been picturing since I first set eyes on the quad bike actually happens.

I mean, come on. We're town dwellers from England, with a good few drinks inside us, on a powerful quad bike, at dusk in an unfamiliar desert. What would any sensible person say? *What the hell were you thinking, you absolute muppets? How was that ever going to end well?*

27
MARGOT

Margot knows from the slow speed at which the quad bike engine is turning that something's happened. The sun's completely disappeared, and a glorious rising moon lends the bushes sharp, black shadows as she stands at the edge of the campsite and peers into the gloom. When she finally identifies the dark shape of the bike idling on the sand, she's relieved to see there are still two figures on it.

'Flynn!' she calls as he comes into hearing distance. 'Are you okay?'

'Had a small accident,' he says as he draws up.

'Oh my God!' Liv cries as she surges towards Flynn, but Margot is more analytical. She notes that neither is holding a broken limb at a funny angle, both of them appear to be conscious, and she can't see any blood.

Celine climbs off the back of the bike and flops into a chair. 'Fuck, Flynn! Talk about a wild ride!'

Margot's eyes flick to Flynn in time to see him exchange the briefest of glances with Liv, who bites her lips together.

'What happened?' Guy asks. 'Were you being an idiot? I told you to be careful.'

'Most important thing,' Sara interrupts, 'are either of you hurt?'

'I'm fine,' Flynn says, but he's rotating and stretching his neck as if checking it works properly.

'We'll live, won't we?' Celine says with a laugh. 'What doesn't kill us makes us stronger, eh?'

'What happened? Did you lose your balance?' Margot asks Celine, thinking about the amount of alcohol Celine had necked before she got on. She's never seen anyone drink faster, and that's saying a lot given who she's married to.

'Margot!' Guy snaps. 'You can't blame the victim!'

'It was at the top of that huge dune,' Celine says. 'Verstappen here decided to do a ninety-degree turn and over we went! I mean …' She shrugs as if it were obvious.

Guy looks carefully at Celine, his eyes travelling up and down her body as he scans for injuries. 'Are you really okay? Nothing hurts? Head, neck, spine?'

He raises his hands as if he's about to put them on her lean, tanned back to check, and Margot's breath catches – but he stops himself in time.

Celine nods. 'Yeah. Maybe a bit sore tomorrow but nothing a few painkillers won't solve. I'm young. I bounce!' She picks up the remains of her drink. 'Cheers to that!'

'As for you,' Guy jabs his finger at Flynn. 'What the hell were you playing at? Imagine the bike had overturned! Imagine we had a spinal injury – or worse – on our hands! Out here in the middle of nowhere! It would all be your fault! You can't act the fool on these things, not with a passenger.'

'Are you going to ask your son if he's okay?' Margot says.

Guy glares at her and she raises her eyebrows back, telling him silently to calm down. The 'nice guy' facade is slipping, as it so often does when he's been drinking.

'You're all right, aren't you?' Guy says tersely.

Flynn flexes his neck again and rubs at the side of his head. 'A bit sore, but nothing's broken, so ... yeah.'

'Okay, great,' says Guy. 'It seems you got away with it. Right, let's get on with the evening.'

'Actually,' Sara says, 'head injuries aren't always obvious, and necks are not something you should take chances with. Maybe we could drive to—'

She hasn't even finished her sentence when Guy holds up his hand.

'Nope. Stop right there. No one's driving anywhere. We can't. We're in the middle of nowhere. We'll never find the road in the dark and, if you're thinking about going to a hospital, the closest one that'll be covered on insurance is probably in Muscat.'

They all stare at Celine and Flynn for a moment. They really do look okay. Margot knows she would never forgive herself if there was a serious injury that they missed but, equally, she knows Guy is right.

'I used to be the office First Aider,' Sara says. 'I mean, I'm not medically trained, but I know how to check for concussion if that helps.'

Margot nods. 'I'd feel better if you do. Do you mind?'

So Sara peers into Flynn's eyes then starts asking Celine about pain and stiffness. She checks her reflexes and asks her what day of the week it is, to which Celine responds, 'President Clinton?'

For a moment, Sara looks appalled, then Celine roars with laughter and Sara slaps her playfully on the arm.

'Okay, you're all right! I think they're both okay.'

'Oh, come here, you fruitcake!' Guy says, and wraps Celine in his arms and it's then that Margot realises that maybe this was all deliberate. She doesn't believe Flynn would have taken a silly risk with a passenger, so she wonders if Celine threw herself off the back of the bike – onto a soft dune – deliberately. But why? To garner sympathy with Guy? Really? Margot doesn't want to deal with this. She just has a few more days to get through and they'll be back home and she'll never have to see Celine Cremorne ever again.

'Is the food ready?' Celine asks.

'Yes, everything's done,' Sara says. 'Come on, before it gets cold.'

Guy releases Celine and claps his hands together.

'Yes, let's eat! We have enough food here to feed an army.'

At the thought of food, the spell is broken and the accident dismissed. The evening carries on and Margot has to admit that once she's eaten, she starts to relax. Maybe she was overreacting about Celine. It's liberating to be out in the open – just them pitted against the environment trying to achieve some semblance of shelter and sustenance under the limitless sky. And there's something extra-special about eating honest food that you've prepared yourself, with your hands, in the open air. Everything tastes extra-delicious. Maybe it's gratitude, Margot thinks as she looks up at the stars. Gratitude that's ingrained in us since cavemen brought home a meal and the family gathered around to feast on it.

By the fire, Guy keeps the others entertained with stories

and Margot watches as they all fall under the spell of his bonhomie raconteur act. What would they think if they saw the real Guy? The one she lives with at home?

The fire crackles and spits, then Guy opens yet another bottle of wine and dad-dances out from the tent with his mobile speaker. As the moon rises higher and the stars twinkle down, they DJ their way through their phone playlists, dancing to their favourite songs from the eighties, nineties and noughties, the niggles that separate them temporarily forgotten. Later, they all move closer to the fire and tell ghost stories till they peel off one by one to go to bed. And, Margot thinks, despite everything, it actually is the most magical night.

28
SARA

I never sleep well when I've been drinking, and the night under canvas is no different. Sleep comes in fits and starts, and I wake frequently from short, turbulent dreams. The snap of the tent in the wind takes me by surprise, and the moon casts a strange glow through the canvas. Outside, the unfamiliar sounds of the desert seem magnified, and the chittering, shuffling and scampering of creatures I imagine have beady black eyes cause me to lie rigid, holding my breath, as I wonder if they're able to breach the tent.

I wish I'd paid more attention to Guy when he was telling us what wildlife we might see as I picture snakes, scorpions, cockroaches, lizards and spiders stalking me: eyes watching me; legs tangling in my hair; scales touching my face. It's cold, too, way colder than I imagined, and the air holds a clamminess that tries to claw its way into my bones. Despite the duvet, I'm fully dressed, lying on my mattress, and that, too, feels alien, my skin protesting at being so smothered.

What Liv said about Celine being a fake friend is playing on my mind but, after I've rehashed almost every conversation I've had with Celine, I decide that I don't really care. Yes, she can be superficial but she's, what, twenty-eight? Thirty? I shudder to think what I was like at that age. But if she's being a fake friend to anyone, it's to Margot because, if I'm right about the chemistry I sensed after they played golf and in the car, there's something between Celine and Guy. If not now, then in the past, and maybe that's what Flynn is unconsciously picking up on, too.

Anyway, I tell myself as I sigh and roll over for the millionth time, in the general scheme of things, it doesn't really matter whether or not Celine likes me. It's not like I'm planning to be best friends with her. I'm under no illusions that I'll ever see her again once I'm on the plane home.

I fall asleep properly some time just before dawn because when I wake, the tent is stuffy with the warmth of the rising sun, and the light's bright against the tent wall. Outside I can hear voices: Guy and Margot must be pottering about as I hear the chink of a teaspoon on a tin cup and the clack of plates being stacked, so it's guilt that gets me up and out. Wearing the clothes I slept in, I unzip the tent and emerge into the sunlight, blinking like a mole.

The site looks as if it's had an overnight visit from the cleaning fairies: the rubbish is in black bags, the empty bottles stacked back in a box ready to be loaded into the car and the fire pit safely cleared. Guy's bending over the camping stove; Margot over the barbecue. Both turn and wave. How they can be so fresh I have no idea: my own throbbing head reminds me of the skinful I drank so recklessly the night before.

'Morning!' Guy says. 'Just in time for breakfast. We've got eggs, toast, beans and croissants. Sleep well?'

'Well enough, thanks.' I roll my shoulders. 'Though I could do with a Panadol. How about you?'

'So-so,' Margot says. Now I'm closer, I can see she looks tired. 'Here, look, we've made coffee – it's keeping warm in the Thermos. Help yourself.'

'Thanks – how about the teens? Are they up yet?'

'They've gone to make TikToks on the dunes,' Guy says, and I laugh.

'As you do. And Celine?'

Margot shrugs and I look over at her tent, which is still zipped. I pour myself a steaming cup of black coffee and cup it in both hands as I breathe in the aroma.

'Thanks for clearing up.' I picture all the empty bottles we'd left lying around, the dirty plates, the simmering coals. 'What time did you get up to do all that?'

'Oh, you know Margot,' Guys says. 'Up with the bloody larks.'

'Well, thanks for doing it.'

'You're welcome. Right: eggs are ready. Beans are ready,' Guy says. 'Margot, if the toast's done, we should eat while everything's hot. Sara, why don't you see if you can get Celine up?'

'Oh. Okay.'

I go over to her tent, squat down outside and call her name. I wait but there's no sound from inside. 'Celine! Wakey, wakey! There's breakfast if you want it!' Still nothing. I lean in closer to the zip, my mouth almost touching the fabric. 'Yoo-hoo! Celine! Are you even in there?'

'Just open it!' Guy shouts.

I unzip the bottom of the tent and peer in. I can see one socked foot poking out from under the duvet. 'Celine?'

There's no movement, so I unzip more and crawl half inside the small space. 'Celine?'

She's lying on her back with her eyes closed. I reach out and touch the sleeve of her fleece, but there's no movement at all. I shake her by the arm and it's as heavy and unresponsive as one of those dummies I learned mouth-to-mouth on years ago. I touch her hand but it's cold. I shake her more vigorously, and then I back out of the tent not wanting to admit to myself what my mind already knows.

'Guys! She won't wake up!'

All my First Aid training deserts me. I stand there, useless, my hand over my mouth. I'm aware of someone saying, 'Oh my God' over and over, and I realise it's me. Guy reaches me in a heartbeat, both his hands steady on my upper arms as he tries to calm me.

'She's probably just passed out from all the booze.'

But I'm shaking my head. I just know: Celine is not all right. My eyes search Guy's in panic.

'Why isn't she waking up? Something's wrong. Really wrong.'

I pull away from Guy, intending to go back in, but he's there before me, pushing past into the tent. He crawls inside and the flap falls down after his feet disappear. Margot tries to go in after him but can't – the tent's too small for three bodies.

She drags her hand through her hair. Her eyes are wide with alarm.

'Do you think she's …?'

I can't speak. I just shake my head, then turn away as my insides squeeze, saliva floods my mouth and suddenly I'm hunched over, heaving onto the sand, painful retches that bring up water and bile and then the acidic tang of last night's alcohol. Margot's hand rubs my back and, when I straighten back up, spitting, she hands me a crumpled wad of tissues from her pocket.

I want nothing more than for her to tell me I've made a mistake but, after a few moments, as Margot and I watch, stupefied, Guy backs out of the tent and I see by the thin line of his mouth and the small shake of his head that I am right: no amount of effort is going to wake Celine Cremorne ever again.

29
MARGOT

For once, Margot actually needs Guy to do what he does best: to take charge. She needs him to say that Celine is not dead; that there's a way they can save her, a way they can breathe life back into her or rewind time and change what's happened but, when he emerges from the tent, his eyelashes are clumped together with tears Margot does not want to see. He gives a tiny shake of his head, then stands with his head bowed for a moment, his face a mess of emotions.

'Too late,' he says blankly. 'She's gone.'

'No!' Sara wails.

She tries to push past Guy to the tent, but he holds her off.

'Don't.'

'I can do mouth-to-mouth!' Sara cries. 'I have to try! We can't just let this happen!'

'Trust me. It's happened,' Guy says. 'It's too late.'

'No!' Sara sobs. Again, she tries to fight Guy off, but he holds her arms around her, pinning her like a straitjacket, and manhandles her away from the tent.

'All you're going to do is upset yourself. She's gone.' His voice breaks and he covers his face with his hands and turns to hide his tears.

Margot's thoughts are a maelstrom. On the one hand, it seems that Celine is dead. Really dead. Margot's nemesis – the person she has hated for so long – no longer exists. Which is shocking but a thought she boxes up to examine later on. More pressingly, she knows that, no matter what caused Celine's death, Flynn is going to blame himself because of the accident the day before. Already her mother's instincts are kicking in. Her son cannot be burdened with this for the rest of his life. She grabs Guy's arm and yanks him to face her.

'We should have taken her to a hospital! It's on you that we didn't!'

'Don't,' Guy says, and his eyes are dark with anger. 'Don't you dare turn this on me. You know we couldn't.'

They're staring at each other, breathing hard. Margot looks away.

'We cannot let Flynn feel responsible for this,' she says.

'Hey, hey, no one's blaming Flynn,' Sara says, holding her hands up.

Margot whirls on her. 'He was the one driving yesterday. How do you think the authorities will view that?' she says. 'Can you tell me that they won't blame my son? A teenager without a licence driving a quad bike? And that's without factoring in the drinking. I've a fair idea of how that will go down with the police here.'

'We could say someone else was driving.'

'It won't change a thing. We still have a dead body on our hands.' She gasps. 'And what if there *was* an invisible injury?'

Sara swallows. 'Maybe there was,' she says. 'As I said yesterday, I'm not qualified. I did my best, that's all.'

'It's not your fault in any way,' Guy says.

'He's right,' Margot says. 'If we had concerns, we should have taken both of them to a hospital last night, and you're the one who said we should. But...' She looks at Guy as she says this, 'we decided that wasn't necessary.'

'We couldn't drive anywhere.' Guy puts his hands on his hips defiantly. 'We were pissed. We would never have found the road – you saw how dark it was. We'd have killed ourselves trying. And where is the nearest hospital anyway? One that's open that time of night? Tens if not hundreds of kilometres away. We did all we could.' He holds his hands up, palms facing the two women. 'Look, none of us is to blame. What we need to do right now, before the kids come back, is come up with a plan.'

Sara looks at Guy as if she's never seen him before. 'What do you mean, "a plan"? Surely we have to call the police?'

'Uh-uh,' Guy says, shaking his head. 'Nope. We need to think very carefully how we're going to handle this. There are two things to think about. One: what we do about Celine. And two: what we tell the kids. They're going to be back very soon and ...' He pauses and looks from Sara to Margot and back. 'I, for one, don't think they need to know about this.'

'What?' Margot says. 'How? How can we possibly not let them know one of us is dead?' But even as she says it, she wants to know the answer because if she can protect Flynn from this, she'll do anything. Anything. She swings her arm towards the tent. 'How can we pretend this didn't happen?' She pictures them propping up a dead Celine on the back seat as they drive back to Muscat and shakes her head. 'You're out of your mind if you think they won't notice.'

'Even if we somehow hide it from them here, surely they'll

find out eventually?' Sara says. 'It'll be in the news. The papers love stuff like this.' She wipes the corners of her eyes with the back of her hand. 'Trust me, when she's reported missing, it's going to blow up. The kids will ask why we didn't tell them. We'll look like we lied to them – or worse, that we were covering something up. How can we possibly keep it from them?'

'Listen to me,' Guy says. 'For now, let's buy ourselves some time. Then we can decide what we're going to do about … her. Okay?' He pauses and waits till he gets a nod from Sara and Margot. 'Okay, good. So, when they come back, we tell them she's still sleeping. Sleeping off her hangover or whatever. Sara, you "take another look" at Flynn to check for concussion, and you find that his pupils are enlarged, or something. Or you tell him he's looking peaky, or his reflexes are slow. Say anything. I'll say why don't one of us take him and Liv back to Muscat early to get him checked out while the others clear up the camp and follow.'

Shocked as Margot is with the speed at which Guy's come up with this plan, she's already on board with it. She'll do anything she can to keep Flynn from blaming himself. She watches Sara's eyes narrow as she processes the idea. Guy's words are bound to hit home with her, too. It's always about the kids.

'And you'd actually take him to the hospital?' Sara asks. 'Because if you arrive at the hospital talking about a quad bike accident, and Celine is dead in our desert camp …'

'Okay,' says Guy. 'Good point. So, when we get to Muscat, I'll ask Flynn how he feels. He'll say he's fine – *because he is fine*. And we know how much he hates hospitals, so I'll check his pupils or whatever, say I agree, and suggest we skip it. It's doable. He won't want to go any more than I want to take him.'

'What if he's not fine?' Margot interrupts. 'I mean, she clearly wasn't.' She indicates with her thumb towards the tent. 'Maybe it was a lot worse than we thought.'

'He's fine,' Guy says firmly. 'This is probably nothing to do with what happened yesterday. She could have had alcohol poisoning for all we know, or mixed medication with all that booze. But that's not the point right now.'

'So, one of you takes the kids,' Sara says slowly as she figures out what Guy's proposing. 'And then what? The other calls the police and stresses that it was an accident?' She frowns then looks from Margot to Guy. 'Look, I'm not one to cover things up, and of course I'd normally never consider doing anything like this, but maybe we could move her to the dunes so it looks like she went for a walk last night, while we were asleep, and we only found her this morning?' She grimaces. 'I mean, it's a bit dodge but it might mean we're not implicated so much when the police come ...' She clucks her tongue. 'But then we'll still have to tell the kids about Celine when we get back to Muscat and they'd be suspicious because they know she fell off the quad bike...'

But Guy is shaking his head firmly. 'Stop right there. Sorry, but we can't call the police. Absolutely not.'

'Are you serious?' Sara says with a hand over her mouth. 'Like, just do a runner?'

It sounds appalling, but Margot knows Guy's right. It's the only way if they don't want to end up in jail. They have a dead body on their hands. The police will have questions and who will they turn to if not the people who were with Celine when she died? If they call the police now, they won't be home any time soon. Flynn will likely blame himself for Celine's death, and neither of the kids will be sitting their mocks in January. They'll all be held until the police have answers and, should Celine be found to be injured … Margot can't even bear to think how that would play out. Flynn's nearly eighteen. Nearly an adult.

She's about to say this but then she hears voices. She turns and sees the kids loping back across the sand, holding hands and laughing, ready for their breakfast.

'They're coming! What are we going to do?' Margot rarely panics but now she's rooted to the spot, unable to think, her brain a cup of noodles.

'I'll handle it,' Guy says. 'Act normal. Both of you.'

30

SARA

Neither Margot nor I move when Guy tells us to act normal. It's as if my brain's forgotten how to function, but Guy makes a motion with his eyes that says, 'get over to the food table, now!' and so I force myself over and it's like walking on the moon. My feet just don't want to move.

Margot reaches the table before me.

'Coffee?' she asks as brightly as a Stepford wife. 'It'll be ready in a minute.'

'Thanks.' I'm not even sure if the word comes out. My mouth is dry; my stomach convulsing.

'Morning!' Flynn and Liv say as they reach the camp.

'Good morning!' Margot says. 'Did you get good content?'

The teens look at each other. 'No. We, umm, decided to live in the moment and absorb the beauty of the desert,' Liv says with an ironic eye roll.

'Aka our phone batteries died,' Flynn says.

'Oh. Never mind,' I say, because I'm trying really hard to act normal. 'Main thing is you had a nice time. It's good you got up early and got some steps in. We'll be in the car a long time today.' I'm aware I'm talking rubbish.

Guy blocks the way to the table. 'Kids, the food'll be a few more minutes. Why don't you make the most of being here and take the quad bike out again?'

'Really?' Flynn looks at his dad like he misheard. 'Are you sure? You said last night "no more".'

'Well … how long will the food be, love?' Guy asks. 'Twenty minutes? More?'

Margot looks down at the food that was ready ages ago and nods. 'At least that. The stove is really slow to heat up. Take your time. Enjoy yourselves. But be careful, okay? Flynn? Really careful.'

'Okay! Thanks, Dad!'

Liv and Flynn hightail it off before we can change our minds, and we reconvene around the table.

'So,' Guy says. 'As I was saying. We can't call the police.'

'What do you think?' I ask Margot.

She blows air out through her teeth. 'I think he's right. It's not going to go well for us if we call the police. It's not really lying. It's just not telling them everything.'

I look from one to the other, genuinely taken aback. I wouldn't have expected this from either of them.

'Sara, love, this isn't the UK,' Guy says. 'If we call this in, we can kiss goodbye to going home. The police are not going to say "thanks for the intel", buy us some duty free and wave us off on the plane to Blighty. They'll take us straight to the station, and they'll interrogate us one by one until they're satisfied with how and why she died … And, let's say she has a head injury… if it comes out about the quad bike …'

'The point,' Margot says, 'is that she's dead. It almost

doesn't matter why. The police have a duty to find out what happened, and that will take time. And we will have to remain here.'

'Probably in prison,' Guy says.

'How many days till the mocks start?' Margot says and raises her eyebrows at me as she waits for that to sink in. 'And, listen, maybe I'm being selfish here but the chances are that Flynn will be found guilty. He was driving a quad bike that Celine got thrown from. She's now dead. Case closed. Sara, I'm his mother. I can't let that happen. You understand that, don't you? You'd do the same if it were Liv.'

I swallow. Bile's rising again, though there's nothing left to throw up. I don't want Flynn to go to jail for this any more than they do.

'We don't have to tell them about the quad bike,' I say.

'Doesn't matter. If we call them here, we'll be riding a police car straight to detention today. The kids, too. I'm sorry to say, we have no choice but to leave her.'

'Is there an option where we wake up and it's all been a dream?' I close my eyes and shake my head, just in case, because the idea that none of this happened is so appealing but, when I open my eyes again, I'm still there, in the desert trying to decide what to do with the dead body of my new friend.

'What I'm saying is that one of us takes the kids, and the other two bury her, get the hell out of here and never speak of it again. That's what I'm saying,' Guy says.

I slump into a deckchair, my brain worn out. The problem of what to do with Celine's body feels insurmountable – I need time to think it over, to work out all the ways Guy's plan could go wrong. But the kids won't be long and we need to have made a decision by the time they get back. My head feels as if it's going to explode.

'Actually dig a grave and bury her?' I say. 'And pretend it didn't happen? That's what you think we should do?'

Guy nods. 'That's what I'm saying we need to do. Are you on board?'

'So we'll just bury her and leave? And that'll be it?'

Guy closes his eyes and pinches the top of his nose, and I realise that his patience with me is running thin.

'Yes, Sara,' he says. 'The chips are down for us – in the worst possible way. We're in a country whose laws we don't fully understand. We don't speak the language, and we have a dead body in our camp. Any way you look at it, our situation isn't good. But we have a chance if we act right now, and if we act together as a group, to save ourselves. To prevent who knows how much future heartache and misery.' He pauses and looks at me, then Margot. 'We have a chance to get away before this escalates. Have you never watched *Banged Up Abroad*? Imagine this drags on for months. A year. Longer! And we're held here, our lives in limbo, waiting for a verdict? And what if they find us guilty? Because there's a chance they will. There's plenty of circumstantial evidence! We were the only people here! Come on, Sara. You're a sensible person. You can't tell me that's what you want. All of us – the kids included – jailed for something we didn't do? Forget *Sara Says* – Guy says "get outta here!"'

I stare at Guy as he speaks. He's framed against the red

sand and the deep blue sky, our hire cars parked jauntily where we'd left them less than twenty-four hours ago. Suddenly it all looks so foreign, so wrong. I'd give anything now to be in the grey skies, the coldness and the familiarity of home; of the relative security of the UK.

'Let me think,' I say.

31
MARGOT

Over the top of Sara's head, Margot catches Guy's eye and he gives her an exasperated look. Margot shrugs and mouths, 'give her time'. Guy taps his watch and mimics pulling his hair out. They step away from Sara and form a huddle, with their backs to her.

'Can you try talking to her?' Guy says quietly.

'She needs a minute.'

'But you're okay with … what I said?'

Margot snorts in an approximation of a laugh. '"Okay" is an overstatement. But I don't see what choice we have. I'll do it for Flynn.'

'Agreed. But we need her to be on board or we can't do it. All three of us have to be one hundred per cent behind the plan if we're going to get away with it. All for one, and one for all.' He gives an ironic smile.

'Why do you think she died?' Margot says. 'Do you think it really was the accident?'

A look Margot doesn't like flickers across Guy's face before he wipes his hand across his mouth. His eyes don't meet hers.

'What? You think *I* did it?' she whisper-shouts. She throws her head up. 'I had my reasons not to like the woman, but you think I'm capable of crawling into her tent and killing her?'

'I never said that!'

'But you thought it.'

Guy shakes his head. 'I didn't. We don't know what happened. Maybe she had some kind of brain or spine injury we couldn't see. A bleed on the brain. We'll probably never find out. But the best thing we can all do going forward is to tell ourselves that it wasn't caused by the accident or we'll torture ourselves. Maybe she had an underlying condition. Or, as I said, it could have been alcohol poisoning – I mean, we all put a lot away last night. Or maybe it was just her time. If this had happened to her in her villa in Muscat, we wouldn't be having this conversation. It's just that we happened to be the only ones with her when it did happen, and now we have to deal with it.' His voice softens as he reaches out and touches her arm. 'It's not our fault, Mar.'

Margot smiles weakly. That's probably the most reassuring thing he's said to her in years.

'And,' he adds, 'if it *was* the accident, then she got on that bike through her own choice. No one asked her to get on with Flynn. She knew the risks, she knew how old he was, she saw him drinking and she chose to do it. Remember that.'

Two long minutes pass. Margot stares at the sand while she draws arcs in it with her toes, then Guy says, 'Please go and talk to her. We're on a ticking clock here.'

'Fine.' She drags a deckchair next to Sara, sits down and leans in.

'Hey. Any thoughts?'

Sara looks up and her eyes are teary and bloodshot. 'So

many thoughts. I'm scared that if we do this, we'll get caught and end up in an even worse position.'

'I hear you. But look at it this way. How would we get caught if we bury her properly? No one knows she was here with us. No one knows where we are. As far as the world's concerned, we were literally never here.'

'I'm just trying to run through what could go wrong.'

'Look, if we do this, we'll do everything we can to minimise the risks of being caught. But at the moment we only have two ways this can go.' Margot counts off the points on her fingers. 'One: we tell the kids and call the police. We all go in for questioning. No two ways about it. The issue is only for how long: anything from days to weeks to months of detention – or maybe a life sentence. Yes, exactly,' she nods as Sara gasps. 'They might even have the death penalty here. I'm not sure.' Sara's breath hitches and Margot continues. 'Two: we do what Guy suggests, hide it from the kids, so they don't have it hanging over them – also, the fewer people who know about this, the better – we bury her and disappear.'

'I see the logic. I do. But we need to think through every step. How can we possibly get away with it?' Sara says. 'People will notice she's missing. There'll be a search … it'll probably be in the papers. The kids will find out. Someone will connect us being here to her.'

'We just say we were in Muscat, but we didn't see her. No one else was in the compound. No one saw us. And we absolutely don't mention that we went camping. Then the search will focus on Muscat.'

Sara gives a tiny nod, so Margot continues.

'Look, it boils down to this: what are the chances she'll be found out here in the middle of nowhere? Ask yourself that. I'm not sure we could find this spot again, even if we tried.'

Sara sighs. 'Okay. But what about her family? They won't have any closure. She'll just go missing and never be found ...'

Margot shrugs one shoulder. 'I know. I feel the same, but ...'

'Collateral damage,' Guy says. He sits down on the sand opposite Sara, his knees bent up. 'Look, if it's between saving us and *our* kids from a potential life in jail, or her parents from a life of worry – I'm sorry it's not nice – I know which I choose.'

'You know they'll start making those appeals on telly,' Sara says. 'How will we feel then? When we see them weeping and begging for leads and we know where she is and we can't say anything? What are we going to tell the kids then?'

'We'll act. We're shocked that she went missing. But look: neither of the kids liked her that much anyway. I think you're overestimating how much they'll care.'

'I worry how Liv will take it,' Sara says. 'I really hope it doesn't trigger her anxiety again.'

'We'll handle it carefully, don't worry,' Guy says. 'And we'll also have to tell them that we can't admit we were with Celine. I'll explain how it works out here. Say we'd be wanted for questioning if we admitted we'd been hanging out with her and, as we don't know what happened to her, we're better off staying out of it.'

Sara doesn't argue, so Guy continues. 'Look, when we get back, they're going straight into their mocks. They're going to have other things on their minds. This will all fade away.'

Margot's not sure he's right about that but she stays quiet.

'At the end of the day,' Guy says, 'I'll do what I have to do for my family. As will any parent.'

Margot closes her eyes. She doesn't like it, but shielding the kids from what's happened is a really good call. All Margot wants to do right now is get them safely out of the way, so they can't find out, and there's no possibility that Flynn can be blamed. She'll deal with the emotional fall-out and the explanations later, and she wishes Sara would stop overthinking it. It's clear to Margot what needs to be done, however unsavoury, and they really need to get on with it.

Guy peers back towards the big dune then looks at his watch. 'They've already been gone ten minutes.'

'And what if we do as you say and still get caught? Then what?' Sara says. 'It's going to look a million times worse if they find her and it comes back to us. It'll look like we murdered her.'

'How can we possibly get caught?' Guy says. 'When she's reported missing, they'll be checking Muscat, maybe the surrounding areas – the police are not going to drive randomly all this way, to this exact spot and start digging. They're just not.'

'Okay, what if we cleared all evidence of our camp and just left her in the tent?' Margot says. 'Made it look like she was camping alone? So at least someone might find her and her family would have closure? Maybe some other campers?'

Guy shakes his head. 'We can't leave her out in the open. She'd be savaged by wild animals.'

Margot thinks about birds of prey pecking and ripping at Celine's body.

'Look,' Guy says. 'Whatever happens, she's going to end up buried. She's dead! We've got to do what's right for us. So, what do you say? Do we have a plan?'

Sara stands up. 'Give me a minute. I need to go through this in my head one more time. Make sure we're not missing something crucial.'

32
SARA

I need to get away from the Forrests. Their constant ear-bending is stopping me from working out my own thoughts and I need to think through every angle of this for myself; I need to figure out what we need to do and what could go wrong. I need to be sure that they have my back; that they won't turn on me once we're home. And I need to know that I'm good with my decision because I'm hardly going to be able to change it later.

Holding up my hand to stop the Forrests from following me, I stumble through the sand and find a shady spot under a tree where I sit, leaning against the trunk, and hug my knees. I feel like I'm holding the nuclear codes in my hand while the world waits to hear its fate. I should have listened to my gut yesterday. We should have turned back after the tyre blew out. The universe was sending us signs. I knew it and I ignored it. Never has the phrase *Sara Says* haunted me more.

When I consider the Forrests' arguments, it's obvious what we need to do if we want to get away scot-free, and the idea of that is very, very attractive. But *Sara Says* is the sensible voice. The angel on your shoulder – not the devil. And the problem here is that the 'right' decision, the thing the angel voice would tell you to do, is to take the difficult route: to stay and face the consequences. But the consequences of me 'doing the right thing' will impact all of our lives, possibly forever. Until Margot mentioned it, I hadn't even thought about the death penalty, but this is the Middle East, so who knows? I shudder and squeeze my knees even tighter as my thoughts run in circles. Whatever I decide, we three adults have to be in agreement. We have to stick together or all five of us will find ourselves in trouble – way deeper than we can imagine.

'Sara?'

It's Guy, walking towards me, his feet causing little flurries as he struggles through the dry sand. 'What are you thinking?'

'What to have for dinner,' I say. 'What do you think?'

'Sorry.' Guy sits down next to me and wipes his forehead. The sun's higher in the sky now, beginning to give us the full force of its heat. I pull my right foot back into the shadow of the tree before it starts to burn. My pulse throbs at my temples. 'I came to say that the kids are back on the dune now. We can see them. So … uh.'

I shove my head between my knees as if I can block it all out.

'Do you really think we can get away with this?'

'I do. But we need to act quickly and get the hell out of here. Not just the desert; the country.'

I turn to look at Guy. He's staring into the distance. My eyes follow his. He's watching the kids on the dune. Every now and then I catch a note of the engine sound as Flynn opens the throttle.

'We're leaving in two days anyway,' I say.

'But still … staying in the compound where she lives …

lived. It depends how quickly she's reported missing. If it's while we're still here, the police will be everywhere, knocking on doors, asking questions, and then we're in the firing line. Best we just leave. We can change our flights online and get out of here.'

'Oh my God. I mean, shit.'

'We're lucky her flatmates are away. But they might start coming back soon. Every moment longer we stay, the more complicated it becomes. And let's not forget the neighbours. Everyone'll ask "where is Celine?" I mean she was hardly a wallflower, was she?'

Was she? Guy's use of the past tense jars me as it brings home the fact that she's dead. I swat at a fly that buzzes around my head, mirroring the thoughts buzzing in my mind. Stay; go; be responsible; run away. I can think of another option, but it would involve one of us sacrificing themselves – but who?

'We could do it another way?' I say. 'One adult could stay. The other two could leave with both kids. The person who stays could call the police and explain they were camping alone with Celine and she died in the night. Then the kids get to go back home, and only one of us faces the music.' I pause. 'It's a compromise.'

Guy looks at me with his mouth hanging open.

'Are you absolutely nuts? That's insane! So, you want one of us to just wave goodbye to our kid now and maybe never, ever see them again? Because, honey, if that person is found guilty of causing Celine's death, they're looking at life. We've no idea why she died. If there's evidence of an injury, the police'll want answers!'

I swallow. He's right. An injury. Oh, God.

'You want one of us to take that risk? Gamble their life on this? No way. I won't allow it.' Guy's talking so intensely that spit gathers on his lips, and he stops to lick it off. 'Sara. Listen to me. I know this isn't how we would normally behave but these are extenuating circumstances. Trust me. We are not phoning the police.'

I stay silent.

'Whatever we do, it isn't going to bring her back. Think about it that way.'

'Do you promise that you and Margot won't ... turn against me?'

'Sara,' Guy says. 'Hand on heart. We're in this together. All three of us.' I can feel the heat radiating off his body next to me. He puts his hand on my bare knee, which startles me, but then he gives it a gentle squeeze and it's strangely soothing – a human touch in this terrible moment. A touch telling me that he's here with me, that I'm not alone. But it undoes me and my head collapses into my hands.

'I just feel so guilty,' I sob through my fingers. 'She was fine last night. Everything was fine – we were dancing. And then ...' I shake my head, trying to understand, but it's too big, too serious.

'Hey, hey, hey,' Guy says. 'It's not your fault. Are you worried because you said she was okay last night? Is that what this is about? Because, listen to me: she said she was fine and she acted like she was fine. She didn't even want you to take a look at her. It isn't your fault. You're as innocent in this as we all are.'

I can't speak.

'We'd all been drinking,' Guy continues. 'No one was in a

fit state to drive, certainly not through the desert in the pitch black. That would have been incredibly risky. Not to mention that we'd have been drink-driving – which is also a crime here.'

'Leaving a body in the desert probably racks up more of a penalty than drink-driving,' I say facetiously.

Guy clicks his tongue. 'Stop it. This is no one's fault. It's nothing to do with her falling off the quad bike. Nothing to do with us at all. Maybe she had a health condition, something none of us could have known about. A weak heart. A brain aneurysm. She could actually have died anywhere. But the point for us now is that this has happened. Nothing we can do will bring her back. So this is the situation we're in and there are two ways we can deal with it. Wait around and face unknown, possibly very serious, consequences, or get the fuck out and get on with the rest of our lives. And I hate to rush you, but the kids are heading back this way.'

33
MARGOT

With the breakfast reheated and ready, Margot is watching the kids on the dune. She sees them turn and head towards the camp. Guy and Sara are still talking intensely under the tree.

'They're coming!' Margot calls as she hurries over, slipping and sliding in the loose sand, her breath hitching and her heart ramming in her chest. 'Guy!'

'Celine is dead,' she hears Guy saying to Sara. 'She's not going to know what we do. She doesn't care.'

'Do it for Liv!' Margot cries as she glances over her shoulder at the advancing quad bike. 'She has her whole life ahead of her. She needs to be back at home, in school studying and looking forward to university, not tied up in a criminal case in the Middle East.'

She sees, by the way Sara closes her eyes and pulls her hands through her hair, that she's hit home. Sara, she knows, is a woman who'll do anything for her child. Even if it means covering up a death.

'Okay,' Sara says, heaving herself up to standing and brushing sand off her backside. 'If you two promise on your lives that we'll stick together, I'll do it. For Liv. All right? But, if either of you ever turns on me, I'll tell the police it was all you.'

'Done,' Guy says.

Margot nods, her hand pressed against the thumping in her chest. 'Okay.'

Guy grabs each of their hands and squeezes. 'We're in this together, okay? The three of us. We stick together. Whatever happens. Understood?'

'Understood,' they echo.

The quad bike is almost on them. Margot can hardly breathe. They're planning to cover up a death and they have about twenty seconds left to finalise their plan.

She speaks quickly and quietly: 'So, who's leaving with the kids? You?'

'I thought I'd be more useful here,' Guy says. 'You take the kids.'

'No,' Margot says. She knows Guy will be strong and efficient at digging the grave, but she doesn't trust him to tie up all the loose ends in the way she would, and there's so much at stake. 'I'm staying. I'll do it with Sara.'

'Okay. Whatever. We don't have time to argue. Now, come on,' Guy says. 'Action.'

By the time Flynn slows the quad bike, Guy is standing directing him towards the trailer. Margot is serving up portions of beans and toast and handing it out with a smile that she hopes looks genuine.

'How was your ride?' she asks. She peers at Flynn's face and sweeps his sweaty fringe out of his eyes. He swipes her hand off.

'So cool!' he says.

'Brilliant,' Liv adds. Her eyes are shining. 'I loved it. But it's starting to get hot now. That's why we came back.'

'Hmm,' Margot says to Flynn. 'You look a bit pale. Sara, do you think Flynn looks pale?'

Sara turns, then walks closer and peers at Flynn's face.

'I'm okay!' he says. He's wolfing down a plate of beans on toast in a way that says he's absolutely fine, but Sara shakes her head.

'I don't know,' Margot says. 'You look at little peaky to me.'

Flynn sighs and rolls his eyes.

'Are his pupils dilated?' Sara asks.

'Look at me,' she says, and Flynn obeys, widening his eyes dramatically while still chewing. 'Hmm. Guy! Can you come here a minute?'

Guy comes over and the pair of them go through the motions of looking at Flynn once more.

'You don't want to mess around with head injuries,' Sara says gravely. 'There could be a brain bleed or something. Honestly, Guy, I think it'd be best to get him checked out as soon as possible. I could never live with myself if this turned out to be something serious.' She has to turn away as she chokes on the words.

'You could take Flynn straight away,' Margot says, 'and Sara and I will clear up and follow, if that works. I mean, the sooner you get him seen, the better.'

She realises her omission at the exact moment that Flynn says, 'And what about Celine? Where is she, anyway?'

34
SARA

Flynn looks over to the closed tent and there's a beat of stunned silence before Guy replies.

'Still sleeping off her hangover!' He laughs. 'We tried waking her but she told us where to go in no uncertain terms. Maybe leave her as long as you can,' he says to Margot. 'Okay, so is that decided? Liv, will you come with us? We'll get going right away and stop at an emergency department at the first hospital we come across. In Muscat, I imagine.'

Liv looks anxiously at Flynn, her face genuinely pale. 'It's best to get it checked out, babe,' she says. 'They'll probably say you're fine – but, if you're not …'

Flynn sighs. 'All right. My neck is a bit stiff to be honest and we're done here, anyway, I guess.' He looks around fondly. 'It's been brilliant. But will you be all right clearing up?' he asks his mum.

Margot and I are possibly too enthusiastic in our eagerness to reassure him that we're perfectly capable of packing up the entire camp. Not to mention digging a grave.

'There are three of us,' I say, avoiding Guy's eyes as I lie. 'We'll be grand. Now, off you go.' Now that everything's decided, I can't get them out of here fast enough. Thankfully, within ten minutes, they're in the Land Cruiser and Guy's gunning it over the sand away from us. Margot and I look at each other, hands on hips.

'Right. Let's do it,' she says. 'Let's pack the car first then we can deal with …' She nods towards Celine's tent.

I can't even begin to imagine what it's going to be like, dragging out her body and burying it so I scurry around doing everything that needs to be done as quickly as I can. I shove things into random boxes and bags; I scrunch up my tent and ram it in the car and then work my way around the big tent pulling out the pegs until the whole thing collapses. Margot and I scramble to fold it up as best we can and we don't speak bar what needs to be said. The contrast from the happy vibe as we'd set up camp yesterday, anticipating the sunset, our sundowners and the barbecue ahead, couldn't be starker. I glance over my shoulder like a nervous tic, checking to see that no one's coming. *Who's going to be coming?* We're about to bury a body. I can't let myself think about it. Will we be looking over our shoulders forever?

When the car's loaded, we survey the remains of the campsite. The single tent stands lonely, and the sand around it where we'd cooked and eaten and danced looks disturbed, but I hope the wind will erase the last traces of us.

'Right,' I say. 'Shall we start digging? Where do you think? Over there by the tree?'

'Wherever,' Margot says, as if my question's irritated her. I don't have the energy to care if I have or not.

'I'll start. We can do five minutes each.'

I take the spade and start digging but the top layer of sand is dry and slippery and my progress is scant. Margot grabs the trowel we used to cover our toilet holes and starts to sweep the loose sand away so I can dig down to the colder, darker sand below. Within minutes, I'm panting and sweat's dripping down my temples and stinging my eyes, and I wish so much that Margot had driven the kids and that Guy was here to lend me his strength.

'Your turn.' I hand Margot the spade and straighten up, flexing my spine and rubbing the ache in my lower back.

Margot digs like the devil, powered by I don't know what, and that energises me enough to take my next turn. By the time the hole is resembling anything large enough and deep enough to pass as a grave, the sun is notably higher in the sky. We stand back and look at our handiwork.

'Is it deep enough?' I ask.

'Apparently some graves can be as shallow as two feet,' Margot says. 'I googled. I mean, as long as she's in the hard sand, we should be able to get a solid layer over her. That's the main thing, I think. Is it long enough?'

'Maybe if we bend her legs? If they're not stiff yet.' I stifle a sob.

'We need to be sure. Because we don't want to get her out here and then have to carry on digging with her lying there in full view.'

I look at the hole. I'm not sure. There's only one way to find out. Margot gasps as I slither into the hole and gingerly lie down. Flat on my back with my legs slightly bent to the side, I fit. The sand is cold. I can't believe this will be Celine's final resting place. I sit up quickly as I picture sand being thrown over the top of me; being buried alive.

'Happy?' I ask.

Margot covers her mouth and I see her shoulders shake. I'm not sure if she's laughing or crying but then she moves her hand and I see she's laughing. That type of shocked, horrified, hysterical laugh.

'I'm sorry,' she says. 'It's just ... morbid. You in the grave. Come on, get out. Let's get her.'

At Celine's tent, I drop to a squat, bopping away the flies that are buzzing around, and pull up the zip. Celine is on her back with her eyes closed. If it wasn't for the colour of her skin and the incredible stillness about her, she could be asleep. She looks small, childlike.

'Sara, wait!' Margot calls, so I reverse out of the tent to where Margot is hovering behind me.

'What?'

'We can't bury her!' Margot says. 'That's actually the last thing we should do.'

35
MARGOT

Margot's mind is racing.

'Think about it,' she says. 'If we bury her and, somehow, she's found, the police will realise that someone somewhere knows what happened. Because someone will have to have buried her. But, like I said earlier, if we just leave her, fully clothed, in the sand, it'll look as if she was out here on her own. Maybe she wandered away from someone's camp looking for the perfect photo, or got separated from a desert safari trip …' she trails off.

'And just collapsed here on her own?'

Margot nods. 'Exactly.'

Sara rakes her sweaty hair off her face. 'But Guy said we should bury her. The point is we don't want her to be found by random campers. We stand a much bigger chance of not being discovered if her body is hidden. Underground.'

Margot looks at the desert around them. 'There's nothing here. Who's going to come to this exact spot and find her?'

'We're not *that* far from the track,' Sara says, and Margot remembers bumping along it before they let down the tyres and headed into the deep sand. The two women stare at each other, lost in the horrors of their thoughts. Then Sara speaks.

'We made an agreement with Guy. We agreed to bury her. Like he said, we can't just leave her here to be torn apart by falcons and eaten by desert foxes. Come on. The least we can do is give her some dignity in death. She deserves a burial. Let's at least be human about it.'

She turns back to the tent, takes a deep breath and crawls in. There, she wraps Celine's sheet around her body, then Margot drags her feetfirst out of the tent. They try to lift up an end of the sheet each but Celine's too heavy for them. Neither wants to carry her with a fireman's lift so they're forced to drag Celine over to the hole. By the time they get there, Margot is drenched in sweat and panting. She's got black floaters circling in front of her eyes and a headache. She knows she's dehydrated and remembers that Guy took all the water in his car.

'We can brush over the tracks later,' Sara says, wiping her brow with the back of her hand but then she stops and stares into the distance. 'What is that?'

Margot shields her eyes from the sun and squints towards the horizon. There's dust rising into the blue of the sky.

'Cars, maybe? I can't tell if they're coming this way. We need to hurry up.'

Somehow, Margot finds strength and endurance that surprise her. The hole isn't as deep as she'd have liked it to be, but it'll have to do. She and Sara roll Celine's body into the makeshift grave as gently as they can but, even so, the body hits the hard sand at the bottom with a muffled crunch that Margot knows will haunt her dreams.

Sara looks sadly into the hole. 'You want to say anything? Any final words?'

Good and *riddance* come to mind, but Margot shakes her head.

'Okay. Well, RIP, Celine,' Sara says. 'You were, um – it was nice getting to know you. Uh, fly high with the, uh, angels.'

I wouldn't count on it, thinks Margot.

One of Celine's hands has come out of the sheet.

'Should we try to get that back in?' Sara asks, but Margot's had a realisation that's turned her insides to ice.

'We don't have time,' she says. 'I've just realised what those cars are. They're the Jeep Jamboree. I saw fliers for it. There are hundreds of them on a desert drive today. We need to get out of here!' She grabs the spade. 'Come on!'

They shovel, scrape and kick the sand onto Celine as fast as they can, while also glancing over their shoulders at the advancing plume of dust.

'They're coming this way,' Sara says and Margot looks up. Now it's possible to make out the line of vehicles, the sun glinting off bonnets and windscreens.

'Oh my God. Right, you collapse her tent and get it in the car and I'll finish up here.'

Margot smooths over the top of the grave and the surrounding footprints with the side of a piece of wood, then she stands back and tries to look critically at her handiwork. The area clearly has been disturbed, the damp sand from underneath is darker in colour, but the sun's hot – it'll dry out in minutes. She just hopes that the Jeep Jamboree doesn't pass this way.

She hurries over to the car and swings herself in – every overused muscle in her legs, back and arms sore and protesting. Sara's already seated. She's holding an iPhone.

‘We forgot her phone,’ she says. ‘What the hell do we do with it?’

‘Is it off? Turn it off. We’ll chuck it out of the window or something. We need to go.’

She guns the engine and doesn’t look back.

36
SARA

We follow the tracks left by Guy, and I see that I'd been right earlier: it's really not that far to the sand track. As Margot bumps the car onto it, I swivel in my seat, looking back towards the trees where we'd camped.

The trees by which Celine lies buried.

'Can't see anything unusual from the road,' I say.

Margot's face is grim. 'Good.' She nods to the right, 'Looks like these guys are coming this way, though.'

'Sod's law, isn't it? You go to the desert to get away from people and meet a thousand.'

We watch in silence as a convoy of Jeeps approaches like a swarm of locusts, growing larger in size and noise until they reach us, barrelling past us on the sand on either side of the track.

'Don't smile,' Margot says as we enter the dust cloud kicked up by the convoy. 'Don't draw attention to us in any way. White Toyotas are practically invisible. We could be anyone. There's nothing memorable about us at all.'

I'm still holding Celine's phone and I look down, pretending to fiddle with it. My breathing starts to slow as we put more distance between us and the camp site. Our speed is limited by the tyres we deflated to drive on the sand, and we make slower progress than I'd like until we get a chance to refill them properly. Margot's staring straight ahead.

'Thank you for agreeing to do this,' she says. 'It might not feel like it right now, but it was the right thing to do.'

I stay silent.

'The accident wasn't Flynn's fault,' Margot continues. 'He doesn't deserve to go to jail. He didn't even ask her to get on the quad with him!' She swipes a hand across her face.

What I need right now is time alone to process all that's happened; time to make peace with the decision I made out there in the dunes, not a heart-to-heart. There's not much left inside me to comfort Margot. I search for the right thing to say.

'We don't even know if the accident was the cause of Celine's death. As Guy said, it could have been anything.'

'Right?' Margot whips her head to face me. 'So why condemn Flynn?'

'Well – exactly.'

'I mean, it was deep, soft sand on the dune. You saw it. There was nothing she could have hit her head on. It's like falling into marshmallow.'

'It does seem unlikely that a fall like that would cause a life-threatening injury,' I say carefully. 'But you never know. You've got to admit it looks odd. Fall off a quad bike and die that same night. What are the chances?'

'How about: drink your body weight in booze and die that same night?' Margot says. 'Or: go into the desert with an underlying health condition and die randomly in the night?'

'I guess ...' I say, but I'm thinking that Celine likely drank her body weight in booze most weekends. She had good tolerance. 'So, is that what you think happened? She had a health condition?'

Margot blows air through her lips. 'Who knows? Could have been anything. Maybe even a snake bite. Or a scorpion.'

'Yeah. I didn't think of that. Did you wake up in the night at all? Did you hear anything?'

Margot frowns. 'Like what?'

'Well, anything. Voices? A commotion? I don't know. Anything that would give us a clue.'

'Not that I remember. You?'

I shake my head. 'No. Nothing. I was flat out. Literally. So weird, isn't it?'

'Yep.'

We drive in silence as I think back over the events of the night and the horror of finding Celine dead.

'You don't think one of us had something to do with it, do you?' I ask.

'God, no. Not at all.'

'Good. Because the last thing we need to do is start blaming each other. Like Guy said, we need to stick together.'

'And we will,' Margot says. Her hand seeks mine and squeezes it. I squeeze back. It feels like we're Thelma and Louise.

We see a shop with an archaic-looking petrol pump out the front and, thankfully, an air pump too. While Margot's snaking the hose around the car to top up the tyres, I jump out to buy some much-needed water and, when I'm back in the car, my phone pings. It's a message from Guy.

I presume Margot's driving. Reached the villa. Didn't go to hospital. Flynn's fine. Everything okay your end?

Yes. On our way, I type.

Just rebooked our flights for tonight with a short layover in Dubai airport and the early flight to Birmingham. There's still availability as of now. I'm sending you the details. Please change yours.

I frown as I look at the messages. Won't running away make us look more suspicious? But, if Guy's changed the Forrests' flights, what's the alternative? To stay alone with Liv, waiting for a knock on the door from the police? It dawns on me again that we're actually committing a crime by burying a body and fleeing the scene of a death. Bonnie and Clyde with their friend and kids. I open my browser and get on the website. Thank heavens I booked with the airline rather than through a travel agent.

My phone pings again, three more times.

It'll cost a bit extra but I'm happy to pay you back.
I think we all need to leave together.
And I can't leave you behind.

I send a thumbs-up to Guy and, as Margot pulls out of the petrol station, I update her on the plan as I search for availability.

'He's right,' she says. 'Whatever it costs, you need to be on those flights with us.'

'Done,' I say, a few minutes later. 'I hope the airline doesn't question why we all changed our flights so suddenly.'

'People do it all the time,' Margot says. 'It's no biggie.'

'I hope not. So that's it. We take off from here at four-forty in the morning, change at Dubai and take off again at seven-fifty. We'll be home in our beds by tomorrow night.'

'Let's hope we don't get stopped at immigration,' Margot says.

'There's no reason why we should be,' I say, but when I look across, her face is grim.

37

MARGOT

As they come into the outskirts of Muscat, Margot takes a small detour along the seafront, where it'll be possible to hurl Celine's phone into deep water. She stops the car and looks at Sara.

'Here's good, I think. Ready?'

But Sara is leaning forward, peering into the footwell. 'I can't find it. Can you put the light on?'

Margot clicks it on and searches around the seat area. 'Where was it? Were you holding it, or did you put it in your bag?'

Sara rummages through her handbag. 'I didn't put it in my bag. I had it on my lap.'

'When did you last see it?'

'Umm. At the petrol station. When we stopped, and I got out to get the water … oh, shit.'

Margot breathes out a shuddering breath. 'No. It'll be here. Come out, move the seat.'

She uses her phone torch and they both examine as far as they can under both front seats and finally Margot has to accept that they've drawn a blank. 'Jesus. Now what?'

Sara shrugs. She looks as if she might cry. 'I'm sorry. I,

just … Guy was hassling me about changing the flights and I was distracted. Now I think about it, I can imagine how it might have fallen out. Shall we go back? Do you want me to go back in a taxi? I will if I have to. You can go back to the villa and just say that I met a random friend or something?'

Margot stares at the sea, her hands on her head as she thinks. The phone should be out there, under that mass of water, being destroyed, never to be found. Now it's at a petrol station somewhere in rural Oman. Incriminating evidence. But what can they do? She goes back to Sara, who's standing by the car looking utterly destroyed.

'I'm so sorry,' Sara says. 'I don't know what else to say.'

'Come on, get in,' Margot says. 'There's nothing we can do now. Going back will take time we don't have and if we start looking for a missing phone we're only going to draw attention to it and to ourselves. We just have to hope no one finds it. Or that it's damaged. Or for a miracle.'

'Are you sure?'

'Yep.' Margot starts the engine. 'But one thing: don't tell Guy anything about the phone. Please? Do that for me?'

'Sure,' Sara says. 'Thank you.'

Guy must be watching for them because when Margot and Sara reach the villa, the front door swings wide and he's there in the doorway.

'All okay?' he asks.

She nods. 'Yep.'

'Well done,' Guy says and he gives them both a nod.

'How are the kids?' Sara asks.

'Fine,' he says. 'They're disappointed about leaving early,

but I said we needed to get back for an urgent work meeting – a VVIP house commission I couldn't talk about. And that, Sara, you'd decided you may as well come with us. Hope that's okay. And they were more than happy not to go to the hospital.'

Later that day, Margot and Guy take the cars to be valet cleaned and return them to the hire company, so they have a smoother journey through the airport in the morning. Margot then throws together supper from the odds and ends left in the fridge. As she lays the table for the final time, Sara hesitates over the sixth place.

'Lay it,' Margot tells her. 'The kids will wonder if we don't.'

It's ironic how happy she'd be to see Celine now, Margot thinks, given how she used to dread her appearing from across the pool at dinnertime with her wearisome predictability and chirpy yoo-hoos. The weather's absolutely perfect, the air warm velvet on Margot's skin as she bustles about, but she can't look at the pool. Is she the only one who sees the shape of Celine stretched out on a sunlounger, ghostly in her white swimsuit?

'This is good,' Guy says, nodding, as they place the food on the table. 'Just like any other night. Nothing out of the ordinary. Good work, ladies.'

'What did you say to Diane and Tom when you gave the camping stuff back?' Sara asks.

Guy had vacuumed the tents and packed them up properly, refilled the quad bike, and taken everything back that afternoon.

'Nothing. They weren't home. I left the stuff in the garage for them.'

'Should we tell them not to say anything about us borrowing

the gear if anyone comes asking questions?' Margot knows that the British expat community in Muscat isn't that big. One degree of separation, if that. Once Celine is reported missing, it's bound to come up in conversations with Tom and Di.

'No,' Guy says. 'We'll look like we're hiding something. It's suspicious. Trust me, they're cool. They won't say anything. Tom and I go way back. The things we know about each other …' He laughs to himself. 'Anyway, look, to be honest, by the time anything's found – if it's found at all – it'll be incredibly difficult to pinpoint when it happened exactly. And we've only been here for a week.'

'A week. Imagine,' Sara says.

'I know!' Guy says. 'It doesn't seem like it, does it? And we flew in during a massive influx of Christmas holiday tourists so *if* it comes to it – and that's a big if – finding out who did this is going to be like looking for a needle in a haystack.' He summons a smile. 'Right, shall we call the kids? Remember, Celine came back with you two and, as far as we know, she's in her villa. Okay?'

Flynn and Liv don't need to be called twice; they fall into their seats and start passing round the dishes. To an outsider, all would look normal, Margot thinks. Two families eating on the terrace on the last night of their holiday, with the fairy lights twinkling and the garden lights reflecting off the gleaming surface of the pool. Happy memories.

Only not.

'I don't wanna go back,' Flynn says. 'Why can't we stay with Sara while you two go back?'

'Yeah,' says Liv. 'Please, Mum?' She gives her mum a puppy-eyed look.

Sara examines her fork as she loads it with vegetables. 'I'm sorry,' she says. 'It's all booked now, and I can't change it.'

'Really?' Liv puts her head on one side like she doesn't believe her.

'Really,' Guy says. 'Now eat up. I think there are ice creams that need finishing after this.'

'Should we wait for Celine?' Margot asks.

Guy looks over to her villa. 'I gave her a shout but she's probably had more than enough of us by now!' He gives a little shrug. 'She'll come if she wants. Dig in.'

They pack after dinner, then the adults clean out the villa, empty the bins, and finish everything up ready for their departure. By the time that's all done, Margot's so physically tired she thinks she might never wake up again, but then she remembers Celine's phone. Will the person who finds it just take out Celine's SIM and put in a new one? Will they wipe it and sell it? Celine won't be reported missing for a day or two. There aren't yet any dots to be connected to a crime. Could it be that simple?

The alarm's set to go off in the middle of the night, and she dozes fitfully, her mind going down a rabbit hole of what will happen if this is ever traced back to them. Aside from the legal ramifications and the terrifying possibility of extradition and jail, if it comes out that the Forrests have anything at all to do with a woman going missing – let alone a dead one – the media will destroy Margot's Mansions. It's a business built on trust and word of mouth; built on the wholesome image she projects on social media, and the media loves it when people like her fall from grace.

Next to her, Guy lets out an enormous snore and then a fart rumbles out of him. Margot sighs and rolls over to face the other way as another even more devastating thought hits her. What they've just done binds her to Guy forever. If she ever entertains the idea of leaving him, he'll hold it over her, she knows he will. Perhaps that's why he was so keen to cover it up and run. It's one more tool he can use to control her.

38
SARA

It's 2 a.m. when we rouse ourselves to go to the airport, eyes screwed up against the electric lights. We move largely in silence, each of us lost in our thoughts and anxieties as we close up our bags. We pre-booked two cabs before we went to bed and they arrive early, waiting outside, engines running, as we do a last sweep of the rooms, checking we've left nothing behind.

Nothing at all. Not a hair. Not a nail clipping. Nothing that could be traced back to Celine's presence in the house. I'd even disinfected every surface and mopped every floor. The Forrests go in one cab, and Liv comes with me. We agree we'll go through check-in, passport control and security separately 'just in case' – 'just in case' what, no one wants to say. We'll meet again once we're airside. Liv and I ride in silence, each of us looking out of our respective windows at the passing landmarks. As we draw closer to the airport and see the tail fins of the airplanes on the ground, I realise that my mouth is dry. I'm scared: scared that they'll look at my passport and call us into a private room with no windows. Scared that we'll get a tap on the shoulder from a uniformed official. Scared that they'll whip out handcuffs at the boarding gate and put them on us right there and then.

I'm scared, yet I know my fear is illogical. Celine hasn't been reported missing. No one could have reported us. I place my hand on Liv's.

'Had a good holiday?' I ask.

'The best,' she says. Her face is grey in the half light. 'I wish we weren't leaving early. We could have stayed. You're always going on about value for money, but leaving early isn't.'

'I know, I know. It's just that the Forrests had already changed their tickets and I thought you'd like to travel back with Flynn. Shall we try to get into a lounge when we're through? Would you like that?'

'Whatev.'

Liv closes her eyes and turns away with a small exhale, the poor, hard-done-by teen. I squeeze her hand, and the returning squeeze is so faint I may have imagined it. Then we're there. The taxi driver opens the boot and pulls out our bags, and we join the bustle and clusters of people heading into the terminal. Ahead of us, I spot the Forrests already at a check-in counter. Liv and I wait patiently in the queue.

'Here for a holiday?' the woman at the check-in asks with a bright lipstick smile as she opens my passport. 'Did you enjoy it?'

'It was lovely, thanks,' I mumble with a faint smile. She stares at my passport long enough to make me squirm, then repeats the process with Liv's, looking at her and then down again at the passport photo.

'Olivia,' she says. 'Lovely name.'

My smile is tight and then she's printing out baggage tags and dispatching our bags and I'm clutching the boarding passes and the baggage receipt like they're hard-won treasure as we turn away from the desk. There isn't much of a queue at passport control, maybe four people ahead of us, and we stand in silence while we wait our turn.

'Morning!' I say with a smile as I hand over the passports. The official smiles back absently, her mind on her task, while my heart thumps like a bass drum. Why is it you look shifty when you try too hard to look innocent? The wait for the computer to process our passports seems interminable. But then it's done and she's holding out our passports without calling the police. Of course she is.

'Have a good flight,' the official says, and my knees almost buckle with relief. Security is quick and easy and then we're airside.

'Give me a high five!'

Liv smacks my hand lamely, not understanding my relief.

As significant journeys go, our flight's distinctly unremarkable, which is exactly what we need. When we reach Dubai, Guy doesn't want any trace of us checking into a lounge together, so we eat whatever breakfast we can force down at a restaurant close to the departure gate, and pay in cash. The Birmingham flight's on time. The ground staff wave us through, and the cabin crew welcome us on board with painted-red smiles. Despite our late booking, the five of us sit in one row: Flynn, Liv and me on one side of the aisle and the Forrests on the other. I distract myself with movies and, before I know it, lunch is served and then we're landing in Birmingham. The sky outside is bleak, raindrops streaking across the window, and the sight fills my heart with joy. Despite my little fantasy about moving abroad, when the chips are down, this is home.

We've made it. We're safe. As the plane taxies towards the stand, I look across the aisle at Guy and gurn a relieved face. He widens his eyes in agreement, then the intercom crackles and the captain speaks.

'Good morning once again from the flight deck. Just an update on landing. I've been informed that there's going to be a police check at the aircraft door so we'll be disembarking from the front exit only. Please have your passports ready to present as you disembark the aircraft. Thank you.'

39

MARGOT

Margot stares straight ahead at the seat in front of her, wondering whether it's an option to hide in the bathroom. Claim she's got food poisoning and not leave the toilet till the police are gone. She's shaking – not just her hands, but everything. This is it, she thinks: game over. She wonders if it would be better if they just confess and get it over with. Would the police be more lenient on them? She feels Guy squeeze her hand, and she knows it's meant to be reassuring but all she can think is: this is how it ends. The feeling of inevitability she has is acute: how did they think they could get away with leaving a dead body buried in the desert? The idea is incomprehensible now.

Around Margot, people are standing up, stretching, rummaging for passports, opening baggage racks and pulling down their bags.

'Ready?' Guy pats her knee. 'Come on, Mar. Time to go.'

He sounds calm, but Margot can see from the tic in his jaw that he's as tense as she is. He stands, stretches extravagantly – which is another 'tell' to Margot – opens the overhead bin and heaves down their bags. Margot sees Sara, looking perfectly relaxed, doing the same with hers and Liv's. When Margot notices that she's the only one still seated, she realises she has no choice but to move. She stands up slowly and puts her hand on her belly, half thinking she might actually make a dash to the toilet, claiming diarrhoea. Then she realises that they need to stay together and gathers her things then waits in the aisle for the queue to move forward.

'Odd, isn't it?' a woman with wispy grey hair says to a well-dressed man next to her. 'Passports, now? I've never had that before.'

'It happens,' the man says. 'I had it going to London from Hong Kong recently.'

'What are they looking for?' the woman asks.

Good question.

He shrugs. 'Could be anything. Asylum seekers, criminals, drugs. They must have had a tip-off.'

'Oh, wow,' she says, looking around the cabin. 'Imagine you were sitting next to a criminal and didn't know. Why don't they just catch them at the boarding gate?'

He shrugs again. 'Who knows. Anyway, look, we're moving.'

And so Margot falls into line and moves slowly forward, shuffling with her family like prisoners to their execution. The cabin crew at the exit beam and wish them a safe onward journey. At the plane door are two uniformed policemen.

Sara goes first. She hands the two passports over with a tight smile. One of the policemen flips through them and hands them back.

'Thank you, madam. Next.'

Guy hands over his and Flynn's. A quick look at the identity pages and then: 'Thank you, sir. Next.'

Margot isn't breathing as she hands over her passport. She doesn't meet the man's eyes, just looks at a spot on the floor as he flips the pages and peers at her. *I'll take the rap*, she thinks. *I'll go to jail if you spare my son.*

'Thank you. Next,' he says and Margot practically falls onto Guy.

'Come on,' he says as she wobbles up the air bridge on legs shaking with relief. 'Time to go home.'

Never in her life has Margot been so grateful to arrive back from a holiday; to be in a taxi on the sodding M5. The things that usually annoy her – the rain, the dreariness, the roadworks, the traffic, the boring monotony of the tarmac – she sucks them in greedily, savouring the fact she's able to see them once more. And, as the electric gates to their house slide back, she finally relaxes against the seat. Home. Margot taps the entry code into the front door and breathes in the familiar smell of their home, and she thinks she'll never again complain about living in the UK. Never again will she yearn for the blue sky and sunshine of Oman. She had more than enough of that relentless sunshine during those desperate hours in the desert when she and Sara had buried a body.

God help them. They've buried a body and done a runner. She and Guy are criminals.

Standing in her kitchen, looking around at the familiar gleaming appliances, the glossy island and the huge cooking range she loves so much, she puts her hand over her mouth and shakes her head, her eyes wide. Everything's the same but everything's different. How can this have happened in her perfect, ordered life? She has the horrible feeling that she's sinking. Or that she's living in a kind of parallel universe and she needs to snap through some invisible fabric to get back to her real life – her proper life – the one where she's a model citizen who makes doll's houses and is interviewed in the local paper.

Margot's hands work on autopilot as she fills the kettle. Everything in her kitchen is so mundane: the coffee cups still on the drying rack where she'd put them the day they left; the butter, the eggs, the cheese still in the fridge; the sourdough in the freezer. They belong to another life. An innocent life.

Guy takes the bags upstairs.

'Cup of tea, Guy? Flynn?' Margot calls up the stairs, but Flynn's door is already closed and he doesn't reply. 'Tea?' she yells again and still gets no response. So she makes one for everyone anyway, because that's what she does and, right now, she needs to cling on to as much normality as she can.

She carries Flynn's tea up to his room, perches on the bed by his feet and mimes asking him to please take off his headphones.

'What?' he says, pulling only one off an ear.

'You okay?' she asks. 'Glad to be home?'

'Uh huh,' he says.

'Missing Liv?'

'Uh huh.'

They sit in silence for a few moments. There's so much Margot wants to say. She wants to gather her son in her arms and hug him tightly and tell him everything's going to be all right and that it wasn't his fault. But she can't because he doesn't know what happened. He doesn't know Celine is dead in the desert, and he doesn't know how close they've come to losing everything.

Flynn stretches and runs his hand through his hair and Margot glimpses a mark on his arm. She pushes up the sleeve of his T-shirt to look more closely: four little bruises, like fingerprints. Flynn swipes her hand away.

'What happened?' she asks, trying to keep her voice light.

He gives a dismissive shake of his head. Could it have been Celine? Out of nowhere, a memory surfaces: the slow tick of a tent zip opening in the middle of the night. Was it real, or is she imagining it? Could Flynn have gone to see Celine in the night? He'd been uncomfortable with the attention she was giving him – is it possible that Flynn went to have a word with her and they had a tussle? A brick of dread settles in her stomach. Surely not.

She stands. 'Well, I'll leave you to it,' she says, although she can see all he's doing is scrolling TikTok.

''Kay,' he says, and puts his headphones back on.

40
SARA

Liv asks to go straight back to her dad's.

'You sure, baby? You're welcome to stay,' I say, but she nods.

All her stuff is at his. I walk her to Michael's door, then retreat back to the cab so I don't need to exchange words with whoever opens the door. It's Nancy. She blows me a kiss – typical Nancy – I wave back, and then the front door closes. My daughter is gone, and I'm alone with the horror of what I helped to do.

Back home, I go through the motions of unpacking and putting on the washing. I check my emails and my website, but I can't focus on answering any questions right now. I haven't got any online clients booked till tomorrow. I get up, walk around, fiddle with things, sit down. I make tea and forget to drink it. I'm jittery and distracted. Waiting for something to happen. And then something does happen. Guy pays me a surprise visit.

'Come in,' I say.

Standing in my doorway he looks strange. Wearing a jumper and jeans, he's not the Guy in shorts and linen shirts I got to know in the sunshine. I see how England reduces him to something less than he was in the desert. Something mundane.

'How are you, Sara?' he asks. I lead him into the front room and dither about what to offer him.

'Oh, I'm all right. You know.' I shrug. 'Glad to be back! I suppose!' I put my face in my hands and laugh. 'I mean, not glad to be back, but you know what I mean.'

'I know exactly what you mean,' he says.

'Can I get you anything? Some tea?'

'No. Thanks, but I won't stay. I just wanted to pop in and check that you're okay. Not having any second thoughts or anything? Because we did the right thing. You know that, don't you?'

I turn away. 'I do. Of course I do. But – I don't know. Why does it have to be so difficult?'

I feel his hands on my shoulders, and he turns me around.

'Look at me.' I meet his eyes. Dark, dark brown, almost black. 'We did the right thing, Sara. It's time to look to the future. Forget what happened. Just get on with our lives. All right?'

'All right.'

He pulls me into a warm hug then releases me. 'Good. We've got this. Okay? Everything's going to be fine. Margot and I are with you. We're all in this together.'

The days that follow are more of the same as I go numbly through the motions of my life. I keep busy with my clients, my YouTube channel and the website but, while I'm coaching people through their problems all I can think is: how long until Celine is reported missing? How long until the story makes the news? What if her body's found? Every day, I wake up with dread writhing in my stomach and wonder if this will be the day the news will break. There's no chance that Celine won't be missed. Her usually active social media is left hanging. She won't be responsive on WhatsApp. It's just a matter of time till her housemates return to the villa and raise the alarm.

I know I can't google her name or even search her social media in case the proverbial shit hits the fan, and my computer and phone are seized so, every day I scan the major newspapers online, and check the world news pages, expecting to see a story about a missing Brit. There's nothing, which you would think might make me feel relieved, but it leaves me even more jittery and wretched because I know that, of course she'll be reported missing. She's a Brit abroad: of course there'll be something in the papers.

I struggle with my work. How can I advise people on their inconsequential problems when I have far bigger worries myself? The teen problems I deal with on YouTube seem so trivial: kids who can't focus for their exams; friendship issues; boyfriend problems. Absolutely no one is dealing with the guilt of hiding a dead body and making a run for it.

I try to reframe it in a more positive way – I now have more empathy with those who find themselves in a bad situation not of their own making. But, still, I can't concentrate. All thoughts lead back to the desert; to that impossible decision made in the heat of the moment. I eat only what I need to, taking no joy in food. My only solace is those few hours I manage to get some sleep, and that's chemically induced.

I do nothing to mark New Year. I call Liv to wish her a Happy New Year, and she's cheerful on the phone. New Year's Eve was great. Her revision's going well. Flynn's brilliant. The

Forrests are fine. Everything's good. As it should be, given the decisions we made in the desert to ensure that it would be.

And then, just shy of six days after we land, there it is: *British expat missing in Oman.* Just a short story, a few lines.

> A 32-year-old British expatriate has been reported missing in Muscat. Friends of Celine Cremorne alerted authorities when they were unable to contact her. The Royal Oman Police have launched a major search.

My instinct is to pick up the phone and message the Forrests. I want to ask if they've seen the story, but Guy's told us we mustn't communicate about this on our phones. I wonder if he and Margot are as obsessed with it as I am, or if they've somehow managed to put the saga behind them. At least they have each other to speak to. Who do I have?

No one.

41
MARGOT

Guy shows Margot the news story.

She's working on a stately home. It's a commission Guy pushed and pushed to win – for the kudos and potential future business more than for the money. It's been complicated, though. Even once the contract was signed, there had been all sorts of protocols to follow before Margot was given access to the home and she'd even had to sign an NDA about everything she saw inside. But now everything's approved and Margot is measuring out the frame. This is a part of the process that she enjoys, but it's also a difficult part of the job. Errors at this stage are difficult to correct later, and no one wants to balls up such a big commission.

'It's hit the news,' Guy says, appearing suddenly at her studio door and startling her so much her pencil slips on the wood she's marking up.

'What has?' she asks. When she's creating, Margot is genuinely lost in her work, not thinking about anything else, which is some blessed relief.

'Turn your phone off,' he says, and she complies like a robot, her brows furrowed in confusion. Once her screen's dead, Guy carries on.

‘Headline today: “British national missing in Oman”. This is it, Mar. It’s starting.’

She feels the blood drain from her extremities. ‘You’re joking?’

‘Why would I be joking? She was always going to be reported as missing. It was just a matter of when.’ Guy throws himself onto the sofa Margot uses for creative breaks and lets out a huge sigh. ‘Now this shit gets real.’

‘Did they say who she was?’

‘They state her name, but nothing more. Give it another day and there’ll be pictures, trust me.’

Margot stares at her work board, the complex measurements, that make sure the house will be perfectly downscaled, fuzzing in front of her eyes. A tiny part of her hopes, in a childlike way, that the fact Celine’s missing will somehow just blow over. There might be a fuss for a while, but when nothing is found and the phone doesn’t turn up, the case will go cold. The media reports will die out – it happened a long way away and it isn’t very interesting. Something more exciting will capture the public’s imagination. And they’ll get away with it.

Guy comes over and starts to knead Margot’s shoulders, hard, in a way that hurts more than helps. She’s not even sure if he intends to soothe her or himself. She holds herself still, enduring it.

‘Things are likely to be tough for a while,’ he says. ‘We just need to hold firm on the course we set. We need to stick together.’ He lets go of her shoulders and paces the studio. Tension radiates off him, disturbing the calm, creative energy she likes to nurture. ‘Do you think we can trust Sara not to talk to anyone?’ he asks.

'It's a bit late to question that now.'

'Are you blaming me for making the decision? Out there in the desert, with the kids coming back any second? Are you saying it's my fault where we are now? Because I know what the alternative was – and it wasn't pretty.'

'No, I—'

'You were on board with this, Margot. And so was she. Don't forget that. You had your chance to speak up and you said nothing. Your hands are as dirty as mine.'

'Guy, I—'

He shakes his head. 'What's done is done. It's no good looking back. We're going to have to check in constantly with Sara. I'll do it. I'll go over now and then to keep reminding her that she can't talk to anyone except us about this. We can't have her going rogue and shooting her mouth off.' He sighs. 'We chose this path, and we need to stick to it. For all our sakes.'

'I know,' Margot says.

She can feel him staring at the back of her head, his eyes boring into her scalp and she thinks about the tent zip she thinks she might have heard going down in the night. Slowly. Carefully. She supposes there's a very tiny possibility it could have been Sara's or Celine's tent, but Margot's hearing really isn't sharp enough to have picked that up from across the campsite. Considering the distance alone, it must have been Guy, Flynn or Liv. And then there were the bruises on Flynn's arm. He'd told her he didn't like Celine. Was there more to that than he'd let on? Had he been in a tussle-gone-wrong with her? That evening in the kitchen, he'd asked why Celine was spending so much time with them. Had he realised his dad was attracted to her? Now he's reaching adulthood, he's very protective of his mum. She stares at the house frame in front of her then turns slowly to face Guy. She's got to ask, or she'll drive herself crazy.

'Guy, please don't shoot me down, but you don't think there's any chance at all that Flynn could have done it, do you?'

'You mean crashed the quad bike deliberately? Why would he do that?'

'No, not that. I meant – maybe accidentally?'

Guy's eyes flash. 'What, killed her? Are you seriously asking me that?'

Margot's left shoulder shrugs, just a small movement, even though she wills it not to. 'Of course I don't think he did it,' she says. 'I was just asking what *you* think.'

There's a moment's silence, then Guy speaks.

'One: he absolutely didn't do it. And two: let's not start pointing fingers at each other because that way madness lies. I think she died of natural causes.' He waits for Margot to say something, but she doesn't. He taps her shoulder. 'Right, I'll let you get back to work. We're on a tight schedule. No room for errors.'

The door closes behind him and Margot's shoulders relax back down but her focus on work is gone. She starts wondering what she'd do if she met Guy for the first time now. If she had the chance to pick her husband again, would she pick this man? She stares at the pieces of wood she's laid out.

She knows the answer.

She just doesn't want to admit it.

42
SARA

Michael drops Liv at mine for the weekend. I'm sitting downstairs scouring the news when I hear the familiar rumble of his car. From the living room, I watch Liv get out: one scuffed trainer followed by the other, a swish of hair, the haul of a backpack onto her shoulder. Nancy, wearing tone-on-tone neutrals with a slash of red, clops around the back of the car, envelopes my daughter in a bear hug then whispers something in Liv's ear that makes her smile. Then she climbs back into the front seat. Liv hugs Michael tight, which gives me a visceral memory of what it feels like to be in his arms. She picks up her bag and turns towards the house and Michael comes up the path behind her. He loiters after she steps inside.

'So, how was the holiday?' he asks.

I shrug. 'Great. Liv had a good time, I think.'

'Yeah. She said. Well done. Good call.'

'Thanks.' I'm fluffed up like a robin redbreast with this hard-won praise, though, in my soul, I know it's built on a false premise. 'Doing anything nice for the weekend?'

'Nance and I are going away for a night. You know. Hotel, spa. She could do with a rest.' He shrugs as if we both understand the stress of Nance's life, though I think I could probably beat her if it were a competition right now.

'Lovely,' I say. 'Well, enjoy.'

'Yeah, thanks. Anyway.' He looks towards the house. 'Tell Livvie I said bye.'

'Will do.' I close the door after him and call up the stairs to Liv. 'Your dad says bye!'

'Bye!' she yells back, even though he's gone.

'You all right up there?' I shout. 'Need anything?'

'No!'

So, I go back to my search of the online English-language Omani papers, and it's only then that I notice a snippet of a weather report.

Heavy rains lash Oman as police warn residents not to use wadis

> Thunderstorms are set to sweep across the Sultanate of Oman from today, bringing torrential rains and high winds. Authorities warned of flash floods, hail and dust storms as well as high seas. Residents are urged to avoid wadis, stay out of the sea and take care on the roads. The stormy conditions are expected to last for three days as a low-pressure system passes over the region.

I'm never one to pay attention to weather conditions in far-off countries but, as the significance of this sinks in, it sends me off on a spiral of worry. All I can picture is how shallow the grave is; the erosive nature of high wind and heavy rain on hastily packed sand; and the hand that slipped out from under the sheet. Is the grave deep enough? Why hadn't Margot let Guy be the one to stay and dig?

Are we going to be undone by a storm? How often do they get weather like that in Oman, anyway? Of all the luck. Next to me, my coffee grows cold. The little bit I've already drunk roils in my stomach, no doubt like the Arabian Sea three thousand miles away

I'm pulled from my thoughts by my phone ringing. It's Guy. I stare at the screen, paralysed. One of our rules of engagement is that nothing related to what happened is ever to be discussed on the phone, on social media or on WhatsApp. So it must be about something else. Still, my mouth goes dry and my heart pounds. Perhaps he's worried about the storm, too.

I swallow before picking up and answer with the breeziest 'Hello?' I can squeeze out.

'Good morning, good morning,' Guy says smoothly. 'How are we today? Over our jet lag?'

'We're good, thank you,' I say carefully. I smile to myself, hoping that will make my voice sound like I haven't just been obsessing over my lack of finesse as a gravedigger and whether the weather conditions in Oman are severe enough to uncover a body in a shallow grave. 'Liv's just arrived for the weekend. How about you?'

We chat a little about this and that. I ask if Flynn will be coming to mine this weekend, too but he's going to a sports fixture. He plays basketball – very well, apparently. A-team.

'Well, the reason I'm calling,' Guy says, 'is about the school fundraiser. Will you and Liv be going?'

'Oh,' I say. In all the time Liv has been at that school, I've never been to the fundraisers. I never really think of myself as the sort to get dolled up to bid for things at an auction. I'd rather donate to the charities anonymously. 'I haven't really thought about it.'

'I'm buying tickets and I wondered if you and Liv would like to join the three of us on a table. It's always a jolly evening. Lots of fun, though the wine's usually a bit of a plonk.'

'Oh,' I say. I don't know how much the tickets are. But I know it's a three-course dinner with wine, then there's outfits for Liv and me. Plus nails and hair, at least for her.

Guy's voice drops a notch. 'I think you should come. Margot and I would love to see you. So that's a yes, then?'

'Err, well, thank you.'

Guy runs through the details with me. Then I simply can't help myself.

'Did you see they're having storms in Oman?' I say. We've just been there on holiday, I reason. It's not suspicious for us to talk about the weather in a place we've recently been, is it? It isn't an admission of anything.

'That's interesting,' Guy says. 'It can happen this time of year. I guess we were lucky with the weather.'

'I'd say.'

'Anyway,' he replies, 'I'll put your names down for the fundraiser, and I really look forward to seeing you there.' That's the subject closed. But at least I know we both know about the storms.

I wonder if Margot is as worried as I am.

43
MARGOT

Margot's always had the ability to lose herself in her work. There's something about focusing on fiddly, physical tasks that enables her to control her thoughts. She spends the morning cutting out the frame of the house she's making, then fitting the pieces loosely in position, ready to start gluing. All the while, she tells herself a different version of what happened in Oman. A version in which they never set eyes on Celine; one in which they didn't know her and didn't see her, didn't go camping with her and certainly didn't bury her in the desert. As fast as images from the real holiday flash in front of her eyes, she replaces them with alternatives; ones she can try to believe in – for her own mental well-being.

But her morning is interrupted when Guy steams into the room and slaps a newspaper down on her work bench, causing the tiny beams and boards to scatter every which way, wasting her entire morning's work.

'Guy!' she snaps.

'Have you seen this?'

'What is it?' she asks, but she knows what it will be. Of course she does. The feeling of dread has been in her belly for days. There's only one reason Guy would buy a paper copy of a newspaper and bring it to her.

As he picks up Margot's phone and turns it off, she reads:

Fear for missing expat

Fears are currently growing for the safe return of the 'fun-loving' British expatriate who was reported missing in the Sultanate of Oman five days ago. A local police investigation has not drawn any leads in the hunt for Celine Cremorne, and friends of the missing woman have launched an appeal on Facebook. Cremorne was last seen getting into a taxi to go home after a celebration on Christmas Day. The family declined to comment at this stage.

'Oh,' Margot says.

'Turn the page,' Guy says. 'There's more.'

Reluctantly Margot turns the page to be assaulted by a montage of images of Celine. She's pictured in skimpy shorts, dresses and even swimwear. She's on the beach, on a yacht with her hair flying in the breeze, holding a glass of champagne and cuddling a cat. In one, she's in running gear wearing a race number and a T-shirt emblazoned with the name of a charity. In another, she's surrounded by small children. In all of them she's smiling, tanned, sunlit and happy. Margot looks up at Guy, appalled.

'Read it,' he says.

Exclusive: Who is Celine Cremorne?

The Briton missing in Oman is a fun-loving primary school teacher who makes time for everyone, concerned friends told the *Daily Mail* last night. She moved to Muscat, the capital of Oman, seven years ago, and works in an exclusive private school, teaching the children of wealthy expatriates.

'We are devastated,' says Lara Peters, a friend and colleague. 'You couldn't find a nicer person. Celine has time for everyone, and is incredibly popular with the children. She's such a vibrant person. It makes no sense that she's disappeared. I can't get my head around it.'

While many expatriates in the Middle East fly home for the Christmas holidays, Cremorne chose to remain in Oman for the school holidays, telling friends she was tired after the autumn term and wanted to enjoy the sunshine. Peters recalls her friend saying she would stay in the luxury three-bedroom villa she shares with friends and make the most of the pool and beach. Average daily temperatures in Muscat at this time of year can be expected to reach a balmy 27°C (80°F) with just one day a month of rain.

Young expatriates living in the sunny Sultanate often share rented villas on private compounds, giving them access to facilities such as a swimming pool. Expatriate teachers in Oman can earn up to £2,600 per month, and there is currently no personal income tax.

Celine is the only child of Howard and Philippa Cremorne of Guildford, Surrey, who are believed to be flying to Oman to help the search.

'We are deeply concerned, and are assisting police with their enquiries. It is all our hopes that Celine is found soon,' headmaster Timothy Jackson said last night.

Margot hands the paper back to Guy.

'I guess it was bound to happen.'

Guy throws himself onto the sofa. 'Yep.'

'But what can we do?' she says. 'We just have to sit tight, right?'

'Yep. Business as usual. And we need to keep an eye on Sara. Last thing we need is her cracking.'

The memory of the tent zip opening in the night comes back to Margot. The tick-tick-tick she thinks she heard. If it wasn't Flynn ... She doesn't want to, but she has to ask.

'Can I ask you something?' She keeps her voice steady; doesn't want to imply any sort of accusation.

'Fire away.'

'Please don't get angry, I'm not accusing you of anything, okay? But on that night – the night we camped – I thought I heard the tent zip go down?' She pauses. It's out there now. She has to say it. 'Did you get up for anything?'

His eyes narrow. 'What are you asking?'

She holds her hands up like a surrender. 'Nothing. I just wondered if you saw anything – if you did get up?'

He angles his head at her like he's having trouble understanding. 'You think I wouldn't have said by now?'

Margot closes her eyes and exhales through her nose, aware that one wrong word will trigger him.

'But, in answer to your question, no,' Guy says. 'I slept straight through. Drunken coma. You know me.'

It wouldn't be the first time he passed out through alcohol.

'I just wondered.'

'You'd drunk a skinful, too, to be fair,' Guy says. 'If you heard something, it could have been an insect or anything.'

Margot twiddles her pencil in her fingers. 'So, do you think they'll find her?'

'Honestly? The chances are minuscule. We were a hundred and fifty miles or more from the city, in thousands of square miles of sand. She's a needle in a haystack.'

Maybe, but maybe not. This is no longer a tiny story in a newspaper in a foreign land. Celine is pretty and led a photogenic lifestyle, and there's not much else going on in the news right now. For sure, the police will push and the tabloids will run with the story until someone, somewhere remembers or reveals something. Margot imagines that the next few weeks and months are going to feel like driving a dodgem blindfolded, never knowing when something will ram into her. The thought makes her want to throw up.

'Well,' she says. 'We'll need to tell Flynn something because he's going to see this.'

'She went missing after we got back. It's sad, but nothing to do with us. Keep it simple.' Of course he assumes that she'll be the one to do it. 'Just drop it in the conversation when you see him. Don't make a big deal of it.'

Margot starts to rearrange the scattered pieces of wood back into the rooms of the mansion and Guy comes to stand behind her. He towers over her, watching while she works. It's his way of reminding himself that he's her manager, her boss. That he's the power in the company she created. How did it come to this?

'Don't forget we've got a deadline,' he says, as if he hasn't just ruined her morning's work. 'You can't afford to lose any more time on it.' He drops the newspaper onto the sofa. 'And one o'clock for lunch today, please. Something nice.'

44
SARA

I've just finished reading the morning's colour pieces on Celine when Margot phones. She's going to tell Flynn that Celine is missing straight after Flynn's basketball practice. Liv is usually there, watching him, she says, so would I like to come too?

I find my way to the gym where Flynn's playing a training match and spot Margot and Liv on the shallow bleachers to one side of the court. Like every secondary school gym, the smell is of disinfectant and stale sweat. Both Margot and Liv are on their phones. I'm hopeful that Liv will take the news about Celine relatively well, given she didn't really like her. But I'm also aware of the tendency Liv has to make everything about her, so I'm steeled for a bit of drama.

'Hey,' I say, touching Liv's arm as I slip into the seat next to her.

'Mum! What are you doing here? You don't usually come to school.' Suddenly her face clouds. 'Is Dad okay?'

'Yes, yes. Nothing like that. Hi, Margot! How are you?'

This is the first time I've ever spoken to Margot at school, and some of the glossy mums in the bleachers look over to see who it is that's friends with Margot Forrest. I can't say the thought doesn't give me a little buzz.

'All right, thanks. How are you?' she asks. She looks me up and down as if examining me for signs of psychological damage. Or maybe I'm just projecting because it's what I'm doing to her. She looks okay. Though a little tired and thin, maybe. But not like someone who's recently buried a body in the desert.

'I'm good, thanks. Keeping busy.' I try to communicate with my eyes that I'm not really looking forward to telling the kids about Celine, but that I'm glad we're in it together. Margot, on the other hand, seems completely unruffled.

'That's good. Me too. Look, they'll be finished in a minute. I was going to take them both for a coffee and cake after – why don't you join us?'

'Thanks,' I say. 'I'd love to.'

And so we find ourselves at a sticky table in a nearby coffee shop, the teens with iced lattes, Margot with her sparkling water and me with a cup of tea and a ginger biscuit. I realise it's the first thing I've eaten all day.

'So, what's up?' Liv says when we're settled. 'Why are you here? You never come to pick-up.'

I look at Margot and without saying a word we agree that she's going to speak first.

'There's something we want to tell you before you hear it from someone else,' Margot says.

'You're getting divorced?' Flynn says.

Margot tuts. 'It's about Celine.' She pauses. 'I'm sorry to say that, since we got back to England, she appears to have gone missing.'

'Missing?' Liv asks.

'She didn't turn up to work on the first day of term,' I say.

'Probably forgot,' Flynn says. 'Hungover.' He snickers.

Margot clucks her tongue. 'It's actually quite serious. Her friends can't find her. She's not at her villa. They've reported her to the police as a missing person.'

'The police have launched a search,' I add.

Liv looks at Flynn, her hand over her mouth. 'Oh my God. Like, properly missing?'

'Oh, right,' Flynn says with a slow nod.

There's a pause while they digest the news. I sip my tea. Liv stirs her latte.

'So – I mean, does it have anything to do with us?' Flynn asks.

Margot shrugs. 'No. It happened after we left. But we just thought you'd like to know, since she's a friend.'

'Wow,' Liv says. 'Like, we were just with her. I hope she's okay.'

'Me too,' I say, exchanging a quick smile with Liv.

'Well, we just wanted you to know. Fingers crossed they find her safe and well,' Margot says.

'Exactly,' I say with a nod, and I'm pleased I came. Team Margot and Sara.

We've got this.

45

MARGOT

Margot sometimes jokes with herself that she's missed her calling. She should have been a magician because creating an illusion is one of the things she does best in life. If any observer were to see the Forrests in those early January days, they would never guess what was lurking beneath the happy facade Margot presents – both in real life and on social media because she is an absolute pro at showing off Guy's best side in public as well as keeping up appearances. Now she adds a new feather to her bow: being a pro at pasting over the fissures in her marriage. The downside is that the more she has to hide, the more it stresses her out. But when she's stressed she works – and so, with the pressing deadline of the stately home to deliver, she throws herself into work. And tries not to let any thoughts about camping, sand, deserts, shovels and bodies distract her.

After the frame of the mansion is finally complete, the next step is to gather a file for each room containing paint swatches, samples of the wallpaper and photos of every fixture and fitting. She'll use these files to recreate the tiny pieces of wooden furniture, the lamps, the rugs, the pictures and all the minuscule paraphernalia that fill the real house. She enjoys this work and she does it humming along to the radio, which is on softly in the background, until her concentration is broken. An unfamiliar ring is coming from her iPad. Her dad's calling on Skype – for the first time ever.

'Dad!' she says as she accepts the video call. 'You've discovered Skype?' Her view is right up his nostrils. 'Move the iPad away from your face.' His face comes into proper view.

'Hello, dear,' he says. 'Can you hear me?'

'Yes. Can you hear me?'

'Yes! Are you impressed?' His eyes twinkle and she can see just how pleased he is with himself for working this out on the iPad. She bought it for him for Christmas so he could be a bit more connected.

'Of course!' she says. 'It's lovely to see you.'

'Yes, I thought it would save you driving over here all the time if we could chat like this every now and then. Arthur showed me how to do it.'

Margot can just imagine the two old men sitting in the residents' lounge or the conservatory with their iPads, and the thought makes her smile.

'So how are you?' she asks. 'Still enjoying life at Buckingham Palace?'

The door to her studio bursts open behind her and she spins around. When she sees the look on Guy's face, she says gently to her dad, 'Dad, can I call you back? Just give me a couple of minutes.'

'What's happened?' she says when she's hung up the call. A vein in Guy's neck is pulsing and his eyes are narrowed. Her insides clench. Guy's temper is never pretty.

He thrusts his phone so close to Margot's eyes she can't read what he's showing her.

'This,' he says. 'This is what happened.'

Margot pushes the phone away so she can focus on the screen. It's a 'missing person' appeal about Celine and Margot sees with a sinking heart that Liv has reposted it on her own Instagram account. Liv's added a prayer hands emoji with her own addition: Anyone seen her?

'What the fuck is she playing at? I thought you spoke to her!' Guy says.

'I told her she was missing. Guy! Calm down.' She drops her voice to a whisper because Flynn is at home. 'You can't expect her to know anything! Okay? Think about how it looks from her point of view. Please.'

'Why would she even get involved? Is she really that stupid? For fuck's sake, this is serious!'

'She doesn't know we had anything to do with it. Get a grip!'

'Don't you dare speak to me like that!' Guy snarls.

'Or what?' Margot says.

Guy storms towards her breathing hard as he backs her up towards the shelves, and raises his hand as if to slap her. Margot jerks away, out of reach.

'I'm trying to protect us, that's all,' Guy hisses. 'There is no room for mistakes!'

Margot takes a deep breath in and notices that it judders as she lets it out. She's sweating. Guy's never raised a hand to her before, but she can see now just how stressed he is about the Celine situation. He's been hiding it well.

'I mean, reposting is the natural thing to do if you're not involved. And we're not involved,' she says as gently as she can, because she doesn't know where in the house Flynn is.

'Get her to take it down,' he growls.

'But—'

'No "buts".'

'Guy, please. You're overreacting.'

'She needs to take it down right now,' he says, 'and she needs to wind her stupid neck in or I'll go to her house and I'll shut her up myself.' The strangling motion he makes with both hands shocks Margot. Even more than the hand he raised a moment ago.

'I'll speak to Sara,' she says with both palms up in surrender. 'I'll ask her to take it down. Okay?'

Margot makes a mental note to tell Sara but then her iPad rings. She and Guy both stare at it, then Guy says, 'You gonna get that?'

'Er, sure,' she says, but she waits till Guy's out of the room before she reconnects with her dad.

Her mind's not on the things he tells her about – the theatre trip to see a play by the local amateur dramatics group, the keep-fit classes he's joined and the art club he's enjoying.

'Margot,' he says after she's responded with yet another automatic 'nice!' 'What's wrong? Is everything all right with Guy? He sounded angry earlier.'

'Oh, nothing. Just work stuff,' she says, but her dad is peering at her through the screen, his eyes close to the camera.

'Baby girl, you know I don't have to live in this place, don't you?' he says gently. 'It's nice and everything, but it's not the be-all and end-all. The main thing is your happiness.'

'Oh, but Daddy, you love it there. You're so happy. The pool, the gardens … your friends.'

'They'll still be my friends wherever I am. I'm just saying:

don't let this arrangement with Guy hold you back from … anything you might want – or need – to do. We'll find a way.'

Margot frowns. 'What are you saying?'

'I'm saying I know he's your husband, dear, and I know that you're very loyal and you try to make the best of things. But, at some point, you have to ask yourself: at what cost, Margot. At what cost?'

46
SARA

After Margot calls me, sounding distressed, I get Liv to take the appeal straight off her socials but I don't know how many people saw it. Did anyone screenshot it? Forward it? Repost it? In the time it was up, did someone see it and connect the dots that we were there? I don't know how they'd know, but I'm always surprised by the strange and rather random connections that happen on social media. A couple of days pass by uneasily and I know something's happened when Guy's name appears on my phone. I stare at it for a moment before picking it up. I'm so jumpy I'm almost expecting the police to hammer on the door. Will they have sirens on when they come to get me? Probably not. They could be surrounding my house right now.

'Hello?' I say tentatively.

There's a pause then Guy says, 'Hello, Sara. Margot and I wondered if you fancied meeting us for a coffee?'

'A coffee?'

'Yes. A coffee.' His voice gives nothing away. 'How are you fixed today? We're actually at that new coffee shop just down the road from you right now, and we thought we'd be spontaneous for once. *Carpe Diem* and all that. Are you free?'

The Forrests wouldn't drive from Charlton Kings to my

neck of the woods to visit the mediocre coffee shop at the end of my road for no reason. They just wouldn't.

'Okaaay,' I say. 'You say you're there now?'

'Just got here.'

'I can be there in fifteen minutes?'

'We'll wait. No problem.'

They look, when I arrive, like any other middle-aged couple enjoying a Sunday coffee in a café. Guy has a newspaper in front of him; Margot's looking at her phone. But, knowing them as I do, I can see tension in the pinch of their faces. Margot's deteriorated since I saw her at school. She looks worn, like an old kitchen table that's been scrubbed too many times, thin-skinned and pale, and her eyes are bloodshot and haunted. It makes me wonder what's being said between her and Guy at home. She pulls me into a silent hug, and clings on for a few extra seconds, as if trying to communicate something. Guy gives me a distracted half hug.

'It's a beautiful day. Why don't you get a take-out, and we can walk?' he says. He's already over by the counter. 'What do you fancy?'

And so, cups in hand, we exit the coffee shop and head, without discussion, towards the park.

'Couldn't hear myself think in there,' Guy says. 'Much better to be outside.'

'What happened?' I ask.

'Do we need a reason to spend time together?' Guy says, indicating with his eyes that he's not going to say anything while our phones are on so we juggle each other's coffees while we switch them off.

'Okay, what is it now? I'm dying,' I say as we set off towards the long path around the perimeter of the park; the one where no one but dog-walkers go. I haven't been on a recreational walk in months.

Guy lets out a sigh that's half a roar of frustration. 'It's Tom and Di. Fucking stupid Di. I swear.'

'Guy,' Margot says warningly. 'She didn't know.'

My breath catches. 'What? Did she say something?'

'They phoned,' Margot says. 'Tom and Di. Happy to tell us how we might be able to help the Omani police with their search for Celine.'

'Oh, God.'

'Just wait. It gets worse.'

'What can be worse than us helping with enquiries?' I stop walking, but Guy and Margot carry on, and I scurry to catch up.

'It seems the Omani police are way more efficient than our lot,' Guy says. 'Not to mention that a missing Brit doesn't look good on them. Seems they've been going door-to-door, asking questions. Hotels, businesses ...'

'Car-hire firms,' Margot adds. 'Homes.'

'They want answers.'

'Oh my God,' I say again. 'I saw that article, but I didn't think about Tom and Di.'

'Yep. They knocked on their door.'

'And?'

'Di was home,' Guy says. 'Jesus, if only Tom had opened the door, he'd have handled it. So they ask if they know Celine, then mention the compound where Celine was living, and Di recognises that it was where we were staying – at the same time that Celine went missing.'

'And she told them that?' My mouth's open behind the hand that's covering it.

Margot nods sadly. 'She thought she was helping.'

Guy takes up the story, his voice high-pitched and sing-song to mimic a silly woman.

'So, she's all like, "Oh, yes! My friends were staying there around New Year! Definitely the same compound. I think they even used to know Celine Cremorne when they lived here. I'm sure I remember them mentioning her. Maybe I'm wrong but I think they were actually quite close! They've moved back to the UK now. But they were out here for a week and I'm sure that if Celine was there, they'd have seen her. Maybe you could speak to them."'

'Shit,' I say. 'What about the camping gear? Did she remember that?'

'Oh, yes,' Guy says. 'She left nothing out. "Guy borrowed our camping gear," she told them. "He was planning a trip to the desert."'

I realise that I'm shaking. 'What do we do now?'

'Well, I think it's a matter of time – and maybe not long – till we get a visit from the police here.'

'Really? Do they communicate like that between countries?'

'I should imagine so, if there's a Brit involved.'

'So we need to plan what we're going to say if and when that happens?'

'And stick with it,' Guy says. 'Are we all in?'

'All in,' I say.

47
MARGOT

Margot, Guy and Sara sit in a row on a cold bench facing the sweep of muddy green that is the park and go through the story they'll stick to should the police come knocking. They go over and over it until it comes naturally to them. Yes, Margot and Guy used to know Celine. Yes, they'd been saddened to hear that she'd gone missing. But no, they hadn't seen her at the compound. They hadn't even known she still lived there. Margot and Guy hadn't been in touch with her for years – they hadn't told her they were coming out to Muscat and they'd just assumed that she'd moved on. Like expats do. No one stays still for long. It's news to them that she still lived there. She must have been away the whole time they were there as they hadn't seen anyone. If it comes to it: yes, they borrowed some camping gear, but they hadn't actually managed to go camping in the end. Hey ho, maybe next time.

Thank God no one else was at the compound over the holidays,' Margot says. 'And at least Land Cruisers are so generic that the Jeep Jamboree guys won't have any memory of seeing us that day.' She recalls how she stared straight ahead at the road, trying not to look conspicuous while Sara looked down at Celine's phone.

Thank God Guy doesn't know about the phone.

They sit in silence for a few moments, and Margot goes over the story one more time in her head, looking for potential tripwires.

'Plot twist,' she says. 'Instead of waiting for the police to come to us, do you think we should actually go forward and tell them all this off our own bat? Because it's what an innocent person would do – right? Otherwise, surely, when they track us down, they're going to ask why we didn't say anything?'

Sara's mouth falls open. 'I thought we'd agreed just to stay quiet. I mean, surely they'll ask why it's taken us so long to come forward?'

Margot pulls a face. 'We lost touch with her after we moved. We didn't know she still lived in the compound until Tom and Di mentioned it. I mean, we didn't see anyone there, did we? We've no idea who was living there.'

The more she thinks about it, the more she knows it's the best course of action. She just hopes Guy agrees. He grimaces at her.

'You might be right. It's not ideal, but it might actually be the thing that saves us.'

'I agree,' says Margot, nodding. 'Transparency. But it would have to be one of us who contacts the police, though, because Sara didn't technically know her.'

'Good point,' Guys says. 'So are we all agreed? We saw nothing. And please, Sara, it's more important than ever that you just stick to the story. Okay?'

They leave the park largely in silence. As they hug goodbye, Sara says, 'Are you absolutely sure about this? Because I'm trusting you.' And Guy nods.

'Don't worry. We'll keep you posted.'

*

'Fuck's sake,' Guy mutters as he and Margot head back home. He's driving jerkily, aggressively, throwing the car around corners in a way that makes Margot cling on to the door handle, and braking only after she's stamped her foot to the floor herself in panic. 'Last thing I want to do is give our names to the police and flag up that we were there but you're right.'

'I know.'

'So who's gonna do it?' He doesn't smile. 'I'm guessing me, right?'

'Who's the better liar?' Margot asks innocently.

'Hmm. Okay. Let me get my thoughts together at home then I'll go.'

And go he does. Meantime, Margot sits at home trying to work but her mind is with Guy and what might be going on at the police station. Her husband's a persuasive speaker – one of those people who can pull you in with his tone and his body language. She imagines him going in, doing the 'good citizen' act to a rather disinterested duty officer who probably won't really care that someone in Cheltenham used to know a person who's now missing in Oman and that they hadn't seen her in Muscat during a recent short holiday. When Margot looks at it like that, what they're telling the police really isn't a big deal. But she feels coming forward is definitely the right thing to do so there's a record of it – however useless the information – for if or when the Omani police contact the UK police.

Around 7 p.m., Guy strides into the house, straight through to the kitchen, where he opens the fridge, pulls out a beer, bites the cap off and drinks steadily in one gulp until the majority of the bottle's content is gone. He smacks his lips and lets out a satisfied sigh.

'Aaahhhhhh. All done.'

'How was it?'

'Fine. The guy acted like I was wasting his time, which is exactly how I wanted it to be. But we're all above board now.' He pulls Margot into his arms. 'We did it, Mar. I think we did it!'

'Great. Well done!' she says, pulling away. 'Let me tell Sara. She'll be waiting.'

We'd agreed that the coded message would come from the phone of whoever didn't go to the station in case the police started monitoring the phone line of the one who did.

Is there a parents' evening this term?

She types the innocuous phrase designed to mean: *He's been to the police and told them and he's back home, everything's fine.*

The ticks turn immediately blue and within seconds Sara responds with the real date of parents' evening, which means: *Message received, loud and clear. Well done, phew.*

Margot sags against the counter in relief. Another day done ... a lifetime to go.

48
SARA

Celine's parents, I discover from continuing news coverage, live in a picturesque house in the country. Even their floof of a cat is cute. All emotion aside, it's a story the media, currently starved of anything more interesting to report on, is salivating over. I'm staring into space catastrophising about where it'll all end when my phone rings: Margot. She has never, ever phoned me.

'Are you free to meet this evening? For a chat?' she says after the preliminary pleasantries. 'It'll be good to see you.'

'Sure.' My stomach clenches with nerves. Has something happened? The phone? 'What sort of time are you thinking?'

'About seven? I'll come to yours if that's okay? I'll bring nibbles.' I notice the 'I' rather than 'we'. If I was less anxious, I'd smile at the nibbles.

'Okay. Seven. Sure,' I say. 'See you then.'

'Looking forward to it.'

As seven o'clock approaches, I rattle around the house trying to see my humble home through Margot's discerning eyes. I clear all of the dishes from the rack and hide the washing-up liquid under the sink along with the dishcloth – as if the Forrests don't use such things. Then I pre-boil the kettle in case she wants tea with whatever 'nibbles' she's bringing, though I'm rather hoping it's wine o'clock not tea time. The fact that she wants to see me alone makes me nervous – we're all in this together, so why is she coming without Guy? Does she have something to tell me about him?

She's prompt. When I open the door and see Margot standing in the rain, her jacket hood pulled over her hair, the first thing I notice is that she's lost even more weight off her face, and that does little to put me at ease.

'Hey,' she says, with an uncharacteristically nervous smile as she proffers a Waitrose insulated bag. 'Forgive the wrapping, but I bring sustenance.'

She's brought a chilled bottle of Sancerre, a tub of olives, a tub of tiny red peppers stuffed with soft cheese and a box of biscuits actually called Cheese Nibbles.

'Well, I did promise nibbles!' she says, and we laugh fragile laughs. I arrange everything on a platter, get out my best wine glasses and clumsily open the wine, then we move into the living room.

'Lovely home,' she says, and I shrivel inside myself. You could fit my entire house in the entertaining space of theirs.

'Thanks. It's enough for me. Anyway – listen – how's Flynn? Mocks going well?'

'Yeah. He's okay,' she says. 'Obviously shocked about Celine, but he hasn't questioned the timeline of when she actually went missing.'

'Same with Liv.'

'Good. It's good we didn't tell them.'

'I agree. That was a good call of Guy's. One thing we did do right in this whole sorry mess.'

I perch on the edge of the sofa with my wine glass and wish she would come out with whatever it is she's come to tell me. But she doesn't reply. She picks up her phone and switches it off, rather theatrically. Then she points to mine and mouths, 'Sorry.' I widen my eyes and cock my head at her – what on earth does she have to tell me? But I do as I'm told, and only then do her shoulders relax.

'I'm sorry,' she says. 'Guy's drilled it into me not to talk about anything with the phones on. I suppose we can't be too careful. I was going to suggest we meet outdoors but ...' she nods to the rain sliding down the windowpanes.

'Mmm,' I agree. 'Bit wet. Not to mention dark.'

'The day ran away with me. As Guy takes great joy in reminding me, I'm on a tight deadline at work.' She lets out a sigh. 'So, look, I just wanted to come and see how you really are. Sometimes it's hard for us to talk in front of Guy.'

I know what she means. When it comes to what happened, he's all business, all action. Everything is done to his agenda; no time for the emotion of the situation.

'I'm okay, thanks,' I say. 'I can't believe Celine's phone hasn't turned up yet. I'm so sorry about that, Margot. I just ... I don't know what happened.'

She waves a hand. 'Nothing we can do about it now.'

'I'm on tenterhooks every day, though. Did you tell Guy?'

She snorts a laugh. 'No. I'm not a masochist. But I agree – someone's going to find it at some point. The question is, what's on it? I never messaged her – did you?'

'Nope. I had a quick look on her Instagram and she didn't post anything that showed us, so there's that at least.'

'Well, let's hope she wasn't messaging my husband,' Margot says, her lips pursed.

She catches my eye and I look away. 'So, uh, how are you, otherwise?'

She takes a huge slug of her wine. 'I'm surviving. It's not easy, though, is it? I have moments when it hits me and I actually can't believe what we did.'

'I know! Same! I feel so bad for her, and for her family. They think she's alive. They're still hoping. That's the worst bit.'

'I know. I just can't.' She shakes her head and covers her face with her hand for a moment. 'I mean, imagine it was Flynn or Liv missing. You'd be going insane.'

'It was us or them, though, wasn't it?' I say. 'Brutal choice, but – what was it Guy said?'

'Collateral damage,' Margot says bitterly.

'It all feels like something I dreamed, or a horror movie I watched,' I say.

Margot nods. 'Yes, exactly! Speaking of which: do you dream about … it? Her?'

'Oh my God. Every night! I dream that I'm burying her but she's not dead. She tries to get out of the grave and I push her back in and I'm throwing sand in her face and she's blinking it away and she just keeps coming up at me.' I shudder. The feeling of throwing the sand onto Celine's body is visceral.

'I have one where she's alive but we shove her in anyway and she's begging us to stop.' Margot pauses. 'I hear her voice. It's so real. And then I wake up and realise the *real* nightmare is actually my life. I can't believe we did it, Sara. We buried a body. I just can't process it.'

'I'm here if you want to talk about it.' I pause. 'I mean, I have some experience. Mates' rates!'

Margot smiles at my joke, then her face changes. 'Really, though? Are there any techniques I can use? Because the memories are haunting me more than any ghost.'

'Hmm. Well, the easiest one is reframing, I suppose. When negative thoughts pop into your head, like "we buried her", try to reframe them as something like "she died of natural causes, and we gave her a decent burial". Does that make sense? Try to tell yourself a more positive – kinder – story.'

'Does it work for you?'

I laugh. 'Not as much as I'd like.'

'Well, thanks anyway. I'll try anything.' She looks around and lets out another sigh as her shoulders visibly drop and she sinks back into the sofa. 'Thanks for letting me come over. There's such a nice energy in your home.'

I look at her in surprise because my house is nothing if not humble, but then I understand what she's really telling me: that the energy in her own house is not nice.

'How's Guy?'

Another huge sigh. I top up the wine she's just finished and she nods her thanks.

'He's … Guy,' she says.

'I see.'

'His coping strategy is staying busy and blustering through.'

'Do you ever talk with him about how you feel?'

'Guy Forrest? Talk about feelings?' Margot's laugh is tight. 'No. He's decided that we must put it behind us and move on, and so that's what we do. On we go: the Guy and Margot show! Oh, don't get me wrong, he follows the news like a bloodhound – he's in and out of my studio like a yo-yo, talking incessantly about the case. But it's as if it happened to someone else; as if we weren't involved at all. We sweep what *actually* happened under a great big carpet. Only ...'

She shrugs then dips her head but not before I see her eyes shining with unshed tears. I think she's going to pull herself together but then her face crumples and the tears start leaking through her hands. I scoot over and pat her back. I can feel the knobs of her spine through her top.

'It's okay. Let it out.'

I bite my lip, embarrassed that tears are gathering in my own eyes, too. I've never seen Margot let emotion out like this, nor let herself be so vulnerable. The back of my throat burns with the effort of holding back my tears. After a few moments, she looks up, regaining control as she scrambles in her bag for a pack of printed tissues.

'I'm sorry,' she sniffs. 'It's just nice to be able to talk about it with someone who understands.'

'I'm always here for you.' I squeeze her hand and try to imagine what life's like for Margot in that big house – with a husband like Guy.

49
MARGOT

'I am strong. I am good.'

Margot chants the mantra to herself as she makes a late lunch for Guy and herself. She's putting together a spicy salmon salad with cucumber, rocket, peppers, feta and a sprinkling of peanuts – one of Guy's favourites. He's battling middle-aged spread and is consequently keen on cutting out carbs, although he and Margot both know that he might get better results if he cut out the bottle of red he's taken to drinking most nights since Oman, not to mention the whisky chasers that come after. Only they don't talk about that.

Since her chat with Sara, Margot's experimented with the reframing technique and decided that the only way she's going to be able to move forward is to pretend that none of it ever happened. She's also going to try to focus entirely on the future, and not dwell on the past. As she chops the veggies and mixes up a spicy-sweet dressing to drizzle over the salad, she practises rewriting history in her head, summoning up new images in her mind, that she hopes will record over the existing ones.

'Nothing happened,' she chants. Chop. 'We had a lovely

trip.' Chop. 'We didn't see Celine.' Chop. 'She was never there.' Chop. 'We never went to the desert.' Chop. 'There was no quad bike.' Chop chop. She still feels guilty about that. 'There was no quad bike,' she says again, stronger. Chop. 'There was no camping trip.' Chop. 'Shit!'

The knife comes down in the wrong place, slicing the pad of Margot's fingertip, and the chopping board turns red almost instantly. She lurches for the kitchen roll, reels off four or five sheets and wraps them around her now throbbing finger without looking at the damage. The pain and the blood make her think she's chopped off the entire finger, but she can't see anything on the chopping board so maybe she hasn't.

She stands squeezing the kitchen roll around her finger as the pain really kicks in. Already the blood is visible through the layers of kitchen roll. She folds six more sheets and wraps those over the top, turning her finger into a fat wad of tissue. Then a wave of heat flushes through her and her knees go weak.

Margot sinks onto a bar stool at the island. She takes juddery breaths – in and out; in and out – to regain her composure. To distract herself she continues her mental refrain: Celine was never there. They didn't go to the desert. They had a lovely holiday. They barely left the villa.

Sitting there, in between squeezing her finger and holding it above her heart to hopefully stem the bleeding, she pours herself a large glass of wine, aware that it will probably put paid to her doing any work that afternoon. But she also enjoys the numbness it brings; the way it slows down her thoughts and makes everything in her head seem less … jagged. Her chanting slows and a feeling of warmth spreads through her. Daytime drinking is so underrated.

'Is lunch ready? I thought you were going to call me!' Guy bounds into the kitchen but stops abruptly when he sees the blood-soaked chopping board and the nearly empty wine bottle. 'Jesus, Mar. What happened?'

Margot lets her heavy head hang as Guy takes her hand and unpeels the layers of the kitchen roll, then examines her finger. Her limbs are floppy with wine, the pain of the cut now fuzzy around the edges.

'Okay,' he says. 'We'll need to strap that up properly.'

He gets out the First Aid box, picks a dressing and a bandage, cleans the cut and starts to dress it. Margot can feel his breath on her hand as he works.

'Thanks,' she says. She much prefers this gentle version of Guy than the bullish one she sees most days.

'Why are you drinking at lunchtime?' he says without looking up. 'We have a meeting this afternoon.'

'Tis only us,' Margot slurs. It isn't a customer meeting. Just a progress report from her to him. 'No biggie.'

Guy finishes dressing her finger and gently places her hand back on the table. 'There we go. Now what happened? You mustn't be so careless. We need your fingers, Mar. They're precious.' He kisses the tip of the bandage.

'She was never there,' Margot murmurs, trying to claw her way back to the place she'd been before the accident.

'Who was never there?' Guy frowns then he catches on. 'Oh, Celine?'

'Celine who?' Margot says and smiles at him, a big, beautiful, but rather drunken smile.

Guy echoes her smile then he cocks an ear to the radio that's been playing softly in the background and his face changes. 'Did you hear that?'

He leaps over to the radio in two strides and smashes the volume button till the presenter's voice is clear in the kitchen: 'Coming up next: hope at last for the family of missing Briton, Celine Cremorne.'

Guy's eyes catch Margot's and they stare anxiously at each other.

'What the hell?' Guy says. His face has drained of colour.

Margot can't focus. The kitchen is starting to spin in front of her eyes. The only thing she can think about is that they somehow found the body. But surely not.

In the hallway, the front door slams. Guy puts his finger to his lips, telling Margot that they need to stop discussing this now. Flynn saunters into the kitchen and does a double-take at the bloody scene that greets him.

'What happened? Mum, are you okay?'

Margot may be woozy, but she sees her son's eyes flick from the knife to Guy to the blood-soaked kitchen roll and back to her, and she realises with a sobering jolt what he's thinking.

'Cut my finger by accident,' she says, and even though it's true, she's not sure she'd believe it herself. 'Chopping veg.'

'But you're okay?' Flynn asks, his eyes moving anxiously from her to Guy and back.

'Yes, fine, thank you, darling. All good. Nothing serious. Dad patched me up.' She beams at him.

'Okay. Good. I just came to grab my sports kit before basketball. Did you see the news? They've detected activity on Celine's phone!'

There's a beat before Guy says, 'Well, that sounds positive, doesn't it, honey?' and Margot nods.

They hold their positions in silence while Flynn runs upstairs, clatters back down and yells, 'Bye!' from the hallway. Then, when the front door slams, Guy turns to Margot and says, 'What the fuck?'

50
SARA

So, it finally happened. Someone found Celine's phone – whether at the petrol station, the car-hire company or anywhere in between – and turned it on. I can't believe I was so careless. I can't believe I didn't take out the SIM. Why didn't I do that the moment we got into the car? Why didn't I take out the SIM and hurl the stupid phone into the mountains?

It's not clear from the news report if the police have the phone or if someone else has found it, but her parents clearly feel positive because they release another video appeal that's suddenly all over the news. I click on the story and see the Cremornes sitting behind a table at a press conference. Then the strangled voice of Celine's father spills out of my phone.

'The last few weeks have been the worst days of our lives. As you may know, after Christmas, our beloved daughter, Celine, disappeared from her home in Muscat, Oman, where she's lived for the past four years. We've been suffering sleepless nights, wondering if our girl is being held against her will, if she is being harmed. Or if she is lying injured somewhere and unable to get back home.' He pauses and looks directly at the camera. 'Activity was detected on Celine's mobile phone earlier today. Obviously, that's given us some cause for hope.'

Howard Cremorne's voice breaks and Philippa Cremorne then speaks, choking back tears: 'Not knowing where our daughter is is unbearable. Celine – baby girl – if you're watching this, there's no judgement and no questions. Please just let us know that you're safe. We love you.'

The hope on their faces makes my eyes well. I sit back with my arms hugging myself. I get it: I'm a parent, too. I know the pain of being separated from your child, and I wouldn't wish it on anyone – yet we've inflicted that on another couple. And like Liv, Celine is an only child.

I'm pulled from my thoughts by the doorbell. Guy's stepping from foot to foot at my front door in an agitated way.

'Oh!' I say. 'Guy!'

'Can I come in?'

He glances up and down the street before stepping inside, then motions that we should both turn off our phones.

'I guess you heard about Celine's phone?' he says when we've done that.

'Uh,' I say. 'Can I get you anything? Cup of tea?'

But Guy doesn't move from the hallway.

'Is it true that you lost it?' he demands. 'Before you took the SIM card out? Because I can't fucking believe what Margot's just told me. Please tell me she's wrong.'

'I did reset it,' I say, but my voice falters. 'I restored it to factory settings. But—'

Guy throws both hands in the air. 'But you didn't take the fucking SIM card out? And then you lost the phone? Jesus Christ, Sara! A child could have done better! Why didn't you throw it in the sea when you realised you still had it? You should have taken out the SIM card and chucked it in the fucking sea! Even an imbecile would have known that!'

He's looming over me, his face red with anger and I'm suddenly aware of his size, his bulk. I back away.

'I … I just … Guy! For God's sake! We'd just dug a grave and buried a body. We weren't at our best, okay? Maybe you should have been the one to stay and help if you didn't trust me and Margot! Instead of pissing off out of there as fast as you could and leaving us to clear up the mess!'

I storm into the living room and he follows.

'You know why I did what I did?' he says and now his voice is all the more terrifying for being quietly controlled. A vein is pulsing in his neck. 'I did it to spare our kids – *your* daughter and my son! *You* could have taken the kids back to Muscat yourself and left me and Margot to clear up. I told you several times you were insured to drive the car, but you refused. Google Maps would have got you back, but no. Scaredy Sara's not driving in a foreign country! So don't blame me before you take a good look at yourself. All right?'

I stare at him, for the first time feeling afraid. He's filling up too much space in my living room, making me feel nervous in my own home. I hold my hands out, palms facing him, partly to keep him away from me; partly to try and calm him. My eyes seek an escape route past him to the door, if it should come to it.

I speak slowly, controlling my anger and my fear. 'Guy. I wiped the phone. When we realised we had it, we planned to throw it in the sea in Muscat rather than dump it in the desert where it might lead people to the site. To do that, we needed to drive back to Muscat because, guess what? There is no fucking sea in the desert. All right? We thought that was the right thing to do. I'm sorry I lost it. I was distracted. Upset. We stopped to put air in the tyres. You were telling me to rebook my flights. I was on my phone. I must have dropped it. I hold my hand up for stuffing up and I apologise for not being perfect under the most extreme stress I've ever been under. But you weren't there, and we did our best.'

We stare at each other and I realise that I'm panting. But something comes over him, as if he sees a reflection of himself in my eyes. His face softens and the breath goes out of him. He runs his hands through his hair then takes two strides across the living room towards me. I edge backwards but he holds his hands out to me.

'Sara,' he says. 'I'm sorry. Forgive me. Still friends?' He holds out a hand, as if he wants me to shake it.

I hesitate but then, gingerly, I reach out, keeping my torso as far from him as possible. He takes my hand and squeezes it. 'I'm truly sorry. I've had a really shit day and now this. I'm stressed. I feel like I'm holding it together for all of us. I didn't mean to snap.'

'It's okay,' I say.

He pulls me into his arms, then holds me tighter, pressing in a way that's not right between friends. Thoughts ricochet around my head like missiles: the way Guy had sometimes looked at me on the holiday; Celine's warning that I was on Margot's radar; the way he appreciated the things I did. But I can't do this. I jerk away and Guy takes a shuddering breath and collapses onto the sofa, his head in his hands.

'I'm stuffing everything up today, aren't I?'

'What's going on? This isn't like you.'

He looks at me and I notice pink spider lines in his eyes, the depth of the bags under them, and the lines etched deeper than I remember. He doesn't look like a man who's sleeping well.

'You think my life's a rodeo? All sunshine and fun?' He scoffs. 'I can tell you it's not what you see on Instagram. You think Margot and I are happy, don't you? Did we fool you in Oman? My God, Sara, you have no idea. Sit down. Let me tell you the truth behind the idyll of Margot's Mansions.'

I look at him warily. 'Hang on. Have you finished intimidating me in my own home now? Because that wasn't very nice, Guy, and I don't appreciate it.'

He bites his lip. 'I didn't mean … I'm just so stressed right now. It won't happen again, I promise. Come and sit with me.'

I hesitate for a moment, wondering if I can trust him, but then I sit a little sideways to him and he begins to speak. What he tells me is the age-old story of a marriage that's run its course; of lovers turned friends turned flatmates until he and Margot are – apparently – nothing more than co-parents and business associates.

'She doesn't love me,' he says when he's finished. 'It's a marriage only in name.'

'I'm sorry to hear that,' I say, although I'm not sure I believe him entirely. I've been around the block enough to know an excuse for an affair when I hear it. It's probably what he told Celine, back when they lived in Oman. And she probably fell for it. 'Guy, listen, I'm just going to spell this out now so there's no misunderstanding. I can't and I won't do anything to hurt or embarrass Margot, no matter how things are between you. So this …' I wave my hand between him and me, '… is a non-starter. Understood?'

He sighs. '"Sara Says" no.' He gives an ironic chuckle and shakes his head. 'You're such a good person. I don't know how you do it. I bow in admiration to your morals.'

We lapse into silence for a minute before I remember what it was that brought him here. 'So, back to the phone, if we can talk about that without you exploding again. Do you think resetting it will have been enough?'

He clucks his tongue. 'I honestly don't know. But it will take time for them to recover anything else. I don't know what she would have had on it anyway. Did you ever message her?'

'No.'

'Good. And I know Margot won't have messaged her. So that's something,' Guy says, leaving me staring at the elephant in the room: was there a train of messages from Guy on Celine's phone? Incriminating photos? After his outburst, I'm not going to prod him. If there was something going on between him and Celine, he probably would have had a burner phone that I sincerely hoped he chucked into the sea.

'So we're all good?' I ask.

My biggest fear is that, for some reason, the Forrests break ranks; that they decide to shop me in and save themselves. I've seen how ruthless Guy can be. I wonder now if rejecting him was a smart thing to do; if it would have been wiser to lead him on a little bit, let him enjoy a flirtation, keep him hooked. I need Guy not to blame me for being the weakest link. I can't believe I lost the phone.

But Guy smiles. 'We're as good as we can be.'

After he leaves, I go to the Facebook appeal page and watch

the parents' video again; it's like a scar I can't stop picking. Maybe I'm hoping that exposing myself to it enough will harden me to their pain. But then I see the comments. The top one – the one getting the most traction with shocked emojis racking up by the second – is from a poster with the profile 'Celine Cremorne'.

> Hi, it's me. You left me for dead. You know who you are …
> Did you really think you'd get away with it?

51
MARGOT

Margot is resting on the sofa in the orangery when Guy comes back from wherever he went. The wine's wearing off and she has a headache. She's getting more of those since she started relying on over-the-counter sleeping tablets to get her through the nights and wine to get her through the days. She doesn't open her eyes when she hears her husband walk in, nor when she feels the weight of him scrunch onto the sofa by her feet. Her finger is throbbing.

'Where've you been?' she asks.

'I went to Sara's to ask her about the phone. She didn't take out the SIM. But she says she put it back to factory settings.'

'That's good enough, isn't it? Maybe it'll be okay.'

'"Maybe it'll be okay" isn't really what I'm aiming for in a situation like this!' Guy snaps. 'I'd prefer "it's watertight", but nothing can be done now. How are you? How's the finger?'

'Agony. Anyway, listen. I've been thinking. About the parents. That video. They're still hoping she's alive, and it's destroying them. I was wondering if there's a way we could tell them that she's no longer alive. To give them closure. Without dumping ourselves in it. Because, at the moment, they have so much hope.'

'Are you insane? No!' Guy's voice is like the crack of a whip, but Margot continues. She's put a lot of thought into this while lying on the sofa.

'Do you remember what Sara suggested at the time? That one of us could stay and explain? Maybe we could still do something like that.'

'Nope. Not happening.'

'Hear me out. One of us could say they were in the desert on their own – they got separated from everyone or went for a walk, or something. Then they stumbled across some disturbed sand that, with hindsight, looked a bit suspicious. At the time, they assumed it was just mess from when someone had camped there, but now being back and having heard about this missing woman, maybe it's worth investigating? The police did say they wanted all information, however trivial.' Margot's even thinking that it could be she and Guy who could go forward. She just wants to alleviate the pain of those poor parents.

'You want to lead the police to where we buried her?' Guy's eyes flash and Margot realises she's on dangerous ground. Guy's so tightly coiled right now. But he turns his back and moves away from her, slamming his balled fist into the palm of the other hand. She watches as he paces up and down. Then he stops and speaks.

'If we wanted her to be found, we'd have been better off just leaving her lying there and pretending we'd never seen her body in the first place. But we decided to bury her. We all agreed, remember? And let's not forget there'll be DNA – I don't know what shit they'll find that could be linked to us.' Guy runs his hand over his forehead. 'Look, this isn't a pleasant situation, is it? And I hate to say it, but it's dog eats dog. Survival of the fittest. Our sanity or that of her parents. And, when it comes down to it, if I'm choosing between them or me, I'm going to pick me every time. Every. Single. Time. Remember, Celine is dead. Saying something to her parents isn't going to change what happened. It's only going to land us in deep shit. Really deep shit. That woman needs to stay six feet under.'

It wasn't six feet, Margot thinks, not even half that – but she's not going to tell Guy that. The whole plan seems so ill thought-out now. Maybe they should just confess. Maybe the police will give them some clemency in return for answers.

'Believe me, I'd like to help them,' Guy continues, 'but there's nothing we can do without compromising ourselves. We can't bring her back to life. You know that. You want to know how I see it? Out there, we were caught in a difficult situation and we did what we had to do in order for us all to carry on living our lives. To give our kids the chance to fulfil their destinies. The Cremorne family is unfortunately the collateral damage. That's all. Sadly, they're going to have to come to terms with the fact that she's gone. And we need to stick to the plan we agreed on.' He pauses. 'Now, are you still with Sara and me? Or do you still want to blow up all our lives?'

He's interrupted by the buzzer ringing from the gate. Guy goes to speak over the intercom. Margot hears some sort of high-pitched crackly commotion and Guy say, 'Okay.'

'Who is it?' she calls.

'Sara. Sounds upset. She was okay when I left her.'

'Has something happened that we don't know about?' Margot checks her phone. It feels as if it's never out of her hand these days. 'There's nothing on Breaking News.'

Curiosity brings her to the hallway as Guy opens the front door. Sara almost falls through it, mascara streaked down her blotchy face, and gasps: 'Have you seen Facebook? Celine's left a comment! She's alive and she knows what we did!'

'What?' Margot's heart thuds.

Guy takes Sara by her upper arms and gives her the tiniest shake.

'Sara, calm down. Look at me. She's dead. We all saw that she was dead.'

'But what if she wasn't?' Sara wails. 'What if she was just unconscious?'

Margot's headachey brain is struggling to keep up.

'We buried her,' she says. 'Under the sand. Didn't we, Sara? It feels like a dream, but it wasn't, was it? We dug a hole. We put her in it, and we filled it in. Right?'

Sara shakes Guy off her and walks this way and that in the hallway. 'Yes! But maybe we didn't do a good job, Margot! I've never dug a grave before! Maybe we didn't pack it tightly enough! It wasn't very deep.'

'It's not like we had a compactor, is it?' Margot says. 'The Jeeps were coming. We were in a hurry.'

'Yes! We were literally just throwing the sand back in as quickly as we could. We should have pressed it down more! And we should have checked she was really dead! All three of us. We should have all stood there and confirmed it.' She flings her hands over her face. 'Now she knows what we did! She'll tell the police and that's it! We'll go to jail and she's not even dead!'

Margot sinks down onto the stairs. Guy is tapping his phone.

'It's on the appeal page?'

'Top comment,' Sara says.

'Got it.' He reads for a moment then scoffs. 'For God's sake, Sara. Clearly a prankster. Set up an account using her name and photos that are freely available. That's all it is. Saw the news about the phone and thought they'd stir it up a bit. People can be such arseholes.'

'How can you be sure?' Sara says. 'Sometimes I have nightmares that she's alive ...'

Guy holds out his arm. 'She's dead, trust me. Come on, let's calm down.' He leads her towards the orangery as if she's a skittish foal, while mouthing to Margot, 'Brandy.'

By the time Margot brings three crystal glasses and the brandy bottle on a tray, Sara's sitting on the sofa in the orangery looking a bit calmer. Margot pours them each a generous slug of brandy and Sara downs it in one. Margot refills it. Sara downs that also, then leans back on the cushions, her hand on her chest.

'Even if it is a crank, they're not wrong, are they?' she wails. 'What if the police get wind of this? What if it opens up a new line of enquiry?'

Guy shrugs. 'Let it. There's nothing to lead them to us.'

'And what if she *is* alive? Margot, you know what I mean? Do you ever have doubts?'

Margot opens her mouth, but Guy beats her to it.

'Well,' he says. 'If she is alive, then there's absolutely no way you should be telling her parents that she's dead, Mar!' He bites his lips, as if stifling a chuckle. 'Imagine.'

'What?' Sara's eyes shoot from Guy to Margot. 'You were thinking of doing that? Why didn't you tell me? I was just with you.'

Guy holds up a hand. 'It's okay. No one's telling anyone anything.'

'We need to stick together!' Sara says. Her eyes latch desperately with Margot's. 'Any decisions need to be made together. Like we agreed!'

But since Sara mentioned the loosely packed sand, Margot's been spiralling.

'What if there was an air pocket?' she muses. She's picturing the loose sheet over Celine's face and the poorly packed sand over the top of the body. Celine's brightly coloured nails clawing at the sand. 'It wouldn't be impossible, would it? Maybe she was in a coma, and she came to and managed to dig her way out.'

'I think it's entirely possible!' Sara says.

Guy slams his hand on a table, causing them both to jump.

'Stop it! Both of you! Listen to me: she's dead. And worrying that she's alive is not going to change anything. And if by any chance she is alive, until and unless she walks into a police station and dumps us in it, there's nothing we can do. All right? This Facebook account is a phoney. It's just some cretin causing trouble. Understood?'

Margot can see that Sara is far from okay and she'll definitely be having those nightmares again tonight. But, eventually, Sara nods, and Guy smiles and slaps his thighs.

'Right. I think we need something to look forward to. Something to take our minds off all of this. Get some semblance of normality back. Agreed? Sara, why don't you and Liv come over for supper one night? We'll have a lovely evening and look only to the future and speak of cheerful things ... current topic banned. How about it?'

Margot looks at Sara and their eyes meet. Margot gives Sara a micro-shrug, a *why not?* Sara nods, and so does Margot, even though she feels as if Guy's dinner invitation is more akin to trying to fix an open wound with an Elastoplast.

'Okay, great,' he says. He makes a show of looking at his watch. 'I hereby declare that normality resumes *now*.'

52
SARA

I'm on pins and needles for the next few days, waiting for the screech of a police car, a bang on the door – waiting for something, anything, to happen. Mentally, I prepare to be arrested. Will I resist? Or will I figuratively roll over and admit it all on the spot? And then something else hits me: what if it's not the police who come? What if it's Celine herself? In my mind's eye, I see her, risen from her grave and covered in sand, tapping on my window with her orange-red nails. The image haunts me, night and day. I might not be in jail physically, but the places my mind goes are far worse than any jail cell.

But, almost unbelievably, nothing happens. The comment is deleted from the Facebook page and I carry on seeing my IRL clients. A stay-at-home mum with a gambling addiction, a woman who doesn't get on with her mother-in-law, a father of four hiding financial problems from his wife, marital issues – the same problems over and over.

The day that Liv and I are to go to dinner with the Forrests finally rolls around. As I get ready, I wonder what it will be like, we adults with the biggest secret in the world acting normal in front of our innocent kids who suspect nothing. To disguise my torment, I pretend to Liv, who's getting ready at my house, that my angst is about what to wear.

'It's not that deep,' she says languidly as I parade choices in front of her while she paints her nails.

'But I want to get it right,' I say. 'I need my outfit to say: casual, didn't make an effort, classy ... does this need a necklace?'

'You're really overthinking it. Just be you. Wear something that makes you comfortable.'

I plump, in the end, for wide-leg trousers and a forgiving top with a chunky necklace and earrings. Liv throws on a sheer mini dress with scruffy trainers and then we're in the cab, on our way, with me clutching the bouquet of flowers and the wine I bought at Waitrose, as if my life depends on it.

'Looking forward to tonight?' I ask Liv when I feel as if I might actually throw up.

She doesn't respond so I jab her with my elbow, and she pulls an AirPod out of her ear with an irritated expression on her face.

'What?'

'I'm talking to you. Are you excited?'

She gives me a funny look. 'It's only the Forrests?'

'Yes, but – you know? It's the first time we've gone to their house for dinner.'

'We spent a week living with them.' She rolls her eyes.

It takes under fifteen minutes for us to get there, then another couple to buzz at the gates and drive up the gravelled driveway that I ran up, so distraught, the last time I was here. The cab comes to a halt and, before I've had a chance to gather myself, Liv's rung the bell, Guy's opening the door and I'm stepping over the threshold while hoping Celine isn't lurking in the shrubbery ready to blackmail us all.

'Sara! Liv! Welcome, welcome. If you just leave your shoes here. Shall I take those?' Guy mwa-mwas me as I struggle with the flowers and wine.

I brandish both at him while I have a full out-of-body experience trying to act normal when things couldn't be less normal. Guy thanks me, Liv disappears up the stairs and I'm ushered through to the kitchen, in the midst of which, with a chef's apron wrapped around her waist and a wine glass in her hand, is Margot. She sways over to me and I realise she's already had a few.

'Sara! Welcome!' She gives me a hug and an air kiss, and whispers in my ear, 'You okay?'

'Mmm,' I nod, and she squeezes my arm. I don't think either of us is okay.

'Sara brought these,' Guy says, placing the flowers and the wine on the island.

Margot examines the flowers as if she's really noticing them. 'Thanks very much, Sara. So thoughtful.' She makes no move to touch them and I see the glassiness of her eyes.

'What can I get you to drink?' Guy asks.

'Whatever you're having,' I say. Guy pulls a bottle of champagne out of a wine fridge, along with three chilled champagne saucers. He pops the cork, fills the saucers and hands each of us a glass.

'Cheers,' he says with an affable smile. 'To friendship, and all it entails.'

'And all it entails,' I echo.

'Cheers,' Margot says. 'Mmm, that's going to go down well.'

*

Somehow, we get through the dinner. The Forrests are impeccable hosts. The police don't storm the place and Celine doesn't bang on the window – so I begin to relax. Maybe it can be like this going forward, I think. I'm bound with the Forrests now; even if Liv and Flynn split up, we'll always have this thing between us, keeping us in each other's orbits. I'm staring into space thinking this over my mint tea when Liv and Flynn burst into the orangery.

'They've found a body,' Flynn says without any introduction. Liv's behind him, her face pale and eyes wide.

'In Oman,' she says. 'It's *breaking news*. What if it's Celine?'

Margot and I look at each other with panicky eyes. Guy shrugs calmly.

'Who knows? Have they said anything more? Is it male, female? Where was it found?'

'Nothing further at this point,' Flynn says. 'But, oh my God. What if it's her?' He flicks on the television and mutes the sound.

'If it's her, then she's definitely dead,' I say bluntly before I can stop myself. I rearrange my face. 'How awful. Let's hope it's not.'

Liv sinks onto the sofa next to me and snivels. 'I'll feel so bad if it's her.'

'You've nothing to feel bad about,' I say.

But she sniffles again into her hand. 'I didn't like her. I asked the universe to make her leave us alone. What if this is how the universe granted my wish?' she wails. 'Oh my God, how will I ever get over this if it's her?'

'Wait! Look!' Flynn says, pointing at the television. 'It's the desert!'

On the screen behind the newscaster is an image taken at the site where the body was found. I don't need to stare at it to know it's the view that's forever imprinted on my psyche: the familiar copse of trees where we camped; the big dune in the distance. Now there's crime scene tape around it. As Liv turns up the volume, I'm transported back into the desert; to the sun, the heat, the dazzling morning light bouncing on desert sand.

'... about a hundred and eighty kilometres outside Muscat in a spot popular with residents for camping and driving on the dunes,' the newscaster is saying.

'That's where we were!' Flynn exclaims. 'Look! The trees!'

'Could be any trees,' Guy says. 'It all looks the same.'

Behind the tape, I can see where they've been digging; mounds of dark sand lying on top of dry, golden sand. I can smell the perfume of the yellow flowers that had been on the trees at the time; I can feel the burn of the rising sun on my bare arms, and the tickle of sweat running down my temple as Margot and I had frantically dug the hole.

'The body is reported to have been found by members of the public unrelated to the search, whose dog came upon the remains,' the newscaster is saying. 'Royal Oman Police have not released any information about the identity of the body but an unconfirmed source said it was female. Should it prove to be that of missing expat Celine Cremorne, it raises more questions than it answers. What was she doing in the desert? Who was she with? And, way more crucially, who buried her?'

Guy clicks off the television once the report ends. 'Blimey.'

'I'm sure that's where we were,' Flynn says.

'Yeah,' Liv says. 'I remember those trees.'

'Desert's desert,' Guy says. 'Trees are trees. It all looks the same. Trust me, I've seen enough of it.'

'I wouldn't be able to identify one bit of sand from another,' I say, looking at the floor.

'Anyway,' Guy says, 'she came back with us. *If* it's her – and that's a big if – she must have gone back later.'

A frown puckers Liv's face and I know what she's thinking before she says it.

'Did she really come back with you? She wasn't up when we left,' she says, as I will her, with every ounce of my maternal strength, to shut up. 'We left early to go to the hospital with your dad, right, babe? Remember? And she was still sleeping. Was she okay, Mum?'

'Yes,' I manage, trying to throw in a nonchalant shrug. 'Hungover like we all were, but fine. Wasn't she, Margot?'

'Mmm-hmm,' Margot nods. 'She re-inflated the tyres.'

'It's probably not her,' Guy says. 'As I said, *if* it's her, maybe she liked where we camped and went back after we left. With friends for New Year or something. I mean, it was the perfect camping spot – easy to find, not far from the road. I sincerely doubt we're the only ones ever to have chosen that spot.'

'Exactly,' I say, and my dinner churns in my stomach.

53
MARGOT

As Margot drives up the sweeping driveway to 'Buckingham Palace', aka her dad's retirement living home, the newly discovered body weighs heavily on her mind. How much will she tell him about what's been going on? She's always been an open book when it comes to him and now she's no longer simply out of her depth: she's actually got no idea how her life can continue on its current trajectory. Even if she tries to keep her worries to herself, she probably won't be able to.

From the driveway, the building could easily be mistaken for an old country house. It's a new build, though, positioned in extensive gardens that the residents are free to tend to or just to enjoy. There's a recreation block with an indoor/outdoor pool, tennis courts and a gym, as well as visitors' suites for when family want to stay over. It should bring Margot joy to see the beautiful house and grounds, but the feeling is bittersweet. Topping up her dad's rent to live here is yet another way for Guy to control her. When they'd returned to the UK, she'd wanted to move her dad into their house – a solution he'd been happy with – but Guy had refused point-blank. The council facility had been grim, and he hadn't been able to afford rent on somewhere as lovely as this – so here she is, beholden once more to Guy.

Margot finds her dad sitting in his sunny living room with a coffee and the papers, having a chat with an invisible person. It happens. He's usually fully lucid and on the ball, but he does sometimes have the odd visit from people who're present only in his mind's eye. While it used to upset Margot to see him talking to no one, she soon realised there's nothing she can do about it, and it brings her dad as much joy – or frustration – as actually having a real person in the room.

'Hello, hello, who's this?' she says jovially as she knocks and enters.

'You know Walter!' her dad says. 'He's just leaving, aren't you, Walter? To what do I owe this honour? I thought we were going to do the iPad these days.'

Margot steps aside to let 'Walter' pass then leans down to give her dad a kiss before sitting down on the chair Walter was presumably just inhabiting.

'I just wanted to see you, Dad. That's all. How are you?' She feels her voice wobble.

Her dad beams and rubs his hands together. 'Couldn't be better. It seems you're the one I need to be worrying about. Look at the state of you. Don't tell me you're doing some new-fangled diet? What is it this time? Not eating from midnight to midnight?'

As much as Margot tries to laugh, she can't stop a sob from escaping.

'What is it?' he says, leaning closer to her and rubbing her arm. 'Hey, hey, hey. You can tell me. There's not much I haven't heard in this life. Not much that'll shock me.' He waits and Margot wonders if she really can tell him. It feels like he's the only person in the world she can talk to right now. 'Can I tell you? Something really bad?'

'Of course,' he says. 'That's what dads are for – no?'

'And you won't judge me? Or dob me in to the police?'

'The police, Margot? What's happened?'

So she unburdens herself of the whole story, slowly and falteringly at first, then faster. Everything – from Guy's affair and why they left Oman, to the holiday, the desert camping trip and the dreadful aftermath of guilt and suspicion.

'And now a body's been found exactly where we were camping. It can only be her. What am I going to do?'

Margot's dad sits back in his chair with his eyes closed. She watches his chest rise and fall, wondering if he's thinking or has fallen asleep. How much of what she just said did he even take in?

'Dad?' she says eventually and his eyes snap open.

'So, either the fall from the quad bike was why she died, or one of you did it?' he asks. She nods. 'And this friend of yours, this Sara, checked her over after the fall and said she was fine. And she looked fine to you?'

Margot nods.

Her dad rubs his jaw in silence.

'What are you thinking?' she asks when she can't bear it anymore.

'Well, what I'm thinking is that it takes a lot of force and strength to kill a person. And I know you wouldn't and couldn't do it. I don't know this Sara person, but I do know one thing.'

'What?'

'That I think your husband is perfectly capable of killing someone.'

54
MARGOT

Another day passes. Guy shuts down any discussion of the body that's been found and Margot struggles to work after what her dad had said. She doesn't doubt that Guy is capable of killing someone, but why would he? The question rattles around in her head, preventing her from focusing on work. There are also aspects of the work she simply can't do with her finger bandaged so, by the weekend, when they're all due to attend the school fundraiser, she's fallen behind on the delivery schedule of the house she's making. Guy's in and out of her studio almost hourly, questioning how far she's got, and it's this high-handed approach that makes her glue the wrong wallpaper into the master suite. It's taken a long time for her to match up the pattern so the model's as good as the real house – a fiddly job that requires her to wear reading glasses. Only when she thinks she's finally done, does Guy spot her error.

'Look at the photo,' he says as he peers over her shoulder. 'Is that the master suite? I don't think it is. That's the paper from *that* bedroom. You've ballsed it up. Margot – seriously?'

Margot's eyes glisten. She doesn't have the energy for this. It's supposed to be her hobby and right now she hates it. She imagines smashing the mansion and walking away.

Smashing up their life together and walking away.

'You're going to have to start again,' he says. 'Strip it. Remake it. And make it perfect. No mistakes. Maybe you should skip the fundraiser. You could use the time to catch up.'

Margot nods. She's fine with that. She doesn't want to go anyway. Guy, she knows, will be his usual charming, flirtatious self with everyone else and she'll be left to deal with the boorish drunk when they get home. She's seen it all before.

'Sure,' she says. 'Happy to.'

But Guy laughs. 'Oh, Mar,' he says, taking the back of her neck in a pincer grip between his thumb and forefinger and giving it a knead while she works. 'I'm just kidding. Of course you're coming. I've got a surprise for you later.'

She works as late as she can, leaving it until the last possible moment to get changed.

'Time to get ready!' Guy's head appears round the studio door. 'There's a glass of champagne with your name on it in the bedroom!'

'Coming!' Margot sighs, tidies up her things and makes her way across the landing. There, on the bed, lies a dress she's never seen before. Beside it stands a very smug husband already in his dress shirt and tuxedo trousers, sorting out his cufflinks.

'What's this?'

'A gift.'

Margot examines it. It's slinky, full-length and shining silver. The type of dress you see on red carpets at film premieres, not so much at secondary school charity functions. It's totally over the top.

'It's lovely. But I was planning on wearing my navy dress – you know, the one I wore on your birthday?'

'Why not something new? It's beautiful, isn't it?'

'Of course, but ... don't you think it's a bit much?'

Guy shrugs. 'You can never be overdressed at an event like this.'

Oh, but you can, Margot thinks. This is a dress he's picked not to make her look beautiful but to make him look successful. It's a dress for his arm candy to wear. Insulting to Margot. Degrading her to a bit of fluff at his side. She studies his face for a moment, trying to judge his mood. Is it worth arguing? It's a delicate dance she does with Guy, and more than ever these days. There's a long night ahead of them. Lots of alcohol – which is good but also bad.

'Well,' she says stiffly. 'Thank you.'

She has a quick shower, gets herself ready and steps into the dress while Guy ties his bow tie. She's at the mirror, putting in her earrings when she hears the click of the lock on the door, then feels him come up behind her. He slides his arms around her, his breathing ramping up as his hands feel their way over her body. Margot puts her hands on top of his and tries to move them off her as she realises what he's doing. But Guy nuzzles Margot's neck, his teeth nipping her flesh in a way she's never said she likes.

'Guy. No.' She tries to wriggle away but he pins her to him.

'Come on, Mar. We haven't done it in ages. I need it.'

He turns her around in his arms and silences her with hard kisses while his hands work to undo his belt and trousers. She tries to push him off.

'I said no. Please.'

But he carries on. It's over in five minutes. Not long to suffer, really, but when she lets herself think about what he's doing, how he knows it's against her wishes and how he never listens to her or respects her, another layer of quiet fury is added to the ball of anger that's gathering in her core.

'Right, chop-chop,' Guy says as he pushes himself off her and does up his flies. 'Get up, sort yourself out. The car's coming at seven and I said we'd pick up Sara and Liv on the way.'

55
SARA

The Forrests pick us up in a luxury minivan. It's plush inside with a uniformed driver, leather seats and a bottle of water for each of us but, when we get in, Margot gives me a wan smile then stares out of the window in silence. She's wearing dark mauve lipstick and a stunning silver dress that sets off her hair and the colour of her eyes in a way that makes her look magnificent, but her face is drawn and I wonder what's wrong. Flynn and Liv bend their heads together over their phones. Guy starts to tell me about the debate there'd been on the PTA about whether to hold the fundraiser at the nearby golf club or the school hall. The consensus was that as much of the money raised as possible should go to the good cause rather than the pockets of the golf club. So the school hall it is, with the food cooked on site.

'It's a shame,' Guy says, 'as the golf club's food is actually quite good. God knows what they'll serve us now. Turkey Twizzlers! Imagine!'

As we make this inane chatter, I nod silently towards Margot and frown questioningly at Guy. He gives an imperceptible shake of his head, which I take to mean I should leave her be. But still, I try.

'Have you ever bid at an auction before, Margot?' I ask. I wait, but she doesn't respond. She's miles away and I notice the whites of her knuckles showing as she squeezes her hands into fists on her lap. 'I'm quite nervous!' I say. 'I'm going to sit on my hands so I don't bid on something by accident!'

My effort garners no response from Margot and a disapproving tut from Liv. I grimace at Guy, who mouths 'don't worry' and then we're approaching the school and I also look out of the window.

There's a long, bright red carpet running up the school drive, fenced by golden poles. Teenagers are all over it, mincing their way up the carpet in micro-skirts, heels and tuxes, like they're arriving at the Oscars, with their phones out to capture the moment for their socials. Liv is no different, deserting me to get her pictures, so I'm grateful to be able to walk in alongside Margot. I touch her arm as Guy goes off to take photos of Liv and Flynn.

'You okay?'

'Don't ask.'

'Did something happen?' I want to pull her away from the crowd and hear what's troubling her, but she gives her head half a shake and turns to greet the person next to her, leaving me with no choice but to do the same.

As we enter the school, I have to hand it to the PTA: the lobby looks lovely. The grand staircase is festooned with garlands, and that seems to be where we're gathering for pre-dinner drinks. Waiters are circulating with trays of glasses and a teen in a tux is valiantly plonking away on the piano, but the sound is largely lost. The noise level is insane as everyone makes small talk at the tops of their voices. I stand in a cluster with the Forrests and mentally pinch myself: I'm standing here, at the school, in evening wear with a glass of fizz in my hand, when the reality could have been so very different.

After we've drunk a couple of glasses, the headmaster ascends to the first turn of the staircase and clangs on the stair rail, and we all fall as silent as a few hundred parents drinking free-flowing fizz can be, while he makes a short speech about the school in Borneo that our donations tonight will help to fund, invites us to take a good look at the auction prizes, and encourages us to bid like we're millionaires – cue lots of guffaws – 'but within your means, of course. I have to say that.' Finally, we're requested to move through to the hall and be seated.

The hall looks splendid, filled with circular tables dressed with crockery, flowers, candles and bottles of wine and water. If it wasn't for the familiar school-hall smell that every adult associates viscerally with tedious assemblies and sweaty June exams, you could probably half-close your eyes and pretend you were at the golf club. I walk through with Margot, hoping to sit with her, but the seats have place names and the other parents at our table are already sitting obediently in their correct places. I nod to each of them.

'Hi, I'm Sara,' I say.

We learn that we're sitting with Freddie and Mary-Jane, who get in very quickly that their daughter is taking four A-levels; Ali and Inaya, who are new to the school and parents to two much younger girls; plus a representative from the PTA called Adele, who laughs loudly at everything anyone, including herself, says – a nervousness thing, maybe.

'So did anyone do anything nice over the holidays?' Mary-

Jane asks when the initial small talk fizzles out. My eyes shoot across the table to Margot, but she's studying the set menu and doesn't look up.

'Nothing special,' Inaya says. 'Family stuff. Aunts, cousins. You know how it is.'

Everyone agrees that they do.

'How about you? Is that a bit of a tan I see – did you go away?' Adele asks me.

I freeze. Of course the holiday itself is no secret, but …

'We went to Oman,' Guy says smoothly. 'Margot and I went with our son, and Sara and her daughter. Our kids are dating, so I suppose we were with the "in-laws" too!' Everyone laughs.

'Which part of Oman?' Ali asks. 'I used to go there a lot. Down in Salalah. It's very beautiful, especially in the summer months when the tropical rains come.'

'Ah, we didn't make it to Salalah this time,' Guy says. 'We were in Muscat. We only had a week and we weren't wildly adventurous. You know, a change of scene. We used to live there, too, so it was a bit of a trip down memory lane.'

'I was desperate for some winter sun,' I add.

'I've never been to the Middle East and I'm not sure I'd ever go!' Adele says with a laugh. She looks nervously around the table, as if she's assessing who'll be on her side.

'I agree it's not for everyone, but it's an incredible part of the world,' Guy says. 'Don't knock it till you've tried it.'

'Hmph.' Adele clearly doesn't agree. 'Well, glad you made it back, eh? Unlike that poor girl who went missing. Did you see about that? Selena or something? Lived out there?'

'Yes, that teacher in Muscat? Yes, we heard about that,'

Guy says without missing a beat. 'Awful for everyone involved. I hope they find her soon.'

'You know they found a body? I wonder if it's her.'

'Well, I hope it isn't.'

'In a way, I hope it is,' Adele says. 'It'd give closure to those poor parents. Imagine your child missing in the Middle East.'

'Mmm,' I say in agreement, although, to my own ears, the sound comes out strangled. Guy picks up the auction catalogue and scans it. 'So, anyone got their eye on anything tonight?'

'The signed cricket bat,' Ali says. 'My dad collects them. I'd love to get this one for him.'

Freddie's index finger lies across his top lip. 'Mary-Jane and I are looking at the luxury weekend break. How about you?'

'I don't know,' Guy says. 'What about you, darling?'

Margot raises an eyebrow sardonically. 'If you're actually asking what *I'd like*, Guy, I'd take the golden cone, thanks.' Her words are strangely weighted but she smiles brightly, takes another sip of her wine and raises the glass in a mock cheers.

'That'll be hotly contested,' Freddie says.

'It's always the hot ticket,' Adele says. 'If anyone's thinking of placing a bid, by the way, the ballpark is about £2,000, going on last year.'

'I'm sorry, what is that?' Inara asks. 'A cone?'

'It's a reserved parking space inside the school grounds at drop-off and pick-up times,' Adele says. 'Like gold dust, obv.' She actually says that – I'd thought it was just a teenage thing.

'And is there an actual golden cone?' Guy asks with a smile. 'Because if I spend two grand on that, I'll want something tangible to show off.'

'I could make sure you have something to show off,' Adele

says flirtatiously. I glance at Margot but she appears not to have noticed.

'Oh, wow, I had no idea there was such a thing,' Inara says. 'Pick-up is *such* a zoo.' She raises her eyebrows hopefully at her husband but, looking at Ali's impassive face, I don't fancy her chances.

'Well, let's see what the evening brings,' Guy says, rubbing his hands together as waiters start to bring round plates of gelatinous-looking starters. 'Now this looks delicious. Does anyone know what it actually is?'

56
MARGOT

The guests are given half an hour after the starters to take a last look at the auction lots and get their bids in. Margot doesn't bother getting up. She can see that there's a cluster around the cricket bat, and she hopes Guy doesn't bid on it when he's not even into cricket.

'I don't know what to bid on. What does Sara Say?' she hears Guy say to Sara, who's seated next to him.

'Well, do you fancy anything?' Sara asks.

'Come with me. Let's go and look.'

Guy holds out his arm like the type of gentleman who would never pin his wife to the bed and Margot turns away, trying to blot him out. She just can't deal with that now – her mind is full of the body found in the desert. Of course it's Celine, she thinks. But then she oscillates the other way: Guy did make a good point when he said it was an obvious camping spot. They're not going to be the only ones who camped there.

But they are probably the only ones who buried a body there.

Of course it's her.

She looks around the crowded room, seeing friends,

community and joy as this body of people comes together to raise money to improve the lives of those less fortunate, and she suddenly feels like an outsider. Not one of them knows what it's like to bury a body and run from the authorities. Compared to what's on her plate, their worries are so trivial. Sitting there, Margot begins to understand that what they did has put a chasm between them and the rest of the world. But they're not bad people. They didn't kill her and neither had they left Celine Cremorne's body to the mercy of the elements, as they could well have done. She sighs inwardly and takes a deep slug of her wine. What's done is done. There's nothing she can do to bring Celine back. She needs to focus her energy on matters closer to home: what to do about her marriage. What Guy did this evening has brought that to breaking point.

Guy and Sara return, giggling, and take their seats.

'Did you bid on anything?' Ali asks, and Guy nods.

'Just a bit, for the craic.' He winks at Margot and she looks away.

'Look at this,' he says half an hour later, as he triumphantly carries the cricket bat back to the table to a round of applause. 'Every signature of the England team from the 2022 Men's T20 World Cup.'

Margot stares at him, aghast.

'It's definitely a piece,' Ali says. 'Congratulations.'

But then Guy grins around the table and holds out the bat. 'I'd love your father to have it. Nothing makes me happier than the charity getting the money, and the bat being with someone who'll appreciate it. So, please …'

Adele's the first to start clapping.

*

The evening comes to a close around eleven-thirty. Margot can't bear to look at Guy as they make their way back down the red carpet. His hero act nauseates her. He'd tried to gift the bat to Ali but, fair play to the man, he'd insisted on paying Guy what he'd bid. Regardless, Guy still came out of the whole thing smelling of roses. Margot's teeth grind together as she yanks open the cab door.

She's relieved that they ride largely in a silence, punctuated only by snorts of laughter from Liv and Flynn as they watch things on his phone. Then Flynn gasps.

'Click on it!' Liv says.

'No!'

They tussle as Liv tries to grab his phone. 'Give it here! Let me look. What does it say?'

'What is it?' Margot asks.

'Wait, wait, wait,' says Flynn. 'It's loading. God, it's slow. Give me a minute.' Then he adds, 'Oh my God. "The body found in Oman has been identified as that of missing Briton Celine Cremorne".'

Guy says very meaningfully, 'That woman who's been in the news? How awful. Her poor family.'

Liv looks as if she's about to ask a question, but Sara discretely pulls an imaginary zip across her lips. Liv and Flynn look at each other with wrinkled foreheads. They're almost at Sara's.

'Umm, would you guys like to come in for a coffee?' Sara says as they turn into her road.

'Great idea, thanks. We'd love to,' Guy says. When the cab stops, they all pile out onto the pavement.

'Why did you want us to shut up?' Flynn asks as the cab drives away. 'What's going on?'

57
SARA

As Flynn asks his question, I'm already up the path, unlocking the front door. So it's confirmed that Celine's body was found at, it's difficult to deny, the very spot where we were camping. What now? How are we going to get around this? Silently, I lead the way into the living room, where Margot takes the armchair, leaving Guy to perch on the sofa. I've had one or two glasses of wine too many for this level of thinking. Flynn hugs Liv, who's scrubbing at her eyes, mascara already trailing her cheeks.

'It's definitely her?' I ask Flynn. 'The body?'

'Celine's dead!' Liv sobs. 'I can't believe it. Like, she was just with us, now she's dead!'

Flynn hugs her tighter.

'Where did you see it?' Guy asks.

'BBC,' Flynn says.

'Okay, phones please,' Guy says, indicating that we should switch them off.

'What?' Flynn scowls.

'Just do it,' Guy says.

'What are you on? Celine is dead and you want us to turn off our phones?'

'Flynn!' Guy barks.

'What's going on?' Flynn says. He looks from Guy to Margot to me. 'What are you hiding?'

'Nothing!'

Liv comes to sit on the armrest of my chair. I try to put my arm around her but it's too awkward, so I give her a pat instead. I want to say, 'She was fine when we dropped her back home.' But the words get stuck in my throat.

'As I said the other day, she must have gone back to the desert after we left,' Guy says thoughtfully, as if he's just piecing it together. 'I mean, loads of people like to spend New Year in the desert.' He finds the news report on his own phone and reads it out.

'Okay, here it is. "Breaking News. Body found in Oman is missing British expat Celine Cremorne. A body found in Oman has, according to official sources, been confirmed as British expatriate Celine Cremorne. The 32-year-old teacher was reported as missing on 3 January when she failed to report for the start of the new school term. The Royal Oman Police said in a statement that foul play is suspected and a post-mortem will be carried out. No further information was made available".'

I wish I could be anywhere but here having this conversation.

Guy switches off his phone and paces the room, his hands steepled against his mouth.

'Foul play?' Liv says with her hand over her mouth. 'Like someone killed her?'

'No, they're not saying that,' Guy says smoothly. 'I imagine that because the body was buried, they think someone must have known she was dead. That's all.'

Liv squeezes her face between her hands. 'I can't believe it. I feel so guilty.'

'Olivia,' Guy says. 'You have *nothing* to feel guilty about.'

'I didn't like her.' She sniffles again. 'What if I wished this to happen?'

'Of course you didn't!' I say. 'We don't know what happened to her, but it's absolutely nothing to do with you. Okay? And, look, I suppose there is a very tiny silver lining to this. As Adele said tonight, at least her parents can stop searching and get some sort of closure. And a body to bury ...' I trail off.

'I don't believe you,' Flynn says. He looks from his dad to his mum. Margot's face freezes. 'We didn't see her that morning. You said she was sleeping, and then you made us leave early. Where was she? Was she actually in her tent?'

'Of course she was!' Guy says.

Flynn stares down his dad. 'This is too much of a coincidence. Her body's buried where we camped. You made us shut up in the cab and turn off our phones. You made Liv take down her post. You're hiding something.'

'I'm not hiding anything! I left with you – how could I have done anything?'

Flynn turns to his mum. 'You and Sara cleared up the camp. Did you see her? Was she fine?' He glowers at her, his hands on his hips. 'Did she really re-inflate the tyres?'

'She was—' Margot says, but she can't meet his eyes.

'Sara?' Flynn says. 'Will you tell me the truth?'

I feel Liv's eyes on me. 'She—'

'Was she alive or was she dead?' Flynn demands. 'Because I think it's pretty easy to tell. And – oh my God – if she was dead, it means you left her there!' Flynn is on his feet, his head in his hands. 'What the hell did you do?'

58
MARGOT

'Flynn, that's enough!' Guy snaps. He grabs Flynn's shoulders and shakes him, his face like thunder.

'Guy!' Margot shouts. Her muscles tense up, ready to intervene, but Flynn squirms out of Guy's grip and dodges to the other side of the room, agile like a boxer.

'Whoah. Talk about a guilty reaction! What's going on? Mum?' Flynn's breathing hard.

'Tell your son the truth, Margot,' Guy says levelly. 'Tell him he's barking up the wrong tree.'

They stare at each other and, in that moment, Margot realises she not only has no love left for her husband, but scant loyalty. She's had enough. The secret's become too big, and it's fracturing both her and her family. She doesn't want her husband shaking her son. And neither does she want to lie to her son. She opens her mouth but finds no words.

'Margot,' Guy warns, and she knows that dangerous tone of his voice.

'Mum?' Flynn says.

Margot looks at Sara, whose eyes skid to the floor. Then Margot opens her mouth and this time words do come out.

'We knew she was dead.'

Liv gasps.

'*What?*' Flynn sinks onto the chair as if his knees have failed him. 'You knew *all this time* that she was dead? What the hell?'

Liv rushes over to Flynn, and they clutch each other as if they're the only two innocents in the room, protecting each other from their murderous parents.

'Why did you lie about it? Did you kill her?' Flynn demands.

Guy breathes in deeply through his nose. He puts both hands up.

'Of course not! Calm down. Everyone, just calm down. No one killed Celine.'

'Calm down?' Flynn yells. 'I've just found out my parents left their friend dead in the desert; hid it from the police; and lied to their child! What d'you expect me to do? Go to bed?'

'Mum?' Liv looks at Sara. Liv's hand is over her mouth and her eyes are huge and questioning. Sara's head drops into her hands as her shoulders slump with the agony of having let down her daughter one more time.

'You knew?' Liv says. 'You really knew, and you let the search go on?'

Sara shrugs, lost for words.

'We didn't kill her,' Margot says. 'You must understand that. She died in the night.'

'You didn't kill her?' Flynn says, and his voice is cold. 'You expect us to believe that?' He looks from Margot to Guy and back. 'I think Dad and I both know why you might.'

'How dare you?' Margot explodes. 'Flynn Forrest, you take that back! As if I would kill someone! *As if!*'

Flynn flinches, but he's not finished. 'I heard the tent zip go down in the night,' he says. 'I heard someone moving about outside.'

'Well, it damn well wasn't me!' Margot snaps, while her mind catches up with the fact that Flynn also heard the zip. It did actually go down. And it was neither him nor her who'd left the tent.

'And it wasn't me!' Liv says. 'I know I said I didn't like her, but I didn't kill her! I wouldn't know how.'

'We know that, darling,' Sara says and tries to smile but her lips wobble too much. 'Was it the zip of your tent you heard, do you think?' she asks Flynn. 'Or could it have been Celine's?'

'Ours,' Flynn says. 'I wouldn't have heard hers across the campsite. So who did it?' He stares at his father.

'No one,' Guy says. 'No one killed her. All right?'

'You sure about that?' Flynn asks. He squares up to Guy, almost as tall as his dad now, challenging him, and Margot tenses herself again, ready to intervene.

'Yes, we're sure about that,' Guy says. 'If you're willing to listen – and that's a big if – I'll tell you what happened. Okay?'

And so Guy explains how, when they woke up, no one could rouse Celine. That she must have died in her sleep. He explains how they sent the kids out on the quad bike while they figured out what to do. How they agonised over making the right decision.

'We wanted to protect you,' Guy says. 'That's all.'

'But you didn't think to call the police?' Flynn says. 'Because that's the most obvious thing to do in that situation.'

'Flynn! We were in the Middle East!' Guy says. 'It's not like the UK. We didn't know how the police would react: we were the only people with her when she died. It's likely they'd have suspected us – possibly blamed us! We'd been drinking. We don't speak Arabic. They would have taken us all back to the station for questioning; maybe they'd have made us sign confessions that we didn't understand. I don't actually know what the process is when you're found in the middle of nowhere with a dead body, but it's not something I felt we should find out. We may have been held pending trial. We'd certainly have been held until a post-mortem was done. It was too risky.'

'And burying her body and going on the run wasn't? What planet are you even on?'

'I can't believe you did that!' Liv says to her mum. 'What about "Sara says"? Where was she? On holiday, too?'

Sara's wiping tears from her eyes. 'Livvie … I …'

'The only thing we did wrong was not calling the police,' Guy says. 'That's the only "crime" – if you want to call it that – we committed. Let's not forget we didn't kill her. We just pretended we weren't there. It was an omission, not a lie.'

'Her family. You hid it from them,' Liv says shaking her head. 'All this time.'

Guy shrugs. 'Unfortunate, I know, but we had no choice. Now – what's been said here tonight isn't leaving this room. Okay? You discuss this with no one. You tell no one. This is our secret and it remains with us. Now that she's been found dead, we'll all be in even more trouble than we would have been when we were in Oman. And, to be clear, I'm talking about life in jail. Understood?'

Liv and Flynn look at each other, weighing up whether or not they can keep such a huge thing quiet. Whether they even want to.

'How do we know what you're telling us is true?' Flynn says. 'I'm not sure I believe you. You covered it up. You didn't tell us. What else are you hiding? What are you capable of?'

'You know everything now, I promise,' Margot says.

'Do we, though?' Flynn puts his finger to his lip as if thinking. 'You sure about that?'

And that jogs Margot's mind. She stiffens as she remembers something. A detail that could be critical: the night-vision trail camera that Guy had bought her for Christmas. She'd taken it with them to the desert and she'd set it up herself. It must have got bundled up with the camping equipment when she and Sara were shoving everything into the car. But she hasn't seen it since. Had Guy found it when he'd taken the stuff back to Tom and Di? Was he hiding it because it showed something he didn't want the others to see?

59
SARA

After the Forrests leave, I try to put my arm around Liv but she moves away.

'Livvie, you have to understand what happened. It wasn't my choice.'

'"You can't choose what happens to you, but you can choose how you react." You're always telling me that. So much for "Sara says",' Liv throws herself onto the sofa. '"Trust your gut." "Do the right thing." Do you actually believe in any of that stuff? Who are you, Mum? I thought you'd changed. After all that happened; all that we went through – your court case, me moving schools. I was just starting to believe that you really had changed. That you'd learned your lesson. And now look.'

The bitter tone of her voice makes my chest ache. I don't know how to put this right.

'I thought you believed in doing the right thing,' she says.

'I do believe in doing the right thing … but sometimes it's complicated. Sometimes the right thing is simply to protect your child.'

'Complicated as in: our friend's died. Shall we call the police? No, let's just bury her and let her parents search for her for weeks! It's not that complicated, Mother! Don't throw it on me. I didn't ask you to do anything.'

'It was the Forrests!' I cry. 'They were the ones who said we couldn't call the police. I said we should.'

'Yet you didn't.'

'Liv! Listen to me! Remember how you came back from your walk on the dunes and Guy told you breakfast wasn't ready? It was because I wanted to call the police! They needed more time to persuade me to shut up. They told me we'd *all* go to jail. You too! Guy was very forceful about it. I believed them. They'd lived there before. They knew what could happen. But, mainly, I was thinking of you. You have your whole life ahead of you. I didn't want you locked up in jail in a foreign country. All I ever do is try to protect you.'

'Well, maybe it's time you stop trying to protect me and started acting with a conscience! You buried her and left her there!' Liv sobs. 'I can't believe you did that!'

'We didn't have a choice! And, just so you know, every day since, I've regretted it. I feel terrible for Celine's family. Dreadful.'

Liv gets herself a glass of water then gives me a withering look as she passes me in the hallway.

'Well, I'm going to bed and I'm going to think about what I'm going to do, now I know that we're all wanted in connection with a dead body. I'm very sorry that you, age forty-eight, couldn't make a decent judgement call for yourself. Sleep well, *Sara*. Sleep well, knowing you were too weak to stand up to your friends!'

She stalks out of the room, leaving me on the sofa in my

evening dress with my head in my hands, my make-up down my face and my nerves shattered. The worst thing is, she's right. I've made a terrible mistake – but now we're all in so deep I'm not sure there's any way out.

60
MARGOT

The trail camera.

That's all Margot can think about as the Forrests take a cab home in stony silence after the explosive revelations at Sara's. Where is the sodding camera? She's replaying in her head the moments when she and Sara dismantled the camp. How they balled up the tents and shoved them back in the car. How they rammed everything in as quickly as they could. How hot it was. How her heart was hammering in her chest with the labour of digging the hole plus the stress of the approaching column of Jeeps. Was the camera there? It must have been, but she's sure she hasn't seen it in England. So where is it? Did they somehow leave it in the villa? Is it lurking on a wardrobe shelf or in a drawer in Muscat? Is that better than Guy having found it and hidden it?

The tent zip.

Surely he wouldn't.

Would he? Did he have a fight with Celine?

Margot's thoughts spiral. Even if she finds the camera, what will it show? Of course the tent zip going down could have been nothing – Guy could have got up in the night for any number of innocent reasons – but she'd asked him and he'd denied it. Why deny it if he has nothing to hide? And then there's the way he was so calm that morning they found Celine; the way he hadn't seemed shocked. Sara had vomited, and Margot will never forget the heart-stopping moment she realised that Celine was not unconscious, but dead.

Yet Guy came up with a plan almost instantaneously and since they've been back, he's insisted on managing all of them. He's been dashing over to Sara's to make sure she's not blabbing to anyone and making them all turn their phones off every time they talk about what happened. Completely paranoid, now she thinks about it.

When they get home, Flynn stalks wordlessly towards the stairs as Margot flicks off her heels in the hallway.

'And you can cut out that attitude, young man!' Guy snaps.

Flynn spins around, his eyes burning with fury. 'You've no right to tell me what to do!'

'I'm your father and I've every right! While you live under this roof—'

'I'm not planning on staying under this roof!' Flynn spits.

'If it wasn't for me, you'd be sleeping on the floor in jail!' Guy yells. 'For life! You've got me to thank for the fact that you're free to enjoy the rest of your life! But go on: throw it back at me! Throw it back at me that I saved you and Olivia from life in jail!'

'Shut up!'

Guy strides towards Flynn, his hand raised as if to grab him. Flynn dodges up a few more stairs.

'Don't you *ever* tell me to shut up!' Guy yells. 'You do know it's probably your fault, don't you? Young healthy people don't die for no reason, Flynn Forrest! You were the one who threw her off the quad bike! Did it ever cross your mind that you killed her? That we were all protecting you?'

Margot sees Flynn recoil as the words hit him. She can see that it hasn't occurred to him till now that Celine may have died because of the fall. His face goes white, and he drops onto the step, aghast. Margot hates Guy in that moment. Hates him.

'She was okay,' Flynn says, and his voice is uncertain now. 'Sara checked her. She was fine. She was talking. She ate dinner ... we were all dancing. It wasn't a bad fall. Mum?' His eyes beseech Margot.

'It wasn't your fault,' she says, because what parent would tell their seventeen-year-old son that he's caused someone's death without any proof? 'Guy, you need to apologise to Flynn for that. You said yourself she could have died of anything. A snake bite, a heart attack, alcohol poisoning, heatstroke, dehydration ...'

'Okay, Flynn. I'm sorry. It probably wasn't that. Okay?' Guy says and then he turns to Margot and his eyes narrow.

Bring it on, whatever it is, Margot thinks. *Let me have it. Just leave my boy out of it.*

'Maybe it was your mother,' Guy says. 'Yes, Margot, let's talk about you. You had more motive to bump off Celine than any of us ...' He glances at Flynn and decides to continue. 'Oh, don't deny it, you knew about Celine and me. I saw how you deliberately tried to wind her up. So, come on: what did you do? A little jibe that went too far? Or was it deliberate? Did you slip something into her drink, or crawl into her tent and intentionally put your hands around her throat while she slept?' He leers. 'Did you *enjoy* it?'

'Fuck off,' Margot says.

'It's true, isn't it?' Guy continues. 'You were jealous, and you killed her!' He pauses. 'By the way, you know that's what Sara thinks,' Guy sneers. 'She asked me if you did it. She thinks she's covering this up to protect *you*.'

That hits Margot like a punch in the gut.

'Well,' she says, 'while we're accusing each other, let's talk about the tent zip both Flynn and I heard in the night, Guy. It wasn't Flynn, it wasn't Liv, and it wasn't me, so that leaves … oh: only you.'

Guy falters for a fraction of a second.

'I went for a wee. Okay? I forgot but now I remember. Don't know what time it was. But I didn't see anyone. Campsite was quiet.' He glares at her, his hands now on his hips. 'In the general scheme of things, the fact that I forgot is hardly a crime, is it? Happy?'

Margot looks at Flynn. Their eyes catch. She'll talk to him later. Just as she'll search for the camera later. For now, she needs to defuse the situation.

'For the record, Guy, Flynn. I didn't kill her. Deliberately or accidentally. To be honest …' She looks from one to the other and back. 'It's a moot point at this stage. We don't know why she died. It could have been any of us or, far more likely, none of us. And on that note, it's been a long night, and I need to get some rest. Good night.'

She sleeps alone in her studio.

And locks the door.

61
SARA

I barely sleep after the fundraiser and, when I do, my dreams are tortured as I flail this way and that, haunted not just by Celine, but by the look on Liv's face when she realised that what Flynn had said was true – we had covered up Celine's death and then lied about it. It stings: the holiday was a means for me to spend quality time with Liv; to rebuild our relationship; to regain her trust. The cover-up had been to protect her and Flynn's innocence.

But Liv's trust in me had been gossamer thin since the court case, despite the years that have passed. After I'd been found guilty of assaulting her teacher, Liv had refused to believe that it really had been an accident. I can see how it looked: the woman was a bitch. She'd been victimising Liv and I'd been at the end of my tether. And, yes, I'd waited for her to pass me on the stairs, that much was true. I'd realised she was coming, and I'd waited for her. "Loitering", the judge had said. I'd wanted to have a word with her; to clear the air after the messages I'd put on the class WhatsApp had been reported to the headmaster, but then she'd seen me and she'd given me that demeaning, dismissive look and … I moved, and she fell. Did I push her? It was a moot point. But when it went to court, the school had to side with the teacher. Of course they did. They supplied witnesses to my so-called harassment of the woman. It was only because my lawyer argued mitigating circumstances, due to the unfair way Liv had been treated, that I got off with a suspended sentence and a community service order.

But that was nothing compared to the punishment Liv handed me.

On the day she'd moved out, I'd thought things could never get any worse. It had been a long road to redemption – a road made of broken glass, over which I'd crawled on my hands and knees. My sole goal was to win Liv back. And I'd been winning. I'd turned it around. Liv was proud of my transformation, of my work, of my YouTube channel. She invited me to come on the holiday and I'd laughingly promised that I wouldn't embarrass her, thinking that the worst thing that could happen would be me looking a bit wobbly in my swimwear. I didn't know the Forrests. I hadn't wanted to go to Oman. I'd scoped out other plans for just the two of us. But as soon as Guy had issued the invitation for us to join them in Muscat, that was all that Liv had wanted and, despite my misgivings, I'd gone along with it.

But what makes it worse is knowing deep down that one of the reasons I agreed to the holiday was because I was hungry for the social validation of the Forrests. I squirm as I think about that. After you've been publicly shamed, a smear remains over you – maybe imagined, maybe real – but it's there, like a physical scar, and an invitation to holiday with the Forrests was like a pretty tattoo over the top of that. People would say the Forrests have invited her to holiday with them: she must be okay. Some of their glory would rub off on me.

So much for that.

In the morning, I'm woken by muffled thumps on the staircase. I throw on my joggers and a sweatshirt and find Liv in the hallway, a heap of bags around her.

'What are you doing?' I say, although I know the answer. We've been here before.

'Leaving,' she says curtly. 'Dad'll be here any second.'

'But you're supposed to stay all weekend. Liv, I …' But the door rattles in its frame as the familiar thunder of Michael's car draws up outside. Liv opens the door and picks up her bags, then she stares me down.

'Any credibility you ever had with me is gone,' she says. 'Destroyed. So don't think I'm ever coming back. We're done. As far as I'm concerned, I have no mother. Goodbye.'

'Baby. No! Wait!' I shout, but I see a flash of Michael's silhouette in the driving seat and then my words are met by the front door slamming in my face.

After a stunned moment of utter disbelief, I tear at the door, fingers fumbling with the catch.

'Liv!' I yell as I run down the path. 'Wait! Michael! Stop! Come back!'

But, almost at the same time as Liv bundles into the front seat, Michael guns the car off down the street, leaving me standing open-mouthed on the pavement.

My world is broken. I can see no way out. If this is how she reacts to the lies we told to protect her, I can only imagine what'll happen if she finds out the truth: that it was me who killed Celine Cremorne.

62
MARGOT

Margot keeps out of Guy's way while she continues her hunt for the camera, her searches becoming more desperate, more oblique, as the damn thing doesn't appear in any of the places where it should or could be. But she has to be subtle about what she's doing because she doesn't want to alert Guy to the fact that she remembers they had it with them – if he doesn't already know.

Guy goes out for much of Monday, and on Tuesday Margot prepares a chicken casserole for dinner, pointedly making only enough for herself and Flynn. Him admitting out loud that he had an affair with Celine is a blow, but one that pales into insignificance against his other revelation: that Sara thinks Margot killed Celine. It's never crossed her mind that Sara might think she's in this mess because she's protecting *her*. That Sara might blame her for everything.

But now Guy's mentioned it, she scrolls mentally back to a couple of months ago, reimagining things the way Sara might see them: the times Margot put chopped celery in the salad because she knows Celine couldn't stand it; her 'accidental' use of full-sugar tonic in Celine's diet G&Ts; the fact that she bought Sauvignon because Celine only liked Chardonnay –

and the dozens of other tiny things Margot had done to amuse herself during that shit show of a holiday.

Yes, she owns it all – but messing with someone's non-allergic food preferences is hardly akin to killing them. But surely Sara understands that? Does she really see Margot as someone willing and capable of murdering her husband's lover? Does Sara even know that Guy and Celine were lovers back in the day? Was it as obvious to Sara as it had been to her?

Margot wonders what Guy's saying to Sara about all this behind her back. He always insists on going to her house alone, claiming Margot's too busy with work to join him. What's he telling her those times he's alone with her? Is he deliberately pointing a finger at Margot to keep the suspicion off himself? Is he setting her up in case the shit hits the fan? Are they now each out to save only their own skin?

Her thoughts are interrupted as Flynn taps on the studio door. His head pops around.

'Hey, Mum.'

'Hey,' she says. 'Come in.'

He flings himself onto the sofa with the deep sigh of a troubled teen. Margot spins her chair to face him.

'Cup of tea?'

'Just had one ... Mum, look, you don't think it was my fault, do you?'

His face crumples and Margot takes him in her arms and hugs him like she used to when he was little. She kisses his hair and pulls it back from his eyes.

'Look at me, baby. No, I don't. I've been going over it in my head and I'm absolutely sure that the fall was nothing. You were fine and so was she. Your dad was just being ... your dad. He was lashing out when he said that.'

Flynn squeezes Margot tighter and bends a little so he can rest his chin on her shoulder. 'Thanks.'

When he pulls away, he says, 'So, umm, you know what Dad said about you ... um ... you know, doing it? I just want to say that I don't believe him and I'm sorry for what I said at Sara's that night. There's no way you would do that, even if ...' He waves his hand unable to give voice to his dad's infidelity and Margot is filled with resentment. This is all Guy's fault. Her son should not be having to acknowledge that affair. Margot's angry – about the affair; angry about the admission that came years too late; and even angrier that Guy dragged Flynn into this mess when she'd sacrificed so much to keep him out of it.

'Thanks, darling. That means a lot. But I'm sorry you had to know. When did you find out?' she asks gently.

'I suppose I was kind of aware at the time that something wasn't right. But it was only in the last year before we left that I truly realised what was going on. But you knew?'

Margot nods wearily. Flynn's old enough to handle the truth, she thinks.

'She wasn't the first, and I'm sure she wasn't the last. Your father, how to put it? He likes the chase. The conquering.' She traces the grain of fabric on her skirt. 'With most of them, though, the novelty wore off quickly. He'd get bored and move on. I don't think he ever thought about leaving me – except maybe for her.' She pauses. 'Please don't be like him.'

'Never! I never want to be like him! Did he know that you knew?'

'I think he wanted me to know – maybe he thought he was

keeping me on my toes. Reminding me that I was lucky to be the one he'd chosen.' She gives Flynn a bitter smile. 'So I used to enjoy making him think I hadn't noticed. The games people play, eh? And look where it got me.'

'Better than where Celine ended up!' Flynn bites his lips to temper a guilty smile, then his face straightens. 'Have you ever wondered if Dad, you know, did it? As in …' He mimes slashing his neck.

Margot frowns.

'I mean, do you ever think about the camping trip?' he says. 'He arranged it all pretty quickly, didn't he? The Jeeps, the tents, all the kit – even a quad bike. Like, within a day, wasn't it? Almost like it was pre-planned.'

Margot remains silent.

'Maybe we were pawns in a much bigger game – a plan to go to Oman, to meet up with Celine. I mean, it was odd that we stayed right there when she was there, wasn't it? And you said she was the only one he might have cared about? Then to take her to the desert and kill her under the guise of a holiday. Wasn't he the one who suggested that Sara needed to see the desert in the first place?'

'Mmm,' Margot nods noncommittally.

'If not that, then it's entirely possible that he went to her tent, they had a row and he somehow killed her. What if she was blackmailing him? What if she wanted him to leave you? She wasn't a good person, Mum, trust me. I told you she was trying it on with me. I'm sure it was to try and make him jealous because he was looking funny at Sara. Oh – shit. Sorry. Had you noticed that?'

Margot sighs. Her son is so perceptive.

'Flynn – I don't know what to think, to be honest. As I said, this kind of speculation will only drive us crazy. When the autopsy results come out, we might know more. It could be something totally innocuous. I don't really want to throw blame around at this point. We're throwing stones here, but we don't even know how she died.'

Flynn crosses his arms. 'Mum. Come on. You've seen his temper. Shall we talk about that, or are you happy to continue skipping around in denial?'

'Flynn, I hardly think ...'

'Because I, for one, am worried.'

Margot opens her mouth to object; to protect Guy as she always does. Keeping up the illusion that everything's perfect. But she can't be bothered.

'I saw him with you the other day,' Flynn says. 'Remember, when he nearly hit you?'

'Flynn—'

'But he had you up against the shelves, Mum! And he threatened to "silence" Liv. I heard him. I saw him do that strangling thing. For your information, that is not normal. It's also not acceptable. And I know this wasn't the first time. I'm not blind, you know. You shouldn't let him get away with it.' He pauses, leaning forwards, his elbows on his knees. 'You know he bullies you, right? And controls you? Do you see that?'

Margot closes her eyes. 'I can deal with it,' she says. 'I'm planning to deal with it. Trust me.'

'Has he ever hurt you? Physically?'

Margot doesn't mean to pause, yet she does, then she realises she's lost the chance to lie, so she remains silent. Her head is suddenly swimming with thoughts. Ideas. A possibility. Flynn swallows and Margot sees his jaw clench.

'What? What is it?'

'You know it's not just you?'

'What?'

'You can't ever tell him I told you this, but do you remember those bruises on my arm? When we got back from Oman?'

The four fingertip-shaped bruises. Flynn's uneasiness when Margot saw them. 'What? What are you saying?'

'That was him. I asked him why Celine joined our holiday. I asked if he was fucking her. Sorry for the word but it's what I said. He grabbed me and shook me. I had matching bruises on the other arm, too. He told me never to talk about her like that again.'

Margot takes Flynn's hand and looks into his eyes. All she sees there is anxiety.

'I'm so sorry, Flynn. Thank you for trusting me with this. I promise I'll make sure he never touches you like that again. I don't know what else to say.'

'What if he killed her?' Flynn said. 'What if he's a murderer? And we're living in the house with him?'

They stare at each other, then the key turns in the front door.

'Did you see the news?' Guy yells from the hallway. He comes crashing up the stairs and shoves open the studio door so hard it rebounds off the door stop. 'They're saying she was strangled!'

63
SARA

Breaking: Celine Cremorne STRANGLED

Authorities in Oman confirmed in a statement today that injuries found on the body of British expatriate Celine Cremorne are consistent with death by strangulation. Detectives have launched a murder hunt and are urging anyone with information to come forward. Police are focusing on leads within the community. Further updates will be provided as the case develops.

I throw my phone down. Of course they'd be able to tell. Even after being buried. After I'd dragged Celine back to her tent and positioned her on the mattress, I'd closed her eyes and used her scarf as best I could to hide the bruising that I realised might come out on her neck. I'd cleaned the sand off her face, but there wasn't anything I could do about the sand she might have inhaled. Thankfully, that morning the Forrests had been too shocked and then too preoccupied to notice anything amiss.

When Margot and I had heaved her to the grave, I'd deliberately taken the head end, making sure the scarf still covered any marks on her neck. Perhaps it had got worse after we'd buried her, too – I really wasn't an expert on the patterns of blood coagulation after death by strangling, and it's not something I dared to look up online. I'm sitting at my dining table thinking all this, not to mention worrying how the news is going to go down with Liv, when Margot calls to invite me over 'urgently' for a chat, which sends me straight into a clammy-handed panic. Has she already figured out that it was me who did it? If she accuses me, will I admit it?

I drive over in contemplative silence, and Flynn lets me in with a nod towards the stairs.

'She's in the studio. Up the stairs, first right.' And so I head on up.

I knock on the door of the room Flynn's specified and stick my head around.

'Yoo-hoo!' I call, trying to lighten the situation. Maybe it would be my last chance to make a joke.

Margot claps a hand to her chest as if she's seen a ghost. 'Oh my God! Sara! Jesus! Did you have to do that?'

She's sitting at the desk on a swivel chair, with an array of fabrics laid out on a large work bench in front of her. To one side stands the frame of an impressive house.

'So this is where the magic happens,' I say to hide my nerves. *Why am I here?* 'It looks amazing! You're very talented.'

'Thanks. It just takes an eye for detail, good eyesight and nimble fingers, that's all. But look. Enough about me. Can I get you a coffee or tea – or a snifter of something stronger?'

I see she has a cut-glass decanter and a half-drunk glass

of something golden on the table. Her bloodshot, puffy eyes make me think it's something strong.

'I'm fine,' I say. 'Is Guy joining us?'

'He's not here,' she says. She gets up and closes the door with a click. 'There's something I want to talk to you about on your own, actually. Sit down.' She points to the sofa, so I take a seat, sitting politely – nervously – on the edge of it and Margot sits on her work chair, facing me. She closes her eyes and takes a juddering deep breath in through her nose then lets it out slowly, her hand on her heart. My own breath is shallow in contrast.

'Okay …' I prompt. My ears are straining for sounds outside the room. Has she called the police? Are they waiting to pounce? I can't see any evidence of wires on Margot but then I suppose they wouldn't be obvious.

'Is your phone off?' I ask, searching for a sign that she's recording the conversation.

'What? Yes.'

'Okay. Sorry. Carry on.'

'So, you saw the autopsy report, right? That she was strangled?'

I nod. 'Awful. So, unless a car full of bandits turned up in the night, it was one of us, I guess.'

My joke falls flat.

'Look, Sara, there's no easy way to say this so I'm just going to dive right in,' Margot says. 'There's something I need to ask you before Guy gets home.'

I hold myself very still. I've no idea how I'm going to react if she asks me straight out if I did it.

'You don't think I did it, do you? she asks. Because—'

'No! God, no. Not at all. Never crossed my mind.' I almost laugh with relief.

'You don't?' She seems surprised.

'No!'

But then I realise that I've made a terrible error. By eliminating Margot, I've just placed the blame on either myself or Guy. And I've seen how ruthless he can be. How he'll put himself above anyone else if push comes to shove. Now that the knives are out, will we continue to stick together, or will he pick himself and throw me – or Margot – under a bus? Is this the moment the gloves come off?

'It's just that, Guy said ... oh, never mind.' Margot flaps her hand. 'Let me ask you another question: which of us do you think is capable of strangling an adult with their bare hands?'

I stare at her. Has she forgotten that Celine was wearing a scarf?

'I have a drunken memory of the night "it" happened ...' Margot's voice is weak, quiet, her lips suddenly trembling with nerves. She takes a swig from her glass and swallows with a wince. 'Obviously we'd all had a lot to drink. I woke up some time in the wee hours. It was still dark ...'

I try to control my breathing and try to look naturally curious, although I can fathom a guess at what she's about to say: she overheard what happened between Celine and me. Or worse: she got up and saw it.

'Do you remember how Flynn said he heard a tent zip go down that night?'

I hold myself very still and nod my acknowledgement.

'Well, I heard it too. The sound of a tent zip lowering,

slowly and cautiously. Like whoever was doing it wanted to be quiet.'

'Okay,' I manage to say on a shuddery outward breath. I'm still not sure where she's going with this. Celine and I both unzipped our tents that night. Is she talking about mine, hers or someone else's?

'But listen,' Margot continues, 'right when we first got back, I asked Guy if he left the tent and he said he didn't. He told me I was wrong and it was probably an insect or something. But then ... when Flynn said he heard it too, Guy suddenly changed his story and said it was him and he went for a wee.' The expression on Margot's face as she looks at me is pitiful. 'Sara, I can't stop wondering. Why did he lie? What if he went out that night for something more than a wee? What if he ...?'

It takes me a moment to realise she isn't talking about me at all. That she's talking about her husband.

'You think Guy's the one who did it?' I rub my chin as I look at her haggard face. The essence of the Margot I know is gone. She's broken, and this is all my fault. I blow air out of my mouth, largely to give myself a moment before speaking. Is this a route I want her going down, or is it my moment to confess my own secret to her? Can I trust her with it?

'Why wouldn't you believe him?' I say in the end. 'If he says he went for a wee, he probably went for a wee. Maybe he just forgot, to begin with. He was pretty drunk, wasn't he?'

The look that flits across her face makes my heart constrict as I remember my own moment with Guy in my house. I lean towards her, my chin resting on my cupped hands which are propped on my knees as I examine her face.

'Margot, what is it? Are you scared of him?'

She closes her eyes and breathes in deeply before sighing the air back out. 'It's just … he likes to be, umm … well, you know Guy.' She gives an uneasy little laugh that I don't return. I feel like I'm only just learning that Guy, the version that Margot lives with, is not the same person as the jovial Guy who'd charmed Liv and me in Oman.

I hesitate. 'You know you can always talk to me, don't you? My house is a safe place if you ever need it.' I hold my hands up, palms facing her. 'No judgement. Any time.'

She gives me a small smile. 'I might need to hold you to that.'

I smile back at her and hope I'm not in jail when, not if, she needs me.

'Listen,' I say. 'Leaving the tent doesn't mean he killed her. It doesn't mean anything. Any of us could have left our tents, to be honest.'

'Is that what you really think?' Her eyes hold mine. 'Do you think I should ask Guy if he did it?' Margot's breath hitches and I realise that she's scared.

My head spins; this conversation is like being on a rollercoaster. If Margot asks Guy, he'll say no. Then she'll know that I did it. I can't let that happen.

'Oh, crikey,' I say. 'I don't know. How do you think he'd take that? Would he …?' I grimace to give the impression I suspect he might turn violent.

She matches my grimace. 'We could do it together?'

No way, I think. Not until hell freezes over am I risking a confrontation with Guy about this. Everything will come out. I know it.

'Look,' I say. 'Think about it this way: would you believe

him if he said he didn't do it? Or would there always be a doubt in your mind?' I pause. 'And if he says that yes, he killed her, what would you do with that knowledge? What would you do then?'

Margot covers her face with her hands then clutches her hands to her jaws as she speaks.

'I don't know! It's impossible. If I told the police, they'd come after all of us. He didn't do it in a bubble. The whole sorry story would come out – how we'd all buried the body and run. Our lives would be over.' She waves at the mansion on her desk. 'All of this, gone. And you'd be dragged into it. We'd all end up in jail.'

I sigh. She's not wrong.

'You know what? I think some things are best left unsaid,' I say. 'He went to the loo; he didn't go to the loo. He got some water. Whatever. Move along. Next please.'

Margot stares at me, her blue eyes two burning holes in the whiteness of her face and, as I hold her gaze, I wish I could see inside her head. Does she really think Guy did it? Or was that conversation a ruse to lull me into a false sense of security while she and Guy work out how to hand me in?

64
MARGOT

Margot hears the scrunch of tyres on gravel and points her eyes to the window to alert Sara to Guy's return. She hopes he burned off some of his negative energy in the gym. The autopsy results hadn't left him a happy man.

'So, how's work?' Margot asks Sara, but she's not capable of listening to whatever it is Sara says in reply. The main thing is that, by the time Guy's head pops around the door, both women are speaking of innocent things.

'Margot? Oh, and Sara! I thought that was your car,' he says. 'Quite the little coven. What's going on?'

Margot looks at Sara but Sara's eyes slide away.

'Oh, I see. Chatting about which of us did it, are we?' Guy says. 'May I join in? My money's on, let's see ... eeny, meeny, miney ...'

'Guy, please,' Margot says.

Guy rubs his hands together theatrically. 'Maybe we should discuss it over a coffee. Will you join us, Sara?'

'I was just going, actually,' she says. 'But thanks!' Sara's across the room like a rat up a palm tree. 'Bye now!' she flings over her shoulder, and Margot hears her feet clatter down the stairs and the front door slam.

Guy looks bemusedly after her. 'So, who do you think's the guilty party?'

Margot remains silent.

'Have you considered it might have been her?'

'She barely knew Celine. And she liked her.'

'So that leaves us.' He folds his arms and stares at Margot. 'You and me.'

'I suppose it does.'

'*Just the two of us*,' Guy sings. 'Romance never dies.'

Margot feels his eyes on her as she shuffles some papers on her desk.

'I know you think I did it,' she says. 'But I didn't.'

'And I know you think I did, but I didn't. So who's lying?'

There's a tense silence, then Guy breaks it.

'Well, I suppose you ought to get on with that mansion on the off-chance that we're not in jail before the delivery date.'

After he's left the room, Margot lets her head drop backwards, drained by the morning's conversations. She'd imagined that Sara would encourage her to ask Guy straight out if he'd done it and she'd hyped herself up to ask him with Sara there as a safeguard should Guy turn violent. She'd pictured the two of them banding together against him, but Sara's response that they should let things lie floored her. Sara *said* that she doesn't think Margot did it, but the fact that she wouldn't agree to asking Guy if he did it indicates that she must have doubts; she must be wondering about Margot. Are the three of them going to be stuck forever in this dance of 'who did it?'

Margot massages the taut ropes of muscle that run up each side of her neck and presses the tender spot where they join her skull behind her ears. She can't do this. Her brain isn't designed for sleuthing. Maybe she should just listen to Sara. Sara's a counsellor who spends her life telling people how to act, and Sara has said that she doesn't think Margot should prod this viper's nest any further.

And maybe she won't. But knowledge is power, and what she suspects after today is that she's married to a man who's not just a liar and a bully but also man who more than likely murdered his lover.

65
SARA

Sitting in traffic as I make my way home from my chat with Margot, I thump the steering wheel in frustration. I don't know what Margot was getting at. Celine was right about one thing: I should never have got involved with the Forrests. I should have stayed in my lane. If Liv and I had got an EasyJet to Munich last December instead of poncing around the Middle East with them, none of this would have happened. None of it.

My mind drifts back to that dreadful morning in the camp. By the time the sun rose, I'd had more than enough time to think about how I was going to deal with the situation. The mess I was in was a galaxy away from pushing a woman down the stairs and pretending it was an accident – and the consequences would be significantly more than a suspended sentence. Celine was dead, I'd done it, and I had a simple choice to make: cover it up or confess.

By dragging the body back into the tent that night and erasing the evidence of a scuffle from the sand in the camp, I'd already begun the process of covering up my crime without even thinking about it. What I hadn't realised was how easy Guy was going to make it for me to continue; and how suspicion wouldn't rest naturally on me because I'd liked her –

and I genuinely had liked her. Right up to those last moments, when – I tell myself – her true colours began to show through. My precious Liv had been right; Celine was a fake friend. The woman I killed was not the saint that the media's been portraying.

The traffic moves forward, and I finally make it past the lights and merge into the lane I need to queue in for the big roundabout. Everything around me looks so normal: the cars, the people wiping condensation from the inside of bus windows, the motorcyclists weaving around the cars. This is my world. This is where I belong. What happened in the desert feels like it happened to somebody else.

That evening in the campsite really had been idyllic. Guy was right to insist we experience the desert at night. I remember the twinkling fairy lights reflecting off the tents, and the delicious aromas wafting off the barbecue. I remember the stars emerging in the canvas of the huge, inky sky; the humming excitement of the teens; and the beat of the '80s tunes Guy played through his Bluetooth speaker. And I wish more than anything that is where it had ended.

After I'd gone to bed, I'd fallen into a drunken sleep but woken later with a dry mouth and a pounding head. I'd tossed and turned for ages listening to the scurries, rattles and clicks of faceless insects before realising I really was going to have to brave going outside the tent to get some water. I undid the zip quietly, trying not to wake Celine, whose tent was next to mine, and crawled out, only to see that she was already up.

I padded over to her, rubbing my hands together. The air was still and very cold. A thousand stars hung in the purple sky above me and the air smelled fresher than any laundry detergent's promise as the sky edged toward the idea of daybreak. From the big tent came the sound of someone's open-mouthed snores.

'What you up to?' I whispered.

In Celine's hand was a beer bottle and it was apparent from the way her body lolled loosely in the canvas chair that she hadn't sobered up at all. Far from it.

'Drowning my sorrows,' she said with a rueful laugh. 'Wanna join me?'

'I need water, actually. Shall I get you one?'

'Nah.'

As I reached across, I saw the glisten of tears on her cheeks.

'Hey, you okay? What happened?' I leaned on the car next to her.

'What we were talking about earlier,' she said as if she hadn't heard me. 'The things you do to protect Liv ... the best thing you can do for her right now is keep her away from the Forrests. Cos I can tell you one thing: that family's fulla shit.'

'They've been perfectly nice to me. I mean, Guy arranged all of this just so Liv and I could experience the desert. I really appreciate that.'

Celine scoffed and took another swig of her beer.

'And Liv really loves Flynn,' I said. 'He's been so good for her. He's really helped her.' A warm glow lit my belly as I thought of how happy Liv had been lately; how settled Flynn had made her feel; how everything was finally coming together. 'Maybe they'll go the distance. And if they do, the Forrests'll be my in-laws, so I need to keep them onside!'

'You don't get it, do you?' Celine said. She hauled herself

unsteadily to her feet and jabbed a finger at me. 'They're toxic. I'm telling you. You need to get Liv away from them or she'll end up like me. Chucked out after the fun's over. Like a used condom. That's all Liv is to her precious Flynn. Like I was to his fucking dad. Yeah, that's right. He dumped me. Tonight. After all this. Arsehole.'

I looked around to check we were outside of earshot of the big tent. We were turned away from it – I hoped our voices wouldn't carry.

'It's none of my business what happened with you and Guy,' I hissed, 'but that's not a fair thing to say about Flynn. He loves Liv. Maybe it's time to have some water and try to get some sleep.'

But Celine carried on. 'She'll never be one of them. You're not rich enough or posh enough. I can't believe you don't see that. I can't believe you're going to let them break your daughter's heart. You, who does anything to protect her! Where's the tiger mum now, Sara? Run away because she wants to hang out with the Forrests?'

'I'm sure Liv can take care of herself,' I said, trying not to let my temper rise.

Celine sneered. 'This from the woman who shoved a teacher down the stairs for making her daughter cry! The Forrests better watch out!'

'What?' Fear lurched in my gut at the thought that she knew my darkest secret.

'Oh, yes! I know all about you breaking that woman's wrist. I know you tried to have it hushed up, but teachers talk. No way that was an accident, and it seems the court agreed. I wonder what the Forrests will think of that when they find out. You're not the kind of person they'd want their son mixed up with. *Persona non grata.* Ha ha ha. You watch how fast he drops her when I tell them.'

'You wouldn't. Celine, please?' I looked at her in disbelief. I knew she was drunk. There was a chance she was ranting and wouldn't remember any of this in the morning. But there was also a chance that she would.

'Why wouldn't I? What have I got to lose? Who are you to me, anyway? You're the one who had an innocent kid removed from a class and shagged a teacher to get your kid into school. You helped your daughter cheat. You're not who you say you are, Sara Says. And I think Margot deserves to know the real you. You're a nasty piece of work, and I bet your daughter's no better!' She lurched towards me and shoved me in the chest.

'Get off!' I pushed Celine back, but she lunged after me again and I shoved her, hard. She staggered backwards, lost her balance and fell onto the sand. I towered over her, fighting the urge to aim a kick at her. My blood thrummed in my ears. If I could obliterate her off the face of the earth, I would.

'Don't you dare tell them,' I hissed.

She tried to stand, staggered again, and fell back down.

'Or what? Fuck off, Sara! I tried to help and you don't want to hear. You do you. I'm going to bed.'

I watched as she crawled unsteadily across the sand towards her tent. She was still wearing the pretty scarf she'd wrapped around her neck when we'd been shivering over the ghost stories. The long ends dragged in the sand. It wouldn't be difficult. She was drunk. I had the height advantage, and she wouldn't see me coming. If I could grab the ends of it, the scarf would give me leverage. Celine would be silenced. Flynn wouldn't leave Liv. Liv would be happy.

When I think about it like that, it really was a no-brainer.

What I need to do now is convince Margot that Guy did it while trusting that Guy thinks Margot did it. If I can engineer that situation, I might just get away with it. I nod to myself as I turn into my road. Liv will calm down; she'll come back. I start to think that things might turn out far better than I could ever have hoped.

And then I see the police car parked outside my house.

66
MARGOT

'Flynn?' Margot can hear her son talking to someone in his bedroom. She knocks and, when there's no reply from inside, pushes the door slowly until her head fits around. 'Flynnie?'

He's at his desk, his back to her, headphones on, on what appears to be a video call – with her dad. That's a new development. She looms into the picture behind Flynn.

'Hello, Dad! What's going on here?'

Flynn spins around, his face for a moment the perfect picture of a kid caught stealing. Then he flicks the call to computer speaker and her dad's voice rings out. Flynn bashes a key to turn down the volume since Guy's in the house.

'Hello, Margot. Very timely! We were just talking about you. How are you?' her dad says.

She snorts. 'Super!' She's being sarcastic, but then she realises her dad might not have heard about the autopsy results, nor connected the case to the one she was telling him about. 'So, er …?'

Her dad sighs. 'Flynn and I have had a lovely chat but, Flynn, maybe you want to speak to your mum alone now? You know what I think and I'm always here if you need me.'

'Okay,' Flynn says.

So goodbyes are said while Margot takes a seat on the end of Flynn's bed and waits to hear what's been going on between her father and her son.

'So?' she says, when Flynn finally faces her.

'So,' he says, and grimaces. 'Sorry. I needed to talk to someone.'

'You know you can always talk to me, don't you?'

'But I did,' Flynn says. 'And nothing's changed. Except we now know that one of you killed her! Mum! The autopsy results? She was strangled! How much longer are you going to ignore the fact that we're living with a man capable of murder? What's it going to take?'

'We don't know he did it,' she says.

Flynn scoffs. 'Who else? You? Sara? Get real!'

Margot looks at the duvet. He has a point, and she wants nothing more than to get away from Guy but she can't see how. The autopsy results have only made it more difficult.

'Gramps says you should leave him. We'll get a place together, the three of us.'

'It's not that simple.'

'Isn't it?'

'If I leave your father, there will be consequences. Financial, lifestyle, the business. Everything. He'll make it as difficult as possible for me.'

'But you make the houses. You don't need him for that. Do you? And we can get a small place. I'll share a room with Gramps if I have to, or sleep on the sofa. I leave school in the summer. I can take a year out, get a job, save for uni.'

'That's sweet of you.' Margot's mind is whirring through the possibility of the three of them living in a small flat. No more Guy. The business her own once more. But then …

'He's a man who doesn't like to lose face, Flynn. You know that. Appearances are everything to him. He would hate for it to come out that I left him. It's what happens to other people, not to us. You know his motto: *all for one and one for all.* He won't like it.'

Flynn shakes his head at her in disbelief. 'Get over it, Mum. Seriously. That is not your problem. It's his. People will admire you for getting out. They never admire the ones who stay with an abuser.'

'Abuser?'

Flynn eyeballs her. 'Gramps said it, not me.'

'He said that?' Shame creeps through Margot's veins. She knew her dad didn't like Guy, but that he thinks she's putting up with an abuser?

'He told me he's already said you should leave. Is that true?'

'Err, not in as many words … but, yes, I suppose he's hinted at it.'

The door bursts open. 'Who's leaving who?' Guy says. 'Is this a conversation I should be in?' He steps into the room and takes in the sight of them both on the bed. 'Oh, look at this. A cosy mother-son chat. How lovely. What did I miss?'

Margot and Flynn remain silent.

'Well,' Guy says, 'if what I just overheard is right, someone's planning on leaving someone. And let me just say, Margot Forrest, if you ever entertain the idea of leaving me, I will be in that police station telling them the sorry tale of how my wife strangled the woman I was in love with.' He glowers at her then at Flynn. 'So I would think very carefully before making any decisions that might separate you from your son for life.'

He slams the door as he leaves, and Margot looks at Flynn. 'See what I mean?'

67
SARA

Before I have time to think, instinct takes over. Fight or flight. I check my mirrors and reverse carefully back out of the street. Then I drive forward again, smartly past the end of my street and, like a machine, to the car park behind Sainsbury's, where I collapse onto the steering wheel with my head in my hands. What would I say to the police? Would they come right out and accuse me? Or would they ask all those clever questions designed to trip me up and confuse me until I make an error? I've watched crime shows. I know how they operate. Will I be able to carry on with the lies, or will they smell the stench of guilt oozing out of me? Will it look worse if I try to cover it up but then break? It's four o'clock; Liv will be on her way to Michael's. Is there a police car waiting there, too? Should I warn her? Should I warn the Forrests?

I get out of the car and walk numbly down the narrow lane towards the shops, passing on my way the usual population – the elderly shuffling along on their daily errands; harassed mothers; kids just out from school, people walking their dogs – people who haven't killed anyone. *I walk among them*, I think. Little do they know how closely they're mingling with a killer. I stand on the street corner and take in the familiar shopfronts – the baker's, the Cancer Research shop with its bright display of dresses pointing optimistically to spring, the Post Office with its piles of stationery supplies and the Co-op with a golden spaniel waiting patiently outside. I wander into the Co-op intending to look in the bakery baskets for a psychological pick-me-up, but my eye's drawn to the display of newspapers.

Who killed this woman? the headline screams, with a headshot of Celine laughing, her long hair blown back by the wind.

The words are nothing more than black ink on white paper, but the pattern they're in is one that threatens to see me incarcerated.

I can't help myself. I pick up the paper and turn to the story. The police are trawling through the social media accounts of those Celine had known, looking for clues as to who she could have been with. In addition to the house calls in Muscat, they're considering that the killer might have been a tourist. They're examining entry and exit records at the airport and talking to travel agents about people who'd booked hotels in Muscat the week Celine went missing. The Oman police are determined to find who did it.

My hands shake so much that the paper trembles. I put it back. I don't need anything more to worry about. The message is clear. The police aren't giving up on this. What will be will be and I have to go home at some point. I head back to the car.

The police might not even be looking for me, I tell myself as I start the engine. It could just be a coincidence. But, as I turn back into my road, the squad car is still there, and I can make out the shape of two officers through the back window. I drive slowly down the road and pull into the vacant space in front of the police car. Then I take a deep breath in, get out of the car, and throw what I hope is a vaguely bemused look in the direction of the police car as I walk up my front path. Hand me that Oscar right now.

They catch me before I've unlocked the door.

'Good afternoon, madam.'

I spin around to find the two officers, one male and one female, standing behind me on the garden path. I smile and try to look surprised.

'Oh, hello. Can I help you?'

'I see that you've just arrived home but, if you can spare us two minutes of your time, we just have a few questions we'd like to ask.'

Now I try to look quizzical. 'Can you say what it's regarding?'

The female officer nods over her shoulder. 'A car was stolen from across the road in the early hours of this morning. We see you have a smart doorbell and we wondered if we can check the footage as it looks like it might have caught something?'

'A stolen car?' I say weakly. 'Across the road? How awful. Yes, yes, come in.'

I usher the police into the hallway where the doorbell monitor sits.

'This is it. Do you know how to use it? Just – I think that button rewinds but I'm not sure as I've had no need to look at it,' I say. I sink onto the stairs and hug my knees while they poke buttons and peer at the screen.

They aren't here for me at all. But I could really make their careers by telling them some different information. My mouth twitches with the absurdity of it. Bubbles of what I know would be hysterical laughter start to gather inside me. I hug my knees tighter and hide my face against them willing my mouth to stay straight.

It takes the police a few minutes to establish that, while my view of the road would have been perfect, my system isn't set to record, only to show in real time who's out there, so there's nothing to see.

'Sorry I couldn't be of more help,' I say as they leave.

68
MARGOT

'Margot!' Guy bellows as he blasts into Margot's studio. It's the first word he's spoken to her since he threatened her over leaving him and she's been walking on eggshells around him ever since.

'We need to talk to Sara,' Guy says. 'I've arranged to meet her on Cleeve Hill in half an hour.'

'Why?' she asks, grateful for once for his ability to compartmentalise his life. It's as if he's told her not to leave him, so she won't. Job done. Move on.

'Margot! Get with the programme! The police have launched a murder hunt! We've told them we were there. The net is closing in. We need to make doubly, triply sure we're all on the same page. Ensure that no one is going to the police. And that we're all on board with what we need to say if the police come knocking. As they very well may.'

It's a bright day and the wind buffets the car as Guy floors it up the single-track road far faster than Margot thinks is safe or necessary. Her grip on her handbag is as tight as the silence between the two of them is tense. Margot wonders what'll happen up on the hill. Might Guy actually confess? When they pull into the car park by the radio masts, there's just one car there and, inside it, Margot can make out Sara's profile. She's staring pensively straight ahead and Margot's heart aches for the pain that her husband's putting this innocent woman through.

Guy cuts the engine and sits with his head bowed and his eyes closed for a moment, then he takes a deep breath.

'Ready?'

'Yep.'

'Okay, let's go.'

They get out and Sara nods hello to them, the strained formality of the greeting many times removed from the familiarity they'd had in the warmth of the Omani sunshine. Even in her leggings, boots and a big, padded jacket, Sara looks thin and grey. Her bony knees protrude from legs thin as sparrows; the hollows of her face are pronounced, her skin tight on the bones; and the weak smile that she offers the Forrests is brittle. She's lost a lot of weight since the holiday and all of their tans have faded. None of them look good in the cold, flat light of the British winter.

'So,' Sara says. 'Here we all are.'

'Indeed,' Guy says grimly. He nods towards the path that leads to the fields beyond. 'Shall we?'

They set off, manoeuvring their way through the gate onto the common, then walking in single file with Guy in front. Margot focuses on the path ahead, not wanting to slip and sprain an ankle, or worse. This is not her natural habitat, not by a long shot. The icy wind bites into her cheeks and wails a ghostly song as it tears through the radio masts.

'Let's not go too far,' she calls, only now wondering if her husband's brought them up here to silence her and Sara once and for all. There's no one around, not even a dog-walker, although hoofprints show that horses sometimes come this way. Perhaps it isn't the smartest idea to be somewhere so isolated with him. Maybe she should have told Flynn where they were going.

They walk in silence a little further until they reach a plateau. Guy stops and they all stand and look at each other. Guy takes out his phone and switches it off. After a moment's pause, Margot and Sara do the same. Guy nods and rubs his hands together. The wind bites through the layers of Margot's clothes, cutting straight to her bones. Not usually much of a smoker, she's suddenly desperate for a cigarette but it's too windy to light one.

'I just wanted to get you here today to warn you that, at any point, we could find ourselves answering difficult questions and I want to make sure that we're all prepared for that. We all saw the news that the police are looking at tourists as well as residents, and I've heard from several people that Adele – remember that woman from school? – has been joyously telling everyone that we were in Oman over Christmas, so it's not something we can hide.' Guy breathes in, his jaw tight. 'I know, right. But anyway, it's no secret that we were in Oman at the time, and we've even told the police here that ourselves – if they bother to pass that on to the Omani police. So I don't think we have anything to worry about but the fact remains that it's possible they might well question us, and I just want to make sure we're all on the same page. That we know what we're going to say when they ask us.'

'I thought they came for me yesterday,' Sara says. 'I came home and there was a police car parked outside my house. I nearly died.'

'What did they want?' Margot says.

Sara's hand's on her chest and her knees wilt like warm spinach as she talks about the relief she felt when she realised they were only there to ask about a stolen car.

'I drove away! But then I realised I had to go back at some point,' Sara says. 'If they want to talk to me, they'll find me, no matter what. Right?'

'Exactly,' Guy says. 'Best to have an answer prepped. So, let's recap. We stayed in a villa in the compound that we – Margot and me – used to live in quite a few years ago. We now know Celine was still living there, but we hadn't been in touch and she wasn't there while we were there. Everyone was away. We never saw her. It's as simple as that. You don't need to say anything else. Just that. Okay? And Sara, you don't even know Celine, okay? You've never met her. So that's easy.'

Sara nods and holds up two sets of crossed fingers, almost blue with cold.

Guy's gaze scans from Sara to Margot. 'Funny to think that one of us did it.'

Margot looks at Sara. She's got to give it a try.

'I was wondering if the person who did it should hand themselves in to the police with a story that doesn't implicate the others,' she says, and a shard of hope glimmers within her at the thought that Guy might actually do this. That would solve all of her problems. 'It might be a way to put an end to all this so the others can get on with their lives.'

Sara looks at the ground, then back up. The wind lashes her hair across her face and she turns her body slightly to let it whip the other way. Her teeth are chattering. She looks utterly haunted.

'It's taking a toll on us all,' Margot adds.

Sara shivers and starts to say something, but the wind snatches her words and Guy interrupts her.

'No!' he says. 'Absolutely not. Out of the question. And, furthermore, I don't think we, ourselves, need to know who did it. Am I right? Us knowing who did it doesn't change a thing. In fact, it makes it harder if we're questioned. Best we don't know. So let's just carry on as before. No one needs to confess to anything to anyone. We just keep going as we are. The police might come sniffing around but we've covered our tracks. They have nothing on us. It'll all blow over. Eventually.'

'We hope,' Margot says.

Guy gives her a sharp look. 'The last thing we want to do is start pointing fingers.' He swivels his gaze from Margot to Sara. 'So, that's it. We're none the wiser and I think it should stay that way. Sorry to have dragged you up here on such a cold day. I thought it would be a nice walk but I swear that fucking wind is from Siberia. Let's go.'

'Wait,' Sara says. She sucks air in through gritted teeth. Her eyes are watery, from the wind that tears at her hair, sending it wild above her head.

'No. Come on! We're done. This is ridiculous. I'm freezing my bollocks off. Let's agree to keep quiet and just say a prayer that whoever did it doesn't turn into a serial killer.' His laugh is hollow. Back at the cars, Guy gives Sara a hug, then beeps the car open. He accelerates away before Margot's sorted her seat belt.

'I think that went well. Don't you?' he says.

'Hmm?' Margot says absently. She's checking her emails. Her courier delivery's finally arrived at the collection point.

69
SARA

The meeting on Cleeve Hill leaves me feeling even more uneasy than I felt after I left Margot's house. The Forrests are up to something, I'm sure of it. I can't get past why Guy, who knows himself that he didn't do it, doesn't want to know if it was me or Margot. And then there's what Margot said. I'm still reeling from her suggestion that the murderer confess to save the others. There are two things to unpack from that. The first is that she's so desperate for this to end that she thinks it's worth taking the risk of implicating all of us if one of us confesses to the police. And the second is that she's willing to sacrifice either Guy or me to a life in jail in order to bring an end to the situation. I think about that again: either she knows it was me, or she's potentially willing to lose her husband to a life sentence. So which is it?

Does she actually think that Guy did it? Celine's words come back to me again in a way that makes me queasy. If Celine was right, the Forrests don't like me. I'll never be one of them, she said. So why would they have any loyalty to me? Maybe Margot was bluffing that day at her house; trying to lead me to believe she thought it was Guy.

I sigh as I go over it all again in my head. She'd seemed

scared to ask Guy if he did it. I didn't think that was an act. But what if it was? What if the two of them had discussed it rationally and honestly and had realised that I was the one who killed Celine? That little chat in her studio had been designed to keep me feeling safe while they decide whether or not to hand me in themselves.

Technically, they could do that and come out of this smelling of fresh air if not roses – and that must be a tempting thought. Margot, I saw today, is desperate for this to end. But, if they were to hand me in, would it be better for me if I'd already gone to the police myself, voluntarily? I could make up a story about it being a drunken accident. Celine somehow got her scarf caught on something and tripped and hung herself by accident. Maybe I saw it and covered it up because I was scared, but I didn't do it. I don't know; something.

It all comes down to Guy. Who is he? The charming, jovial man I saw on the holiday, or the bully that Margot's hinted he might be at home? Is she really scared of him, or is she in cahoots with him? My head sinks into my hands. A counsellor? I'm a disaster. I can't even manage my own life.

The ring of my phone jolts me. It's Michael. I pick up the phone wearily.

'Hey,' he says. 'How are you?'

'Oh, fine,' I lie. 'You?'

He talks for a moment or two then gets to the point. 'Look, I want you to know it's not from my end, but Liv's asked me to let you know that she won't be coming to yours this weekend.'

'Oh. Right.' I mean, I knew she wouldn't, but it still hurts to hear it out loud. Then a more pressing concern. 'Did she, umm, say why?'

Michael sighs. 'Not really. She said something about wanting to work and being able to concentrate better at ours. But I'm not sure. She was very vague and she hasn't been herself the last few days. Really quiet, just in her room. Has anything happened?'

I swallow. 'Nothing I can think of. Maybe problems with Flynn? Or just school pressure? It's a tough year.'

'Hmm. Maybe. Anyway, look, thanks for understanding. Hopefully we'll be back to normal by next week.'

'Yeah. I hope so. I miss her. Give her my love.'

I hang up and then the tears come. My baby doesn't want to see me. If only she knew that everything that's happened has happened because I love her. Meeting the Forrests and going to Oman. My fight with Celine. Us covering up Celine's death – everything was done for Liv yet all I've succeeded in doing is driving her away. She's moved out and she doesn't even want to see me. My efforts to love her, make her happy and protect her have left me in a worse position than before the stupid holiday.

Everything I've been bottling up since the moment I pulled that scarf around Celine's neck and ground her hateful, drunken face into the sand comes out – everything. The pressure, the worry, the anxiety, the nightmares. The ever-shifting sands of the cover-up and the stress of living in a world of murder and subterfuge. It all comes out in one huge, sobbing mess.

And, when I can cry no more, I open a bottle of wine and sit staring mindlessly at the television, balled-up tissues scattered around me as my body calms back down after the maelstrom. I'm not aware of what's on the screen. I mute the sound and I drink and think, and drink and think, while my mind runs in circles.

That meeting on the hill was weird. Something was really off. Maybe I'm paranoid, or maybe it's my suspicious nature but, despite all their talk of sticking together and keeping quiet, I don't think I can trust the Forrests not to hand me in if it gives them a chance to save themselves. If that's the case, my best chance of coming out of this with the least possible damage is if I go to the police with my own story before they get there. I don't want to spend the rest of my life in jail, and neither do I want to abandon Liv, but what choice do I have? It's the best thing I can do for Liv. If I step forward, she'll be free to get on with the rest of her life. Margot will get the end she's craving – and Liv, eventually, might even come to thank me. The more I think about it, the more I realise that I actually have no choice but to go to the police.

Tomorrow, I think.

Tomorrow I will.

70
MARGOT

Home from Cleeve Hill, Margot and Guy go their separate ways. When she hears him start to work through the list of phone calls on his to-do list, she grabs her keys and nips into town to pick up her parcel at the lockers. It's an incongruous place to collect an item, especially one that could prove to be her husband's downfall. Still, she doesn't want Guy to know that she's contacted Di and asked her to look through the camping gear for a camera that may or may not have got tangled up with the other stuff. That may or may not prove that he killed Celine. Guy's no stranger to opening Margot's mail. Heaven forbid he were to open the package with the camera and watch the footage before her.

The package is an encouraging weight, and she smiles to herself as she slips it into her shopping basket and buries it under a loaf of sourdough and the flowers she picked up in Marks. The bag swings on her arm as she hurries back to the car. Thank goodness Di's such an innocent. She'd swallowed the story that they hadn't gone to the desert and she hadn't put two and two together when Margot asked her to look for, 'anything that may have got tangled up with the camping gear in the boot of the car including – maybe? – "Flynn's" camera?'

All Margot had to do was intimate that Guy was furious that Flynn had lost it, and Di was on board and happy to keep the secret. Maybe others notice his temper, too.

Back home, Margot arranges the flowers and tries to get on with her work but her mind's racing. Will there be any footage at all? Was the camera running that night? Did the battery last long enough? What will the footage show? The biggest question of all: what will she do with any information she discovers?

Finally, Guy shouts across the landing that he's going to the gym. Margot hears him clatter down the stairs and then the front door clicks shut. She listens as his feet crunch over the gravel, then the car door slams, the engine rumbles and the gravel scrunches more consistently as he drives away, pausing at the gates. She peers out of the window to check the gates close behind him then springs into action.

She opens the parcel with shaking hands then turns the camera this way and that, confused: it doesn't have a viewing screen. Quickly, she googles how to view the footage on the damn thing. Aware of the fact she has less than two hours – and that's only if Guy stays at the gym for a shower – she researches how to access the content, locates a USB cable and manages to connect the camera to her laptop.

After a false start, she manages to get the file transferred over to her laptop, and gasps as she sees the date is December and the opening image is in darkness. Could it really be?

'Breathe, Margot,' she says. 'Be methodical.'

Her heart skitters like a goat on a mountainside. The answer to everything could be right there. She doesn't even ask herself now if she wants to know. There's absolutely no question of her not looking at the footage. It could be the only way out of her marriage. With a trembling finger, she clicks on the first video and, oh, God, there's the campsite. She'd fixed the camera to a table where it gives a view of the area where they'd eaten and danced, one of the four-wheel drives and the entrance to one of the single tents, which Margot remembers is Celine's.

Eyes peeled, she scrolls through the short clips of video, as the camera's triggered by little scurrying things, with eyes lit up white, in the night-view vision. She realises she's going to have to work more quickly, so she fast forwards in bursts, trying to find something that looks larger. Then there it is, on the screen in front of her, clear as day: Celine emerging from her tent, stumbling about, opening a beer and slumping into a chair. In the next burst of video, a figure crosses the sand and joins her. She watches as the two figures interact and then, with her heart battering her chest, Margot sits back in disbelief.

Well, well, well.

She finally knows who killed Celine Cremorne.

71

SARA

I wake just as determined to go to the police as I was the night before. I've never liked being in a state of indecision. Knowing what to do is always better than not knowing, even if the way forward won't be easy. But I'll explain. Tell them it was an accident. That I panicked and covered it up. Yes, ultimately, I'll probably go to jail, but Michael is a good dad, and, after the initial shock, my sweet Liv will be able to get on with her life without looking over her shoulder. Just living in fear of the police for these miserable weeks has worn me down. I can imagine the relief the others will feel if they're no longer suspects.

I get up slowly and take time to savour my last coffee in my own home. I make myself a breakfast of Greek yoghurt and fresh fruit – things I doubt I'll get in prison – and tidy up the house so it looks presentable for whoever comes in next. Who will that be? Liv? Michael? I flick though the folder I've made with all the house and banking information for Liv, checking I've included everything because I know I'll fret in jail that I've missed out something significant, like the code to the safe or the PIN for my bank cards. Then I place it on the kitchen table where it'll be easy for Liv to find. I clear the fridge of perishables and empty the bins, the task reminding me too horribly of when we'd fled the Muscat villa.

I dress in comfortable clothes, expecting that I'll be in them for quite some time, then I compose a WhatsApp message to send to Margot. She'll be so relieved to be able to put this behind them and finally move on.

> Morning. Shock news: I'm going to the police station to hand myself in. Don't worry. All will be well ☺

The last bit is meant to convey the fact that I'm not going to dump them in it. God, it's difficult talking in riddles. I send the message, shove my phone in my bag and leave the house. It's about a twenty-minute walk to the police station and I value every moment of it, breathing in the fresh air, looking at the trees that line the roads, still in their bleak, twiggy winter state but beautiful all the same. I pay attention to the clack of my boots striking the pavement, the feel of my heart rate rising with the exercise, and the warmth that tingles through my body to my fingers. Is this the last time I'll ever walk along a street in the winter in Britain? What will it be like in a jail in Oman? It's not like inmates post pics on social media: I have nothing to go on.

'You're doing it for Liv,' I say out loud because I can feel myself faltering.

My steps slow as I approach the police station. I stare at the windows of the building as I wait at the lights to cross the busy road. How will the people inside that building take my confession? Will they know what I'm talking about? Will they believe me, or think I'm delusional – looking for my five minutes of fame? What'll happen next? Will I be extradited to Oman immediately? Or not at all? Will there be a trial? Here or in Muscat? I have no idea. The traffic stops, the crossing beeps, and I walk the final few metres towards my fate … and straight into Margot.

72
MARGOT

Margot grabs Sara's arm, spins her smartly away from the police station and marches her towards the back street where she's left her car. The traffic was dense when she left home and she'd thrown the car through all the wiggly streets she knew, abandoned it in a side street and run the last bit to the police station. It was stressful but she's grateful beyond words that Sara chose to walk, and that she was held up at the pedestrian light because, if Sara had gone into the station and spilled her guts, Margot doesn't know what would have happened. Thank God she reached her in time.

'Oww!' Sara tries to yank her arm free. 'What the hell?'

'Go with it, please,' Margot hisses. 'You need to hear what I have to say, then you can make your decision. But I'm not letting you hand yourself in without listening to me first. Okay?'

She frogmarches her to the car in silence then barks, 'Get in.'

'What's going on?' Sara asks. 'I feel like I've been kidnapped.'

'You have been kidnapped,' she says. 'Kidnapped before you could make a huge mistake. Why in God's name do you want to hand yourself in?'

'I'm handing myself in before you and Guy do it for me,' Sara says.

'We …' Margot begins, but Sara holds her hand up to stop her.

'I know you think it was me, and you're partly right. I know what happened, and I can't put us all through this anymore so I think it's best if I just tell the police myself. Don't worry, I'll say it was just me and Celine in the desert. You won't be implicated. I'll tell the police what really happened. It wasn't murder, by the way.'

'And what exactly are you saying did happen?' Margot asks.

'It was an accident! You know how drunk we were? You'd all gone to bed and we stayed up for another drink … the stars were amazing. We were spinning around and looking up at the sky – her scarf got caught up and we were too drunk to notice. I passed out. She must have carried on spinning until … uh, oh, God, when I came to, I realised she'd got wound up in her scarf and I couldn't revive her. I panicked and put her back in the tent. I couldn't deal with it. I felt responsible even though it wasn't my fault. I'm a coward, Margot, and I should have admitted what I knew, but I'm not a murderer. Hopefully they'll be a bit lenient on me if I come forward. I want this to end. We can't live like this, looking over our shoulders all the time. You said it yourself. The police know we were there. It's only a matter of time till they come asking questions. Liv has disowned me. Everyone's living on edge. It's destroying us. If I do this now, everyone can get on with their lives.'

'Very noble,' Margot says. 'But I don't believe for a minute that's what happened, and neither will the police. Her scarf got caught? On what? Pull the other one, Sara. If you tell them that, you'll be spending the rest of your life in jail. You understand that, don't you? You'll never see any of this again.' She indicates the world outside the car. Unfortunately, it's a dank street of terraced houses, parked cars and bare trees that don't look so very enticing in the flat winter light, but Margot hopes Sara can see the vision. 'I refuse to let you do it.'

'I've always taught Liv to do the right thing,' Sara says, and her voice wobbles. Her head tips forward into her hands and Margot realises she's crying. She looks at her, aghast. She hadn't realised she was so close to the edge.

'What if the police come calling? What if they question Liv?' Sara wails. 'She's a kid who went on a holiday – not a fugitive! I don't want her to go through that.' She inhales snot with a gulp. 'I need to do something. I need to put this right for her – and for you. We can't live our lives like this, one step ahead of the law; questions hanging over us the whole time.'

'You want to put this right for me?' Margot asks softly.

'I do. Yes! For you and for Liv and for your family. I bet you wish Guy had never invited me to Oman.'

Margot lets her head slump forward, resting on the steering wheel for a moment. 'No. It was lovely to have you both there. I might not have shown it, at least to begin with, but I was really glad you were there. I'm just sorry that it ended up like this.'

'It's not your fault. Really, it's not.' Sara tries to smile but doesn't quite achieve it. She blows her nose and her hiccups start to slow. A jogger runs towards them and past, his feet slapping the ground. A delivery van shoots past them, unseemly fast, up the narrow road. Sara folds up a clean tissue and puts it in her pocket.

'Well, if that's all, I've a police station to visit.' She moves her hand to the door handle, but Margot leans across and slaps it back down.

'You cannot hand yourself in,' she says. 'I won't let you.'

'Why? Is Guy there doing it for me now? Is that what this is about? Make yourselves look good in return for leniency?'

'Sara! We were never going to hand you in! Why would we?' Margot closes her eyes as her stomach lurches. 'I won't let you step up for this because I know you didn't do it.'

There's a stunned silence in the car, then Sara speaks.

'What? You don't believe me?'

Margot breathes in deeply and lets the air out. She's gripping the steering wheel, her knuckles white. There will be no going back once she says what she's about to say.

'Sara. It's very noble of you to want to get us all off the hook with that cock and bull story, but I know who really killed her. And I don't want you going to jail to protect them.'

Sara whips her head around to stare at Margot. 'What? What do you mean you know who killed her?'

Margot closes her eyes and mouths the word. 'Guy.'

'Guy?'

'If you agree not to go to the police right now, I can explain.'

'You can explain?' Sara's suddenly laughing, her hand over her mouth to try to stifle it, but it's a giggle that gathers pace until it sounds quite out of control.

'Sorry,' she says, when she's regained herself. 'I know there are lots of circumstantial things that could be seen to make him look guilty, but it's a big jump to hang the whole thing on him.'

'Sara. You need to stop this now. Come with me and I'll show you the evidence.'

'Evidence?' Sara echoes like a confused child, her face suddenly serious.

'Yes: evidence,' Margot says. 'And once you've seen that, we can decide what we're going to do with it.' She smiles as she clicks her seat belt into place. It seems the power is finally in her hands.

73
SARA

Well, that silences me. Evidence. What can she possibly have on Guy that doesn't incriminate me? Would it stand up to examination? In a court of law? I have questions I can't voice so I sit with my thoughts as Margot guides the car through the morning traffic towards Charlton Kings. Around us at the traffic lights sit parents coming home from the school run and people driving to work, to the shops or to meet for coffee – all of them going about their normal business with no clue of the tension in the Audi next to them. And, all the while, I'm wondering what proof Margot could have. Is there really a way out of this? A way that the situation can end without me spending my life in jail? Margot seems to think so, and I'm both dying to see whatever it is that she has to show me and, equally, terrified.

When we pull up, Guy's car is not on the driveway.

'He's gone to see a supplier in Bristol,' Margot explains. 'He'll be gone for hours. Come on in.'

I follow her into the house, shedding my coat and shoes at the front door like she does, and through to the kitchen. We face each other across the kitchen island.

'Coffee?' she asks, turning on the chrome café-style machine.

I shrug. I'd been picturing, if I was lucky, an instant coffee in a paper cup at the police station, not a soy milk latte in a multi-million-pound home in Charlton Kings.

'Sure. Thank you. Whatever you're having,' I say, so Margot goes about preparing our drinks while we make small talk about things I don't care for. Finally, she joins me sitting at the island and I cup my hands around the Hermès mug she slides over to me and inhale the welcome aroma of the fresh coffee.

'So,' Margot says. She sighs.

'So, indeed,' I say, waiting for her to spill the beans. 'I was expecting to be in a cell by now.'

Margot gives me a kind smile. 'It would have been so wrong for you to take the blame.'

I look at her, barely able to conceal how baffled I am.

'What a thing to do,' she says. 'I mean, I want this to end as much as you do, but I won't voluntarily put myself in jail over it.' She laughs to herself. 'Look. I don't know how much you know, but I haven't been that happy with Guy in recent years.' She chews the inside of her lip, her beautiful, usually inscrutable face showing the strain.

'I … I did wonder,' I say, glossing over the fact that Guy himself had told me – not that I believed him at the time. 'There were a couple of moments when I suspected that things might not be as good as they looked. But, I mean, from the outside, you look as if you rub along all right?'

'Not these days,' she says. She pulls her sleeve down and my eyes shoot to her wrist. She realises why I'm looking.

'No. Not that. Nothing visible.'

I think about him looming over me in my living room. How intimidated I was.

'Let's just say there's a lot you don't know,' Margot says.

'He's not the easiest person to be with, I imagine.'

'He's *Guy*,' she says. 'Do you know what I mean? He's too much. He's always in my face. Controlling. Bulldozing. Belittling me. Always telling me what to do. He always has to have the last say. And he's always right. He's always goddamned totally right. Even when he's not. I hate the effect it's having on Flynn.'

Memories of Guy taking charge, forcing things to be done his way, insisting that his way is the only way chase each other through my mind's eye, and I nod.

'I liked his swagger to begin with,' Margot says. 'I hadn't known anyone like him. I found it ... compelling. He was the first person I'd met who knew what he wanted and how to pursue it. He was a force of nature. It's a powerful feeling to be pursued by someone like that. It was sexy.' She shrugs and stares into her coffee, her eyes misting over with the memories. 'But now? After twenty plus years of marriage? I've realised he's just a bully.' She gives her head a little shake. 'I'm not a quitter, but I've reached a line in the sand. I want a different life. One where I can make my own decisions without having to go into mental battle. And I want to show Flynn that this is not how a successful man treats a woman. My biggest fear is he'll turn out like Guy.'

'Flynn's lovely! You don't need to worry about that. He's so sweet with Liv.'

'Thank you. I've done my best.' She sighs again. 'I don't know why I'm telling you all this. It's not really relevant. The point is, Guy's finally pushed it too far. He killed someone, and I have proof.'

My face scrunches up. 'What proof?'

'Let me show you. Just be a sec. It's in the safe.' She slides off her stool. 'Can't be too careful,' she throws over her shoulder as she leaves the room.

Wow. Proof in the safe. What could it be? Could it be possible that I hadn't actually killed Celine? Had Guy finished her off? I mean, I'd known deep down that she was dead when I left her in the tent – but I don't have a lot of experience in that department. Maybe I'd been wrong.

I look around me. Sitting in Margot's kitchen with her and potentially planning Guy's downfall feels Shakespearian. All we need is a cauldron, a newt and a strand of Guy's hair. Margot interrupts my thoughts. In her hands is neither a smoking gun nor a newt but a strange-looking chunky camo-coloured device, which she holds up for me to see.

'Ta-da!' she says. 'It's all on here.'

'What?' I ask, as shock jolts through me like electricity. Is that a *camera*?

'Trail camera,' Margot says. 'Night vision. Christmas present from Guy. For him more than me, as is always the way. Completely forgot we had it. It'd got caught up in the camping gear. I had to get Di to courier it over.'

My mouth falls open as what she's going to say starts to dawn on me.

'It was on that night,' Margot says. It has a motion detector, so it videos each time something moves. And guess what it caught, along with a desert fox? It caught my husband fighting with Celine in the wee hours, shoving her into her tent, then coming out half an hour later. How's that for proof?'

I suddenly can't breathe. It had been 4.30 a.m. when I'd left Celine's tent myself. I press my hand to my chest to hide the thumping that must be so obvious, but Margot takes my reaction as relief.

I swallow. 'Did it run till morning?' I manage to say.

'I set it when we went to bed and the batteries ran out soon after Guy left her tent – but I got the main act, didn't I? Here, let's watch. We can see it on my laptop.'

'And what happens when the batteries run out?' I say, my voice barely more than a whisper. 'It just cuts out? Stops working?'

'Yes, but it doesn't matter. I got the important bit,' Margot says. 'Are you all right?' She peers at me.

'Yeah … I'm just …'

'I know! I couldn't believe it either. Talk about getting hoisted with your own petard.'

She brings over her laptop and connects the camera while I try to regulate my breathing. Until I see it with my own eyes …

Margot clicks the mouse. 'Okay, here we go. Come closer.'

74
MARGOT

Sara peers at the screen. Margot selects one of the videos.

'Right, here we go. First the fox, then Celine, then Guy.'

Despite having watched this video several times, she's still transfixed to see the campsite again. There it is in black and white and grey, and it all comes back viscerally. She can feel the warmth of the daytime sun; the softness of the sand underfoot; and the chill that descended once the sun went down. She remembers the cold crispness of the gin and tonic; the lurching fear when Flynn had fallen off the quad bike; the giddiness of having had too much alcohol a bit later; and the sound of the tent zip slowly ticking open, which she now knows she had neither dreamed nor imagined. She really had heard it. And Guy really had said he just went for a wee – nothing about seeing Celine, arguing with her, et cetera et cetera ...

'It's so clear,' Sara says, 'Not grainy at all.'

'It's a good camera. Right ... hang on, we're nearly there. After the fox ...'

As if on cue, a little desert fox trots across the sand, pauses and stares at the camera, its eyes glowing like white orbs, then exits stage left.

'Now,' Margot says, and Sara leans in a little more, her

breathing fast and shallow. The two women watch as Celine's tent opens and she staggers out, grabs her beer and slumps in a chair. Then Guy suddenly appears from the bottom right, looks back at his tent, then creeps across the sand with a finger on his lips.

They watch in silence as he stands next to her while they talk, then suddenly the body language changes. They gesticulate more, then Celine stands up, steadying herself on the back of the chair. Guy takes a step towards her so he looms over her, but she holds her own, trying to draw herself up to her full height and jabbing her finger at him.

'They're fighting,' Margot says. Sara has her hand over her mouth, her eyes huge as she stares at the screen.

'I didn't hear a thing,' she says. 'They must be whisper-shouting.'

In front of them on the screen, Guy grabs Celine's arm but she shakes him off. She starts to walk away but he grabs her again. They struggle and she breaks free and walks back towards her tent, sticking her middle finger up at him. Guy stands with his hands on his hips as if weighing something up, then he leaps after her and shoves her into her tent. He looks quickly around the campsite, then follows her in and the tent zip comes down. The time on the screen says 02.45.

'Oh my God,' Sara says faintly. 'And then what happened? Can you tell?'

'There's a bit where the side of the tent ripples but who knows what they're doing in there. Maybe they argue and he tries to silence her by strangling her. Or maybe he fucked her and then strangled her. Perhaps it was always his plan to do her in. Nothing surprises me about Guy anymore. I guess we'll never know. But look …' she moves on to the next video. 'Now he comes out.'

And so Sara watches while Guy's head pops back out. He looks around, wipes his brow with the back of his hand, then crawls out of the tent and scampers back across towards his tent.

'Did he really not know the camera was on?' Sara asks.

'I set it up while he was out on the quad bike. He was busy trying to impress you all. I don't think he noticed.'

Guy's face looms close then disappears off camera. Margot stops the film.

'So that's it? That's all you have?' Sara says. She's frowning intently at the screen as if staring at it hard enough will show her what happened inside the tent. 'There's absolutely nothing else?'

'It's all I need,' Margot says. 'It's enough.'

'But, after that? It just ends?'

'Nothing happens. There's no more movement and then that's it. Nothing else triggers it. Then the battery ran out. But look at that! All I was hoping for was a sand cat or a jackal!' Margot chuckles. 'Who would have thought I'd catch my husband? Not even cheating – but killing someone!'

'So what now?' Sara asks. Her voice is faint. She looks as if she's seen a ghost.

'Look, I know it's a lot to take in. It took me a while to process it myself and I've been agonising about what to do with it. I wasn't going to tell anyone about it but then you came up with this crazy idea to hand yourself in! What were you thinking?'

Sara just shakes her head.

‘Obviously I can’t let you do that, not knowing what I do. But the question is: shall we hand over the memory card, or not?’

Sara sighs deeply, then she looks at me with a strange look on her face.

‘Margot,’ she says, and it sounds as if she’s got the weight of a thousand years on her shoulders. ‘Tell me this honestly. Do you *want* your husband to go to jail?’

75
SARA

Margot's eyes continue to hold mine as we stare at each other.

'I mean, you could just divorce him like a normal person,' I say. I have to give her the chance, but every ounce of my body is urging her to say yes, she wants him to go to jail. I cannot believe she's found this video. This is my chance; my salvation. I could actually be off the hook. Thank God I'm sitting down, because my legs really are shaking and I can feel sweat beading at my hairline. I try to keep my breathing as normal as I can.

'I know he's my husband,' Margot says, 'but Guy has a terrifying and dangerous temper, and I think he should pay for what he did. It's only a matter of time until the police come asking questions. I don't want Flynn and Liv questioned any more than you do, and I also think that Celine's parents deserve answers ... which I have. As a parent on both counts, handing over the footage is the right thing to do.'

'I agree,' I say, frowning as if I'm weighing up the issue, but actually now that Margot's dangled the carrot of escape in front of me, I will do anything to pin it on Guy instead of me. 'But how can we hand this in without incriminating all of us?'

I ask. 'The police will want to know why we never admitted that we were camping with Celine.'

'We could send it anonymously …' Margot says. She's obviously thought a lot about it.

'To the parents? Or the police?'

'To the parents.' She bites her lip. 'That might be better, actually.'

I roll the idea through the mental processing unit. An anonymous memory card lands on the parents' doormat. They pop it into the computer, watch it, realise that they can see someone arguing with their daughter then shoving her into a tent in the middle of the night, in the desert where her body was found. They take it to the police.

'It's got the date on it, hasn't it?'

Margot nods.

'And you can see Guy's face clearly enough?'

'We could send his name along with the memory card, just in case.' Margot pulls a face then laughs. 'It really sounds like I want to shop him in, doesn't it?'

'No,' I say, because I don't want to look too keen, but she's right: it really does.

'I keep reminding myself that he did this! Not only did he do it, but he dragged us all into it. Which is downright selfish and cowardly.' Ouch. 'And, if I don't shop him in, we're all going to be pulled into it, which is wrong and unfair. He did it! He was sleeping with that … that woman and then he killed her!' Margot sits back, shaking her head, her voice having reached a crescendo of outrage.

'So, you send the card in anonymously, the police will come to talk to Guy, and we'll deny any knowledge. We were all together at the villa that night, but Guy went out to meet an old friend or an ex-colleague. That's all we know. We haven't told the police because we never saw Celine. We're just like every other person who was in Muscat at that time who didn't see Celine. After that, just block, block, block.' I speak slowly as the thoughts come to me. 'I suppose it's easy to find out that Guy was planning to go camping – those friends he borrowed the gear from will confirm that. Tom and Di? But ... he was alone when he asked them for the gear, so they don't know for sure who he was going with. And we didn't know at that point that he'd borrowed any equipment. Are you with me?'

'Yes. And the video only shows Celine's tent,' Margot adds. 'No one knew Celine was with us. Not a soul.'

I replay the tape in my head. She's right. With the positioning of the camera, you can only see Celine's tent and the one four-wheel drive that Guy had rented himself.

'He rented two cars, though? Wasn't one in your name?'

'It was. I can say I used it to get around Muscat? Gave you guys a little tour? I mean ... why not? I'm not confident enough to drive in the desert ...'

I nod slowly as I start to see how the pieces could potentially fall into place.

'Okay,' I say slowly, as my mind works furiously overtime. It seems to make sense, but is the plan fool proof? I rub my chin.

'It'll be our word against his, and all we say to the police is that we stayed in that compound where Celine lived, but that we didn't see her,' Margot says. 'I mean, the fact that he booked the compound where she lives really makes him look guilty. And then, on the night Celine dies, he said he had to meet someone and went off on his own.'

'With borrowed camping gear from Tom and Diane.'

'Which we didn't know about.'

'They might contradict that. I bet he told them we were going together.'

Margot speaks firmly like a schoolteacher. 'He may well have done. But Sara, he's an adulterous murderer. It'll be obvious to the police that he was lying to cover his tracks.'

I nod as I bite my lip. It really isn't looking good for Guy.

76
SARA

Margot and I leave it that we'll each try to work out any potential pitfalls in our story and, as she drives me home through the lunchtime traffic, we exchange the odd silent sideways look. Collaborative. Disbelieving. Thelma and Louise. The decision appears to be made. It's just a matter of firming up the details. My belly flutters with nervous energy that isn't necessarily the good kind. Have I really got a chance to end this us without me going to jail?

As I slide the key into the front door and step into the home that, just a few hours earlier, I believed I was vacating forever, I feel like I'm trespassing. The house looks like it does when I get back from a holiday – all neat and ordered – the only difference being that the smell of my morning coffee still lingers in the air. I pad upstairs and change into the soft loungewear I thought I'd never wear again, then I put the 'house' folder I made for Liv away with my other files. That done, I sit down to think, and I realise that there's something troubling me.

Margot seems hellbent on handing Guy in to the police – and there's nothing I want more than to be able to put this behind me and get on with my life – but Guy's innocent. I'm the only person who knows that – the only person at this point who could truly advocate for him. And, apart from that one time he lost his temper with me, he's always been lovely to Liv and me. He may not be the perfect husband, and I'm in no doubt that Margot has her reasons for wanting to get away from him, but can I live with knowing that I've sent an innocent man to jail? I've done some appalling things in my life, but do I have it in me to let this happen to Guy?

I bite my lip as I mull it over. Me or him. Him or me.

But then I realise it's actually about me and Liv.

If Margot and I can 'prove' that Guy did it and hence enable the kids to get on with their lives, Liv will surely start to forgive me. I'd have a lifetime to make it up to her. We'd get things back on track, I know we would. In many ways, I admire Liv's strong moral code; the stance she takes on things she feels are wrong. But, as I sit there mulling it all over, I begin to understand one thing: she didn't get that from me.

Margot phones just as I finish my lunch. Beans on toast as I have nothing else in the house.

'Did you have any more thoughts?' she asks. 'I've gone over it from every angle and I think it's definitely what we need to do if we're to get the police off our backs. Agreed?'

'Agreed,' I say. 'But look. We do need to be absolutely sure this is watertight otherwise we'll end up in even deeper trouble.'

'Okay. Tell me.'

'The video doesn't prove that Guy killed her,' I say. 'It just shows him going into the tent. The police could argue with that? Say that, umm, someone else went in later?'

'Sara! You saw the video! He argued with her, shoved her

into the tent and climbed in after her. It was the night she was strangled in that very tent! Come on! Wake up! We need to face the truth. Guy is not the man you think he is.' Her voice drops. 'You want the truth about the golden boy, Sara? My husband is a philanderer, a narcissist and a bully who left bruises on Flynn's skin. He and I no longer feel safe in the same house as him. Is that enough for you?'

Absolutely.

'Or do you need me to tell you about the night he raped me?' she continues. 'Before the fundraiser. I decided not to resist. But, when the chips are down, Sara, my consent was not there, and he knew it. If that's not rape ...'

'Margot. I ... I'm so sorry. I had no idea.'

'Why would you know?' Margot says. 'I said nothing. I don't believe in airing our dirty laundry. As it is, I've been preparing to divorce him. I've been speaking to a solicitor and getting my affairs in order before I tell him because I know that once I do, he'll fight very, very dirty. He's a man who doesn't like to lose. Anything.'

'Margot.' I try to convey a hug with the word.

'But now I have something better. The man deserves to pay. And the sooner we get on with it the better. I don't want to spend another day under the same roof as that man so we need to tell the kids. I was actually calling to say I'd like to pick up Liv with Flynn from school this afternoon, then come to yours so we can break it to them together. What do you think? Shall we do it today?'

'I'm in,' I say.

77
MARGOT

Margot tells the kids as little as possible in the car on the way to Sara's – just that she and Sara have something to talk to them about. Liv starts to kick off about not wanting to go to her mum's but Margot cuts her off.

'This isn't about you, Olivia,' she says. 'Can you please just grow up?'

The car journey after that is quiet and Margot doesn't bother trying to engage them in chat about school. Sara gives them a guarded smile as she opens the front door.

'Come in, come in,' Sara says. 'I'm just making tea.'

She tries to give Liv a hug, which Liv shies away from, then exchanges a grim smile with Margot and shows everyone into the living room. They take their seats while Sara goes off to get a tray with the tea things. Margot tuts to herself. It's not a social occasion; they just need to get this ball rolling. Still, Sara sets about serving everyone a cup like she's the hostess with the mostest while Margot wonders if she's the first person in the world to tell their child that their father is a murderer over a cup of Earl Grey tea.

'So what's this about?' Liv says when they're all seated. 'You know I didn't want to come, but she made me.'

Sara opens her mouth to speak, but Margot answers first. Her husband. Her story. She's telling it.

'It's to do with what happened in Oman,' she says. 'Some evidence has come to light.'

Liv gasps and her head swings from Margot to Sara to Flynn and back.

'Do you know who did it?' Flynn says.

Margot nods. 'I do.'

'Well then? Was it Dad?' Flynn's on the edge of his seat, his leg jiggling with nervous energy.

Suddenly heat flushes through Margot making her wipe her brow with a hand that comes away damp. She blows air out like she's been exercising and ploughs on before Sara can say anything.

'Do you remember the night-vision camera your dad bought at Christmas?'

'The one that was supposed to be for you but was really for him?' Flynn asks. Then his eyes widen as he realises the implication. 'Wait. Was it there? You mean ... fuuuck! Was it on?'

Margot nods, ignoring the profanity.

'And what's on it? Can you see what happened?' Flynn leans forward.

'No, you can't see exactly what happened. But what you can see is that your father argued with Celine outside the tents, then shoved her into hers and went in after her at 2.45 a.m. and came out half an hour later ... which, of course, doesn't "prove" anything ... but also does ...'

Liv's hand is over her mouth; her eyes glued to Flynn.

'So, he did it?' Flynn asks.

'No one else went into her tent and she didn't come out alive.'

Flynn flings himself back in his seat. 'Why didn't you tell us this earlier? Why only now?'

'I actually forgot about the camera,' Margot says. 'And when I remembered, I couldn't find it. I searched everywhere. You have no idea. I thought your dad had hidden it.' She shakes her head. 'But then I emailed Di and she found it with the camping gear.'

'Did she watch it?'

'No. She wasn't suspicious. You know Di. Anyway, then, when I found it, I looked at the footage, and it's all there.'

Liv's face is white.

'Drink some tea,' Sara says to her. 'You're in shock.'

Tears well in her eyes. 'I can't believe it. I can't believe any of it. Guy wouldn't do that. Flynn …?' She turns to her boyfriend, her mouth working but no words coming out. But Flynn shakes his head.

'I can. I knew it. I always knew it,' Flynn says. 'So, what are we going to do? Are you going to tell the police? Or what?'

'Well,' Margot says. 'I think we have to. I know your father thinks this will all blow over but, in my opinion, it's only a matter of time before they come after us all, and a way to stop that happening is to tell the truth.'

'But what'll happen to him?' Liv asks.

'He'll be questioned and charged for what he did.'

'Will he go to jail?'

Margot nods. 'If he's found guilty.'

'Which he will be,' Flynn says.

'But I need for everyone to be in agreement with this if

we're going to do it. If any one of you doesn't agree, speak up now.'

'I agree we should go forward,' Flynn says. 'It's so stressful wondering when the police are coming for us. I'm a nervous wreck, Mum. Every time the gates open or the phone rings.'

'I know, babe. I'm the same,' Liv says. 'I'll go with what you think. It's your dad.'

'Sara?' Margot asks.

She bobs her head. 'Yes.'

'Okay, agreed,' Margot says.

'But how can you hand in the memory card without all of us being in trouble?' Flynn asks, and so Margot explains how she plans to send the memory card anonymously to Celine's parents but, before she gets to the end, Flynn stops her.

'No,' he says. 'Not like that. Don't do it anonymously.'

'What? Surely if I just send it to the parents with Guy's name, we'll all stay out of it.'

'That doesn't work,' Flynn says. 'Think about it. Who would have sent the memory card to the police? If Dad was there alone and set up the camera himself, he'd hardly send it to the police, would he? Someone else would have sent it, and that someone else is pretty much only you.'

Margot stares at Flynn, astounded, because he's totally right.

'They'll know you were involved,' he continues. 'Either you were there yourself, or you found the memory card and sent it in. It's far better that you own it. Hand it in to the police yourself. Say Guy went out for the night and left us in the villa – where, by the way, we had never seen Celine – and you only found the camera and memory card just now. You watched it and pieced together that he'd lied to you to meet Celine and go camping with her. You admit that he's had an affair with her. You're horrified that your husband had taken up with her but it makes sense that he went into the desert with her when you thought he was in town meeting an old friend.'

'Okay,' Margot says, frowning as she follows Flynn's logic. 'I could say that it's Guy's camera – he bought it, after all, if they check. And that he went into town for a night – said he was meeting a friend or something. Some sort of cover story a man would give if he was taking his lover to the desert for the night. What do you all think?'

'It's the best plan, Mum,' Flynn says.

'I'd believe you,' Liv says, and everyone looks at Sara.

'Sheesh. Hiding in plain sight,' she says, shaking her head. 'Isn't that always the best policy?'

'Okay,' Margot says, 'so we just need to agree to stick to that story ourselves. As far as we're concerned, we never saw Celine the entire time we were in Oman. We slept in the villa every single night. Guy stayed out for one night. We thought nothing of it. I only just found the camera. It'll be our word against his, and all the evidence they need is right there on the screen. Done. And maybe this whole thing will finally be over.'

'Amen to that,' Sara says.

78

SARA

Margot goes to the police station that very afternoon. The kids and I stay at mine, expecting a long evening while we wait. I call Michael to tell him that Liv is revising and might stay the night, and he accepts it without question. That seems odd to me, and I have to remind myself that he doesn't know a fraction of what's really been going on.

It's really not that much later that we're scrolling through Deliveroo, debating Five Guys versus tacos for dinner when the doorbell rings. Seeing Margot's distinctive shape through the glass, I rip the door open and throw my arms around her, suddenly overtaken with the most unexpected emotion. I'm also wondering why it's so quiet. I'm half-expecting sirens, handcuffs, news helicopters overhead and Guy arrested on the spot. But, of course in real life, things just aren't like that.

'How was it? How are you?' I stammer, realising that Margot is as surprised by my hug as I am myself. But she's precious to me now, and I'm glad to be able to express that properly for once. Margot gives me a squeeze and I get a grip of myself and bring her through to the living room, surreptitiously wiping my eyes.

'Mum!' Flynn's on his feet and in her arms as they rock

together and she kisses his hair, then he pulls Liv, who's been dithering about, half sitting, half standing, into the hug. Then Liv looks sheepishly at me and extends her arm, welcoming me into the group and we all four stand there for a what seems like ages, hugging each other with tears running down our faces, even though we still don't know what happened at the police station. I break the hug first – I really, really need to know – but keep my arm around Liv. Now I've got her, I'm never letting her go.

'So, what happened? What did they say? Tell us everything.' I'm imagining the gratitude of the officers having evidence handed to them on a plate; their eyes gleaming as they picture the recognition they'll get for solving an international murder case.

'Are they going to arrest Dad?' Flynn says.

'I didn't hand it in.' I can't tell if Margot's laughing or crying. She fishes in her handbag. 'I've still got it!'

My body sags onto the sofa. '*What?*'

'I went in and, look, it's just a local police station. I didn't want to hand it to just anyone and risk it being lost in the system. I realised that we need to get it to the people actually working on the case. Right? Wasn't there a number you had to contact if you had information? Maybe we should do that. So I brought it back!'

We all look at each other. Now we've come this far, we want a solution. As quickly as possible. We're all psyched up for it. Waiting is torture.

'There was a phone line for the incident room,' I say. 'We could call that and say we've got a strong lead. But, in the meantime, Margot, you're going to have to go back home and continue living with Guy. How do you feel about that?' Flynn and Margot glance uneasily at each other.

'You could stay here,' Margot says to Flynn. 'I'm sure Sara won't mind, given the circumstances.'

'Of course. You're always welcome. You know that.'

But Flynn is shaking his head. 'No way. I'm not leaving you, Mum. If you're at home, I'm there, too. He's killed someone! I can't leave you alone with him.'

Margot's face is grim. She clearly doesn't want to be there either.

'Could you … invent an urgent work trip or something?' I say, speaking my thoughts out loud. 'A supplier problem with a mansion or something? That needs you there to sort it out?'

Margot nods. 'Maybe. And then what? Just stay in a hotel …?'

'I guess. I'd invite you to stay here but … I mean, I could sleep on the sofa and you could have my room.'

Margot throws me a quick smile. 'Thanks. It'll look more convincing if I'm in a hotel near to where one of the suppliers are, for sure. Rather than staying down the road with my friend. Or maybe it could be a new client. Yes! There could be a prestigious client who's reached out to me in confidence and wants a personal visit, like, *now*. You know how clients can be like that. And it's too far to go in a day.'

I nod. 'Sounds like a plan. So what are we going to do with the memory card?'

'We save a copy of it. And we hang on to it,' Flynn says. 'We can't give it to anyone until we know it's in the right hands. Like Mum says, we can't risk it getting lost.'

Liv shudders. 'I can't believe this is our life. That we're

sitting here in Mum's living room discussing how to get your dad taken down for murder.'

'I can't believe my dad murdered someone. Someone we know!' Flynn says, and they stare at each other, aghast.

Margot's just shaking her head slowly, looking baffled. 'Right, Sara, would you mind having a look for a place for me to stay in, umm, say, Oxfordshire? I don't have the mental space to deal with hotel bookings right now.'

'Sure. Buy do you actually have to go that far?' I say, 'I mean, you could *say* you were there but actually be much closer ... he's not going to check, is he?'

'I guess not ... in that case, somewhere reasonably close but not too close? Just somewhere simple.'

'Do you need to pack?'

'I suppose I need to go home and pack a few bits, yes.'

'I'm coming with you!' Flynn says.

'Okay. Here's the plan. You two do that first. Before we do anything else. I'll book you a room. Then, once you're both safe, Margot, we'll call the incident room.'

'Okay.' Everyone nods.

Sara the sensible one. Sara the rescuer. You couldn't make it up.

79
SARA

I book Margot into the Holiday Inn in Gloucester. It's close enough for her to be reachable, but far enough away that she's unlikely to bump into Guy. I also save on my laptop a copy of the video, which Margot decided to leave with me 'just in case'. Then I look up the number for the incident room. Detective Sergeant Margaret Ward is the name given.

'Great,' I say. 'So now it's just a matter of waiting for Margot and Flynn to get back.'

Liv orders dinner for us, though I doubt either of us taste any of it. After we've eaten, she gets up and looks out of the window. Then she starts pacing the room and chewing the skin around her fingers in a way that makes me nervous. I gather up the detritus of the Five Guys meal and pack it into the largest paper bag.

'I hope they're all right,' Liv says. 'They'll have to be so careful. They mustn't give anything away or he might …' She shudders.

'He's not going to do anything to them,' I say.

'But if he finds out that they know, and they're planning to hand him in, he'll be desperate. He might do anything. I mean, he's a ruthless person. We know that now. But I'm so shocked,

Mum. Before Oman, I used to think Flynn was so lucky to have him for a dad. He was more like a mate than a father. In a good way. I can't believe it.'

'Well, as you go through life, you'll learn that people will surprise you. You think you know them, then they reveal a whole new side of themselves.' I stop. I have more important things to talk about with Liv than Guy's personality. 'Livvie,' I say. 'While it's just us, I want to say I'm so sorry that you and Flynn had to go through this.' Oh, God, the guttural sound Celine had made as I'd pulled that scarf tight around her carotid arteries. 'All I ever wanted was to protect you. I want you to know that. That was only ever my intention. And always will be.'

Liv stops pacing and looks at me. 'And I'm sorry. I get that. I realise that he manipulated you. You had no choice. Flynn made me see that. I'm sorry for what I said.' Her mouth wobbles. 'Really sorry.'

'It's okay, Livvie. I'm always here for you. Okay?'

'Thanks,' she says. 'Can I have a hug?'

We lapse into silence after our hug. Liv continues pacing. I refresh my WhatsApp constantly, checking to see when Margot was last online, as if that'll tell me anything other than that she's still alive.

'Do you think he'd take them hostage?' Liv asks.

'You mean if he finds out about the memory card? He doesn't even know the camera was there.'

'What if he remembers?'

'Let's think positive. Margot and Flynn are popping home to pick up their stuff. Flynn's coming to stay with us, and Margot's got a meeting with a potential new client who may or may not be royal. Guy'll probably be glad to have a night to himself ... we're overthinking this because we know what's at stake. But you've got to remember that Guy knows none of this. For Guy it's just a normal Tuesday.'

It's well over two hours before we hear from Margot again.

On our way, her message says, and Liv and I both slump back with relief.

'How was it?' I ask as soon as I open the door.

'Oh my God. Farcical,' Margot says. 'Flynn and I deserve Oscars. I actually cooked him dinner and we all sat at the table. I barely ate a thing, but he didn't seem to notice.'

I nod appreciatively, although the word 'seem' sticks in my gut. Could Guy be playing a game here, too? If I'm not careful, I could really spiral. I'm so far out of my comfort zone my brain feels fried but I can't let on, not with everyone depending on me to be the guiding hand on the tiller of logic and reason.

'Nice,' I say calmly. 'Nice touch. So, he doesn't suspect anything's up?'

'He doesn't suspect a thing. He's actually pleased about the new client lead. He's in front of the TV with a bottle of red wine.'

'Amazing. Right – you're welcome to stay as long as you like. If you want to make the call from here?'

'Let's do it together,' Margot says. 'Then I'll go to the hotel. Because if, for any reason, he comes here, my car can't be parked outside yours.'

'Well, we've got the number of the incident room, so ...' I bite my lip as I look at Margot. 'Shall we? Are you ready? Everyone ready?'

'Hang on. I can't call them from here,' Margot says. 'They'll be able to see my location, won't they? I should do it from the hotel, shouldn't I? Otherwise, they'll come here, and you'll all be implicated.'

I frown. 'But wouldn't you have told us? Because we were with you in Muscat. We're a part of the story. We're witnesses that you were home in the villa that night ... We can be with you, I think? And it isn't such a stretch that you'd have come running to a friend if you'd found this out,' I say. 'Maybe Liv and Flynn should go upstairs, but I'll sit here with you if you want me to.'

'Okay,' Margot says rather breathlessly. She fans her face with her hand and tries to calm her breathing. 'I can't believe I'm about to do this.'

'He deserves it,' Flynn says. 'You can't let him get away with it.'

And so Margot dials the incident room. The call handler answers the phone sounding, according to Margot, tired and fed-up, but snaps to attention the moment Margot blurts out her story. She then waits while she's transferred to DS Margaret Ward herself, and I follow the conversation through Margot's nods and affirmations.

Margot hangs up the call. 'She's coming here. Now.'

'What?'

'The Detective Sergeant – Margaret – she's coming to collect the memory card and take a statement from me. Oh my God, Sara – this is it. I've done it.'

I get up to hug her and she clings to me. I don't know who's shaking the most, me or her.

It takes about an hour for DS Ward and another detective

to drive up from Oxford. They take accounts from Margot, me, Flynn and Liv, view the video, and take it away. Early in the morning, Guy – vehemently protesting his innocence – is taken into custody. Within twenty-four hours he's charged with the murder of Celine Cremorne and imprisoned pending trial.

It's finally over.

EPILOGUE

When Margot arrives at The Ivy, the hostess tells her that her companion's already arrived and leads her to the table where Sara's waiting. Sara stands when she sees Margot and the two women hug before taking their seats.

'What a lovely place,' Sara says. 'I've walked past it so many times but never actually been inside.'

'In a previous life, it used to be the original spa of Cheltenham Spa,' Margot says. 'The rotunda was added later, I believe.'

'Then how fitting that we're here. I feel like I have a previous life, too – and I've certainly added some rotunda! It must be the relief! All that weight I lost has come straight back on.' Sara pats her belly and chuckles. 'So that's it? He's gone?'

'Yep,' Margot says. 'He flew out last night.'

Guy's extradition has been a long and gruelling process. At times, Margot would find herself waking up in a cold sweat, having dreamt that he'd somehow wormed his way out of the penal system and was free. That he had come home and was back in her house, ready to punish her for handing him in. But it hasn't happened. All the evidence, including his DNA that was found on and inside Celine's body, points to him. There's no alternative scenario to consider. He's really gone.

'Shall we start with a glass of champagne?' Margot says.

'Absolutely,' Sara says. 'It's such a relief, isn't it? To be able to draw a line under it all. I still can't believe it. Even now it's signed and sealed, I can't actually believe that Guy's going to jail for murder.'

'Well, you know what they say: if you can't do the time, don't do the crime.'

'I guess!' Sara smiles brightly. 'Anyway, how's your dad?'

'He's doing really well, thanks. It's good for him to feel useful, and it's great for me having him around since Flynn left for uni.'

'I'm so glad it worked out,' Sara says with a smile.

The champagne arrives, and they clink glasses before talking more about their children. Liv and Flynn are at different universities and are no longer together. They'd been very level-headed about not wanting to be tied down when they began university, and neither mum had tried to persuade them otherwise. The most interesting thing to come out of that relationship, though, is that Margot and Sara no longer need their children as a tie. Their friendship has developed from morning coffees to weekly lunches in bougie restaurants around town. It might seem an odd match from the outside, but Margot likes Sara. Likes her sharp edges and the rawness of her. Her mother's instinct. Sara's turning out to be the best and closest friend Margot's ever had and, with Guy safely behind bars, she thinks it might finally be the right time for her to make her own confession.

'I still can't believe how it all turned out,' Sara says as

they enjoy a bottle of Sancerre with their salmon. 'Imagine you hadn't remembered about the camera. Imagine you hadn't thought to email Di. Or Di hadn't found it.' She shakes her head. 'We'd all still be suspecting each other. Wasn't that an awful time? It's so good you found clear evidence of what actually happened.'

'I know! Imagine you'd handed yourself in that day,' Margot says. 'You'd be the one extradited and facing life in jail, not Guy.'

Sara gives an exaggerated shudder. 'And now everything's worked out. Liv and I have become close again. That's all I ever wanted. And you and Flynn got away from Guy. So all's well that ends well, eh?'

Margot plays with her dessert spoon as she looks at Sara mischievously. 'Guy might disagree with that.'

'Well, yes, of course,' Sara says. 'No one wants to spend the rest of their life in jail. But – I mean – he did kill her. You can't really go around getting away with things like that, can you?'

'I guess not,' Margot says thoughtfully. 'But, you know, Sara, he chose that trail camera himself. He put a lot of research into choosing it. Compared a whole lot of them. Picked the one with the highest spec – in terms of resolution, battery life, memory.' She elocutes the three things slowly and clearly with her eyebrows raised.

'I can imagine,' Sara says. 'That's Guy all over, isn't it?'

'Indeed,' Margot says. 'But that was actually the first time we'd used it.'

Sara grimaces. 'Eek. Probably not what you imagined filming when he bought it.'

Margot fiddles with the spoon and waits for Sara to

connect the dots. To figure out that the battery was top-of-the-range and brand new; that it didn't run out after Guy came out of Celine's tent; that it was Margot's decision to delete the subsequent clips that showed very clearly what happened next.

And, when Sara looks slowly up at her, her brow creasing and then her mouth opening in a questioning O, she sees that Sara finally understands. That she realises that Margot knows exactly who killed Celine Cremorne. And Margot raises her glass to her with a smile.

'Cheers.'

Acknowledgements

This book was a long time in the making. I started two different stories, got a long way in and abandoned both of them. I tied myself in knots trying to come up with ever more twisty plots but, when the words failed to leap off the pages, I realised my heart wasn't in those early ideas, so I took a step back and then wrote something completely different: a 'what if that happened to me?' story set in a part of the world that's close to my heart. I hope I've managed to convey a fraction of the beauty of Oman and the glorious feeling of being out in the vastness of the desert. If you get a chance to visit, I'd recommend it. Just don't act like my characters did!

The novel went through more rewrites than I want to count, first under the skilled eyes of my agent, Luigi Bonomi, and then of my brilliant editor, Cicely Aspinall. Thank you both for your patience and guiding hands. Thank you to Lisa Milton at HQ Stories for your support and for believing in me, and thank you to everyone behind the scenes at HQ who played a part in helping turn this author's manuscript into a beautifully packaged book you can buy in the shops.

Thank you to all my friends for your encouragement, support, WhatsApp voice notes, lunches and chats. Thank you for being there for the lows as well as the highs. Particular authorly thanks to Bernadette MacDougall, Lisa Hall and Darren O'Sullivan as well as every author, industry professional, librarian, and book blogger and Instagram book reviewer who's engaged with me and encouraged me on social media. This can be a lonely business, and your words, jokes and pet photos keep me smiling.

To my readers – thank you for keeping reading alive. We wouldn't be here without you.

Sam, this story wouldn't be what it is without that evening spent drinking rosé on the balcony of our Muscat hotel. Maia and Aiman, each of you has shaped this book in ways you probably don't know. Thank you for the plot ideas, the twists and for understanding when I sometimes had to put work before doing more fun things. And, finally, to Mum, thanks for waiting for this. I hope you like it.

Don't miss more gripping and suspenseful novels from Annabel Kantaria …

Your parents make you who you are. But how much do you really know about them?

After her father unexpectedly passes away, Evie returns to England to her pristine family home, which is filled with her mother's unspoken grief for Evie's brother, who was killed as a child in a tragic accident. She soon begins to realize that everything she thought she knew about her family has been one big lie.

In a family built on lies, who can you trust?

Audrey plans a once-in-a-lifetime cruise around the Greek isles with her twin children. On the night of her 70th birthday, she goes missing just hours after she breaks the news that the twins stand to inherit a fortune after her death. As the search of the ship widens, so does the list of suspects – and with dark clues emerging about Audrey's early life, the twins begin to question if they can even trust one another …

Available now in paperback, ebook and audio.

By Annabel Kantaria, writing as Anna Kent

Once you let her in, she'll never leave …

Abi Allerton is happily married, and her past is firmly behind her.

When her old university friend Grace gets back in touch, Abi is hesitant. Their friendship was intense and all-consuming. But with her husband away for work, Abi could use some company, so she agrees to let Grace stay.

Before Abi realises her mistake, it's too late. Grace is back to her old ways and Abi is losing grip on her calm, well-ordered life. Because Grace knows Abi's secret – and she'll never let her forget it.

Available now in paperback, ebook and audio.

ONE PLACE. MANY STORIES

Bold, innovative and empowering publishing.

FOLLOW US ON:

@HQStories